Cold War, Hot Pursuit

by:

David R. Dye

MAPLE
PUBLISHERS

Cold War, Hot Pursuit

Author: David R. Dye

Copyright © David R. Dye

The right of David R. Dye to be identified as author of this work has been asserted by the author in accordance with section 77 and 78 of the Copyright, Designs and Patents Act 1988.

First Published in 2024

ISBN 978-1-83538-162-5 (Paperback)
       978-1-83538-163-2 (E-Book)

Book cover design and Book layout by:

White Magic Studios
www.whitemagicstudios.co.uk

Published by:

Maple Publishers
Fairbourne Drive, Atterbury,
Milton Keynes,
MK10 9RG, UK
www.maplepublishers.com

A CIP catalogue record for this title is available from the British Library.

Dedication

This fictional novel is dedicated to my beautiful, intelligent wife who passed away in June 2021.

She was a very accomplished equestrian with a very deep love of horses, and dogs!

To ride horses, and care for horses, you have to be brave. Her bravery surpassed everything I have ever experienced. She fought an exceptionally cruel cancer for 10 years. She cared for our severely disabled son for almost 20 years, always with a smile and a humorous quip.

She happily accepted travelling and living around the world with me due to my work. And several of the situations in my novel involved her. See if you can spot a few!

Dedicated to Karen.

Disclaimer

Out of complete and utter respect for Ford Motor Co. Ltd , the author of this fictional novel wishes to state that all events, situations and characters that reference Ford Motor Company Ltd are therefore, also completely fictional.

CONTENTS

Chapter 1 – Are You Being Served 8

Chapter 2 – The Thin Controller 12

Chapter 3 – Is Driven A DNA Thing? 18

Chapter 4 – Red Light Shopping 22

Chapter 5 – I Saw Her Standing There! Love Me Do 32

Chapter 6 – Glenn Wanted To Be A Pilot 43

Chapter 7 – Message In A Bottle 49

Chapter 8 – Yes Minister! 53

Chapter 9 – Up On The Roof! 59

Chapter 10 – On The Loose In Sousse 65

Chapter 11 – Reverse Somersault 69

Chapter 12 – She Decided To Sit On It 73

Chapter 13 – Death In Paradise And More 77

Chapter 14 – Oh De Cologne Dinner 84

Chapter 15 – Down To Earth Comedy 90

Chapter 16 – On Fire In Valencia 96

Chapter 17 – The Bottom Line 104

Chapter 18 – The World Is Your Oyster 111

Chapter 19 – Everyone Needs A Rest 119

Chapter 20 – Now We're Up The Pole 124

Chapter 21 – It's First Class 127

Chapter 22 – Girls And Gifts Galore 132

Chapter 23 – Not A Hit For Everybody 136

Chapter 24 – Disappeared Among The Stars 140

Chapter 25 – To Be Frank, London Is The Best! 143

Chapter 26 – Mistaken Identity In Lon...Don! 147

Chapter 27 – Who Is Frank 150

Chapter 28 – They Seek Her Here, They Seek Her There . 158

Chapter 29 – Down To Earth 164

Chapter 30 – Gunfight At The Ok Coral 172

Chapter 31 – Swimming With Seals 181

Chapter 32 – They Fired Their Guns 190

Chapter 33 – The Alcatraz Tour 199

Chapter 34 – The Chaps In Wickenburg 206

Chapter 35 – Chaps Look Great And Prevent Chaps 210

Chapter 36 – The First Roundup 213

Chapter 37 – Lets Have Shagging At Our Party 217

Chapter 38 – Sunset Ride 223

Chapter 39 – Ding Dong The Bells Are Gonna Chime 241

Chapter 40 – We Were Climbing The Walls 248

Chapter 41 – Where We Began 261

Chapter 42 – With A Little Help From Her Friends 265

Chapter 43 – Looking Back Helps Going Forward 269

Chapter 44 – Goodbye – Wipe A Tear From Your Eye 274

Chapter 45 – Every Time We Say Goodbye 278

Chapter 46 – Frozen Theme Or Canadian Dream 290

Chapter 47 – Anya Getting A Memorial 297

Chapter 48 – Dragging On A Fag...301

Chapter 49 – Toronto, In The Big Country 311

Chapter 50 – Our Dreams Come True – To Be Frank..........322

Chapter 51 – A Baby, To Be Frank..327

Chapter 52 – Heading To The Demise Of The Wall..............330

Chapter 53 – All The Presidents Men.......................................335

Chapter 54 – Start By Doing What Is Necessary...................345

Chapter 55 – Next, Do What Is Possible 350

Chapter 56 – Now We Are Doing The Impossible................352

Chapter 57 – Prologue To The Wall's End 356

Chapter 58 – Home And Dry 359

Chapter 1

Are You Being Served

The street lights reflected on the rain soaked pavement. It was a cold, wet, winter morning. But I had to get on because I had a full bag of papers to deliver. With the bag swinging on my back, I scooted the bike with one foot on the peddle and mounted on the move. On these cold mornings it was best to keep moving. There was no talk of power or energy crises in the newspapers because there was hardly any to be used. No fire at 5am. Certainly no central heating. Not even tea bags to make a cup of tea. It was, make a full pot or none!

Strangely, we never really thought about it. We just wore thick winter clothing to make us warm. And kept moving, working, breathing the cold air and watching the steam from our mouths float away in front of us.

I hadn't long left school. About 9 months, but I had already had three paid jobs. They had all been great but something about them did not quite join the dots. That's not quite true as the first was the only one I had seen as a future. Football, but my body, not all of it, just my knees, let me down.

After finishing my morning round, I rushed to get changed and then catch the Underground to Piccadilly. I needed to get to my third job by 8.45am. The store, Simpson (Piccadilly) Ltd opened at 9am. I was domiciled in the East End of London. Yes, a true Cockney. So I considered myself very fortunate to get a job in such a salubrious, posh store as Simpsons. At the time it was well known as the Outfitters to the Queen and Duke of Edinburgh.

Although it was a fabulous job that I enjoyed immensely and which taught me so much about business, it also opened my mind to the possibility of finding a lucrative career and, with it, a lifestyle that I had never ever contemplated before. Most of the time my role involved credit control. Among the rich and famous that shopped in Simpsons, it was generally accepted that they would require a credit account and pay for what they purchased at the end of the month.

I quickly started to memorise and recognise areas of the country where the rich congregated. Places such as Iver(Bucks), Cheyne Walk (Chelsea), Hampstead, Chester and so on! Furthermore, most of the staff came from monied backgrounds, it certainly was a magnet for debutantes, actors' children and sons' and daughters' of nobility.

Unexpectedly, I was soon getting invited to parties in London, surrounded by people out to enjoy life, and beautiful girls that made my mind explode with excitement. As a naïve, young and different class lad, I became somewhat of a target for some of the older women. More to challenge my sexual interest and stimulate excitement. For example, at the corner of the store, Simpsons had a boutique. I had to go to the boutique first thing in the morning to set up the till with the cash float. There was a very glamourous and beautiful assistant there, about 25 years of age. Mostly, without speaking, she would tease me with an intensity that almost daily caused a sensual eruption. She would lift her skirt to adjust her stockings and suspenders, bending forward to show me a glimpse of her perfectly formed breasts. But it was more the wild look in her dark eyes that stared straight at me and then would trail down to my trouser hump that always developed. I could not wait to get to my task in the Boutique each day!

However, despite all of these reasons to love the job, the pay was relatively poor, as it was in most department stores.

I certainly had a mental struggle convincing myself to overcome these human urges and emotions but I had a stronger urge for fortune. I wanted badly, very badly, a career which would take me into the sort of riches that I saw around me every day. On a Monday morning I would chat with colleagues who had spent the weekend on a Lord's country estate. I would sanction account bills for Roger Moore that would charge a £20 shirt to a Theatrical Costumiers Account. During a stint on the sales floor, I witnessed a gay colleague selling Peter Sellers a Vicuna overcoat with a price of £1095. Don't forget, this was in the 1970's, so these amounts were only spent by the very rich.

I saw and even spoke with people such as Sophia Loren, John Wayne and The Beatles. On occasions I was required to chase debts incurred by other very rich people. Some saw themselves as far too famous to pay a bill or return goods obtained on approval. To this day, I continue to remember Account Numbers of the rich and famous. Also, I constantly reminded myself that one day I wanted to be a person with a Simpsons account. Little did I know that one day Simpsons would be characterised in the TV comedy" Are You Being Served"

One last anecdote before we leave Simpsons. Having just mentioned steps, I once had occasion to use a small pair of steps to solve an unusual circumstance for one of my male sales colleagues. I had been seconded to work for our Security Department. My colleague, Mr Charles, came to me at the point the store was due to close. He had a male customer with his supposed wife from mid-afternoon. The store closed at 5.30pm except that the policy allowed an over-run if customers were still in the store. At 5.45pm Mr Charles was continuing to pass suits into the changing room where the man had stayed for some hours with his supposed "wife". I was asked to get involved and have a gentle word with them.

I proceeded to tap on the changing room door several times and each time the response was "won't be long". I ran out of patience, got a small pair of steps, stood on them and peered over the side of the changing room. The man and woman were having almost raging silent intercourse. I had never seen any such thing before and certainly had not imagined this was going to be what I would find. I subsequently got accolades from my boss as everybody was relieved that they could go home. However, I was sworn to secrecy! Until Now! But that lingered in my mind forever. The main thing it taught me was not take what you see at face value. Secondly, men especially, but not just men, never stop thinking about sex. But, as a man, I accepted at an early juncture that if you want to make real progress in work, you have to find a way to suppress it. It's difficult but if you don't, it will seriously divert you from your ultimate objective, progressing in business and making money.

My days at Simpsons were definitely memorable, comical and valuable in terms of learning about the world, the wonderful people in it and how business reacts as an interface.

Now to my next job at Ford Motor Company. I certainly never expected it to be as exotic, flamboyant and colourful as it was around the SOHO area and Simpsons.

Chapter 2

The Thin Controller

On my interview day, I was wearing a hand-me-down suit, it was in no way well fitting, however, I knew this and used my hands, arms and every other extremity as camouflage.

I drove up to the security gate just before Engine Plant. It was a grey winter's day and the place looked even greyer. I was directed to a car park which was almost full – probably over 400 cars. From there, I walked in, back through security, always staring at the Dickensian – looking massive building. The windows were the large type but separated by small panes that looked like they had never been cleaned. The main entrance into the building was half way, about 100 yards along the west of the building. I entered, but nothing improved!

Tentatively climbing these flights of grubby grey melamine stairs, I couldn't help but notice the dismal green walls. I surfaced into a very quiet but well inhabited area, both to the left and right of me. The glare from the hundreds of fluorescent ceiling lights did not reflect on anything. Nothing had a shiny enough surface. The windows looked even worse from the inside. The place felt like a massive prison cell.

Then I was immediately faced with a short fat man with greying hair. I looked around just at the point he was asking if he could help. There was a complete herd of dirty green desks with people at them heads bowed, buried in paper and computer tabulations. Other people were walking the aisles between the rows of desks and small groups milled around.

I asked for the Controller's Office and was politely directed to the right of the stair gangway. Now I was walking towards a large singular office on the front wall. All the desks faced away from this office. I later was told that this geography was so that the Controller could stand at his door and quickly assess who was working – or not! Next I was walking past a group of desks all inhabited by young women, and one older grey haired lady. They tapped and rattled away on an unknown machine.

In total, there was about eighty desks in the office which included the ten comptometer lady personnel. By now, however, I wondered if I should stay or run for it. The impact of what I had witnessed around me was in stark contrast to the stunning décor of Simpsons; no marble staircases, no lift attendants dressed as footmen, no beautiful mirrors and lighting. And stunningly dressed glamorous people. That said, the Ford people were smartly dressed and personably polite.

Especially the Controller's secretary, who immediately asked if I would like tea of coffee. I smiled as graciously as possible in the circumstances but refused as my hands were too shaky and clammy to hold the cup.

She then ushered me into the inner sanctum. The Controller's office was impressive. A large oak desk, large leather office chair. At the back a library of meticulously organised books and binders. Around were four red cushioned chairs, but the windows remained grubby with dirty streaks.

The Controller sat behind the desk, furiously writing without even looking up. His secretary interrupted his flow by announcing that I was there for an interview. I first noticed his stature, he was thin but tall. His face was thin and pasty. He said hello, stood up and held out his hand. But it was his gaze. It was steely eyed and imposing. When he spoke, he had what I now recognise as an air of authority. He had brown thinning hair and spoke with an Irish accent which was quiet and soft and almost lyrical.

An HR person joined us, but didn't say much other than to introduce himself. In those days, that department was named IR – Industrial Relations.

The interview commenced. I don't remember much of it because those steely blue eyes dominated. I was tutored on this by a wonderful Manager I had at Simpsons. Before I left, and we did have a fantastic rapport; he said that in interviews you need to keep a friendly gaze straight into the interviewer's eyes. I felt this had worked because during the interview the Controller's gaze softened and became warm and welcoming. I am now going to name him as Paul, as his unknowing tuition throughout my time in the Engine Plant, and I say unknowing mostly because it came from watching him and listening to his summaries of what needed to be improved, that helped me immensely.

So there I was, feeling elated. Nobody had said I had got the job but I was confident. I said thank you to the Secretary and left the building. Then as I walked to the car park, I saw and smelt smoke. Felt the grime of industry. Saw the hundreds of cars in the car park. Is this really for me?

I heard a shout, it woke me out of my world of thoughts about my take on what I was feeling. The differential between the opulence of Simpsons and the graft and grime of Dagenham. It was the HR guy running towards me!

He skidded to a halt beside me. Said "Matthew, I have been talking with Paul and would like you to know he wants to offer you the job" I was taken aback, but as it sunk in, I was elated. He carried on, "Pay as we said is £16 per week and we would like you to start on April 18th." It needed a little thought, but not a lot. This was almost twice what I had earned at Simpsons. He continued, you will be salaried staff so pay is monthly and there will be Pension Contributions. I accepted immediately. Didn't really understand all the other guff. Just kept thinking about the £16 per week. Finally, he smiled and said "you did very well and doing it verbally like this will save us all a lot of letters, paperwork and time".

April 18, a Monday, came in the blink of an eye and I was back in the same Ford car park. I had a second-hand Ford Popular that did not look out of place.

The working hours were 8.15am to 4.15pm. On this first day, despite some very heavy traffic, I was only a couple of minutes late. At the top of the entrance stairs sat a man on a green tubular chair. He said I was expected and should turn left at the top of the stairs and ask for Harry. He was the Supervisor on the section I would be working in. A very approachable, friendly, character who knew the job inside out. He spent time with me over the rest of the week, after which I was left to get on and ask for help when I needed it.

The guys in my section were all very welcoming and helpful. One person, Peter, who was about 23, stood out as knowledgeable and likely to be going places. The rest were the usual mix of people happy to walk the marathon and maybe even just trudge along!

At the end of my first month, I, along with two others, was called in to see the Controller. Putting it bluntly we were all given a severe rollicking. Lateness was not to be tolerated. I was berated for being late 3 times in the month.

All occasions were five minutes or less. However, Paul made it very clear that this was not acceptable. From that day on I was always early or on time. As he said there is never a good reason for lateness. Always start out leaving yourself plenty of time to cover unforeseen events.

Next there were vacancies with higher grades in Cost Analysis. This was a fairly regular occurrence because most of the people in these grades were competitive. It was never stagnant. I had done my best previously in lobbying for a promotion to a higher graded job but never been successful.

Now the time had come. I had made a bit of a name for myself reducing the amount of scrap components, so it was promotion into Area Cost Analysis. I would now work for the Controller, jointly with an Area shop floor Manager. My luck was in! I would be working with a Manager I really liked. He was comical and assertive with it. He managed Crankshafts, Camshafts, Pistons and several other components. We got on like a house on fire. I had come to know him in the scrap job and all the management that worked for him. They were all different characters but I really did like them all.

The factory production area was enormous. For me it was an Aladdin's cave of exploration and continual learning. It did not dawn on me at the time but my mind was gradually seeing that learning about this and listening to the shop floor operators was a treasure trove for my future career development.

The front perimeter of the production area was amazing. This was piston manufacturing which probably stretched a quarter of a mile, whirling and twirling carousels and gravity conveyors loaded with pistons. Behind were crankshafts, camshafts and small components such as conn rods. The spectacle was analogous to a vast fairground. The smell of coolants (chemical fluids used in machinery) and oil will stay in my nostrils forever.

I found that sometimes comedy can get you out of trouble. We were set to have a cost review with the Director of Manufacture. A most senior and extremely feared member of Senior Management. A particular graph to be shown in the meeting reflected very poor cost control by one of the Superintendents I worked with. I warned him that he could be in the firing line when this was shown. Several times I did this. Again and again because I was so worried by the Director's reputation. The only response I received was "don't worry I will handle it" in a gruff, cockney voice!

On the day, the slide came on the screen showing the distressful zig zag graph. The Director retorted "Bill, what the hell is that, it's disgusting!" my superintendent took a deep breath, then replied "Sir, right now that is my heartbeat". After, he smiled at me and said "see I knew I would get through!" nothing more was said and the Director laughed and moved onto the next subject. My Superintendent had found the nugget. He was a solid, genuine character with so much knowledge, and there were so many more people like him throughout my time at Ford.

Chapter 3

Is Driven A DNA Thing?

From that day my mind-set became more focused. In that conference room I had witnessed senior management of the company in action. Their power and commitment to finding improvements, making change happen and above all, communicating in a way that they believed was necessary to motivate people was all too obvious.

Indeed, it appeared to me that these senior guys were in a different league to my peers and most of the junior management in terms of their analysis of problems and situations, their thought processes and their reaction to the whole community.

My next steps were, therefore, to improve my speech (my cockney accent was strong). Concentrate on thinking things through before speaking. Attempting to see and use the comical side of situations. But lastly, to grasp every opportunity to progress with every strength I could muster.

With hindsight, I suppose I was always ambitious and "driven". But now the foot was on the accelerator and, in consequence, there were very positive results. However, one thing was missing. Qualifications at a higher level!

If you are going to win a battle you need sufficient arrows in your quiver. At this point in my career I was competing with good players. But they had greater stamina in the long run because they had either degrees or professional qualifications. I only had the memories of my final year at school doing extremely well at football, applause in assemblies and a glut of girlfriends. I left school with only 3 GCE's (expected eight) and no mathematics or English Language. What a plonker!

I had a real mental battle with the thought of going back into studying. It was going to be really hard as I needed the two important GCE's before I could even commence on a professional accountancy qualification.

But then one evening I sat down and looked back at how far I had got. I had been, as a young teenager, very close to taking the wrong road. We lived in the shadow of the Krays. Every teenager was expected to be in a gang. So of course, I drifted into one. I was respected for my football and that elevated me in the gang. They were all West Ham supporters. Fights between gangs were commonplace involving knives and coshes.

I came very close to being arrested on a couple of occasions. Kids today have it even harder. It's not the people. The kids are the same kids. Largely it's driven by drugs. I always avoided drugs but they were prevalent in my era. Now it is a million times worse. But I don't see much being done to eradicate it.

So this was crunch time. I definitely would not want to go back to that type of life. And I did not want to get stuck in the rut. So, there was only one choice. Start studying again. I made all the arrangements and Ford agreed to help financially.

In the meantime, the grimy windows and dusty fluorescent lights of the Controller's department had developed a sparkle. I was getting on well with the bosses and had received three excellent annual reports. "Excellent" was the rating, but the one to get was the one above "Outstanding".

Next I was selected to join a Group Office Team to work on a major investment project which went extremely well. My name was getting around! Then suddenly I was called by a guy who had been my previous supervisor to say he wanted me to join him in a new operation that had been set up ! It would be grade 8, magic to my ears, just one step from Management Roll. This was my key aim. With grade 9 came a car!

However, there was a major sized hurdle to get over. My boss, Paul in the Controllers Department, had become so reliant on me that I was finding it difficult to make progress. I had applied for several promotion jobs but he had blocked them. It did not sit well with me, but I decided to talk directly to them. They gave me the job. Paul was magnanimous. He accepted it and I was elated.

The new job I was acceding to involved a new organisation which would consolidate the manufacturing of all truck variants within Europe, including overseeing the development of heavy tonnage trucks. An area of the truck market in Europe that Ford had not previously participated in on a Europe-wide basis.

My first day was a bit of a shock. It was a new six-story office building, but with only twenty or so people in it. My department was a grand total of four people and two were managers. However, within six months there was over one hundred and by now I was starting to grasp the job. It was a fascinating time as we took over and began to build the autonomous truck business.

I was assigned to work on the basics of profitability for three large factories in our responsibility. There also was a small group working on developing a plan and programme to launch heavy trucks, 40 ton plus, to compete with the leading French, German and Dutch companies. These guys had been progressing this development for some years in a different part of the Company, but had now been centralised with the rest of the necessary functions.

So there I was having made quite a lot of progress in this new organisation. Then the boss rang me. He was the new boss on the block. A German who I liked and admired. His energy for everything was almost unbelievable. He was like a Duracell bunny. If I met him at the bottom of the stairs early morning, he would challenge me to race him up the stairs. And this was most mornings.

As instructed, I went off to the boss's office. He was a small agile man who was always on the move. While walking around, he explained in semi-broken English that he wanted me to go to Amsterdam on a fact-finding mission. Absolutely nothing was going well out there. They were not producing any volume and resultant costs were through the roof. This was not new to me; I obviously said yes I would go. With that, his response was "stay out there if you think you can help".

The thing I was primarily concerned with was how to get there. After taking advice, mainly from engineers that had been, I decided to go via Harwich – Hook of Holland. First Question, where is Harwich? I was going to be driving. When I think back it was like the "only Fools and Horses" episode.

I eventually ended up on a boat at Harwich. Had something to eat then got my cabin for a night's sleep. The whole night was like living through an Orange Mans parade in Belfast, constant loud drumming so I did not get much sleep. Then it was the drive through Holland which I managed using maps. No SatNav. Just a brain, eyes and ears.

Chapter 4

Red Light Shopping

I was booked into a superb hotel on the edge of the red light district. I was not aware of this until I went for a walk in the evening. What an eye-opener! Next day I drove to the factory on the outskirts of Amsterdam, met the people who were all English speakers. They gave me a very warm welcome, then escorted me to a quite large block of offices to meet the Senior Management. On the way we walked past about fifty trucks. All were in a bad way quality wise. Bonnets up, wiring looms hanging down, some without seats etc. They were clearly in the midst of an assembly and quality crisis.

I was taken to meet the Sales Director but first met the usual guard dog secretary. But she was not in any way usual. She was absolutely beautiful, gorgeous, so much so she took my breath away. Then had a brief meeting with the Director who did not seem to have any knowledge of the casualty vehicles and their quality issues.

That evening, after dinner, I decided to take a walk by the river, parallel to the Red Light District! This was destined to turn into an amusing, and later, embarrassing situation. In fact, it would create a complete change in my life!

It was early evening, still light and not many people around, except scantily clad girls sitting in shop windows. I had only walked past six or seven of these exotic shops when, approaching the next, the beautiful woman behind the large plate glass window was smiling, waving and then beckoning to me. This was to be a turning point in my life! My focus would move from being DRIVEN to being smitten!

I approached, almost tripping over my own feet. Her smile said everything. There seemed, at that moment, there was nothing more to life. She was perfection. My brain seemed to ignite as if it was made of phosphorus. She had long black hair, down to her shoulders. The innocence in her eyes was partly deflected by a naughtiness in her expression. But somehow, the combination of the features in this beautiful creature created an uneasy feeling in me.

I wanted to look at her lingerie clad body but my eyes were fixed on hers, as if she had put me in a trance. Then in an elegant but sensual motion she moved to the door, getting nearer with every second. Her movement seemed to break the embarrassment spell on my eyes and I glimpsed pristine underwear covering some of her exquisite contours.

In that moment a tornado of feelings got the better of me. A very strong sense of knowing the features of this nubile, sent my mind into a tailspin. I turned and ran down the road adjacent to the river. It was more a pathway for cyclists than a road. In my haste, I turned a corner and crashed into one of the many bikes securely parked at the end of the street.

Lying dazed on the cobbles it dawned on me that the girl was the same one, the secretary, I had met at the office the previous day. But there was a massive doubt. She looked very different. Her hair had been short, like Audrey Hepburn, not long., And certainly not black, more a light brunette. I think the clothing also provided camouflage. The thought occurred to me; perhaps she wore a long black wig, moreover, she was a well-paid secretary! Eventually I gathered myself enough to walk back toward my hotel, all the time analysing what had just occurred. I was at the point in my life that was the edge of success. A great salary, travel, company cars and substantial bonuses. I remained totally driven, but I was aware that a new and unavoidable distraction may just have entered by life.

Next morning, in complete trepidation I headed for work. No breakfast so my stomach was churning all the way. I desperately tried to walk into her office looking confident, with an upright gait. Somehow that turned to jelly. I managed to say "good morning" and in return she gave me a wry knowing smile.

As I waited to see the Director, she passed me a slip of paper which read " lunch at 12.30 outside the main gate". I smiled at her, although inside my heart was beating out of my chest and I really wanted to jump on a desk and scream with delight.

It was a short meeting outside the perimeter fence at a small coffee shop. We got the introductions done, her name was Anneliese. She would be finishing at the Red Light District that night but asked if I would take her for dinner the next night, Friday. Then we had to get back. I was in seventh heaven.

Friday at work seemed a whole year long. I left early to preen myself. We met at a dimly lit restaurant close to my hotel, The Sonesta. I started with an attempt to charm but Anneliese wanted to get straight into explanations, personal information and gradually more relaxed getting to know you stuff.

She was in the sex business to save more money. So far, she had done very well in a short period of time. She was leaving on Saturday to travel to Hammamet in Tunisia where she had inherited a printing/publishing company that predominantly provided travelogues all across the

Middles East and Africa. She loved travelling so this was her dream. I asked why she didn't have much of a Dutch accent. Apparently she had been educated mainly in USA. She had an MBA in Business Studies which took us into several short discussions. I suppose I was really in awe of this woman. A woman of astounding beauty, intellect, and cosmopolitan to boot.

I tried to beef up some of my background and it seemed to be well accepted. At the end of the evening she said she would like to keep in touch and when she was settled, possibly have a holiday in Tunisia. We exchanged numbers and I also gave her my home and work address and phone numbers. I threw all caution to the wind!

As we left there were just polite kisses. No hint of passion or possibility of future sex. But she said an interesting thing. She earned much more under the red light than she did at Ford, but now her target was to take the publishing/printing company into millionaire land. This girl was DRIVEN but without any paradigms, which can be dangerous!

I left the next day to return to my perfect life and exhilarating job. But I'm human, so for 2 or 3 weeks I could not think of anything else other than Anneliese.

She also left to go to Tunisia. From that moment it seemed it had all been a dream, a dream that ended badly. However, there were things in the pipeline that would reduce the negative impact of this flirtation.

About three weeks went by then I was told by my boss that I was being promoted into a grade 9 position in the European headquarters. My reports on Amsterdam had hit the spot and I was moving onwards and upwards.

I was quickly promoted again, now a Senior Supervisor, Grade 10. My target now was grade 13. Private Salary Roll.

Almost everything one could wish for, two company cars, free fuel, private health insurance, substantial bonuses etc etc.

During the preceding year I had been going through an acrimonious divorce. To keep myself sane I'd thrown all my time and effort into my job. It clearly was getting recognition.

Ford had just launched the Fiesta in Valencia, Spain and the whole European team were on a high. All products, but especially Fiesta saw sales on a steep incline. Ford was top seller, and therefore, had great market shares.

Sale analysis had become the be all and end all for the Senior Management. Consequently I was promoted into this area of the business. All the jobs I had done previously I had thoroughly enjoyed. They all provided something tangible to get your teeth into. But not this one. It was real CORPORATE. Purely monitoring sales statistics for all the different European markets. Both for Ford and its competitors. A significant amount of the work involved forecasting future sales.

Indeed I found it difficult to maintain motivation. There were many important things about the markets that I placed in my memory bank. Lots of useful information about our own and competitors upcoming new products. Extremely valuable to any company in the European Car Market. Also, suppliers would give their right arms for most of these revelations. Another interesting element was the niche sales. For example, US imports, mostly destined for US servicemen in camps around Western Europe.

Due to the success of off road and 4 wheel drive pickups, US Imports were projected to have strong growth.

Notwithstanding the sickening predominance of boredom, I pressed on regardless determined not to let my guard drop.

I thank my lucky stars that, once again, I was about to be on the move. This was a Grade 12 job. The initial task would be to centralise the different groups of Cost Estimators. These personnel were a clever combination of an Engineer and a Cost Analyst. Most of them had started work in the Company as engineers and for numerous reasons had chosen to accept training in costing.

These people were all over the place, In the UK, Germany and Spain. And once I got a feel for them, they were definitely the most unusual set of characters I had ever had the good fortune to meet.

In essence, the role involved estimating the cost of components in all our vehicles. Each Estimator was a specialist in his particular family of components. Next, they would attend Negotiation Meetings in support of the buyer. Their responsibility was limited only to purchased parts. Nothing manufactured in-house! The meetings were with Suppliers to agree pricing.

I had the last say in who would attend the Negotiations. If it was of substantial value I would often go myself, or if it needed any special analysis or strategy.

We would often use our own factory costs as a benchmark or comparator. We had several small electronics factories, pressings, forgings etc which gave us good information.

I had not been in the job more than a couple of months when I received a telephone call from Anneliese. I was overjoyed to think she had thought of me. We exchanged pleasantries then she got down to business. She needed a Transit Van but a very cheap one. I explained that the only possibility was what was known as a "scrapper". I would do some digging and call her back as soon as possible. She was such a clever businesswoman. Always looking for opportunities! Best of all, I now had her number, and to add to the euphoria my divorce decree-nisi had come through a month or so earlier. Maybe the talk of a Transit Van was just a way of talking to me. Who am I kidding?

About a week later, my contact gave me the good news and I rang Anneliese. She said she would call me straight back as she wanted to clear the decks and have a longer chat. I put the phone down and 2 minutes seemed forever. Then the phone rang. I was in a fairly quiet general office which had my own separate manager's office.

I got straight into the substance of it. Southampton Plant had a "scrapper" but it was only because the paint job did not meet the quality standard. The rest of the vehicle was brand spanking new and she could have it, as long as it was collected for a price of £1000. An absolute bargain! But it was red, except the paint had a pigment problem and it had turned orange. The heater had not been fitted but the rest of the interior was immaculate. She was over the moon. She did not need or want a heater. Not much call for it in the Sahara.

We had lots of chat. She needed the Transit to travel Tunisia, the rest of Africa and the Middle East. Then she asked me the question that started my heart racing. "Would I meet her to get the Transit and drive it back with her to her home in Hammamet?

Later that day I phoned by boss who operated out of the Cologne office in Germany. I knew I had plenty of holiday to come as I had not used any so far that year and had some carryover from the prior year. He was fine with it! Actually commented I deserved a break, except he said that he needed me at a negotiation meeting in the next couple of weeks. It would be in Bologna, Italy. I would get dates and details from our Purchasing colleagues. Of course, I agreed immediately.

In the back of my mind I knew Bologna was close to Genoa where Anneliese would get the ferry to Tangier.

In the next few hours I would get things moving. I talked with purchasing and got times, dates, travel itinerary. Then phoned my Southampton contact. Apparently there was no urgency on his part. Just needed to get the funds transferred and let him know the collection date.

Now I had to make the call to Anneliese. The phone call cut off twice and in between I heard lots of strange background noise, mostly clicking. The next call got through. Anneliese was very understanding about my work and how it would be an expedient opportunity to dovetail with the Bologna business trip. I asked what date would suit her to meet me in Bologna. She gave me a date that worked well and allowed her time to get from Southampton. She would transfer the funds as soon as she could get to the bank which was in Sousse, probably around the end of that week. So everything was arranged. I said I would stay about ten days and was really looking forward to it! More than that, my heart was beating out of my chest! She was fine about driving from Southampton to Genoa. It was much less of a drive than to Malaga and she had done it before. So all was looking very special.

Come the day, I had not had much sleep for excitement. I was at Heathrow early. I had two travelling companions. Mike, a buyer and Richard, the Power Train Purchasing Director. I had done my homework on the subject of our meeting and was confident with the pitch and our planned tactics.

Had quite a laugh on the trip. Mike was a small Jewish guy who had a fantastically dry sense of humour. He kept us smiling all the way. Richard was the epitome of an English Gentleman. Kept pulling Mike back to talk about work and the subject meeting. Along the way he made strenuous efforts to include me and get my thoughts on various Company topics.

He quietly detailed to me various new product programmes that were in the pipeline and explained that I most likely would be required to go to the US with him to progress the "global" programmes. That was fantastic to hear. I had never been to HQ in Detroit but from what I had heard in the past, if you fitted in it was a superb fast track for Europeans.

Getting my feet back on the ground, we arrived in Bologna about 8.30am. No Luggage, I just had my pilot's briefcase full of paperwork.

The Italians were there to meet us at the gate. Three of them and three of us alighted a luxurious Mercedes people mover. Actually it was more like a coach built for someone like George Bush. They explained they wanted to take us on a quick tour to see some of Bologna before heading to their office. I was delighted. Richard and I looked at each other and agreed it would be rude to refuse.

After not too long of a drive from the airport, we arrived at a Piazza. A large beautiful square with medieval and renaissance type structures. How lucky am I, a kid from the East End in Italian grandeur. They named the place as the Piazza Maggione. This confirmed what they told us. Bologna is one of the most beautiful cities in the whole of Italy.

I was in awe of the place. I remember studying at school and being so fascinated by what I read and heard from teachers, that this place was near the homeland of the notorious Medici family. Like all teenagers, growing up in earshot of the Krays, the word "notorious" awakened my spirit. The Medici family originally lived in the Mugello region of Tuscany. Serene Valleys between Bologna and Florence. They chose to move into Florence and became the Italian banking and political dynasty. They ruled for centuries. Very organised, sometimes cruel, but very successful.

Getting back to our hosts, who obviously had a strategy to occupy us as long as possible and get us as inebriated as possible. They had arranged superb and ongoing hospitality. We went to a restaurant in the middle of the terraces in the piazza. The welcome was generously extravagant. We sat on a very large table in an annexe to the main restaurant. The food was fabulous complemented by several toasts interspersed between the various courses and copious bottles of glorious red wine that arrived with regularity, delivered by our waiter Francesco, on an engraved silver salver.

Eventually Richard called everybody to order. We had the business over in about half an hour. They accepted our re-pricing clearly due to the pressure that had been applied regarding a Ford factory that was available to take their business and consequential possibility of re-sourcing – better known as integration. This remained a possibility in the near future, however, we did not play that card.

All the while I kept my eye on the time. The Ford team had to leave for the airport by 4.30pm. I had asked Anneliese to try to arrive about 5.00pm and park somewhere in the airport and meet me in departures.

Chapter 5

I Saw Her Standing There! Love Me Do

Then I saw her! The Ford team had just headed into the departure lounge. She came into the hall, stood at the doorway and glanced around. She spotted me and started walking towards me.

I should say it was more a glide than a walk. She was even taller in her high heels and had a proud, classy, upright gait. She was stunning. Nubile perfection.

Every man in the hall seemed to stop and stare. As she came towards me she was wearing a thin cotton knee length dress that had a button front. My eyes were magnetised by her body shape and as she neared me, the dress at the last button flapped open to reveal legs caressed by nude coloured hold-up stockings. I felt as if I was a coca cola can about to have its ring pulled!

As we met, she embraced me and gave me the continental double kiss. Although her firm body pressed against me, the kisses felt more like those you get from a female relative than one from a female with thoughts of love or passion. I had felt the same in Amsterdam but continued to exorcise it from my brain and live in hope.

We talked as she walked me to the Transit van. Don't remember what was said other than mine seemed polite gibberish. She said she would drive as she knew the way and as she sat in the driving seat she took off her high heels and put on some pale blue trainers – that matched her dress. Once more my eyes were drawn to the flappy dress and her beautiful thighs as she lifted each foot off the ground.

She drove away from the airport at speed. Once we got on the dual carriageway she said she had picked up my suitcase from my flat in Deal as I had requested. Then went on for a while about what a lovely place it was and that she would like to stay with me sometime in the future. Another carrot for the Donkey!

About 3 ½ hours later we arrived in the port of Genoa. The sun still seemed exceptionally hot and the surroundings did not ease that feeling of intense heat. It was a typically ugly dock area. There was no Customs or ticket drive-through area. Instead Anneliese, who seemed to know all the procedures, jumped out of the Transit and headed towards a small office building. I knew that if men were in the office, there would not be any problems.

As she walked towards the door, the soft cotton of her dress folded in between her buttocks. The flickering breeze from the harbour had decided to mesmerise me for that 50 yard glide across the tarmac.

Within half an hour, we had boarded a vessel that seemed pretty archaic. It seemed reminiscent of the "African Queen" but ten times larger. I guess that was appropriate as we were on our way to Tangier!

With all the chatting we had done on the trip so far, the atmosphere was getting much more relaxed. After we left the port, Anneliese immediately dragged me into the small dimly lit bar. The barman knew her. She explained that with all her travels for the travelogue company, she used this ship regularly.

It was nearly midnight before we gave up drinking, or at least, our bodies and mind couldn't take anymore. Anneliese drank vodka like a fish gulps water. My drink is whisky. But all they had was Canadian Club. Not a brand that I like but it got much better as the evening wore on.

And so did we! It started to glow with a warmth. Most of our conversation was about my work. I suppose I enjoyed that. Made me feel important. Made me feel that she thought I was important and worth her efforts to get close. Really, she didn't need to try so hard. Having said that, I managed to keep in mind that she was an MBA. She was interested in all the details. Literally all the detail.

There was some humorous dialogue about me recording work and leaving it for my staff to work with, mostly done when I was in the bath because I seemed to get my best ideas then. I explained that I had a Dictaphone that I used for every meeting and other important information and that I kept it in my flight briefcase. That is a large briefcase usually called a Pilots bag. Everything I was working on was in the Pilots bag and I needed it in case any issues arose at Ford while I was away. It went everywhere with me and was in the back of the van behind my seat.

So, around midnight it was off to the noisy cabin for bed. Once again, a sister's kiss with an almost sensuous embrace. But I decided not to push it. It would be about another 15 hours before we arrived in Tangier.

Next morning we took it easy. I definitely had a hangover. Anneliese did not seem too bad. Had some breakfast which was good considering we were on the "African Queen". We then did several turns around the deck, talking constantly about her work, but mostly mine. She was really interested in the topic I had raised previously about US imports. Sales of American cars and trucks to mainly European based servicemen.

As we neared the coast of Morocco, early afternoon, Anneliese was getting closer and closer to me. Breathtakingly clingy. Then she whispered that she had a seed corn of an idea regarding the US Imports and it could make us both a lot of money. She said that we should talk some more when we were in Hammamet. The intervening period would give her time to develop her idea further!

I remained driven but now I was also severely distracted. It can happen. It did happen to me.

We were on deck as we started to dock. Then I noticed she had pulled out a tin, yes a tin, of cigarettes. I had never before seen her with a cigarette in her hand. It was black with a gold band. I asked what make it was, she said "Oh, please excuse me but I really fancied one before the drive". It is a Sobranie cocktail. I had never seen it or heard of it. Being black and gold made it unusual and exclusive. She held it so elegantly and hardly seemed to draw it. Just appeared to excite it so it glowed gently. I smoked, not very often, but of course, mine were the good old fashioned English John Players, or sometimes, when I wanted to appear cosmopolitan, it would be Gauloises, but they did make me cough!

We docked and I thought it was time I took a turn at driving. We had a long drive ahead of us. Tunis was a full 24 hours plus drive away. Anneliese said she had a single mattress in the load compartment and so to take turns driving and sleeping. My thought was let's rest at hotels on the way. This was not Anneliese's thinking. She was concerned about her parents and wanted to get back to Hammamet as fast as possible.

With her guidance I quickly got out onto the A1 road. It was a good road but the further we went, the more boring and laborious it got. Anneliese was sleeping by now, but I could not stop thinking about her. I was under her spell. Now I'm older, I understand that women can be likened to a drug that you cannot get out of your system. They manage to create that constant craving that is similar to the feeling leading to orgasm but continuous and constant!

With Anneliese in the driving seat we reached Tabarka in the light of day. Until recently, not a tourist resort and relatively unknown. But as we drove the coast, it was an amazing spectacle. Probably enhanced by the dark drive through Northern Tunisia, but nevertheless entrancing in its own right. Especially, the Aiguilles Needles which are fantastically eroded, 60 foot stacks that punctuate the coast close to the town centre.

I would have loved to stop and explore but we were on a mission. We had another 3 or 4 hours' drive to Hammamet, depending on lots of things. The roads, according to Anneliese were not great and agricultural traffic may slow everything down. The A1 had been good but somewhat mysterious. Every so often I am sure I saw the same white BMW E9 tailing us. It would come and go. Perhaps just another long range traveller!

So far we had made really good time. The A1 had been almost clear and almost nothing reduced our speed below 120km per hour. There was the occasional piece of bad road but it was mostly surprisingly good.

We reached Hammamet in daylight. I was in the driving seat, with Anneliese beside me. She had prepared herself and had the look of a lady on a night out at the Ritz. Her perfume was arousing and I found it difficult to concentrate on the road. She gave me strong directions, taking me off the main road onto a dirt track that eventually came to an end.

There was no sight of the town itself. I would see that tomorrow, she said. Along the dirt road was a swathe of citrus green. Olive and Orange groves clad both sides of the road and directly ahead of us was a solemn line of cypress trees that seemed to add dignity to the opulence of nature around us.

At the cypress trees we had no choice but to come to a halt. The smile on Anneliese's face said this was her garden of Eden. She pointed left to a beautiful white villa. "This is where I live with my parents". She then pointed right, once again a beautiful white villa. "This is where you will be staying for your holiday. If you fancy exploring this evening, the beach is just beyond the cypress trees. Hope you don't mind sharing with my best friend Anya. It's a very large villa, so you won't get under one another's feet"

Just then, Anya appeared. Came running to the van. Anneliese jumped out and greeted Anya with extreme and, obvious, sincere affection. Anya then turned to me, clasped my hand, followed by a lengthy genuine show of affection.

She helped me with my two bags while I followed feeling useless! Anneliese shouted that we would all meet for dinner about 9 o'clock in her residence.

Once inside our villa, Anya asked politely about the journey then showed me around the villa. It was very large, four bedrooms and a pool at the back. Anya explained that she had been best friends with Anneliese for many years and that she had spent the last two weeks caring for Anneliese's ageing parents. She loved them like her own!

Anya was also what the Spanish call a "guapa". She was a fare bit shorter than Anneliese, very well proportioned, flowing long blonde hair. A very pretty young lady who, to most men, would be called a hotty or "guapa" in Spain. But, and I can't really explain it, she was not my type. She did have a wonderful, almost continuous smile, with blue eyes that seemed to search your soul. However, the real reason probably was that I was so infatuated and fixated with Anneliese. It was more than that. There was a negative I could not pinpoint.

One really intriguing thing was Anya's accent. It was fairly strong in contrast to Anneliese who carried an almost English aristocratic accent. And I was relatively sure that Anya's accent was Eastern European. But I thought it would appear impolite to ask this early in our meeting.

We went our separate ways to shower and smarten up for dinner. I had brought lightweight summer clothing including a casual unstructured cotton jacket. Light blue and loved by me. I thought I should wear it to show respect for my hosts. The rest of my attire would be described as Colonial!

Once ready, I was feeling good but also hot! I walked out to the pool and Anya was already there, seated with a glass of red wine. She asked, then poured me one. It hit the spot and lessened my nervousness. Not that I suffer from nerves, but this was all out of my league!

We sat in leisurely oblivion as far as the rest of the world was concerned. Another glass of wine and my inhibitions were a distant memory. I asked where she had grown up. Those eyes were penetrating me. She explained that she was Russian and decided the freedom of the West was for her. She had managed to get herself a Dutch passport. Anneliese, had a similar journey. She was born in Holland then went to boarding school in France. That explained why she was so chic and classically educated. She had pulled all the necessary strings when she was at University in the USA to get a US passport. I'm still not sure what strings you pull but good luck to her.

Then Anneliese wakened us out of the increasingly in-depth detail of our lives. My answers to Anya's questions were embellished. I had to or I would have appeared a totally inept character. But Anneliese's call to the table was my saviour!

As we left to cross the road, I noticed that on the edge of the beach was a beautiful Eucalyptus tree, so expansive that many branches were only two feet from the ground. With the sun starting to set it was a fabulous memory that I would, and have, kept forever.

At the centre of the road Anneliese grabbed my arm and we walked together. She was brushing against me and almost snuggling up to me as we entered her garden. I felt on top of the world.

It was almost a replica of our villa. A beautiful pool but we were eating inside because the cold evenings might affect the parents. It was 25c plus. We entered the dining room. Passed the dinner table which was smothered in beautifully colourful salad and seafood.

Mum and Dad did not appear as old as I had imagined. They both stood up to welcome us. Both were extraordinarily smartly dressed. Dad's suit was clearly hand made. Superb stitching on lapels and pockets. Mum, similarly had a Jean Patou suit with fantastic jewellery to set it off. At least I did not feel over-dressed.

The parents seemed lovely people. As you know, I had spent quite some time in Holland and know that they are generous, polite hard-working people. We talked a lot about families and education, which is where I felt exposed. Both Anneliese and Anya were talking Universities. I could only talk about leaving school at sixteen and playing football. The saving grace was that Dad was big on football. We got on like a house on fire and ended the evening on Brandy, even though I don't like it much!

Just as the evening was ending Anneliese announced that she had to be at work the next day. I could go into Hammanet if I wanted to. There was a car in the garage I could use. Dad, his name was Joe, would give me the keys. Anya asked if she could come to do some shopping. Apparently it was only about 3 miles away.

Anneliese followed that by saying that she and I were invited to Tunis on Thursday evening for a dinner party with a member of the Tunisian Government and, she thought, the US ambassador to Tunisia was also a guest.

Her parents were obviously so proud that she had kept their business going. Apparently her travelogues were on sale in several airports and widely on sale throughout Africa and the Middle East. Father actually said that the money he had invested in her education had been returned tenfold due to her business acumen. He stressed that it was done for love of a daughter, not the investment return. His Dutch accent seemed to add to its sincerity.

Anneliese explained that her dad had retired early because he had become asthmatic. They came to Tunisia in 1967 because it is believed that a warm climate by the sea reduces its impact on the body. Dad had, in his first work life in Holland, been a Director of the Delft Pottery and China Company. He had obviously done very well out of it as it enabled him to buy the small publishing and printing company in Hammamet. It was not so small now, so that had been a good decision and Anneliese, with her travel and expertise to pinpoint the important and interesting areas to visit, was growing the business.

Now the parents were in their sixties and Mum, Frederika by name, had developed health problems. She was such a lovely peaceful lady, but had, for some years, suffered severe Arthritis, mainly in her knees. She had a wheelchair but needed assistance moving into it!

They were such gracious people that clearly loved one another. But I was also suffering from serious niggles in my conscious thought patterns. I was excited by the prestigious invitation to the dinner in Tunis. What seemed questionable was the reason we had been elevated to attend with such esteemed company. I tackled Anneliese on this diplomatically. She was not phased at all by the question; we had taken a break and stood together in the garden.

Simplistically she said and without appearing pretentious" I believe it is because I am considered very successful here in Tunisia. I am extremely well educated and can talk knowledgeably about most things. I am streetwise and I can read who is worthy of my trust and who is not".

"However, because of the way mens' minds are wired, I am beautiful, and have a body that most men desire. I can make love better than any woman. I know the facial expressions that increase the intensity of passion and I know the sounds men need me to make while love making. And so I can get almost anything I want from a man! In a nutshell, that is why we have been invited to dinner with the Tunisian Minister for the Interior and the US Ambassador".

She carried on " I am not telling you this because I want to make you jealous which, again, is natural. I know you have feelings for me. But I need you to understand that love is totally different as far as I am concerned. It is special beyond belief! I have not yet experienced that feeling but I sense that I may be heading towards it with you and I don't want to spoil it by rushing things"

"Well, I suppose I have stumbled into this monologue from the simple question you asked, but it all needed to be said. You know that I have had sex with many men. But they were just work, not a relationship. A way to look at it which you will relate to is that I am no more than a professional footballer using his athletic toned body and elite skills to achieve a positive outcome. I may eventually use these attributes with you, but only when I am captivated by love! Not because the Team Manager says I have to win!"

We went back inside to the dinner table. Anya and the parents were chatting and there were a few giggles and looks. I had the impression that the parents thought we were becoming an item. They seemed pleased and coffee appeared momentarily. The strong small cup Arab type thick dark coffee with an astounding aroma. Anya decided to call it a day, said good night and went back to our visitor's villa.

The four of us sat and sipped the brandy and coffee as well as some very sweet chocolates. The conversation was lightweight and so I slipped in the question "which University did you attend Anneliese?" She had graduated and completed her MBA at Ann Arbor University. I excitedly said "that's not far from Detroit where Ford has its World Headquarters". That rounded off the evening very nicely. The parents gave a knowing smile. We all embraced and I made an unsteady exit due to the effect of the brandy.

As I reached the ornately carved rear door, Anneliese said she would return early Thursday morning so to be ready to go on the visit to Tunis. She continued " you can have Anya all to yourself tomorrow, but no flirting". I smiled a semi-inebriated smile and lurched off to our villa. It was now a very dark but starry-lit night. The moon shone over the villa and as I approached it, I stopped for a moment to appreciate the Moorish arches across the front, the carving of the window frames and generally enjoy the glorious surroundings and warmth of the evening air.

⊷⊶◅❉▻⊷⊶

Chapter 6

Glenn Wanted To Be A Pilot

I slowly sauntered in through the open rear doors. Initially I was confused by what I saw. Anya was kneeling on the large Moorish carpet. On her right hand side was a pile of files and papers. My files and papers! Anya seemed to be sifting through my pilot case. I was so shocked I just stood still for a few seconds. She sensed someone was there behind her and swiftly turned to face me. Her expression was somewhat startled but she made a good job of covering it up with a smile.

Trying not to use an offensive tone I said "can I help, Anya?" Her response began with a slightly muddled stutter. "Oh sorry, you gave me a shock" she then managed to pull it together. Her explanation was plausible to the point of being believable. "We have a Gecko living with us. He has been here quite some time, even before I arrived. He is very quick and although he is carnivorous, seems to eat almost everything."

She was convinced she had seen him slide under the lid of my pilot case and was worried he might settle in there and eat my papers. But there was no sign of him, she continued, he was as fast as lightning, so agile and could climb anything. And because he was so quick and could climb straight up, she had named him Glenn, after John Glenn the astronaut.

We both broke into simultaneous laughter. Anya went straight for the red wine and two glasses. We continued to talk about Glenn for a few minutes then Anya said she was looking forward to tomorrow. As the alcohol took hold, I just wanted bed, so I made my excuses, scrambled my paper back into the case and went off to bed. Another intriguing evening!

In the morning I awoke about 6.30am. The sun was pouring in through the shutters. I caught a glimpse of Glenn at the top of the white stone stairs leading to the roof. It was going to be a hot day! I was feeling full of vigour. Maybe the climate agreed with me, so I decided to go for a short run along the beach and combined it with a bit of getting to know the area.

I ran out of the garden, noticing the tremendous colour with Hibiscus and Oleander all in full bloom. It was only about 50 yards through the cypress trees and past the glorious Eucalyptus. I jumped a couple of its low branches and then I was on the beach.

Looking both ways, it appeared to stretch for miles. Pure white fine sand that did not grip my feet. I ran down to the water's edge. The sea was still, and so clear. I could see small fish only a few feet out. The colour of the sea almost merged with the sky. I started running left on the hardened wet sand at the edge of the incoming tide.

There were several well-kept small boats on the beach and as I got nearer I could see a figure laying sunbathing. Beyond was a spectacular hotel which I decided was my target for the length of my run. It was about three quarters of a mile from where I started.

When I was about seventy yards from the figure on the beach, I could see it was female. The shape is unmistakable. A bit further on I realised she was completely naked. I slowed almost to a halt.

As I paced slowly nearer she pushed up on her elbows, turned her torso slowly toward me and smiled. All I could think of was to say good morning. She just nodded and watched as I passed by. She was a very fit lady. Completely suntanned and probably mid-thirties. Later Anya told me that it was quite usual on this beach for ladies to discard their clothing to get an all over tan. I carried on jogging!

My mind tripped back to Anya's account of Glenn the Gecko and my pilot bag. I know the bag had been closed, lid down with the handle inserted through a cut out section in the lid. This secured the lid. I could not figure how she could think the Gecko could squeeze under the lid. But still, women sometimes have inexplicable imaginations.

Ahead of me now was an exotic Moorish style hotel. I wanted to get near enough to read the hotel name on the ornate board in the garden facing the beach. It read Hammamet Marhaba. I had the thought that it looked luxurious and worth a visit in the near future. As I turned to begin my run back to base I caught sight of the car park at the side of the hotel. At the end of the first row of cars was a white BMW E9. Just like the one I had seen a few times on the road from Tangier to Hammamet. Probably a coincidence that these people were staying just along the beach from us.

I was back for breakfast by 7.30am. I had worked up an appetite so, thankfully, Anya was up and had set a breakfast by the pool. It looked superb, fruit, pastries and handmade bread and cakes.

Anya was very welcoming. Almost too much so. As I sat down she flew around the back of my chair, put her arms around my neck and kissed down the side of my face. Then she moved away to our coffee and I started to feel flustered. She was wearing a tiny bikini which was almost covering nothing. Over this she had a flimsy beach negligee. That's the only way I know to describe it. And that seemed to cover even less.

After the nude beach goddess, I had now been presented with a further beautiful female and it was only breakfast time. Whilst I consumed coffee and pastries, I did my very best to pull myself together. That seemed more than the two girls had managed this morning.

I chatted about incidentals with Anya and I could tell by her expression that she knew I was flustered.. and she was enjoying it. We agreed to leave to go to Hammamet at 9am. She said that on the way we would need to stop at a bakery to get more bread, pastries, cakes etc. all of these were food for the Gods, especially the bread so I put this at the top of my priorities for shopping.

We got together again at 9am. Anya took me to the car. It was in the garage at the back of the villa. We opened the doors. I was in my element. It was a 1970 Mercedes 280 SE. Beige colour. A fabulous car that was never, at that time, seen in the UK.

We got in, the key was in the lock. I turned it and it started first time with a roar then a purr. I was on cloud nine. We set off. It was no better than a Granada but it was bigger and it was different.

Anya gave directions. Occasionally her hand would drift onto my thigh, usually when we cornered. After about 3 miles we pulled up outside a non-descript building with a door that was literally a hole in the wall. This was the bakers.

We ventured inside. It was almost like a small cave. The two men behind the counter clearly knew Anya and were very cheerful and friendly. She made her purchases and we left waving vigorously to the two guys.

We arrived in Hammamet and Anya told me to stop and park anywhere. We were opposite the Medina. It was the only real landmark in Hammamet. The Medina is lapped on one side by the sea and its walls back onto a cemetery. Here it faces the sweep of beach that is colourful with fishing boats and curves south to the hotels past our villas. The ramparts of the Medina were first created in 904. Can you imagine that? To look at the Medina it is like a castle with castle ramparts. In the Medina, which is now commercial, are the Suqs, a series of small shops and merchant stalls, some very brightly painted.

Viewing the Medina with the scenic coast and sea as its background presented an exquisite panorama. As we strolled through the elaborate arch into the Medina we could see the stalls and shops, the Suqs with all types of trinkets, caskets, glass, pottery, leather goods and various other merchant's wares. Apparently, Hammamet is famed for its bridal dresses which predominated.

Some shops and stalls exhibited their goods by hanging them festooned outside their properties. This certainly added to the colour vista. The perfume created by incense, herbs, henna and flowers of different varieties, combined with the colour palette, gave a sense that was almost overwhelming.

Anya lagged behind throughout, viewing everyone's wares, chatting to the touts working for the merchants. However, there were a few occasions when negative aggressive voices were directed at us. The reason for this, according to Anya, was that this was a time of increasing unrest throughout the Middle East. This was 1980, the Lebanese civil war was raging, Yemen had serious problems regarding rebellion, Iran was threatening a revolution, and so on. The West, Europe and North America were bound to get some heat from all this.

We just ignored it and strolled on. Anya found a small butcher's shop and decided to purchase a chicken. I stood by, watched and listened. There were several crates with chickens in. They were alive and well. Anya pointed to two that she favoured. The Butcher was literally that! He dragged the chickens out, rang their necks and walked to an enclosed machine at the side of the shop. We both watched in silence as he stuffed them into the machine. It whirred loudly, feathers floated around us. A minute or so later he took them out and very professionally, and with rapid skill wrapped them in thick brown paper. They were very secure. He placed the two parcels in a cardboard box and handed it to me while Anya settled up.

Previously Anya had bought some incense, a few trinkets and some fine lace which she wanted for a beach robe or coverall. As we walked and talked, I could feel heat from the chickens through the box. The thought of the treatment of these poor birds had done damage to my appetite. So when Anya asked if I wanted to get something to eat, I said I would prefer to take our fine bread and pastries and go back to the villa to eat. She agreed without hesitation.

As we were leaving the Medina, turning a corner I caught sight of two Western looking men, smart in casual attire, one small with a face like a ferret. The other, big, strong and bald. Both had a white complexion. Not the normal tourists, although there did not seem to be many tourists anyway.

Intuitively, I could not help but fear they were following us. But once out of the Medina and pacing towards the car, they disappeared out of sight. Perhaps our chicken fiasco had been enough for them also!

❈

Chapter 7

Message In A Bottle

Back at the villa, we had the fabulous bread and pastries for lunch with a glorious red wine called Rioja, a Spanish wine that was Anya's favourite. Before the food, she changed into that itsy bitsy tiny bikini. How lucky can you get! After the food and a full bottle of Rioja, Anya said she wanted to show me the roof terrace. The gecko had been there before, but now it was my turn. There were luxurious sunbeds and it wasn't long before we both dozed off.

When I awoke, it was approaching dusk. Anya was nowhere to be seen. But then, about five minutes later, she appeared. Apparently she had been to the parents' villa to check on them and help prepare their dinner. She was still in her itsy bitsy bikini!

With obvious longing, she uncorked a bottle of red wine, said she would leave it to breathe, but two minutes later, poured two glasses. She passed me mine and as she stood behind my chair, started to massage my shoulders. All the time, she would lean on the back of my neck, her breasts now massaging my neck and head.

She stopped and went back to her chair and the wine. Quickly finished her glass and began another. This continued for twenty minutes or so. I was close to finishing my glass as the bottle emptied. Another bottle was opened and Anya continued relishing the wine after topping me up.

We were talking about everything in general but as the alcohol took hold, Anya became more verbose. The first surprise was when she said Anneliese had been, in her youth, a champion high diver. A sport not in my repertoire! The surrounding conversation described her diving and entry into the pool with minimal ripples and so on and so forth. This meant absolutely zilch to me and I could tell the expletives were loaded with wine.

She walked back to me and resumed massaging my shoulders. I commented that she was very accomplished in the art of massage and asked where she had learned to do it so well. By now, she was becoming somewhat slurred and her clear affection for my neck and shoulders was more intense.

She said she had learned this in De Wallen in Amsterdam. I was intrigued, "where is De Wallen?" I asked "You probably know it as the Red Light district "she replied. "I worked just along from Anneliese. We are now like sisters. We share everything, she said with that same soul searching look of hers. Now we are business partners. I work on everything with her. I help with her parents. I run the travelogue business when she is away. We work together on her several other businesses. If you stick with us, you will become rich beyond your wildest dreams. Talking about wildest dreams! Would you like me to take you further on the massage expedition?"

I recoiled into my shell. "Anya, you have had too much to drink and although you are very beautiful, you will definitely regret going any further. It's a beautiful evening and I have thoroughly enjoyed your company, however, I think we should get to our beds. I have a busy day tomorrow with Anneliese in Tunis and you will need a gentle day to get over the wine you have consumed.

Whilst intoxication remained the master, Anya's lips kept moving. I interjected, trying to quieten her "what were the main types of men you met in De Wallen?" "Oh, it wasn't just men, but I prefer men" she said with a cheeky smile. "especially American Servicemen. They know how to lavish gifts on a girl they like. Also, I got a kick out of the famous ones, the MEP's and the like from the Brussels Parliament. They always had loose lips if you got them in the right frame of mind ... and mostly, the right position! Their wallets were very thick so you knew they had come prepared to be generous. Several important ones got to know me extremely well."

We said goodnight and trickled off to bed. Anya tripped on the stairs a couple of times and then groaned as she flopped on the bed.

I woke early, an hour or so before Anya, I dressed in a smart casual way, wearing my beige jacket and blue chinos. We were having some breakfast when Anneliese arrived.

She was dressed in a stylish flowery chic dress. Her hair and make-up were perfect. Her light grey and red patterned dress seemed to complement my attire perfectly.

Anneliese said to Anya that we would take the Mercedes and leave about 10am. We did just that and as we were getting in the car, I heard Anneliese tell Anya that we may be a couple of days, depending on how it went.

We left and had not been driving long, had got just out of Hammamet. Anneliese was driving then she said she wanted to talk about the US imports we had talked about a while ago. She said that she had a pretty solid business idea and wanted to know what I thought. She had worked on it for the last 2 days.

She said she had two people in California and another two in Berlin. She had been at University with all of them. They wanted to set up a company as Ford Agents to sell Ford

US vehicles, predominantly, to US servicemen in Europe. They had done their research and believed the new Ford products were just right. They would act as an Agency, taking a high percentage commission. She would not have to put too much work into it because she could trust the people she had involved. If I would give them US and European contacts, they would handle it. She had expressly asked them to keep me out of it just in case it may be a negative from Ford's perspective.

My reaction was, "I can agree to that, sounds great, get on and push it".

The drive back along the A1 to Tunis was about an hour and a half with a stop for some coffee and water. I enjoyed the drive in daylight which, with the sunshine, was interesting and panoramic throughout.

On reaching the suburbs of Tunis, the thing that struck me was that most streets were lined with Palm and Orange trees. The buildings were various styles and the trees significantly enhanced the impression of an exotic peaceful city. Not in any way like London. Vestiges of Moorish architecture, limited vehicles and traffic noise made it feel very welcoming.

With Anneliese driving there seemed no question of misdirection or need for U turns. We were aiming for the diplomatic and government area of the centre of the city.

Having turned into the Avenue Habib Bourguiba, Anneliese parked right outside a tall building, some four storeys, that resembled the famous Royal Crescent in Bath. In this case not a crescent but a wonderful building with clean lines adorned by Moorish style windows, verandas and iron work.

Chapter 8

Yes Minister!

At the large front double doors, we were met by a Tunisian lady who smiled but did not speak. We entered and walked along a vividly painted corridor into a glamorous sitting room at the rear of the house. There we were met by the Tunisian Minister of the Interior. Anneliese had already coached me on how to address him. As we shook hands, I began to say "pleased to meet you, Minister" but he cut me short and insisted that I call him Khaled.

He explained that his wife and housekeeper were preparing lunch but would not be eating with us as they had two young children who would need to be kept happy and occupied. Next it was straight to the wine. Two large carafes of wine, one red and one white, had been placed on a gigantic hexagonal coffee table surrounded by many splendid glasses.

We sat for about ten minutes exchanging pleasantries. It was noticeable that Khaled had an eye for Anneliese, almost appearing as if he was mesmerised by her. He obviously knew her well as he recounted a couple of anecdotes regarding her assistance in attracting some important visitors to his country.

As we spoke, the door opened and there stood a mountainous man. The housekeeper standing at his side was made to appear dwarfish. He wore a bespoke three piece suit which caused him to perspire just a bit. His grin was from ear to ear. He was balding but with striking side-head flashes of blonde hair.

Khaled jumped up to greet him. They almost wrestled for a few seconds then Khaled turned to us and announced that this person was the US Ambassador to Tunisia. The large American immediately interjected "My name is Harry Grenke and I'm really only a deputy Ambassador. We really all share the work in the Embassy because we need to travel so much in our jobs". Looking straight at me he said "and we really rely an awful lot on Annelieses' travelogues. What is also important in our work is the fleet of Ford vehicles we use to travel all over. So I have the honour of being in the same room as two pillars, vital to support our business."

Now it was time to move into the dining room to eat. As we walked in, we were met and greeted by Khaled's wife who then immediately retreated to the kitchen. The table had already been stocked with "starter" food. That was the first eye opener. And the décor was exquisite. There was an inherent friendliness to it that seemed to demonstrate an edifying attitude to life. Contentment, hospitality and family solidarity exuded from every corner of the room.

I commented on how fabulous this room appeared. Khaled thanked me. On the walls and windows were carved plaster domes and minarets. The plaster reflected white spires and arches set against sky blue doors, dado rails and ceiling carvings. The combination was elegant, tasteful and exotic. In western language, it blew me away!

Khaled requested us to be seated at the dining room table. There was acres of room around the table but Khaled sat close to me, opposite Harry Grenke and Anneliese. The table was filled with very colourful appetising dishes. And the aroma from the various herbs and spices increased the intensity.

Out of respect, I asked what the dishes were. In the middle was a large platter of what resembled white bait. He stated the name of this and various other dishes but I couldn't get the pronunciation. One I did understand was Gazelle horns. However, these were crafted out of dough, Thank God, not the real thing! Another was Fingers of Fatma which apparently was mince meat and seafood in pastry covered in herbs and spices.

And so the dishes drifted on, all over the family table. The one I particularly liked was a vegetarian dish call Farfoncha or something along those lines.

All the while the wine continued to be poured. We, consequently, were all becoming more relaxed and amiable. We were then all encouraged to sample a very large, splendidly luscious looking desert called Mahkouka. It seemed to contain pistachios, hazelnuts and almonds in an incredibly sweet and rich pastry.

Before I even got the first taste, I clumsily dropped my fork on the table and then managed to brush it with my elbow and it fell on the floor. Embarrassed, I rushed to pick it up.

With my eye line slightly below the table top, I glanced across. Anneliese's legs would have been the attraction for my gaze but it was not to be. Instead it was her hand grasping the top of Harry Grenke's thigh, and moving in a motion that ventured into his groin!

My flabber was gasted! I recoiled above the table top and tried to smile but I was sure it appeared an ignominious smile. I felt as though everybody's gaze was on me. Anneliese commented on something. I don't even remember what but everybody started back to conversation. My relief was gradual.

Until then, the conversation and discussions had moved around, but were always agreeable and convivial. There was significant interest in what Ford was doing in terms of new models, new territories and profitability. Mostly, I handled it like a UK Minister, with obfuscation! Khaled spent some time emphasising how Tunisia would provide cheap land and cheap workforce for any type of manufacturing. It would be in farming areas where the workforce mostly earned about $3 per hour. Now, quite a bit less than Spain where Ford had just invested in Valencia. Land also would be inexpensive because the Government would definitely apply substantial grants.

I showed massive interest, but knew that the Ford concern would be the volatility of the Middle East. However, all the while Harry Grenke was extremely supportive of Khaled, indeed, to the point where he appeared overcome with the possibilities. Maybe he was at the point of orgasm but that thought just reflected the jealousy impact.

I suppose I really was in love with Anneliese. I knew very well her history. I knew she would say this was just work and no real feelings were involved. But mine were and I could not just blank it out.

It came time to say farewell. All four of us stood in a huddle at the front double doors. Anneliese announced that she and Harry were staying in the same hotel and she would drive him. I could also go with them but she was unsure if a room was available! So what would I like to do?

By now, I was boiling up inside. Feeling hurt. Brain was in neutral, so I engaged mouth before brain and said I was tired, and would like to go back to our villa.

Khaled immediately said his driver would take me. Anneliese responded with "that's fantastic". Turning to me, she said she would be back by midday.

I slept most of the way back from Tunis. The day had been draining. There was an occasion when we stopped for a coffee and I thought I caught a glimpse of the BMWE9. But not too sure and it was only of minor interest now.

When we arrived at our villa it was dark. I was heading straight to bed when Anya appeared and said she would make me a coffee. I said I was more in need of a glass of whisky and she decided to have one with me. I outlined to Anya in the briefest of ways how the day had gone and then politely exited to bed.

Morning crept up on me quickly. It's hard to be sleepy in bright sunshine. I arose and did my usual morning run along the beach. Each day the panorama would make me feel more alive than I felt back in Britain. By the time I returned I was famished.

Anya had done her usual excellent breakfast. Mostly pastries, coffee and juice. She asked what the plan was and I described Anneliese's plan that gave us a nice relaxing free day. I had appreciated all the arrangements so far, but was really glad of a break.

Anya felt the same. She wanted to spend some of the day on the beach and maybe lunch at the hotel. Morning came with the same glorious weather and comfortable morning warmth. We drifted through breakfast and were talking about whether to go to the beach immediately or wait until lunchtime. Anya said that would give us time to tidy the house, which needed it, but not desperately.

Just at that point Anneliese arrived. She looked as breath-taking as usual and joined in the conversation whilst pouring some coffee. She politely asked if Khaled's chauffeur had got me back ok and then mentioned that she had just had a couple of drinks in the hotel bar and then went to her room for slumber.

The two girls then set about tidying whilst I cleaned the swimming pool. A long handled net was the trick to scoop all the leaves off the top. A barracuda electric pool vacuum was the answer to cleaning the bottom of the pool and was fascinating to watch.

Chapter 9

Up On The Roof!

We agreed to walk down to the beach at 11.30am. We set off together and must have looked like a bunch of giggling school kids going to the lido. In just a few minutes we had jumped the boughs of the eucalyptus tree, ducked under the cypress tree and found an unshaded part of the beach about fifty metres from the water's edge.

The weather was glorious and I was in the company of two extremely beautiful interesting females. We messed around for about an hour. I demonstrated my football prowess with a white plastic frido ball. Anneliese seemed impressed and clearly enjoyed brushing the wet sand off my thighs.

Hunger was now the focus of us all so we took off along the beach to the hotel. We sat outside and, just like the beach, we had the place almost to ourselves. Tourist time was around the corner but we were still in the quiet period.

Lunch consisted mainly of red wine and super-crusty doughy bread. But also, several different fruits, berries and soft cheeses. And as lunchtime wore on and alcohol gained ground, the surroundings, exotic colourful plants and sun glistening on the pool, began to increase my euphoria and well-being.

After about an hour and a half of lunch punctuated by mostly girl talk, it was agreed to go back on the beach and spend some time topping up our tans.

We dragged some sun beds out onto the beach adjacent to the garden white wall surrounding the hotel. After a while, Anya asked Anneliese how the new business with the U.S imports was going. I was surprised as I didn't know Anya knew about it. Anneliese replied that it was looking very promising but it was early days.

I suffered the heat for about two hours. Similarly Anneliese was feeling the heat and had got to the point of surrendering. She said "shall we go back and relax by the pool" I agreed immediately. But Anya said she wanted to stay and have a dip in the sea.

So we said our goodbyes and Anneliese and I strolled off back to the villa. Going through the glorious cypress trees, Anneliese put her arm around my waist and looked directly into my eyes "it will be nice to have some quiet time together" she said.

In the villa it felt so cool. Our little gecko friend seemed to be excited and was charging around, up and down the walls. Anneliese went off to Anya's room to freshen up and as she was going, said "let's go up onto the roof with some fruit and wine and relax there".

I was happy with this, so took the stairs up to the roof. Glenn followed me like a domestic cockapoo! The roof top was inviting with a large double lounger, a coffee table and a large beach chair with arms. The wall surrounding the roof terrace had several electric lanterns which would enhance the atmosphere on a warm dark evening.

I leant on the wall facing the beach and had a beautiful view of the sea over the top of the eucalyptus and cypress trees. I did not hear Anneliese arrive but suddenly felt her arms around my waist. Her breasts were warm against my back. She said "are you enjoying the view?" clutching me even tighter. "You may prefer to look at me" she said as she gently turned me to face her. My heart was beating out of my chest as our eyes met. She was wearing a beach robe which had slipped to show her tanned shoulders and then with a single move, the whole garment fell to the floor. My eyes could not help but explore her body in such an intense way that it generated what I can only describe as an out of body experience. Her breasts were perfection, slightly beyond the size of her torso with enticingly erect nipples. The rest of her body was slim but defined by exaggerated curves with lightly tanned silky smooth skin.

Although my mind had gone into a tailspin, my gaze automatically floated back to her face. She held an innocent but expectant, almost demanding, expression of desired pleasure.

From that moment Anneliese took complete charge of my body, my mind and all my senses. Absolutely every part of my being was completely filled with ecstasy, so much so, that I cannot really remember the physical acts, only the continually heightened concentration of loving emotions.

This woman, Anneliese, was now lying next to me on the double lounger. We had both spent 5 to 10 minutes recovering from this enchanting, almost spiritual experience. She had made me hers! She was there next to me and that was all I cared about. Her head was nestled in my neck, her arm across my chest and it felt so comforting.

I had never experienced anything like this before. It was not in my repertoire. It was unique. I had made love to many women but mostly it had developed from human lust rather than unselfish love. I now knew that I really loved this lady and wanted her in the rest of my life.

As we both slowly emerged from loving recovery, Anneliese sat up and said she wanted a cigarette. "I have never experienced such wonderful love-making" she said. You can imagine the questions that immediately came to mind. She continued" you know of my past and that it was just work. Every second of our time together has been pure. It has cancelled out the prior. I really love you and want to be with you in the future".

I was gobsmacked but managed to find some words "I love you more than anything. I did from the moment I first saw you. Your previous life does not matter. I just want to be with you always".

"So where do we go from here?" I said. Anneliese took a deep breath, gave a glimmer of a smile and said "you are such a caring person I am sure you will understand. I have no choice other than to carry on with my business to support my parents and to ensure they are cared for. And all my other irons in the fire are there to help me guarantee my future, sufficient for us to live on for the rest of our lives together"

"I am sure it will not take more than a couple of years to get things organised. In the meantime we will carry on as lovers. We will meet regularly, as often as possible! We can talk every day and e-mail if we need to. So please be patient, bear with me and I know we can make it work".

"Just one more thing. Anya has the hots for you. She has spoken to me and she is serious about it. She is very important to me. I do not want to hurt her so I have not said anything about us. Therefore if things develop to the point where she wants you, please don't upset her. I will not mind if you have sexual relations but you would have to let her down gently eventually. My love for both of you is too important to risk it in any way".

Anneliese continued "getting away from difficult subjects I thought that tomorrow I would take you to Sousse to see the printing factory. We won't take too long! I don't think you will find it fascinating after enormous car factories. So then we can relax and have some fun at one of the hotels in Sousse." "Anya will come with us tomorrow. I sensed from your expression that you were disturbed by what I told you. Please don't be. Let her enjoy herself tomorrow and most of her enjoyment will come from being with us. We are both modern Dutch women and are more than happy to share you. It will not impede our relationship in any way! Be assured that Anya is the only person in the world that I would agree to share you with. You both mean so much to me!"

These revelations astounded me. I was completely bewildered and uneasy because my initial thoughts asked a very difficult and emotional question. If Anneliese really wanted me as her life partner and had complete love for me, why would she be agreeable to me having any kind of sexual relations with her best friend? My mind began to analyse this in some detail. It culminated in an assessment that evoked a complete review of how life has become and where sex between a man and a woman sits.

In summary, it is clear that Anneliese has had intercourse with many men. That cannot be disputed. In today's world that is not perverse. To her it was just work! Similarly, I have had quite a few relationships and they all involved sex. Nowadays, almost everybody in the country has sex with several people before they find their life partner.

In this instance, Anneliese was doing no more than recognising that we both had a past. More than this, she was placing her love and affection on both myself and her best friend. And she was also doing this without any hidden jealously or potential animosity. She expected us all to be honest and, if I wanted it to develop this way, to manage it and keep us all happily synchronised!

I suppose, in my earlier years as a sexual heathen with continual promiscuous thoughts, I would have been in my element. Two beautiful women willing to accede to my desires.

In these circumstances, however, I concluded that I was not quite on the same page as Anneliese and would ride the white water as it flooded over me. Although I was very well aware of the fact that Dutch people were much more relaxed about sex, cannabis and leisure activities than we were, sexual liberation, to the extent that my potential partner would be happy to share me, was not easily accepted.

But, as they say, tomorrow is another day. Not much occurred for the rest of the day and we had tomorrow in Sousse to look forward to.

⟨⟩

Chapter 10

On The Loose In Sousse

The next morning as we were finishing breakfast and beginning to get ourselves organised for the day out, I found myself looking at Anya in a different way. My psyche was uncertain whether I needed to be reticent or forward towards her. However, my heathen instincts were rising. She was very beautiful with an amazingly proportioned body and a particularly voluptuous bottom, a liking of mine that I always had great difficulty suppressing. In the event, I withdrew, surrendered to my tender feelings for Anneliese and just got my mind back on getting ready.

After a short while Anneliese appeared, casually dressed but still elegantly attractive. She said that we should take swimwear just in case we would have a dip in a hotel pool. We all jumped in the Mercedes with Anneliese in the driving seat. Anya sat next to her and I became the rear seat passenger.

In her usual style, Anneliese went hard on the gas, foot down and more speed than seemed necessary under the circumstances. We drove the A1 again along the coast road south to Sousse. It took just over an hour and when we arrived the midday sun was beating down.

We were in a small industrial development and stopped at the door of a long single storey building. Anneliese led us through the entrance double doors into a small reception area.

The adjoining door opened almost immediately and a well-dressed gentleman greeted my two companions with double-cheeked kisses. Anneliese introduced us saying that this was Yousef who managed the printing side of the business. He was a long serving, highly skilled printer who had also served her father.

Yousef gave us an ear-to-ear smile obviously greatly appreciating these commendations. Anneliese said that we would not be staying long as we had a lunch appointment. A slight untruth but I was glad she had put that stake in the ground. On a hot day like this, I was not over keen to spend too long in a factory.

Once inside the work area, a young lady offered us bottled water or a cool lemon drink to carry with us. For me, the most interesting element of the tour was watching the Compositor setting the type blocks. Moving them around at great speed and accuracy. The rest of what was seen was rows of archaic fast moving-machines and equipment that clattered and rattled and occasionally needed a mechanic's attention.

Tour over, Anneliese explained that the publishing area of the business was essentially a small office block on the outskirts of Tunis. Not much to be seen there, other than six employees who, she said, were absolutely key to success of the business. Their main focus was to make the travelogues very attractive both in words and pictures.

We said our goodbyes and several of the factory staff came out with us and waved farewell. This had clearly been part of their morning drill!

Next, we drove to a hotel, The Khalef, on the edge of the city. There was plenty of parking and we went straight to the dining room for a buffet lunch. There was an amazing choice of fish, seafood, salads with many types of beans, cous cous, rice and cooked meats. I stuck close to the girls and followed their choices. They vocally salivated about most of the offerings and we all sat down with full, colourful platters. Wine followed and we all clearly enjoyed the first taste.

Once we had sufficient wining and dining, Anneliese and Anya chatted for a few minutes with some of the hotel staff. They were obviously well known and liked at this hotel. The staff, apparently, had made preparations for us outside by the pool and we were then shown to rooms for guests to change and prepare for the hot sun with complimentary sun tan lotions and oils.

The hotel itself was typically Tunisian with Moorish arches and domes. All the structures were brilliant white interspersed with some black ironwork and several palms. The building was a quadrangle shape with a gloriously inviting swimming pool in the centre.

One of the hotel staff showed us to our sun loungers by the pool. Indeed they were much more than sun loungers. I think Anneliese must have warranted celebrity tickets. These were in fact, two large double beds dressed in crisp white linen including enormous pillows. The back structure included a white linen canopy which was very acceptable to me as I am not a great sun lover. Especially, really hot sun, and that day it was in the late thirties.

Both of the ladies complained to each other that they wanted to get more sun and then trudged off to find a couple of beach chairs so they could sit outside the canopy and get the rays.

After I had settled, it was time to have a good look around. I was pleasantly surprised that there were so many people around the pool just relaxing on the riff-raffs normal loungers. In the hotel, on our beach, it had been difficult to find a tourist, which I suppose, near our village, was good in every respect!

I got up and decided to go for a wander around. As I strolled past the close-knit loungers, I paced slowly to listen to the conversations. My German is pretty good so I quickly realised that these people were mostly German. And then my searching gaze picked out several men wearing Munich style peaked caps. That was the confirmation I needed. I would bet their towels were the first on the sun loungers in the morning.

When I returned to our honey-mooners beds, my one was occupied. Anya was lying there looking like she was posing for Playboy. She was certainly the right calibre.

I sat on the edge of the bed, feeling extremely nervous. But then I thought, have some guts and deal with it. I lay down next to Anya and in the blink of an eye, her hand was on my chest. She asked "are you enjoying yourself, do you like this place?" I naturally responded with a big smile and "of course, how could one not".

To avoid what I thought might happen, I tried to get Anya into conversation. This had little success! It resulted in one word answers whilst her fingers explored my chest, belly and now at my belly button. All the while, I kept glancing at Anneliese who just smiled back at me, but I could not see her eyes as she was wearing sun glasses. Eyes always give the right answers!

Chapter 11

Reverse Somersault

So now I needed a manoeuvre to get me out of what could be an embarrassing situation. I said "excuse me" to Anya and sat up on the side of the bed. Anneliese, I said, she looked startled. "Anya told me that as a youngster you were a high diving champion. Can you still do it?" Anneliese replied "no, have not tried for years"

I persisted. "This is the right place to try and I would love to be able to boast about it. It's a fabulous pool with a twenty metre board. Is that the sort of height you did in the past? If you have a go for me, I will be so proud and I'll get you a drink as soon as you finish, whether successful or not!"

Anneliese stood up, then stood even more erect. "I will do my best" she said and set off around the pool. I had been devious just to get myself out of this awkward situation. But now watching Anneliese walk around the pool, with everybody watching her, I was so proud, her beauty and glorious figure could not be avoided. She reached the steps to the boards and everybody started to sit up in their loungers.

She started to climb the steps. Past the first board and carried on up to the high board. Now everybody was silent, sitting up and watching intently.

She walked out very gracefully on the high board. Then she astounded us all. She turned around and now was backwards. My pulse was racing. She edged her feet back slowly until her feet were over the edge of the board which now was just gripped by the balls of her feet and toes.

She sort of stretched her calf muscles a couple of times and then stood perfectly still. This seemed a lifetime long. Then with a flexing of her beautiful muscles, she flew into the air, tumbled three times and seemed to enter the water without a splash. I had goose pimples on my goose pimples.

As she surfaced, around the pool was completely silent. It was like we had just had an eclipse and now the sun was starting to shine again. I was ready to run over to her with a towel but the noise stopped me in my tracks. Everybody around the pool, especially the Germans, especially the Germans with Munchen caps, were on their feet applauding. But not just applauding. Whistles, shouts, banging their beer glasses on the side of their sun beds.

It was absolutely spectacular. I did eventually get to Anneliese with a towel and I could see from her smile that she had enjoyed the whole thing!

We got back to the sun beds and as Anneliese and Anya were caressing each other, drinks started to pour in. Almost everybody had bought us drinks. So there was nothing for it other than to get stuck in and enjoy the euphoria. We were all drinking so much, I began to wonder how we would get home, but Anneliese assured me she would be ok to drive.

With that, I excused myself to go to find the toilets. Walking inside the hotel, I overheard lots of Germans gabbling on about the dive "Fantastiches" I heard several times. I was exceptionally proud.

After finding relief, I started to walk outside to the girls. As I reached the first pillar under the hotel, I could see Anneliese and Anya in deep conversation with a couple of guys. They did look familiar.

I was only about ten feet away, so I stood behind the pillar and ear wigged. I thought they were probably Germans talking about the dive. But no, their language was not German. Mine is pretty good having spent a lot of time in Germany with Ford. This was very acute. Almost threatening. But I was sure the language was Eastern European.

I thought I needed to end this and came out from behind the pillar. Seeing me, the two guys turned and walked off. When I asked who they were, Anneliese brushed it off, saying they were a couple of Germans congratulating her on the dive. That was not the accent that I heard, or indeed, the threatening attitude and body language.

I think we were all determined to enjoy the rest of the afternoon. I only had two days left and wanted desperately to make the most of it. Similarly, Anya had decided she would carry on enjoying me. We all chatted and joked constantly, and when the chance came along, Anya would use every part of her body to entice me and stimulate a sexual response. On a couple of occasions, I stroked her body as my response, but mostly I took regular walks around the pool and into the hotel with the excuse that I wasn't much good at sitting still and doing nothing!

After a couple more drinks Anneliese suggested we head back. Anya reluctantly agreed but then said they should both check on the parents and cook their evening meal.

On arriving back, the girls went across the road to do their domestic duties. I had a short walk through the trees, stood on the edge of the beach and just simply admired the view, taking in the beach, the waves and surf and the overall vista. The blue of the sky and sea almost became one and the same, only broken by the white surf.

I returned to the villa, sat on the steps and had a chat with Glenn. Anya returned about half an hour later. She said that Frederika was not very well and Joe wasn't very hungry so Anneliese had prepared them a light meal.

She then asked me if some pasta would suffice for us. She would be happy with that and would begin cooking if I was hungry now. "That's fine" I said and opened a bottle of red. The routine red was taking charge of me!

I poured us both a glass and Anya sipped it as she started to boil spaghetti. Once it was on the stove, she sat on the arm of the settee next to me. We chatted about this and that and then attempted another glass of wine.

Chapter 12

She Decided To Sit On It

Half way through that glass, with the spaghetti bubbling away, Anya slid off the settee arm onto my lap. I held on tight to my almost full glass and instinctively placed by arm around her waist.

Kissing my face, neck and ears she began to whisper. I think it was Dutch or something else, but it was arousing. Her whole body was starting to wriggle, so my groin became awakened, embarrassingly so!

Her body was so soft and warm. Her buttocks were kneading me like warm dough. I was beginning to become a quivering mess. I was squirming in my seat.

I had constantly told myself that I would not allow myself to be indoctrinated by carnal lust which Anya's phenomenal body invited from every angle. My whole being was almost overcome by a clamouring need to dive directly into the inviting intimate pool.

Anya began to cling to me, urging me to quicken my response, hers was dramatic! So much so that I very soon realised that panties did not exist. The extrapolation of the urge to go further translated into deep, stirring kisses, tongues tangling.... But then I shakily came to my senses.

"Anya, please, I am starting to feel a strong affection for you so let's not spoil it with simple raw sex."

Not surprisingly the spaghetti was badly spoiled. Burned, in fact. We both attempted a loving smile and agreed to leave it for now and go off to bed. Another very loving kiss and strong embrace then we headed off to our rooms.

I lay in bed for what seemed like hours thinking about what had occurred. I concluded that I really was getting strong feelings for Anya, but more carnal lust in its strongest form! When I lay there thinking about what had happened all I could focus on was her bottom. It was a sensational shape and seemed to have a mind of its own.

In contrast, lovemaking with Anneliese was exactly that! Lovemaking. It had a completely different emotion and effect. She knew all the same sensual tricks, but there was a special feeling with it... maybe a feeling of love that very few people experience.

Anyway, maybe I am making more of this than actually existed. But all I knew was that both these girls were absolutely fantastic. But Anneliese had found a way to my heart. And I think I had found a way to hers!

We arose about 8pm and had the usual relaxed evening in wonderful surroundings and fabulous company. Both girls were in casual but very attractive outfits. We chatted whilst demolishing another bottle of red, but this time Cabernet Sauvignon. Food was Tapas style, which with the wine will always be one of my best memories.

I only had one more full day and the girls really went to extraordinary lengths to make me enjoy every moment of the evening. About 10pm Anneliese suggested we have a swim in the pool. It was a gloriously warm evening and for most of the swim I enjoyed embraces from both the girls. Next it was dry off and sample some American Bourbon that Anneliese had selected for our last drinks.

I am very capable with whisky but this firewater did some immediate brain cell damage. I became putty in their hands and that was all I wanted. I just wanted to be close to a female, any female.

Notwithstanding my needs, the girls decided to plan my last day. Indeed it really was only the last morning. Not the last supper! So my harem decided we should go and have an exotic breakfast at our neighbouring beach hotel. Due to my intoxication I did not really care. I just wanted my bed, which the girls proceeded to arrange for me.

Their parting shot was that they would get me up at 8am to go to the Hotel Marhaba. Anneliese would book it and we could have a very relaxed gastronomical morning. She would drive me to the airport and then Anya said she wanted to see me off as well. I was clearly a lucky, but drunken fellow. This sounded to be an auspicious occasion. But I went to bed hoping that this was not the end, and feeling pretty sad.

Sure enough, they got me up at 8am. Even helped me dress as I was a relatively drunken drunk. By about 8.30am, closing in on the hotel, I was beginning to feel life starting to course through my veins.

Once in the Marhaba, although my surroundings were hazy, I managed to join in the chat and appreciate that the girls were doing their best to resurrect me. After about 10 minutes, the whole of the bar and breakfast area was full of men in uniforms. A large contingent of the Tunisian National Guard had arrived!

They were interviewing and questioning the staff. I couldn't understand what was being said but could see Anneliese and Anya listening intently. After a while, I asked what was going on. Anya said, not to worry, there had been a road accident.

While this was all developing, we could not get served. I managed to catch the eye of a waiter that had served us before and knew that he spoke English. All I wanted was gallons of their thick dark coffee!

Chapter 13

Death In Paradise And More

He arrived with a big grin but before I could say coffee, he launched into an explanation. Two of the male hotel guests had been involved in a serious accident. But there was more to it. There were suspicious circumstances. They had been driving from Sousse, had gone off the road at a dangerous escarpment, down onto the rocks by the sea. They were Russian tourists and the police had found their hotel keys.

I asked, what was suspicious? The waiter replied that they were in a white BMW and, apparently, the police thought there were some bullet holes in the rear end, but could not be sure due to the significant damage to the vehicle.

My mind started racing. But I was still not in a very capable state. I looked over at Anneliese. Seeing my quizzical expression, she said "they were probably Russian Mafia involved in drugs. If so, they got what they deserved!" I nodded and then left the subject.

I ordered coffee for us and asked the waiter to come back in five minutes. As he left, I looked at Anya. She was looking straight at Anneliese and both of them had seriously worried expressions. My instincts said that this was not just concern for the calamitous situation. This was very real and personal to them. What I saw, without exception, was fear!

The rest of the time at the hotel seemed somewhat difficult. We all tried to introduce light-hearted subjects but mostly it seemed they sank slowly in the quicksand atmosphere.

After the police, the National Guard left. A waiter turned the bar television on. It was all over the news, and, it seemed constant news about this event. But not in English!

We almost ate ourselves silly with the gourmet breakfast. The girls wanted to get away from the news so we went outside, on the beach, for half an hour. Then Anneliese said it was time to go. I did not want to hear it. I wanted to stay forever. But nonetheless I understood we traipsed back along the beach. I had about 10 minutes to pack.

The drive to the airport was uneventful. Anneliese had booked me to fly from Carthage airport which was only about an hour from Hammanet.

We were all in a downbeat mood but on the way, they both promised to keep in touch every week and that they would arrange to meet up soon! What would have been marvellous, would have been to have facetime in those days. But not my luck. Whilst driving, Anneliese kept telling me how much she loved the Transit and that I had done a wonderful thing, getting it for her. She had already done 8000 miles!

We parked up right outside departures. I was dreading this point, I'm not good at goodbyes.

We stood on the pavement beside the Transit, Anya stepped forward first with a long embrace. She whispered in my ear that no man had ever resisted so long. I felt her hand slide down to caress the front of my chinos. A surprising leaving present. She carried on with the whisper "next time I will love you to ecstasy! Physical promises from Anya are hard to ignore!

Anneliese stepped forward. She kissed me with real loving passion and said that we would meet for Christmas. As she held me, she caressed my neck and pressed against me. Love exuded! Her beautiful blue eyes never left mine. She carried on "are you likely to be able to get to Cologne just before Christmas?" "Why yes" I replied, " I am there when I want as I always have work to do there".

Anneliese had a sincere look of happiness, and said she would let me know some dates and we could go shopping in the Cologne Christmas Market. To be honest, that did not excite me. However, a couple of nights with Anneliese was really something I could look forward to!

We all embraced and kissed again, then it was time to head into departures. I attempted to look unemotional, but I really felt choked to leave these wonderful girls.

Come Monday morning, I returned to my world of routine which initially seemed very bland and uninteresting. Then I was given a first piece of news from one of my colleagues. Apparently, the rumour going round was that in the near future the Company would embark on a global program to develop a common car for both the European and North American continents. The board had approved the strategy and we would have to wait for the detail.

The next piece of news that week was a real shocker. On Wednesday afternoon, the payroll cash had been delivered to Dagenham ready for the wage packets to be made up in the evening and next morning. However, overnight there had been an audacious well planned raid on the payroll building and about £800,000 had been stolen.

Some months before, a critical report had been written concerning payroll procedures and security in the major plants. This was in response to concerns raised by the

Security Company and the insurers. This report was sitting in my pilots case and pointed to the vulnerability of the building itself which was situated on the perimeter wall of the Body Plant.

Sure enough, that's how the thieves broke in. They used a JCB to ram the wall and managed to carry away the safe with wage packets and remaining cash. It had been a completely professional job by people that knew all the cracks and crevices in the payroll operation.

Now I carried on working hard, trying to be inventive, but with Christmas in my periscope. It surfaced above the waves about three weeks before Christmas. Anneliese e-mailed me, yes, by this time I had e-mail. In fact, I had had it several months but did not like it. It did not save me any time and most of what I received was cya's. In English "cover your arse" messages.

Anneliese wanted to confirm that I would be in Cologne ten days before Christmas and stay over two nights, I set about arranging it and then confirmed to Anneliese. The company had booked me into the Crowne Plaza but Anneliese thought it best we stay away from the popular hotels and she would arrange a quiet hotel. She would let me know nearer the time and I could cancel the Crowne Plaza. All good so far!

A few days later, she advised she had selected the Hotel Mondial, close to the Altstadt, with the market and many restaurants nearby. She would be bringing her two colleagues, based in Berlin, to dinner on the first evening and hoped I did not mind. These were her people working on US Imports.

That night, thinking about all this, my integrity switched in. Next morning, I moved my flight to a day earlier and the booking at the Crowne Plaza. And for the two days with

Anneliese, I would use vacation days. I had several work things I needed to get done in Cologne and, in addition, taking the vacation days would ease my conscience.

The day at work in the Cologne offices proved to be extremely productive. But every time my brain relaxed, it pictured Anneliese, so it seemed a long day, and the night much longer still. As I lay in my bed, my mind kept digging. Why would such a beautiful, intelligent woman have any feelings for me? Why would she even look at me? I know I looked reasonable but not a fabulous catch. Not exuding sex! Not exuding any form of attraction!

In the morning, I checked out of the Crowne Plaza, jumped in a taxi and ventured over to the Mondial. I was too early to check in, so I went for a walk through the Altstadt... the old town.

I found the walk around exhilarating. I had never really had the chance to absorb the sights of Cologne but this was awesome. I wandered through the Altstadt, admired the historic German architecture. I stopped at Papa Joes, a jazz bar that was alive and kicking at 1.30pm. I went in and it was busy, really busy! Its set up is unusual for a small bar. On the right hand side, they have tiered seats like in a football stadium. And the waiter brought your drinks to you. I had one there and loved the jazz music. I moved on, carried on to the big square by the Dom. That's the name given to Cologne Cathedral. Like the Germans tried to flatten St Pauls Cathedral, we did the same thing to the Dom. If you stand beneath it and look up, all the stonework is chipped and cracked by the bombs we dropped. So maybe God protected these buildings.

Just opposite the Dom is a bar called The Frueh. It is always full. You can have just a beer or a full meal. A full meal may include a pigs head complete with snout and eyes. Not for me, but an unusual spectacle to watch.

There were probably about fifty people just standing and drinking. I had a kolsch and then another. But then I wanted to trek back to the hotel because I didn't want to be drunk when Anneliese arrived. I had not paid a penny for my drinks, but when the waiter arrived he knew exactly what I had drunk and how many. With 50 people in the bar, how do they do that? But anyway, time to move on.

It was a gloriously bright winter's day and I headed back to the Mondial. I sat around in the lounge until Anneliese arrived. She looked and smelled wonderful. We checked in and went straight to the room. Except it wasn't just a room, it was a Penthouse suite. She had arranged our stay in the most luxurious room in the hotel!

As soon as I closed the door, her lips were on mine. Whilst our lips chewed on each other's and tongues tangled, she was taking off my clothes and hers in deft simultaneous moves. We spent the next hour making love. Continuous, spontaneous and completely unified love that culminated in us seeming a singular being.

The subsequent gentle embraces led our minds into generous warmth of feeling and we both nodded off on the luxurious pure white bed linen.

I exited from this snooze about 6.00pm. My mind immediately asked for more but Anneliese, in a hazy state, said that we were due at the restaurant at 7.30pm. I went for a shower. When I came out, Anneliese was recovering with a coffee. This room had all the comforts. I was beginning to dress as Anneliese stripped ready to take a shower. She was pulling on a soft Egyptian cotton dressing gown, and said "whilst I get dressed, why don't you go to the bar and I will meet you there in about 30 minutes. I want to surprise you with what I will be wearing tonight. I am doing it to please you, so look forward to it". I really wanted to get back in the shower with her but decided to go along with her wishes!

I sat in this bar, which I had sat in before, for about half an hour. Anneliese made an entrance. And what an entrance. I didn't even recognise her initially. She was wearing the Amsterdam dark wig and looked fabulous. She wore a fur coat with a bushy fox fur collar of a ginger colour. As she sat on the bar stool next to me, I felt so proud. Indeed I was so proud of how she looked, I was lost for words. She said "I would like a drink" The way she looked numbed my brain. I found putting words together really difficult. The barman overheard and asked "what would you like madame?" She opted for a red wine because she said we needed to go soon.

Anneliese finished her drink and we took off into the Altstadt which was just around the corner. Early evening had some snow, but it was a very clear but cold night. As we strolled through the Altstadt, Anneliese clung to my arm. The cobbles were slippery. She was wearing high heeled boots which did not help. As we walked she said we were going to a Thai restaurant halfway along the Altstadt. Was that ok with me? Well yes, it will be the first experience!

Chapter 14

Oh De Cologne Dinner

The restaurant was colourfully decorated. The waitresses wore bright green high necked dresses. The place certainly did not feel Germanische. We were escorted to a very bright corner and I immediately tried to be gentlemanly polite by helping Anneliese remove her coat.

I was over whelmed with the view. She was wearing a light grey woollen dress. It was so clingy and tight, it accentuated every tiny curve in her body. I could not take my eyes off her. She had a ballerina's waist with a curve in the small of her back that magnified the shape of her bottom right down her thighs. At that point, my eyes captured the soft leather thigh-high boots.

Yes, she had certainly found a pleasing outfit! Indeed, the thought occurred to me that it is somewhat peculiar how the female body, dressed in a certain way, can be sensually more attractive than the naked form.

My mind would have continued to wander through fantasy land had it not been for the arrival of our guests. Anneliese greeted them both and did the introductions. The man was Alphonse and the lady was Mia. She had a strong resemblance to Anneliese except she was blonde and an inch or so shorter. Smartly dressed and definitely beautiful, Alphonse was shortish, stocky and balding with dark hair at the sides.

Everybody agreed to settle for red wine and a jug of water. After the drink arrived, the general getting to know you chat began. Alphonse had been at Anne Arbor with Anneliese. He met Mia in Berlin where she was from. Now they lived there together. Alphonse mentioned how well the US Imports business was going and broke into thanking me for all my help. At that point, Mia pulled a bag from under the table and handed it to me saying it was a well-deserved gift. Inside was a heavy package which I began to open, but Anneliese grabbed my arm and said "no don't open it in here, I will explain later" casual talk continued mostly about how everybody's lives were going. Then I mentioned my interest in Berlin. Alphonse and Mia spent a while explaining how, since 1945, it had been split into sectors. They lived in the North West sector which was under French control. It had fabulous restaurants, night life and the patisseries, cafes and French cuisine which made it more than acceptable as a place to live. I had heard through Ford meetings that there was enormous political and community activity going on within Berlin because Gorbachev seemed to be relaxed and willing to enter into discussions about the future of Berlin.

I then let the wine get the better of my mouth and explained about the Company's plan for a global car and that they were considering opening a plastics factory in Berlin due to the rapid expansion of plastics in vehicle production.

They all listened intently. Alphonse sat very quietly, engrossed in thought, whilst I carried on explaining that my thinking was that a new world car would have developments in plastic to give a more comfortable interior. Soft feel plastics in particular would enhance the modernity of a global car.

Alphonse suddenly came alive "I have some contacts that operate in the world of venture capitalists" he said. "I may be able to put together a small group that would be interested in a joint venture with substantial funding input for the Berlin plastics plant"

He was clearly very intelligent and well versed in the world of business finance. He continued "to go a step further, it possibly could lead to establishing a separate company involving all the Ford component factories. These could be funded from a launch on the Stock Exchange as a major component company supplier to the whole motor industry. General Motors made a similar move a while ago!"

Alphonse's mind had gone through all the gears in quick succession. It was a novel idea but I slowed it down. My initial response was "I think it would be best to start with just the plastics factory first. I will give you some contacts, Alphonse, and I know you will understand that I must be kept out of it. However, all the very best"

Anneliese raised her glass and said "the future will be very bright for all of us". We all joined her in the toast. It was now time to depart. It only took a minute to say our goodbyes and let's meet again soon!" Anneliese almost dragged me out saying she needed to get me to the hotel.

We strolled along the cobbles with a crescent moon shining on us. Anneliese said she would make sure I got a share of any financial reward if a deal made it through. I started to resist that offer but Anneliese assured me that it would not impact my integrity as I would not be involved.

All of a sudden this struck me as funny. I said"I feel like I am involved in a James Bond movie. Three beautiful women orchestrating my life. I said that the latest, Mia, would have a Bond girl name like Mia Bliss. The Bond films that, in the circumstances, came to mind were Goldfinger and Octopussy. We should call our movie "Goldpussy". Anneliese thought this was hilarious. She laughed and giggled all the way back to the hotel which made me feel great as she was normally pretty reserved.

In the bar at the hotel, I looked around before we entered to check that there were no Ford people. All was looking good, so we sat and had a couple of drinks. The banter continued especially as we both had large ones. I had whiskies with a jug of water. This may just be imagination but if I drink it with lots of water, it really increases my virility. And I was glad I did, because with how Anneliese looked, after we entered our room it was totally X certificate. And then the morning was Y and Z.

But, as you can imagine, the next day I felt absolutely drained. I did my very best not to show it and I think I did fairly well. We eventually, after being playful, went off to breakfast. The one thing German hotels do well is a breakfast. We could have anything we fancied, cooked, cereals, fruit, pastries (as good as Danish), lots of different juices and mostly what I needed .... Good strong coffee!

We were leaving today. I'm not goodbye educated, I have said before, so we talked about the future at breakfast. Anneliese was heading straight back to Hammamet and I was going back to work. No question that we would keep in touch. We were now in a long distance relationship. But how did I deserve this with such a fabulous woman.

When we got back to the room, Anneliese held up the bag with the present in. "This is a present from me. I told Mia I wanted to give it to you but did not suggest she brought it with her. It is your contribution to our future, our savings plan. It is 30,000 US dollars!" I started to sound like a motor boat "but, but, but" Anneliese placed her hand over my mouth. "I knew you would be worried about taking this back through Customs, because you are so upright and honest" she said "you won't have to! I will take it back to Tunisia and invest it for us, but in your name. It will be in corporate shares and I will send you the share certificates. Think of it as your share options in our future. I never have a problem with Customs because they know me and I often look after them."

"The taxi should be here by now so let's get going" I was in a haze of disbelief but managed to finish my packing and get everything together. As we went down, Anneliese said she had settled the bill as it was her treat. On reflection, it was definitely a real treat for me!

The taxi was a beige Mercedes, just like Anneliese's. We chatted, held hands and I thanked her with all my heart for the gift and said I would never let her down.

Once on the autobahn, I noticed 100km speed limit signs which were very new. There had recently been a horrendous accident in fog on the ring road, and the speed limits had been introduced, as a response, by the local government.

I glanced at the speedometer. We were travelling at 160km, or close to 100 miles an hour. And our speed was continuing to increase. In the back of my mind was the accident that killed the two Russians. If it was an accident!

I shouted at the driver, "We are not in a hurry. We have plenty of time" He was a big guy with a handlebar moustache. He seemed to ignore me and our speed was still increasing... now 180km. So I shouted "Mein herr ist 100km bitte" He took his eyes off the road, turned towards us, smiled and said" ya per person!"

Anneliese had been relaxed through all this. Now she burst into laughter and I followed her lead. We immediately embraced and noticed the driver's eyes in the mirror smiling back at us.

We got to the airport in one piece. Anneliese's flight was first. I would be about 20 minutes after on the Ford flight.

We sat in a bar and I noticed several Ford guys arriving. I said to Anneliese "its your time to go, but please be careful, I just have this gut wrenching feeling that something bad is following us". Anneliese responded with a glorious smile and said "don't be silly, I have protection with me wherever I go and it's never let me down. God is always with us both because we are God people".

"1 will let you know when I am safely back. So stop worrying. I am a big girl that has streetwise in her DNA. We will soon arrange another meet and talk every week". I said "of course, I have loads of vacation so maybe we can get a few weeks together again soon" I really could not wait for that time. It would seem like an eternity.

Chapter 15

Down To Earth Comedy

I returned to work and made a conscious effort to throw absolutely everything into my work. Man management, or should I say, staff management, took up most of my time but I appreciated that I needed to learn and apply some of the techniques I had gleaned from managers I had worked for. This present position was challenging because of the staff numbers, about 120 in all. But what added to the complexity was that they were in three different countries; Britain, Germany and Spain. Although I had met with some of the Spanish personnel, it had been in Britain. I had not actually been to their home location in Valencia to get a perspective. That was a priority.

The British staff were the most eccentric bunch and I had to solve problems with them almost every day. Having said that, they were also the most entertaining, indeed I could do another book with the stories they created.

As we were approaching Christmas, I will tell this particular anecdote. One of the Cost Estimators never worked as an estimator. He was a comical Scotsman that originally had worked on the shop floor. He had never adapted to the essence of office work. So he had become a gopher. Go for this, go for that.

To say it mildly, he had an unusual look. Suits always appeared grubby and a few sizes too large for him. He had a very strong Glaswegian accent. His hair, at the back, was very long and grey. Down to his bottom, which he would tuck into his shirt. The rest of his head was bald and shiny.

The consequence of all these eccentricities was that he was always excluded from any external meetings, especially those where he would support a buyer in negotiating with our suppliers.

I could not afford to carry him, and he was not the only one I had to evacuate from the doldrums. I persuaded him to change to an almost normal, acceptable, conventional, look. Sent him for a complete makeover. Had his hair cut, nails and skin renovations. Bought him a new suit, I was quite proud of him at the end of all this.

Now came the test! I arranged, more like I pressed hard, to persuade Purchasing to take him on a Negotiation meeting. It was to be in Sheffield with a steel supplier just before the Christmas break.

We saw him off, forgot about it, and then all went for a Christmas break. On Christmas day, I received a call from Sheffield Police. He was in hospital seriously injured. I gave the police all the information I had about his home and also some colleagues' phone numbers that may be able to provide more help.

According to Police, in the evening after the meeting, which I would add he did well at, apparently he had a fear of fire in buildings so went looking for the fire exit in the hotel. Sadly, he found it. Except it was an exit with an automatic folding ladder. He stepped out of the exit door, gravity took hold, he ran down the lowering ladder which stopped six feet from the ground, which he hit with force. Not surprising, the speed he travelled down the ladder! He recovered, and in about a month returned to work.

I spent Christmas with my Mum and then brother and his family. He had two young children which made it more like Christmas should be. My brother and I had a couple of boozy lunchtimes that were a good laugh and it helped pass the time. I was missing Anneliese.

I called her a couple of times over the holiday and on Boxing Day, we had a really long chat. She told me every detail about her Christmas day with parents and Anya. A few of her staff joined in the fun and games Christmas night. It all sounded extremely normal except her sun was shining.

Anya had been a delight, doing almost very chore there is over Christmas. While we were talking on Boxing Day, Anya grabbed the phone, said several romantic things and how much she missed me. She then said "I want to come too". I was about to ask where when Anneliese snatched the phone back.

Anneliese went on to explain "I've had an idea. In mid-march there is a splendid fireworks festival in Valencia. If you can arrange to have a few days' vacation, we could meet there and have a great get-together". Without even thinking, I said "of course we can, sounds a fabulous idea" I continued, after my brain clicked in "that's a definite because I have needed to get to Valencia for some time to meet the people that work in my department. The timing is just right ".

Anya was starting to mean a great deal to me. Not romantically, although under any other circumstances, I could not have resisted her. I've always thought that the face has to fit! It was second over the finish line and the body was almost equal. But now I was realising what a lovely person she was.

On returning to work, I pressed on with several projects that all turned out extremely well. I was now getting invited to Senior Management meetings, sometimes in the boardroom.

At the end of January I called my manager in Spain, Santiago. I have never forgotten him. What a lovely man and his character was the same. I spelled out what I wanted to review with him and that I was planning to go to the Fallas of Valencia Festival (the fire festival). I would be with a couple of friends. He immediately replied "I will make all the arrangements and if you want me to, I will join you to show you around"

However, he carried on that there were some important work issues. He was getting a lot of flack from suppliers because they were not getting paid. He said the reason was that accounts payable and the supporting administrative sections had recently been depleted. He needed at least three new employees.

My life seemed to move like a tortoise as I couldn't wait to get to March and the visit to Valencia. Talked constantly with Anneliese who seemed very happy with the way her businesses were going. She had been travelogueing Kenya and Libya. With the different news reports I had listened to, they sounded like pretty scary locations. I pleaded with her to be careful and she was always upbeat about the places she had visited and blasé about danger. She would say "I always live with danger, it's my profession." That always concerned me.

About a week before we were due to meet, I had a lengthy conversation with Anneliese about Valencia. I gave her a complete round-up of everything. Described Santiago, explained the work staff problems he had and that he would be our guide if we wanted. She said she would prefer it if we just went for a couple of drinks or a meal one evening. She wanted to spend the short time with me rather than entertaining someone she didn't know. To be honest, I felt the same. So I would distract Santiago with work.

Anneliese then spoke about the staff shortages. She had some contacts in employment agencies that may be able to help. "What are the jobs he is looking to fill" she asked. There were three, but I only knew of an accounts payable clerk and a cheque writer. For the life of me I could not recall the third.

I made it clear these were very junior administrative positions but with scope for someone that wanted a career. These were the types of job and level I had started at.

She laughed and said "and look where you are now. I will do something to help through some contacts but I am sure they will find something. Do not say anything to Santiago, just in case it doesn't work out."

At this point I will take an interlude to explain that this was in the days before contactless, bank transfer, phone banking, internet banking etc. In those days, if you had an invoice or a bill, you paid it by cheque. Indeed, even credit cards were only owned by the few. I had one! Because I saw it was the future.

Work was going well. I was making friends in high places. Its true when they say it's not what you know, it's who you know. Well it's only a half truth. You have to prove your worth to the people that are worth knowing.

We had some comical times. One board meeting in particular proved humorous to the board members. Several of us supporting managers were invited to the meeting and some of the Brits got together and, because a lot of Germans were due to be in the room, arranged a surprise. We got there early and placed towels over half of the boardroom luxurious leather seats. When everybody arrived, there was quiet for a moment, then hilarious laughter.

Our German colleagues laughed as much as we did! We had to explain to several of the American contingent, but they also went into hysterics. The whole meeting was jocular and we were earmarked as the ones to watch!

Chapter 16

On Fire In Valencia

The day had arrived. Inside, I was so excited that I was going to see Anneliese. However, I had to contain the excitement for a couple of days as I had some work to do with Santiago.

I set off for Stansted, very early morning. We had our own Ford terminal to check in at. On the way, the radio news forecasts said to expect thunder storms.

Actually, the flight out wasn't too bad, but along the way we had quite a bit of turbulence. I was accustomed to this by now and even though I am not a person that likes heights, flying has never worried me.

It was a very quick check through at Valencia. Again, probably because it was the Ford flight. Santiago had booked us into a beach hotel, but only about 30 minutes' drive from the factory and offices.

From the airport, I took the Ford coach to the plant. It was extremely new compared to most of the Ford factories that I had worked in. Santiago met me and we went straight to his office, met the staff, and then got down to the staff shortage issues, reviewed several financial evaluations of potential suppliers, a quick lunch, met the Spanish Purchasing director and then it was close of business time.

Santiago had arranged a Company car for me which I dented just getting out of the parking space! Managed to drive myself back to the hotel. Santiago told me to be very careful, especially if traffic lights turned red. In this area nobody, apparently, is willing to slow down or stop on the red at traffic lights.

Once again intuition told me I was being followed. This was a small black VW polo that sat about 100 yards off me all the way back to the hotel. As I didn't know where the hotel was, I made a few mistakes which meant U turns, last minute turns and a lot of blaspheming. But he was always there behind me.

Arriving back, I was pleased with the hotel which was very clean and welcoming, with a very attractive bar and waitress. I just had to survive tonight and tomorrow then Anneliese would be with me. That was how my mind was working, I could not think of anything else!

Work the next day was less than interesting. It was mostly about personnel. I was asked by Santiago to review his staff's performance appraisals. We moved onto reading the CVs of the people selected for the three vacant positions. They would all start next week. Their CVs were all pretty impressive, I had a great deal of respect for Santiago's ability to spot people that had drive and initiative. So we were both exceedingly happy with the appointments.

I was really glad to get on the road back to the hotel. The heat was oppressive in the little Fiesta but once inside the hotel, the air conditioning worked wonders.

I made my way to the bar, the barman smiled and said the welcome gift this evening was a carafe of rioja wine. This Spanish wine had become my favourite. When he passed it to me, the carafe was more like a clay jug holding about 2 litres.

Just as I was thinking this was too much for me, Anya arrived at the door. The barman's eyes looked just like an American Bullfrog!

Next came the apex of my crescendo, Anneliese stood for a few seconds in the doorway, then started towards me. My pulse raced. She was untamed teasing elegance with overwhelming poise and beauty of movement, from head to toe. I just cannot describe how she made me feel. There are no words that pay homage to this beautiful creature. Anya was a few paces behind. Both Anya and Anneliese embraced me. My arm was resting on Anya's and I sensed how much she also loved Anneliese. The chemistry between the three of us, at that moment, was explosive.

The girls were sharing a room, so after a couple of Rioja's, they went off to spruce up. So did I, just changed into something casual but retained a jacket. Then we were off to the Fires Festival in, appropriately, the little Fiesta.

After about ten minutes of trying to park, I gave up and did what everybody else did. Parked three abreast in the main street. We set off walking with the hordes of visitors. As we walked, there were bangs and flashes everywhere as people decided to create their firework displays. There were many people representing firework companies, and, of course, they had to demonstrate the loudest and most fearful explosions.

We were heading to the Plaza de Valencia, the largest square, where they display the most fabulous Papier Mache sculptures and effigies. But there were many along the way. Exhibits such as Ronald Reagan, Margaret Thatcher, some celebrities and all extremely life-like. The main effigies were over 15 feet high and in consequence, the Bomberos (firemen) were in position ready to hose down the buildings.

As we were getting close to Plaza de Valencia, Anya stumbled due to an orange tree planted on the pavement. While talking, she did not see the missing slabs surrounding the tree, stepped into the hole surrounding the tree and head butted the tree full on. The impact made a small cut on her forehead and her nose was bleeding. I was so sorry for her. Such a pretty girl and immediately concerned about how she looked.

Rather dazed, she stumbled on with us trying to put a brave, although rather sad, face on it!

We could see the Plaza in the distance with an exact replica of the Disney Castle as the main attraction. We were early, the festival was due to commence at 8pm so we had 45 minutes to go.

At this point, we reached a welcoming Tapas bar so I suggested we go in and aid recovery with some sustenance. Then Anya looked and saw a Pharmacia a few doors along from the bar. She said she would go into the pharmacy, get some plasters and paracetamol. She would meet us in the Tapas bar in a few minutes.

All around us now fireworks were emitting loud bangs and colourful showers. We quickly headed to our targets. The bar was tiny as most of the Tapas bars are in Valencia but we were welcomed in for service.

We were standing close to the bar and just as the barman was passing drinks across to us, there was a gigantic explosion. So loud that the barman threw my drink all over my jacket. Everybody had stunned looks on their faces. There was a lot of Spanish shouting and everybody ran outside and we, naturally, followed.

A crowd was forming outside the Pharmacia, but they all stayed well back. I could not believe what I was seeing. Anya was lying in the doorway. I ran over to her. Whatever the blast was, it had caught her. For a few moments I stood and just stared at her crumpled twisted body. I thought she was dead. The shock, horror and disbelief cleared and, urgent assistance kicked in. I ran to her and kneeled down beside her motionless body. I knelt with a feeling of uselessness, not knowing what to do, what I could touch, what would help.

I was distraught. There was blood running from her mouth and her shoulder was at an obtuse angle, clearly abnormal. I had no idea what to do so I instinctively stroked her face and said "Anya, please open your eyes. Please talk to me".

An onlooker was standing close so I rudely shouted "phone for an ambulance". Anneliese arrived at the scene saying that she had phoned from the bar, but she also was clearly stunned. A few seconds later Anya opened her eyes and had the cheek to smile at me. "Are you ok" I asked in a trembling voice "don't know yet, my shoulder hurts, give me a few minutes and I'll be fine "she said.

Now Anneliese, with relief, knelt down and cuddled Anya. She had tears in her eyes and was visibly shaking. Anya started to get up. "I was just outside the door, there was a massive bang and that's the last I remember".

She must have been thrown like a rag doll at least ten feet. It must have been an extremely powerful banger, almost as powerful as a hand grenade. But that is sort of understandable because these firework companies pride themselves on the intensity of the explosion they can achieve sometimes going beyond the law!

We managed to get back to the Tapas bar. Everybody was concerned about Anya. She had a stiff drink. It seemed a lifetime waiting for the ambulance which never arrived. Eventually, Anya insisted she would walk back to the car. We set off, stumbling together and holding and helping one another. Anya wanted to stop occasionally to dab some gauze on her mouth. I had thought she had suffered internal injuries but instead she, somehow, managed to put her teeth through her lips.

In the city, the traffic was still awful. Nose to tail. In addition to the traffic noise, there were the constant bangs and whooshes from fireworks. The effigies in all the squares we passed were still burning. The Bomberos were literally hosing down buildings, even whilst people were standing on their verandas. It gave a fine spray to everyone walking along and cooled people down as they passed the burning statues.

We managed to find the car which, luckily, was now standing on its own almost in the middle of the road. All we wanted was to get back to the hotel, so we all clambered in and set off for the main highway which traverses several large lagoons that surround Valencia.

As we arrived on the edge of the city, the traffic lights that turn onto the dual carriageway changed to red. Without hesitation, I hit the brakes. A couple of seconds later, we were hit in the rear-end. It wasn't a tremendous crash, more a jolting loud bang that pushed us forward into the dual carriageway. Cars were swerving around us but fortunately, the traffic was relatively light.

A car that was suspiciously familiar, a black VW polo, pulled round us and stopped alongside. The driver shouted something through his open window. I could not hear, so I wound my window down and shouted Que? In the hope he would hear me. He started to open his door to get out. But everything moved onto a new level. There was an enormous crack/bang from behind my seat, I turned to see Anya firing a revolver at the guy! But her repeated shots just sprayed the side of the car.

In the next second, Anneliese was screaming "drive, drive, drive!" she was bent low with her head below the dashboard and Anya was continuing to fire. In hindsight, it must have all just blended with the noise from the multitude of bangs, crashes and flashes from all the fireworks.

I hit the accelerator, swerved then recovered and full throttle onto the dual carriageway. All Anya could say was "nobody is following". Anneliese never spoke. In fact, she looked extremely composed considering what had happened. I never said a word, just concentrated on having my foot flat to the boards. And Anya continued to simply stare out of the rear window.

There was a scary point close to the hotel where we had to travel across a humpback bridge. I was now so confident with my fast driving that I kept pressure on the accelerator onto the bridge. At the top, we took off like Evil Knievel. At the bottom of the slope down there was a sharp left hand turn around a wall. I swerved sharply, almost lost it, recovered and we were safe. I slowed, and we all burst out laughing. Anneliese grabbed me around the neck and smothered my face with kisses.

Anya was also cuddling me from behind. I turned to her and said "thank God for the Advanced Drivers Course that Ford sent me on and the wonderful Dunton Test Track" we giggled and enjoyed the moment as if we had just won the Grand National. In our world, it was even better.

We helped Anya out and all headed straight for the bar. Other than scrapes and bruises, Anya had recovered. At that moment, I realised that Anya was a very strong, fit, well-trained lady who could handle any situation!

We got in the bar and, to be quite honest, I don't remember much more. The adrenalin mixed with the alcohol was very, very potent. I said, what if he finds us tonight! All both girls kept saying was, they will not try, and if they did, they are no match for us! I believed them. But this scorched a burning question into my mind! Who are THEY?

After, I am not sure how many hours, we went to bed. All the time, on the way to our room, I kept saying "you must explain to me what is going on" Anneliese said, they would explain in the morning. All I can remember saying is "it doesn't scare me, I have been in a lot more shit. I know I'm pissed but I can look after myself".

The only thing I can remember after that was saying "if I had listened to Santiago and not stopped at the red light, he wouldn't have rear-ended us" We, by now, were all three in bed together. No hanky panky, we were just too far gone. But the emphasis I put on "rear-ended" set the girls off laughing again. This time, the effort of laughing sent us all off to sleep.

In the morning, the hangover was in charge. We all found it difficult to get our thoughts together on what to wear, and finding the clothes was even more laborious.

I was first down to breakfast. I opted to start with several cups of Spanish thick dark coffee. The girls arrived and we all silently selected from the sumptuous breakfast buffet.

Back at the table, Anneliese looked me in the eyes occasionally, but always had that naïve innocent look designed to divert you away from asking difficult questions. In contrast, Anya's face and expression almost demanded me to ask the question. It was the question that I had muttered in a drunken state at the end of last evening. However, my brain had cleared sufficiently to decide a strategy.

Chapter 17

The Bottom Line

Looking at both of the girls, I forcefully said "I must know what is going on, but we should not talk about it in here. After we have finished, can we go for a walk to the tennis courts at the back of the hotel, in the sunshine, and talk about it"

They both nodded, silently. From that point the silence was deafening. Reading the signs, we had all finished our breakfasts, I stood up and walked towards the door. Both girls got up and followed. Once outside, they both joined arms with me and we sauntered out to the tennis courts. Nobody would be playing this early. I spotted a couple of spectator benches and headed for them.

We sat down, the girls either side of me. A moments silence whilst I gathered my thoughts. I then delivered the question, "Girls, I need, and you must help me to understand, what is going on. Last night brought it to a head, but there have been several unsettling coincidences. So please tell me. And what justified firing a gun? And why did Anya have a gun?"

Anneliese looked at Anya, a determined but authoritative piercing look. I had never seen such a facial expression before and it disturbed me.

Anya looked into my eyes. Indeed her look smothered me and said you must believe me! She started to speak in a way that was strong and convincing "I will try to explain as it really is. You have known us both for quite some time so I am hoping that there is some trust. Anneliese is my boss but also my best friend. You met us both in Amsterdam doing a sordid job but that was part of an overall much larger plan. We were there because we had been sent there by the organisation we work for. It's a long story, however, there will be some gaps. Things we cannot tell you until we are completely sure we can trust you and you have the stomach for what I am about to tell you " I listened intently and was ready to memory-bank every word.

Anya continued "since University we have worked for an organisation, a Government Organisation which has two main objectives. Firstly, to respond and prevent espionage by enemy governments. In a nutshell, we are involved in counter espionage for the West. We are under attack from the East constantly and our job is to neutralise their efforts. I say our job, but my boss, Anneliese, is in charge so perhaps she would like to add something".

Anneliese looked towards both of us and remarked "Anya is doing great without me, so she should carry on" In my mind I wanted to hear from Anneliese but I started to respect her position and authority.

Anya took over again. "I cannot name the organisation we work for yet. That may come later. Some of the incidents you have seen are explainable. Anneliese was set up in Tunisia by Western Governments. Everything there was her cover. The car accident in Tunisia that you saw on the news was due to us. Those guys were Russian Mafia. We had been supplying them with information while we were stationed in Holland. It continued in Tunisia, mainly information concerning financial and fraudulent opportunities. The

Russians have very strong links and interests in those Middle East countries.

Of course, the information we provided had been doctored sufficiently to ensure they only made small gains. However, we were alerted to the fact they had begun to suspect us and so, followed us continually. In consequence, to eliminate the risk, KGB operatives neutralised them!

The attack on me last night at the festival was not intended to kill me. It was just a warning to do as we are told and to do better. The bastards concerned are Russian Mafia. It was their guy at the traffic lights too. The whole event was just an attempt to scare us into providing them with lucrative information.

This whole scenario is like a game of chess. We are clear on who and where our allegiance lies. However, our enemies think we work for them. We constantly feed them titbits of information. Sometimes we give them clues or absolute information that is deliberately inaccurate or misleading so they draw the wrong conclusions.

The KGB are always in our back pocket as they believe we work for them, but now have suspicions. But it was Western Governments that set up the cover for Anneliese in the Middle East. They always maintain a low profile, unless they fear we need protection. The swimming pool incident in Sousse was Russian Mafia threatening us. Our KGB friends heard about it and decided to eliminate the threat. There is no love lost between those two Russian organisations."

Anya now stared straight into my eyes. "You will be going back to your secure British life tomorrow. You have two days to think over our offer for you to join us. We both love you and know you would bring a lot to the party. Yes, it is a party because we are the best there is at our jobs.

Anneliese is already building a fortune for us all to share. If that is not enough of a carrot, then you have the affection of both of us". Anneliese smiled and gave me a very cute wink. Anya carried on "yes and some of that fortune includes significant financial returns on investments you gave us, and we know you will work well in our team and find ways to make even more money!"

We will be in touch and if you are agreeable we will make sure we tell you everything you need to know and how to survive with us.

And there's one more thing. There are two options that will probably be considered. You may think, given your honest understanding character that you should go to the authorities. Don't even think about it. They will think you are in la-la land, and you have absolutely nothing that would be considered evidence.

The other option, and we would never go this route unless you forced us to, would be to expose the financial return that you received for the US imports programme. Your monetary gain has been invested by Anneliese in your name and it can be proven. However, as I said, we both think the world of you and this action would be the very last resort".

Anneliese grasped my hand for a few moments and said "please, please stay with us. You will not regret a moment." Standing by the tennis courts and close to the beach, we all went our separate ways to get to grips with the whole scenario.

After five minutes or so, I became panic stricken. My heart was pounding and I was breathless. I have never really done anything criminal, fraudulent or even dangerous in my whole life, other than a few serious punch-ups in the East End. I have seen friends and other people attacked and even tortured, but only from a distance. However, none of it was on the scale of what was being talked about here.

My brain seemed to gradually settle and the panic moved to disbelief. Was it the case that this was all in Walter Mitty land. It all seemed completely unbelievable. The next phase had more clarity. Of course, this was all real! I had sensed that things were not what they seemed. There had been too many coincidences. I had seen and experienced the collision, the unexplainable fortune that Anneliese had amassed in Tunisia, the results of aggression and Anya firing a gun in the middle of a Spanish city.

As I walked, deep in thought, towards the beach, I could see Anneliese and Anya in the distance. My thinking began to become somewhat composed. The deciding elements were now becoming solidified at the bottom of my mind.

These two women were extraordinary. They were intelligent, composed, unafraid and extremely beautiful. They had given me several exciting and rewarding months. They had enhanced my ability to enjoy life on permanent adrenalin. They had already made me richer than I had ever imagined. I could go on forever, but I had reached the bottom line. My life had been transformed from one with a job that I loved, but that had a high percentage of drudgery.

I still had that job but now it could be under-written by constant excitement, ever increasing wealth, two people that I loved and had the support of an extraordinary secret organisation. Then it struck me. Little nobody me, the paper boy, was being invited to join this team. By now I was ignoring negatives. On that basis, I would be a real plonker to refuse!

I caught up with the girls. As I got close they had uncertain expressions. A few yards away, I almost shouted IDI. Anneliese said "what is IDI" I replied laughing with excitement "IDI AMIN, you know! Its cockney for yes I'm in" They were both totally bemused.

The rest of the day I tried to relax, but the girls asked me several times if I was sure and said they were so pleased. However, this did cause me to go back over it in my mind, constantly analysing all the past events. I continued to respond positively saying it was the best offer I had ever had!

Both Anneliese and Anya pampered me throughout the day. Then over drinks in the evening. Anneliese sat close, held onto my arm and said "we do have to make sure you are prepared to cope with this new career". Her smile loosened me, but not totally. She went on "you will need some training. It won't be too difficult or strenuous. You are a very fit guy, with all the football you played. So you will gobble this up. I will prepare the plan and organise it for you. It will be in America but I know you will be inventive and find a way. Also, I will ensure I am there with you!"

For some unknown reason this conversation with Anneliese seemed to calm me. I was due to leave early and we all had a fantastic evening. Late on, there was dancing at the hotel. Anneliese took hold of my hands and led me onto the floor. It was Spanish salsa type music which Anneliese was superbly competent at. We started slowly and as we did, she looked straight at me and said that she had a lot of administrative things to straighten out and that it would be about three months before we would be together again. As she finished speaking, the music was reaching a crescendo, she pulled me toward her and gave me the most sensual French kiss. As we pulled apart, the music was bewitching. My body took control such that we were sensually synchronised through the closing stanzas.

As we walked hand in hand off the dancefloor, the people all around at the candlelit tables were completely silent. But as we sat down, people waved and smiled at us and a few guys came over and offered us drinks. It was a Valencia farewell.

I spent a very hazy night, once again alcohol, with Anneliese. Anya kissed me goodnight and said she would see me at breakfast. I had to be away to go to Valencia airport by 6.30am. But sure enough, both girls were there with me for breakfast. It was a quick, brief intake of coffee and croissants. Then we said our goodbyes. I was so sad, and they also seemed overcome emotionally. But we had managed to stay together so far, so I kept telling myself this would not end.

Once on the plane, looking around, seeing various work colleagues, I felt different. It seemed I was entering a dual life! Then it dawned on me. I had signed up to a double life, the more it sunk in, the more excited, but also apprehensive, no fearful of what I may have let myself in for.

The office surroundings, and people, brought me back down to earth with a resounding, muted, nothingness. I was getting back into it after a couple of hours, it seemed that darkness had descended. I was fighting back because that's me. Nothing is going to depress me. I am a survivor. I had watched my Mother, a single mother, survive in a world where there was no help! So nothing was going to get to me.

Then the phone rang. It was my German boss. He was a gentle character who always relied on me. He was a very slow English talker. After all the pleasantries, he got down to it. "Matthew, something urgent and important has come up. Can you fly over tomorrow as we need to have a meeting as soon as possible"? "Of course" I said "I will get Jenny to get it booked and I will be in your office about 10am". He continued "but if there are any issues let me know and I will get emergency approval".

⸺◈⸺

Chapter 18

The World Is Your Oyster

That last sentence made me realise this was something big. Thinking it over, I decided in my mind that it was to do with the rumours of a "world car". We had never researched, designed and manufactured a vehicle that was common to the main markets of North America and Europe and obviously, the rest of the world. The potential cost savings, particularly economies-of-scale were enormous. However, on the minus side, the complexities were just as large. There was also the human aspect. People find interference and change difficult to accept.

So we had two teams. The North American team and the European team. Both very strong teams that loved most of how they did things on their pitch. Now, a "world car" would have a severe impact on the thinking and processes of those two individual teams. What a challenge that would be!

I arrived on time. Got off the coach, and carrying my faithful old pilots case ventured into Otto's office. He was waiting. As usual a very polite welcoming boss who always appeared in good spirits. He was much older than me but from his demeanour and way he had handled difficult situations before, a very wise and astute character.

We sat at his visitors table with coffee and chewed the cud for a few minutes. Then he got straight to it. I was right, it was the "world car". It had a code name CDW-27. Careless talk would result in a cyanide pill! He went on that I had been selected to head up the team supporting a new global purchasing organisation. I would need to arrange a system to select the best suppliers in the world from those nominated by North America and Europe purchasing organisations. Most importantly,. This new approach needed to prove it had achieved substantial economies-of-scale.

I asked, "Will I still be working for you Otto?" no, was the answer. "A new Director, an American, will be coming to work with you and the whole team". Otto knew I was dying to ask the next question and so pre-empted it "yes, you will get an upgrade and maybe 2. It will take a while to evaluate it".

"Before I ask you to decide if you accept" he added "you will be required to travel to the USA every couple of weeks or so because you need to lead and manage the US part of your team".

I responded with "may I have a couple of days to think it over" "no" he replied "I must have an answer by close of business tomorrow. "As we finished, I remarked that I was positive. He smiled and said "have the rest of the day in Cologne, enjoy yourself", I thought, not half as much as the last visit!

The next morning in the office, I had just got a coffee when the phone rang. The staff were all starting to arrive, shouting, good morning and smiling at me. My secretary was getting things organised, I answered the phone and it was Anneliese.

As everybody was around, with some taking an interest, I immediately responded with "I can't talk right now, could you call later?" Anneliese said with a dictatorial tone, "you don't need to talk, just listen. That new job, it has been organised for you. There have been a lot of people being encouraged to engineer this for you. Just trust me." She clicked off, the line went dead.

I sat trying to compose myself to think clearly. After a new minutes of replaying all the happenings in fast reverse, I phoned Otto "I willingly accept the challenge" I said. He gave me a great vote of confidence, saying that he was sure I would do an outstanding job and that I could talk to him at any time. His final words were "go and make me proud of you". That meant so much to me.

Over the next few weeks I carried on trying to focus on the job in hand. From various emails, copied to me, I could see things were taking shape rapidly. I suppose I expected Otto to ring me soon to tell me the next steps. However, the surprise came with an email from a name I had not heard before. It gave me a number to call and the time to call.

Later that evening I called the number. A lady answered and said in a very polite way "oh we were expecting you. Gordon does not have long so I'll put you straight through".

A cool, American film star voice answered. "Hello Matthew, this is Gordon, Gordon Rousell. We are going to be working together on this massive programme. I know you are up for it! Listen, I don't have long, can you get yourself over here around mid-May. You may bring one of your staff, the key person you will rely on for admin. I will send an email with info I need. Great to talk, thanks ".

After the call, my mind immediately began to question and research the latest events. How did Anneliese know I'd been offered this job? Who are her contacts in Ford; it seems she has eyes and ears everywhere. The word she used, "engineered", certainly raised many issues in my mind!

The day came, mid-May, and there I was, seated in business class on a Pan-Am 747 taxiing to take off to Detroit.

There had been more mystery just before I left home. Anneliese had emailed saying she would find me in the Hyatt Regency hotel to explain in more detail.

Although I didn't have a clue about where all this with Anneliese was taking me, I had already signed up with her organisation and I do not go back on my word. And in any case, I told myself, they certainly appeared to be organised and know what they were doing.

I caught a taxi at the airport and went straight to WHQ to pick up a car. It was a white Thunderbird with all the trimmings. A fabulous eye catcher!

As I was checking in at reception, Anneliese came over to me from where she had been seated. As usual, she had fabulous poise and charm, but now she added a very professional business-like greeting. Shaking hands but keeping her distance. When I looked closer, unexpectedly she was wearing a business suit which enhanced and portrayed her as a prominent business figure in the car industry.

Anneliese whispered, "Let's find somewhere quiet to talk". We sat at a small coffee table in the corner of a lounge. She started saying, in a very quiet voice "We have to assure everyone that we are just business colleagues. There must be absolutely no shows of affection". She then handed me a mobile phone. "My number is in it "she said, "In a moment you should go to your room. We have separate rooms. Get yourself showered and ready and we can meet for dinner about 8pm. I'll see you in the bar".

I'd not had a mobile before, but it was quite clear this was for secrecy between Anneliese and me. One drink at the bar and we sauntered to the restaurant; a few feet apart. At the entrance the Maître De explained that I required a jacket to enter the restaurant. It was a very warm evening so I had dressed in a crisp white shirt without a jacket.

But as you would expect, the Maître De produced a jacket from a rail, full of jackets for unknowing people like me. It was light grey, but excellent quality and a very good fit. He showed us to a quiet table. The restaurant was very tranquil at that time.

Still using a whispering voice, Anneliese set down some markers. Looking straight into my eyes she said "In the new world you are in, I am the boss. At certain times, we will need to be actors and this is one of those times. While we are at Ford, you are my boss. I am your PA. We have no form of relationship. If anyone hits on me, you sit back and let it happen. No jealousy, no heroics! But you know it means nothing. The truth is; you are mine and I am yours".

"I know you are sitting there with curiosity gnawing away at you. Blank it out. I will tell you some things for now, as much as you need to know for the safety of both of us. And you must trust me, because I am experienced and have been doing this job successfully for several years".

"To begin, we are agents of the West, that is Europe and North America. Our Organisation is CECD which stands for Counter Espionage and Criminal Deterrent. It is the first organisation of its kind owned jointly by America and Europe. So right now we are on home territory. Our cover and support in America is always superb. Companies like Ford are key to the economies and well-being of America and Europe. So getting me into a salaried position at Ford was not difficult, because it is in their interest to assist if they can.

The wider aspect of this is that our masters have unearthed fragments of a Russian plan to infiltrate major U.S. Companies. Ford is a prime objective due to the world car strategy. In essence, the Russians are planning to disrupt the whole program with consequential severe damage to the Ford Corporation.

I repeatedly stated it is a Russian plan as opposed to saying KGB. This nuance is essential because it recognises analyses that has detected collusion between the KGB and the Russian Mafia. And if we are correct, it further indicates that a Senior American Politician is passing secrets to these Russian organisations.

Information, some of it from your Ford involvement, was used to play this politician, he took the bait and now is a Key target. I will not go any further for now. Other than to say do not trust anyone! Obviously, you must have complete trust in me and Anya.

Lastly, and this is very important, I have clearance throughout the Ford system. HR have all my details, education, previous employment and so on. None of this personal data can be seen by anyone without special access. I have a security number and security badge. As you know, these are the only personal details needed to be an employee of Ford.

The bottom line is that all this HR information, personal details etc is false. I think the line goes, all details have been changed to protect the innocent. I have a new passport, driving licence and bank account to support me while I am with you at Ford. But the key thing to remember is I have a new name. It is KAREN FLEMING. Memorise it! Practice it all night. Do not make a mistake tomorrow. We will probably have several meetings and you must not let us down."

Next morning, Anneliese and I were in Gordon's office by 8.00am. He got straight to work with us. Anneliese sat taking notes on her laptop. Gordon set out briefly and succinctly the first phase plan to get things moving. We would meet at 9.00am with the staff he had selected as his support team. He and the team would work directly with the European and American Purchasing organisations. The Board had stressed to these organisation heads the importance of assisting our teams.

He would be joining us in the UK mid-August and by then, it was key that I had my team in place. He thought it should be a team of about 10 people to develop procedures to evaluate and select preferred world car suppliers.

Clearly, this would be consensed with Purchasing. The difficult task for us would be determining targets for the price of key components which would support substantial economies-of-scale. Global single sourced suppliers was the key.

We would all meet in the U.S. just before shutdown, the second week in July, to set out the world car objectives.

Most personnel would go on vacation in shutdown, between the last week of July and end of second week of August. We would all resume business at that time.

Throughout this period I sat listening, intently. But not just listening. I focused completely on Gordon, watching his body movements, every tiny element of his make-up, trying to assess the character of the man.

I decided I liked him, from what I had seen and heard. He had a very vibrant and charismatic personality. His stature was almost as impressive, being about 6 feet 3 inches tall, stocky build with strong positive movement. His demeanour was very likeable and his face, to a woman, probably handsome. Blondish hair with a strong chiselled chin and smiling blue/grey eyes. My thought was that we were going to get on famously well.

Towards the end of our meeting I caught Gordon glancing at Anneliese and, especially, her legs. She had closed her laptop and was moving as if to stretch and with that had crossed her legs a couple of times. It hinted at being deliberate, and I didn't blame Gordon one jot as it was difficult not to look at her.

Chapter 19

Everyone Needs A Rest

The meetings through the rest of the day were largely structured as meet and greet and get to know you meetings. Mostly very boring and with a lunch in the middle which comprised sandwiches and Danish pastries.

Next came my memorable faux pas. At least memorable for the Americans I would be working with. It was towards close of business and most people were getting fidgety. Several people, predominately ladies, left their seats and after a short while re-entered the room.

I turned to Gordon and asked "where do the people keep going?" he responded with "the restroom". Naively I asked "is it a legal requirement to provide staff with a rest during the afternoon?"

Gordon started a low tone giggle which turned into outright laughter. As he calmed, and probably because most of the audience were looking quizzical, he explained to everybody's amusement what had been said! He followed this by saying that in the U.K we do not have restrooms! We have toilets or, and he dragged on the syllables, La-va-tories!

From the chat which followed this meeting, I knew that this mistake had christened me as the "Memorable Manager".

As we left, Gordon asked Anneliese and me if we would join him for an after work drink in our hotel bar. I agreed saying that would be great. Gordon said about 7.30pm to give us a chance to get back and ready. He would not be able to stay long, family commitments, and would bring Bill, the U.S. Estimating Manager, along who I had met during the day.

Anneliese and I met in the bar dead on 7.30pm. She had changed into casual clothes, but they were fairly reserved. About 15 minutes later, just as we had been served our drinks, Gordon and Bill arrived.

They both wanted a small beer and while I was ordering, they started chatting with Anneliese. It turned into a Q & A session regarding her personal history. Both guys seemed extremely impressed with the fact she had attended Ann Arbor, a segment of Michigan State University.

They pressed her on why she had not joined a car company, given the proximity to Detroit. She handled all the questions perfectly, almost as if she was working from a prepared script. Essentially, she used an explanation of needing to return to Europe to care for her family, had got some experience in other Companies, and then used her CV to get into Ford of Europe. So she had got into a car company via a circuitous route.

Both guys hung on her every word. I could see that her earlier assessment of her power over men, due to the way men's brains are wired, was completely true. This may apply to many women but they don't necessarily recognise it, or indeed, know how to apply it. That did not, in any way, dovetail with Anneliese's psyche!

About 9.30pm Gordon and Bill made their excuses for having to leave. They both shook hands with Anneliese and me, then we escorted them to the door. As Gordon was opening it, he grabbed my arm and whispered "where the hell did you find that lady, she is going to be one hell of an asset to you and your team! In fact, I guarantee she will set the whole of Ford alight". As I walked back, my thought was the word "alight". It struck a nerve considering all I'd seen recently.

After a couple more drinks, we said thanks to the barman and paced off to our rooms. We were in the elevator alone, so we kissed but Anneliese made me promise to be good to my word.

When back in my room, I felt completely empty. So I began to get tempted to get my bag and go to Anneliese's room. But no, I told myself, this new job requires me to be professional. I snuggled down in the bed but hated that feeling of total excruciating loneliness.

We had the next day free, but only until our early evening flight. We met for breakfast at 8.00am. I suggested to Anneliese that we should go for a wander in the hotel. I wanted to show her the Rotunda that not only gives you a fantastic view of the Detroit skyline, but also gradually rotates so you get a 360 degree view. After, we would take in Greenfield village which has a superb array of historic buildings, including Edison's house, Henry Ford's first factory and several bars and hot dog stalls.

Following breakfast we went back to our rooms. Then my testosterone took charge. I packed my bag knowing that any Ford people would have gone to work by now. I arrived at her door, knocked and simultaneously glanced up and down the corridor, checking for anybody coming.

She peered through the tiny security peephole, then let me in. We spent over 30 minutes in the shower together. We were both feeling exhilarated but physically exhausted. We lay on the bed together for about ten minutes and in that short space of time, Anneliese recovered. She decided that what we both needed was her very special moisturising cream.

She worked on both of us with such a gentle masseuse ability that I felt just like a new born baby. Again we contemplated the ceiling for about ten minutes.

And then, and I don't know how, her stamina seemed to be completely recharged. "Ok, Matthew" she said "it's time to go sightseeing. We are off to Greenfield Village".

I watched her slowly and seductively dress her body in silk, flimsy cotton, and sheer nylons. It was such a turn-on my whole being awakened. She saw this in its raw form and said in a commanding voice "come on, get yourself going, get your jeans on and get your mind on what we are doing next".

I needed that prod. So we were soon in the car and travelling along Southfield freeway to Greenfield Village. As I drove, the sky began to darken and became threateningly stormy. Thunder and lightning started and intensified all around us.

Then I began to notice cars in front of me pulling off the freeway. In fact, quite a queue formed leaving the freeway at a ramp that led to a tennis club. These people must have known, from experience, what would happen next. As we were inching forward through the entrance to the tennis club, the heavens opened. Loud thumps and bangs which became violent crashes were soon occurring all over the roof of the car. As I turned in, the wind direction caused the massive hail stones to impact the windscreen which cracked and shattered as we drove. Yes it was a hail storm the like of which I had never seen before. These hail stones were the size of tennis balls.

At the entrance door to the club was an awning and lots of cars had managed to get under it. But there was no room for us so we both sat, sometimes with fingers in our ears, suffering the onslaught. Anneliese remained surprisingly calm, and after about 15 minutes the storm subsided.

We both got out and stood staring at the car. The whole car looked like it had been attacked in a war zone. The car was driveable, but vision was difficult so Anneliese used her mobile to contact Ford WHQ security. She explained about the storm and damage to the car. They offered to pick up the car and deliver another one, however, as we were returning to the UK she said it was not necessary. Instead, they very kindly called a cab for us which got us back to the Hyatt Regency. There was no point trying for Greenfield Village as we were not left with enough time, so we went to our rooms to pack and have a short rest.

Chapter 20

Now We're Up The Pole

Although we had plenty of time, we agreed to get to the airport early, intending to have a couple of drinks in the frequent flyers lounge. Reception called for a taxi and it arrived pronto. The driver, a well-built white guy, grabbed our cases and stuck them into the trunk. We were in the rear seat with Anneliese directly behind the driver.

As we drove away from the hotel, the bullet shield arose behind the driver. My thought, initially, was this gave us some privacy. And it's not unusual in America, and especially Detroit, to give the driver security. Also, the sound of the doors locking was not unusual, but we were now firmly locked into the rear cabin!

Entering Dearborn village, the driver did a sharp left turn into a car park at the rear of what appeared, by the neon signs outside the place, to be a girly or pole dancing club. We came to a halt as I was about to ask Anneliese why we had stopped here.

The driver got out of the car and immediately came to Anneliese's door. The doors had automatically unlocked as he got out and he was attempting to open her door, but she clung onto the interior door handle. All the time, he was shouting "you clever f…ing bitch, now you will learn respect".

With that, Anneliese put her foot on the door and kicked it outwards. The edge of the door hit him with force, in the chest. I was rooted to the spot but not Anneliese! She scrambled out of the car and as she did, he grabbed her hair. She then did a full spiral spin and using the velocity of that spin, hit him with a clean karate chop full in the throat. The ferocity of that blow made his eyes bulge and both his hands flew to his throat as he gasped for air.

Now she was free from his grasp, she took half a step back then with tremendous force, kicked him in the genitals. The kick resembled a footballers toe punt using 90 degree ankle angle combined with the hard toe of her shoe. From now on, his proboscis would be one continual oscillating throb.

He fell to his knees, but she didn't stop there. She brought her right knee up under his chin with such speed I swear I heard his teeth shatter. He fell to the ground and lay in silence. As Americans say, her performance was awesome!

The whole event had left me stunned. As my brain began to work again, Anneliese jumped into the driver's seat. As we accelerated away, she withdrew the bullet shield and shouted back to me, with a broad grin into the rear-view mirror "where to sir, the airport?"

On arrival at the airport, she calmly drove into the short-stay car park right opposite departures. We both got out and before anything else, I gave her the strongest, most loving hug and a very tender kiss.

We took our cases from the trunk. Anneliese threw the keys onto the cab's front seat and we casually strolled across the road to departures. As we walked, still professionally apart, I remember thinking that this lady, my lady, was an exceptionally amazing character. She, clearly, had attributes that would continue to surface in the future. Already, she seemed the most exotic and sublimely surprising creature on this planet.

Having checked in, we went to the lounge, got some drinks and sat opposite each other in two comfortable leather armchairs. Anneliese looked into my eyes and read my thoughts "When we settle down on the plane, I will tell you all about it".

Chapter 21

It's First Class

Just as we started to relax and giggle and laugh about the taxi event, the lounge hostess came over to us and commenced with an apology, saying that Business Class had been overbooked! She continued with "Would you two lovely people like to volunteer to be upgraded to First Class?" We looked at each other and burst out laughing. Anneliese looked at the hostess and said "please excuse us but the day could not get any better". The lady smiled, took our boarding cards and in a trice came back with the new ones, the First Class ones!

Very soon we were settling into our First Class loungers, indeed they were almost luxurious bed settees. I had never travelled anywhere first class. This was spectacular. The ambience, the attention from a myriad of beautiful air hostesses, the alcohol, the chocolates and sensational hors d-oeuvres.

We were adjacent to one another with several back boards enclosing us so it would be easy to have private conversation.

Anneliese opened up with a surprise. After what I had experienced I could have a drink because a driver would meet us at the airport. Secondly, she asked if I would spend the weekend with her in London. She wanted to go shopping with me and buy me a few gifts. Was this all a dream and

I would wake up soon staring at the dirty windows in the Engine Plant!

A couple of glasses of exquisite Cabernet Sauvignon later and Anneliese went into tutor mode, "a lot of this is guesswork" she said. She continued, "The KGB and Russian Mafia are everywhere. Although I do my utmost to impress the KGB, they do have agents that work for both organisations. Furthermore, both teams are expert in every type of criminal activity especially extortion, blackmail, coercion and so on. Are you following this? Therefore, wherever you are, whatever you are doing, their eyes follow you. So, putting that into perspective, they may have people working in major blue chip companies, governments, hotel chains and even taxi companies. Bottom line is you must always be alert and vigilant".

"I suspect the cab driver today was paid by the Russian Mafia. The reason he attacked us will become clear. To explain, you remember the new staff that Santiago needed. They were Mafia, infiltrated to the organisation through Mia. I hope you remember her. She works for me. When you get back to your job you will hear that they ripped the company off by about 2.5Million dollars. But that money is with us. They were being paid by us and we are protecting them. They are now down in Brazil in safe houses. The Americans will look after them, as I will!"

"The issue is the Mafia don't know what happened to the money they thought they were getting. So, straight away they suspect me. But they are careful because they do not want to upset the KGB. However, for now the funds are with me, you and me!"

"I realise that you are getting a baptism of fire. But that works. It did for me and you are the same type of person. We will be great together for as long as we want to be, when we go back to Detroit for the next meetings and then you have scheduled vacation with me, I will go with you for some physical training. I had to learn and I know you can too and you will be great! As far as mental and psychological training are concerned, I am convinced you already have capability so I will teach you as we progress".

By now we had both had a couple of red wines and I had moved onto whisky. Special rare whisky that was so smooth if seemed to be absorbed into my blood stream almost immediately. Probably due to the alcohol, my brain started to accelerate through several questions. Whilst we had privacy, I would endeavour to get some straight answers.

"So Anneliese, is Mia Russian Mafia?" I asked. "No, they know she is on my team and, of course, so far I have convinced them that I work with them because I seek to make substantial sums which I share with them. I have done so in the past!"

I followed up with "tell me about the three agents that got away with the 2.5 million dollars". "Well, those guys are our agents, CECD agents. They had infiltrated the Mafia some time ago and had worked for them on several projects. We just sat back and waited for the right time to bring them into a game that was under our control. They exceeded our expectations and are now having time out and living the high life in Brazil. You get a major accolade for providing the opportunity".

"So what did they pull off, how did it work?" I asked. "Before I give you detail" she replied " do not forget that these three guys were selected for their intellectual ability. They are all extremely clever. How it worked was something like this. They researched, interrogated and tested the financial system. They worked as a team and colluded every step of the way. Operative one, the buyer, set up an account for a fictitious supplier. He then issued Purchase Orders showing the parts supplied. He colluded with the Accounts Payable clerk who then authorised payment. These authorisations were issued to the third operative, who simply issued cheques.

The cheques were sent to a company mailbox in Brazil. Once the total reached the target they had set, a colleague in Brazil paid them into a bank account and then transferred funds to other banks leaving a very complicated trail. In the meantime, the three cuckoos flew the nest down to Brazil to collect!"

Staring into her gorgeous eyes, I said "Anneliese, you must really trust me, having given me all that incriminating information. She smiled and responded "Yes I do. I said once before we were good for each other. I have grown into you to the point where I love you more than anything. And I know you feel the same about me. I have never risked everything for a man but I am doing it with you, and more importantly, for us".

Knowing there were no other Ford people in First Class, I leant over, pulled her face to mine and kissed her softly, gently, with trembling love exuding from both our beings.

We were broken out of this ecstasy egg by a stewardess offering more booze and a trolley full of exotic gateaux. I went for another whisky. Anneliese opted for Tropical Baked Alaska. The presentation was out of this world and as I sipped my Dalwhinnie whisky, I was amused by Anneliese's lips covered in cream with her tongue searching around them.

Now the announcements came fast and furious. Landing soon, seatbelts, clear up the mess (not us, the stewardesses) and so on. I didn't want to land as I had had such a great time. And I was close to inebriation.

As the flaps came down and I felt the plane slow considerably, I closed my eyes. My mind, however, continued to analyse the past few days, particularly Anneliese. I kept going over the fact that it had only been half a day ago when I had watched this adorable demure, female work-of-art, use her physical strength and acumen to destroy a brute of a man. What more could possibly emerge from this woman?

Our landing was completely painless. We had circled around over Heathrow for about ten minutes but I was dozing; then when our 747 hit the ground, I sort of came to my senses. I was still under the influence of alcohol but feeling more alive after the ten minutes doze.

Anneliese and I trudged along together, but trudging was more me. She never ever looked like she trudged, she always appeared upright and classical. We found her bag on the conveyor belt quickly. Mine was just a small carry-on and my pilot's case. Next came immigration which was simple. Our organisation had done an exceptional job on her new passport. We carried on walking and reached fresh air, the pick-up zone.

⚜

Chapter 22

Girls And Gifts Galore

Anneliese phoned and a car appeared almost immediately. It was a Bentley with a chauffeur. I stood open mouthed. It was a Bentley Mulsanne, a fabulous car! The chauffeur wore a chauffeur's cap and began to step out. I then realised it was a woman. A very beautiful figure of a woman who was wearing a chauffeur's jacket but a very small skirt that barely covered her.

She walked towards us and with a very slick singular movement, removed the cap. I was astonished. What a special moment. It was Anya staring straight into my eyes! She grasped both of us at the same time. I was overjoyed to see her. Over time I had developed an affection for Anya that could not be surpassed. My love for Anneliese was untouchable, but Anya had a way of reaching a separate part of my brain world.

We all got into the car. Anya took off at speed and we were soon on the M4 into London. I didn't have a clue what these girls had arranged but I was more than willing to go with the flow.

It was difficult to talk to both girls as Anya was driving, so mostly I asked Anneliese things like what have you two been organising? It didn't seem five minutes before we arrived. A fantastic hotel. I had never been there but I had heard about it in Simpsons. This is where the rich and famous stay. Claridge's in Brook Street, Mayfair. I was gobsmacked. I couldn't believe it! As we stepped out of the Bentley, a valet driver took the keys. We had all the luggage and although three of us, there was not much to carry. But before we moved, a porter came over and took charge. All we had to do now was check in!

Even though I was still a little inebriated, I felt very nervous walking into this historically famous establishment. The whole place screamed elegance and opulence. At reception, Anneliese did most of the talking as it was her reservation. The other reason was that I was impacted by nervous tension and could hardly string two words together.

Every staff member was kind and courteous and I began to relax. A porter had already gone ahead to our room with the luggage. We were escorted to the room by a chic lady from reception. But this wasn't just a room, it was a luxury suite with timeless, glamorous design and décor.

I did, initially, feel completely out of my depth. But after taking a deep breath and looking to Anneliese for succour, it struck me that neither Anneliese nor Anya were phased by the grandeur. Anneliese gave the porter and receptionist exorbitant tips. She obviously had learned what was acceptable in these circumstances.

It was early afternoon, but we were all flagging with jet lag. Anneliese said we should have just a couple of hours sleep, took my hand and led me into a bright, vibrant bedroom. We climbed into a bed, although there were two large double beds in the room.

We were just getting comfortable when Anya joined us. With me in the middle, all three of us cuddled up together and soon were all in the land of Nod.

Anya woke about 5pm and started kissing me which woke me from a deep sleep. It also did more than the usual for a man, it aroused me with a vengeance. As Anneliese began to wake, it calmed me and I just gave both of them a loving cuddle.

Everybody arose, started showering and tripping around naked. It was all so difficult to comprehend. Here was I, who 12 or so years ago, had been a paper boy in a less than prestigious East End area. But I had loved where I lived, the people, the paper round and especially my Mum. When I think back, she had put heart and soul into caring for me! There were no benefits, no Dad to help, only constant effort to work almost around the clock. She had six great brothers who constantly helped out financially, and also provided a bolt hole for me when it was needed. How life had changed! Now I was in a hotel that was usually frequented by the rich and famous.

Anneliese woke me out of these daydreams saying to both Anya and I that we needed to have a meeting before we went off out for the evening. She had booked a restaurant which we could relax and enjoy, the Kensington Roof Garden Restaurant. It sounded fabulous, so I asked Anneliese the question "why are you doing all this for me?"

Her reply was short and sweet. "Your work has made us a lot of money and I love you!" "Just check your bank balance when you have a moment and you will see what I mean." I glanced at Anya. She smiled but with sadness in her eyes. I became determined to give her a fabulous evening.

When we were all settled and ready, we sat in the lounge area, Anneliese said "listen carefully, this is important, in fact, crucial, it may save your life" Anya is familiar with what we always needed to do but you, Matthew, are not".

"Now, whatever I tell you get it into your heads that this is important for our safety and however important and crucial you think it is, just double it."

Chapter 23

Not A Hit For Everybody

Our agents that disappeared into Brazil have given our organisation a mass of information about the Russian Mafia. People involved, incriminating evidence, photos and so on. So CECD have been picking off their people one by one. The Mafia are threatened and extremely angry. They are like cornered rats and will come with some form of retaliation.

CECD central intelligence have intercepted recent messages that they believe make us top of the Mafia target list. Also, the Mafia are doing their best to convince the KGB that we are double agents. Clearly, they are not as stupid as I thought!

In essence, the KGB are confused and concerned. On balance they need us so they do not want to believe it. And we have strong support in the KGB due to past successes. In particular, they need us and, importantly, they need Matthew because their strategy to disrupt the world car programme requires their suppliers to be selected as "key" suppliers. They think Matthew will be influenced by you and I, Anya, for good old fashioned sex reasons.

Another angle has emerged. You remember Grenke, the U.S diplomat. They are planning to get us to use our female weapons to get him to guide developments in their chosen direction. Grenke is now back in the U.S in charge of International Business. The bottom line is they want the world car factory to be built in Belarus. Quite a challenge set by the Kremlin for the KGB! They know that I have got Grenke on my hook before and always managed to influence him. So the KGB have faith in me. But they need to be kept sweet and positive about us.

Now, having said all that, I seriously hope you see the dangers, the risks. They surround us. So all three of us must be constantly mindful of this, and watch each other's backs. You, Matthew, are less threatened than we are, but also, you are the most vulnerable because of your inexperience, but your training will come soon, and that will help.

In the meantime, we must all be fixated with vigilance. If you suspect anything or anyone, alert the rest of us. Anya is our most powerful weapon, she will bodyguard us every step of the way and I would bet on her ability versus anyone. So now we will go and have a good time in your home town of London. I have reserved our table for 8pm and our car will be ready and waiting. So let's go, get ready and have a splendid evening! We all deserve it!"

Putting on the eveningwear commenced. Anneliese outlined the dress code. I would be OK wearing my smart business suit and shoes. The ladies were expected to appear smart and elegant, with high heeled shoes, a mini micro or cocktail dress, preferably black, and beautifully defined make-up.

We were on the way down to the car by 8pm. Both the girls looked stunning. Anneliese wore a silver cocktail dress, and Anya a tiny pleated white skirt and blouse. The new driver stood in one corner of reception, held out an arm to escort us to the car. He opened the Bentley's door and as we alighted, I expected Princess Margaret to be in the car waiting.

Anneliese whispered to me that the chauffeur was one of our men and would provide some security for the evening. The restaurant was 100 feet above Kensington High Street on the sixth floor roof top of Derry and Toms. It was a spectacular place with three themed gardens, a stream stocked with fish and even four resident flamingos.

We had a reserved table in the restaurant and from the moment we were seated; opulence, scintillating surroundings and the most beautiful and fashionable people in the Western World were in our gaze. I was mind blown when I spotted Sophia Loren with her entourage seated at one corner and at the next table, Roger Moore and his family. As usual, he was impeccably dressed, probably, all from Simpsons!

The best wine, the best cuisine the whole event seemed an absorbing, fast-moving tornado of enjoyment and spectacle. Then around 11.30pm a waiter asked if we would like to move to our reserved table in the club for music and dancing.

Anneliese and Anya looked at me and asked if I minded going dancing. "Of course not" I said, then Anneliese responded saying that maybe we should not stay too late as tomorrow would be a busy shopping day. Anya started to giggle, took my hand and almost dragged me into the club.

Whilst we were having more drinks, I noticed Anya's eyes constantly, but slowly and carefully, assessing the people in the club. It was obviously a method she had been taught in order to seek out any danger.

As I was starting my third drink, Anya stood up, grabbed my hand and hauled me onto the dance floor. She was a very stylish and accomplished modern dancer. Three dances later, we were still there, then the music slowed down to the song "Stand By Me". Anya moved in closer and we slowly circled with her warm torso pressed close to mine. As we continued, romance poured from her, with her left thigh now solidly planted between my thighs.

Feeling as if I was cheating, I glanced over at Anneliese. She was smiling a loving smile that really said she was glad I was enjoying myself. And yes, I really was! I now was beginning to have strong perfect feelings for both these girls. We had one more dance then returned to our table.

Chapter 24

Disappeared Among The Stars

Anya stood at the table with a worried look on her face. Anneliese was nowhere to be seen. She had disappeared. Anya said she was going to check in the ladies toilet. I could not just sit and wait so I wandered around inside and outside the club trying to find her.

Just that wander around with my eyes checking every table brought superb surprises. As I approached a table near the club entrance, I couldn't believe my eyes. It was the chart topping group, the Small Faces. The Faces I knew were Ronnie Lane and Steve Marriot, the lead singer. I made a beeline for Ronnie as I had gone to school with him and Steve Marriot, although I didn't know him well, had lived in my road in Upton Park. But Ronnie's face was a real treat. The look of surprise was a classic.

As we stood talking about how we used to all sit with him in the Wimpy Bar at the Princess Alice, Anneliese appeared with Frank, the chauffeur. She held my hand and we did polite introductions. She whispered to me to come back to our table, then she sauntered off with Frank.

Ronnie Lane looked at me, as did Steve Marriot, and said in good old fashioned Cockney "Wow what a sort, where did you find her? She is sensational! What is she doing wasting her time with you?! it was said with cockney humour and charm. I apologised and wished them a great evening, but we had to leave soon. "Just keep churning out your fantastic music" I said as I left their table.

When I reached our table, Anneliese, Anya and Frank were in quiet conversation. Anneliese never ever seemed phased or worried by anything. She said "it's nothing serious yet, but Frank is pretty sure he has recognised some people from the other team. Just from photos he was given. So he has arranged for us to go down in the staff lift and meet him at reception. He will have the car ready. Anya will walk some thirty feet behind you and me, and we must behave like lovers. So let's go!"

It all worked perfectly. Frank got us back to the hotel in less than ten minutes. I just wanted a drink to suppress the adrenalin running through my veins. Anneliese and Anya both agreed this would be good to round off the evening.

We sat down in the bar, I took a very deep breath and said to the girls "thank you for a wonderful evening" Anneliese began to stand, smiled and said "ok, what is it, a large Glenfiddich?" I replied that would be great, but I would prefer Bells if they have it. I know Bells is the working class scotch but I prefer it!

She returned with Glenfiddich... they did not stock Bells! The girls had gin and tonics which surprised me. After another drink, we were ready for bed. Anya wanted the toilet, so Anneliese gripped my wrist and said "before Anya gets back, you know how much I love her. And you know how much she wants you. So tonight, I would be very happy if you shared the bed with her rather than me." My mind went into overdrive. Before I could think or say anything, Anneliese said "please do this for me and her. While we have been away, she has put heart and soul into looking after the old folks. She never lets me down. She is my soul mate and I am very happy to share you with her. It will make us both very happy.

And then, I promise, I will give you a day tomorrow you won't forget". We returned to the room.

As we entered our room, I held out my hand and led her to the other bed. I felt marginally ashamed but Anneliese's words were still ringing in my ears. At the very least we had some privacy as the suite was in an L shape so our bed was around a corner away from Anneliese.

For reasons of propriety, I won't go into how the night went, with detailed descriptions, other than to say it seared passion to the point of complete ecstasy. There was a wonderful erotic dimension which Anya orchestrated, just as it intercepted the bonding of our passion.

This time with Anya had fervently increased my feelings for her. They were no longer limited to eroticism, but had exploded into a strong sublime yearning for some kind of love with this amazing woman.

Sleep was now top of the agenda. In the morning, we would go to breakfast about 9am. Theoretically, it was planned as a relaxed day shopping in London. If such a day can be defined as relaxed!

The girls were up long before me, beautifying themselves. I arose much more slowly and spent at least 10 minutes with my head buried under the pillow, to avoid the noise of hair dryers and so forth.

Chapter 25

To Be Frank, London Is The Best!

Frank was outside with the car sharp at 10am. He suggested dropping us outside the Ritz and we could then walk through Burlington Arcade up to Bond Street. We all agreed we would miss lunch and just have a drink in a bar sometime, then meet again outside the Ritz about 3pm.

Anneliese was more than enthusiastic about treating me to some presents, which was a very kind thought. However, as I mostly despise shopping, I will try to keep it to a brief description of how it went.

She was definitely fixated with the presents. First thing was a fabulous, and fabulously expensive, pair of handmade Church shoes. She tried several times to get me into men's clothing shops but I side-stepped by saying I wanted to do that in Simpsons, my old employer, which I was keen to visit.

Next came a silver money clip in Tiffany's. The girls treated themselves to exclusive bracelets and necklaces. After this, I was cajoled to accept a fabulous Mont Blanc Meisterstuck fountain pen. Then the girls bought themselves superb Mulberry bags, in a maroon soft grain leather; also one for Mum, Frederika.

Almost the final present for me was in a Bond Street jewellers. Anneliese wanted me to have a watch. Initially she wanted me to have a Rolex watch. She saw in my face that I wasn't keen. I opened up to her that I much preferred a Breitling and particularly a Super Avenger. I said the nomenclature reminded me of her.

So that was what I got. I admit that I did worry about wearing it for work as it might raise the question of where the money came from!

The girls didn't mind when I asked "shall we walk round to Simpsons now?" Anya said, and Anneliese agreed "never been in that store so it will be a novelty!" I couldn't wait so we trekked quickly through Burlington Arcade and down Piccadilly towards the Eros Statue. As we got close, I recalled there was a bank on the corner, so I said to Anneliese I just need to go in. In my mind, I wanted to get the girls something but had no idea if I had enough in my account.

I went straight to a cashier, gave her my cheque book and asked her if she would give me my balance. Very efficiently, she found it on her spanking new computer and wrote the balance on a slip of paper and pushed it, smiling, towards me.

Other than about fifty pounds, it was almost half a million pounds. I turned to Anneliese, perspiring profusely and showed her the slip of paper. She looked straight into my eyes and said "you earned it and you deserve it" I almost staggered out of the bank. Anneliese held my arm and said "We will be set for life soon. And the pay from the Western Government is not bad either."

As we sidled into Simpsons, I almost could not contain my elation. I suggested we start on the sixth floor and work down. At the top was sports, but the girls were not really interested. Next two floors were for females. They absolutely loved what was on offer.

Both girls started to pile items up at sales desks. They kept them at the desk and then we moved to the next, it was continuous. Underwear, Cashmere sweaters, summer dresses, gorgeous designer jackets and business suits.

We now reached menswear. Anneliese convinced me to buy an unusually different modern style overcoat. Brown with thin stripes, double breasted. As we cockney's say, it was the nuts! Next came suits. I didn't really think I needed any but I was served by my good friend, Mr Charles. What a salesman. And the girls absolutely adored him.

He told Anneliese and Anya the story about the late night, with the copulating couple, trying on suits. The girls were in raptures. As I entered a fitting room with two suits, Anneliese said "hope they were not ones your friend tried on!" Afterwards I did check for any stains. But Mr Charles was ecstatic at seeing me and pleased I was doing well.

One of the suits was fabulous. A DAKS suit in a very modern style, three piece light grey Prince of Wales check. The fit was exact. The other was a more practical dark blue suit, two piece, in mohair. Both were the type of suits I had always dreamed of.

Now we had finished shopping. They would collect all the items together and ship them over to Claridges the same evening. What a wonderful store and a superb, relaxed way to shop. All the bills were collected into one batch. I assured Anneliese and Anya that I would pay this. I wrote my cheque and it went with the bills to the cash office. I did give the men's floor manager my name and address. Mr Charles stood close to him constantly repeating that I was well known as I had worked in Simpsons and that I was a person of integrity!

Just before we got into the lift to the ground floor, I asked the girls to give me a minute. I walked across floor 2 to accounts and peered through the glass door. Most of the people were the same as when I worked with them. I wanted to go in and talk to them but then I thought it would be just an ego trip and the girls were waiting.

I re-joined Anya and Anneliese. I asked if we could walk down to the ground floor, only one floor down. I wanted to sample again those marble steps that I had seen so many celebrities saunter down. We took it slowly. The girls always appeared to be harmoniously elegant!

As we neared the ground floor, several of the sales staff and a particularly brilliant window dresser, recognised me. They waved and smiled with decorum. It took me by surprise and I was close to feeling choked! The girls were pleased for me and waved and smiled back to everyone.

As we walked towards the main entrance doors, past men's shirts, Anneliese stopped me to point out some shirts she appreciated. Anya had stopped by a counter some thirty feet away, talking to Mr Tenby, a very interesting character, who had, before Simpsons, been a member of the Savoy Orphians Orchestra that played most nights in the Savoy Hotel. She has told me since that he was extremely pleased I was doing so well.

Chapter 26

Mistaken Identity In Lon...Don!

Who would have believed it? Even before we got to the exit, which was only about 20 feet away, we would be involved in physical violence!

As Anneliese was trying to persuade me to buy some very nice, very expensive shirts, two people, a man and a woman, approached behind us.

With a very swift move, the man grabbed me around the neck, his arm locked on my throat. He started to say something, but before he could get all his words out, Anya sprinted across the floor, kicked the woman in the back of her knees. She crumpled to the ground. Anya then grabbed the man's left arm, twisted it up his back so forcefully that his torso went with it and he landed flat on his back. She put her foot on his throat and screamed at the woman not to move.

It was all so fast, Anya had used scintillating Jiu-jitsu text book moves. No wonder! She informed me later she was, indeed, holder of a black belt.

With a foot across his throat it, initially, it was difficult to discern who he was. Neither of them struggled. The woman just lay there grasping her knee joint.

At that point, as I stared at the face of the man, the light bulb went on. I cried out "Anya let them up, help them up" this man was Simpsons Security Manager, who I had worked with on several occasions in the past. This was Don, who had been a great help getting me a start in life. I didn't know his assistant who was his backup, a store detective.

We all rushed to help them both to their feet. Don started to laugh. Thank God he wasn't hurt! The whole thing reminded me of a time when we tackled two guys who were stealing Shearling coats, I mentioned this and Don agreed and gave me a hug.

He was wearing a very smart raincoat which was now crumpled and marked. Anya set about dusting him down. And all the time she was apologizing "oh I'm so sorry, I thought you were attacking Matthew. Your move looked so realistic"

Don responded with "your moves were much better and were realistic! Where did you learn that, it was so fast, and superbly accurate? When he was here I taught Matthew some moves and he was good at them. But none of my moves compared with that!"

As calm settled on all of us, Anneliese took Don and his partner to one side and apologised with much defined sincerity. The lady store detective had recovered and said not to worry; she had received worse and it was all part of the job.

Don's gaze indicated he was smitten by both girls. By now we were surrounded by staff with some recognizing me. Everyone started speaking at once until Don, in a very loud voice said "that has given me a story to feed off for the rest of my life. I was attacked by two of the most beautiful ladies I have ever seen! The surrounding company all began to laugh and we all received pats on the back.

Anneliese quickly said it was time we were due to meet Frank. She moved aside and phoned him on her mobile. She struggled to get it back in her bag until she pushed the aerial down. "He is coming to us" she said. A minute later the Bentley arrived at the door.

We all began saying our goodbyes, continuing to apologise as we moved out of the door. I thanked Don for being so understanding. "Don't worry it was all my fault" he said. I continued "and please give my respects to everyone in the store, especially those I worked with".

Moving out onto the pavement, Don and several staff followed. Frank stood holding the rear door open and touched his cap as we got closer.

Don exclaimed "well you really have done well for yourself, what a fabulous car" Frank replied "thank you very much Sir" and helped us all into the seat. Lots of waves as we drove off round Piccadilly. I had the best time ever!

Frank took us straight back to Claridges. The girls both wanted a drink at the bar. Frank was asked to pick us up at 6.30pm, but I asked him to come in for a drink with us. Wrong move.

Anneliese said it would not appear correct and there would be plenty of chances in the future to socialise with Frank. He nodded in agreement and thanked me for the thought!

We sat in Claridges Bar, the girls ordered red wine and I decided to just go for a lemonade as I knew we would be going out again later.

Chapter 27

Who Is Frank

The waiter gave me a smart leather bound brochure which I read with interest. In this bar, they were accomplished at mixing any cocktail and specialised in Vodka martinis in ice-chilled glasses. These were attractive to the girls, but for later. I read on and found they also held a great collection of rare whiskeys, some distilled in the U.S.A. before and during prohibition. These may be a treat for me later.

Meanwhile, the conversation began with what was now perceived as the comical episode in Simpsons. As we trawled up and down all that had happened, my mind kept locking onto Frank. So I asked quietly, "who is Frank? Is he just a chauffeur or what?"

There were quite a few people in the bar, so Anneliese asked the Barman if there was somewhere quieter we could have our drinks. He said "yes of course. I will escort you through to the Snuggery." We followed him through a door to a small discreet room. We were the only people in it. In a flash, he returned with our drinks.

Once he had left us alone, Anneliese said "Frank works for us. He has recently been detailed to be your assistant. He will stay close to you, although you won't always know. He has been a paratrooper and later transferred to the SAS. He is a crack shot! A trained marksman! And bottom line is, he is a fantastic, reliable, chap".

I would like to ask another question. Anya said "of course, go ahead". Anneliese, knowingly looked at Anya with a content smile. "Well, the thing is this, where have all these funds come from that are sitting in my account?"

"It's like this" replied Anneliese. "We are very well paid by CECD. Secondly, we have a good regular income from the agents' fees for the U.S. Imports. Next, you will recall the Dagenham heist by the Russian Mafia. Well our people stole most of it back from them. That is the main reason they are trying to put pressure on us. Lastly, the Valencia fraud revenues predominately came to us. About 30%, plus expenses, was paid to the three guys now down in Brazil. They will continue to be well looked after until we need them again and it is safe to do so! Ford will recover most of their monies either through insurance or the U.S. Government as these were acts of Terrorism by a foreign country. Are you satisfied with this explanation?" I felt comfortable but also somewhat uncomfortable! But "Yes, I am happy with that, thank you. "I replied.

Anneliese gave me a very tender look and said she had planned for us to celebrate on our last night, listening to some jazz music, and asked if I was ok with that "Also, to raise the pleasure stakes, I have invited Frank to join us. I sensed you needed some male company and two men, two women, won't look out of place".

"Frank is a big fan of jazz music. How does it sit with you, Matthew?" Anneliese asked. "Well, I'm not a massive fan but have had some favourites in the past, especially Dave Brubeck, Johnny Dankworth and Cleo Lane. So I am already looking forward to it".

"Now, can I really try to impress you? "I said. "When all three of us were based in Amsterdam, I was invited to a weekend birthday party at my hotel, The Sonesta. It was on a full floor of the hotel and continued almost two days. I had a marvellous time! The birthday boy was Johnny Dankworth and with his wife, Cleo Lane, played superb jazz music for several hours. There were many other jazz artists and so, it was an event I will never forget".

We got a taxi to Ronnie Scott's, on the edge of Soho. Frank would do the same and meet us in there. It was pouring down that night but we got the full VIP treatment with a doorman, complete with large umbrella showing us in.

We were taken to our reserved table and Frank was already sitting comfortably. We all had a bit of a chat and the girls spent five minutes worrying about their appearance as they had felt a few drops of rain.

A waiter arrived, Anneliese and Anya decided upon very expensive champagne. Over this weekend, everything had seemed "very expensive". I just decided to start slowly with a beer, as did Frank.

Then Anneliese decided to explain the arrangements for the next day. Frank would drive us all to Heathrow midday. The girls would be flying back to Tunisia early afternoon. Frank would take me to my flat in Deal and had arranged to stay close in Canterbury. Apparently my mobile had Frank's number in the directory. She had explained this now as she thought she might be worse for wear later.

Looking around, the place was very dark with only table lamps. And to begin with, it appeared a bit dingy. Thinking back I suppose it wasn't so much dingy. It simply had that sort of beatnik cellar atmosphere, although it was not a cellar!

The jazz music began. Various artists unknown to me, but enjoyable. Great background sounds as we all made conversation, Frank was loving it! Then he informed me Stan Getz was on next. I knew this name as his fame went before him.

Stan Getz and his quartet were fabulous. The music had a lush, mellow tone and Stan's individual spots on his tenor sax were spectacular. They moved into bossa nova type jazz and immediately the girls' sprang into action. Their swaying, swinging hips, consistent with every beat, was something to relish. Meanwhile, Frank only seemed to have eyes and ears for Stan Getz.

Although the place was bursting, only a few people were dancing. Maybe out of respect for Stan Getz's music. My thoughts took me back to watching the girls. It was impossible not to watch their bodies moving to this music. It dawned on me that most men at their tables were watching and drooling. They were drooling because both girls were wearing very light coloured short dresses. To accentuate this, there were several spotlights searching around the small dance floor.

Every time the spotlights picked out Anya and Anneliese, their dresses became almost invisible. Both girls were, obviously, wearing miniscule g strings. It has a completely magnetic effect on me, and I know them both exceptionally well. So I can understand the impact on the rest of the guys in the room!

Eventually, they returned to our table. All the while, Frank had been chatting to me, but in between being obsessed by Stan Getz. I was growing close to this guy. He was my type of fella.

We were all continuing to drink. I had moved onto scotch. Frank, however, obviously wanted to stay relatively sober, and I kept noticing his eyes searching the room for anything strange or out of the ordinary.

It's hard to describe Frank, but I feel I need to try. I don't know why, but with our bonding I developed the feeling he would be around us for a long while in the future. It's easier to start with what he was wearing. He had a very smart, what looked like, bespoke tailored suit. It was a strong weave, maroon coloured but with a tiny white stripe running through it. He wore slip on style Chelsea Boots that were immaculately polished. From my training at Simpsons, he was probably a 42inch chest and a 34inch waist. He works out! He had a mid-blue shirt with a fabulous dark blue/red and yellow striped tie. Ties were always the thing then!

He had strong brown hair covering his whole head with sideburns that finished at his cheekbones. His skin was lightly tanned and there was no facial hair. His teeth were not perfect, but he had a smile that gave you comfort.

I was pleased to think I could have found a good mate to help me through this maze that I had got myself into.

I looked across at the girls. They both seemed to be having a great time. They were both just lighting up their special cigarettes from a candle on the table. The whole place, by now, was filled with cigarette smoke so theirs wouldn't make much difference.

Frank pulled his chair closer to mine, got close to my face and said that he had been informed earlier that the Russians were out searching for us. They were not finding it easy because of Anneliese's false passport. So far, they had used her as the key target for their tracking. This information started to cut through my alcoholic mist!

The next question really sobered me up. He asked "Do you know how to fire a gun, a pistol, not a twelve bore." I suppose I was taken aback so it took some seconds to think and answer. "Yes", I said. "My brother took me to Bisley and sort of taught me how to fire a revolver!" Frank's gaze hardened and looking straight in my eyes he said "good because it's getting close to time to leave. In a while I will pass you, under the table, a revolver. Stick it in your waistband, button your jacket over it. Do not be afraid to use it, it could save all your lives".

He continued "when we go, my taxi will follow yours, at a distance. I will be with you all the way. Matthew, just a couple of hours with you and you are like my new brother. Don't let any of this get to you. Always have my philosophy, be measured, be pragmatic, but most of all be the focused dangerous one! One more thing" he said "when you get back to the hotel, remind Anneliese to check the room. If they are determined to find you, they may have already done so. She knows exactly what to do!"

With more drinks and cigarette indulgence, the girls were verging on amorous. So both Frank and I were collared to dance. By now it had moved to more of my type of music. An artist named Art Pepper was giving it large with blues music. It was definitely my stuff. The girls, also seemed to accelerate into the mind absorbing music when a John Lee Hooker special "Put on Your High Heeled Sneakers" was played. I'm not sure that's the title but I can remember the words and the picture in my mind's eye of these two girls bodies writhing with rhythmic movement, and singing these words, in harmony.

They sauntered back to the table when they finished. Both girls were perspiring and needed to sit down for a minute. Then they were off to the girl's room to check their make-up.

Frank nudged me as he leaned forward and quietly said "under the table". My hand found his and I grasped the gun. It was quite light and I then did as I was told. I stretched back in my seat and after checking around, I quickly inserted it in my waistband. Frank whispered that the safety was on and that it was a small protruding switch on the left above the handle. "Don't forget it if you need to use it!" Frank said with strength in his voice and eyes. He made a good teacher.

I buttoned my two-button jacket just as the girls came back. In a sadistic way I felt like Reggie Kray heading home after a night in the Blind Beggars.

Frank had disappeared for a moment, then returned and said our taxis were waiting. We should go first and he would be just a few paces behind.

We three jumped straight into ours. Frank's taxi had parked several cars back and as we left, I checked and Frank was following about three cars behind. We arrived at Claridge's safely. The girls went straight in, whilst I paid the driver. Frank's cab just sat there until I had gone through the main doors.

The girls were just inside waiting for me. Anneliese clasped me with both hands around the back of my head, kissed my cheek and said "thank you for a wonderful time tonight. Shall we head into the bar for a nightcap?" Anya grabbed my hand and tugged me towards the bar. Except this time we went to a different bar, the Fumoir, because Anya thought we might enjoy some snacks. There was no way I wanted snacks. I just wanted a 50 year old "prohibition" whisky. But I went along with their thinking!

We went in this dimly lit, decadently decorated bar with a million percent attentive service. We had a couple of drinks. The girls had decided on Vodka Martini's which came in chilled cut-glass umbrella glasses. I continued with my special whisky and I suppose we were all getting a bit worse for wear.

Anneliese said that we were going to throw our hats in the ring for a couple more hours of enjoyment. She called a waiter over and ordered room service for food, a bottle of champagne and more whisky.

I had reached the point where my mind said, let's not think about how expensive this is all getting. However, as the room service was about to go to the room, so should we. Joining arms, we got to the lift and up to our suite.

Chapter 28

They Seek Her Here, They Seek Her There

I opened the door, letting the girls go first into the room. The chandeliers were so bright after the dimly lit bar. The girls were standing in the centre of the lounge. As I trundled in, I took my jacket off and threw in on the chair.

Both Anneliese and Anya started to giggle. I stood there with a vacant expression, "What?" I said. Anya, with a wonderful grin and wiggle as she spoke said "Is that a Walther PPK or are you just pleased to see us?"

The two girls slumped on the settee together and started to taunt me. They got their drinks and as they sipped them, proceeded to flash their legs in a way that became more provocative by the second.

I was starting to get really excited, but then I remembered what Frank had said about the Russians searching for us. I called a halt to proceedings and said "please listen for a moment. Frank warned me that...." Anneliese chimed in "Matthew, we already know. Central Intelligence warned me some days ago and I informed Anya. Don't worry it is not something we should get worried about. So let's just finish enjoying the final evening of this weekend together. " I thanked them both for their honesty. Anneliese replied that they had not said anything as they did not want to worry me.

She followed that with "now we are going to worry you, how are you going to choose?"

Their performance was way beyond exciting. However, I decided to play it cool. I did not want to be drawn into "choosing". So, I just got stuck into the whisky. "It numbs every part that girls may want to reach".

The music was soft and gentle and they colluded to get me on my feet dancing with both of them at the same time. These girls were teasing me. They both got close and then closer. Their bodies gradually gyrated in time with the music, increasing the tempo constantly. I managed to control myself, more due to the whisky in my blood than my natural instincts.

The music ended and we collapsed onto a settee like a house of cards. Anneliese got into a sensible mood, reminding us that we all had a long travelling day tomorrow. The girls debated having a shower before bed and agreed they should, even though they would also need another in the morning.

I just wanted bed so they slipped off together to the shower room. I pulled myself somewhat together and then, as I was getting up from the settee, noticed the Walther PPK laying there on the edge of a cushion. I was about to pick it up when I noticed Anya's shoulder bag behind it.

Because I am a curious person, I wanted to see if she had her gun. I have always had a liking for guns, probably stemming from watching all those old cowboy and crime films. I opened the bag, peered in, but could not see a gun. I put my hand in and felt around. There was a separate section and as I felt inside, there was a lump! It was a tiny holster and inside was an elegant Derringer. A tiny 357 magnum. The sort of gun that gamblers used on the riverboats that sailed the Mississippi.

Now I knew what she had used in Valencia. It is a fabulous piece of engineering with the power of a full size handgun.

As I returned it to the holster, pieces of paper, mostly folded, moved. I went to push them back down but one paper was thick and embossed. I tugged it up slightly and with what I saw, my inquisitive nature kicked in. It was the embossed White House Pentagon emblem of an encircled Bald Eagle. I pulled it out and clearly saw a signature at the foot of the short page, "signed Harry". I was just about to read the whole thing when I heard the girls returning. I quickly pushed it all back into the bag and flopped on the settee.

Anneliese and Anya walked in. Totally naked. If I had been giving a commentary on horses in the paddock before the start of the Derby, I would have said "What superb specimens". They both have strong, muscular bodies, and incredible hind quarters. They were different, but so attractive. Anneliese has a lithe body with lines that accentuated her tiny stomach, ample breasts and beautiful bottom. Anya had extra everything on bosoms and bottoms. But she was shorter and not the elegant stature of Anneliese. I loved both these girls so much it was not fair to put me in this position!

Out of the blue, a cloud of depression descended on me. I had started to think about tomorrow, the end of a fabulous weekend. So feeling miserable, I said I was going off to bed. The girls agreed it was time to hit the sack, but being in a sad place, I told them I wanted to go in one bed alone! I shuffled off to the bed around the corner feeling I was in a shroud of loneliness.

The lights went out, but I couldn't sleep. I tossed and turned for almost an hour. I was overjoyed when my bedside lamp was turned on and both girls jumped in beside me. We were back in our teenage years, kissed and cuddled, and gradually fell asleep all huddled together. These girls had more heart than Valentine's Day.

Morning broke. I felt surprisingly good, in fact, I was first out of bed. We all began to get ready. It was an exquisite suite so we just got on with it. No waiting for the bathroom or bumping into each other. Although occasionally I caught sight of scantily clad females scooting across the rooms. I suppose they were Anneliese and Anya!

Breakfast was relaxed but the pressure came on when I had to choose. The menu was amazing and extravagant. The girls, however, had their favourites in their head, and despite some things not being listed on the menu, they were told that the chef would accommodate. Then the girls chose as their drinks, Bucks Fizz, I knew I was in the company of lavish up market professionals.

We chatted, laughed and recounted events from the weekend. Then the Maître-De came to us and said that our bags had been taken to reception and our chauffeur would arrive in about 15 minutes. I had never felt so pampered.

Frank arrived at 11am. Our bags had already been put in the Bentley. Said our goodbyes to the staff. One of the ladies on reception, a very beautiful girl named Andrea called out "please come back and see us again". We waved goodbye and clambered in the car. Misery kicked in again, but as I sat with the girls, I thought how could I live in their world if I allowed emotion to attack me? I decided to work on toughening up!

Just getting in the car and all the way to Heathrow, Frank's eyes were constantly scanning our surroundings. He clearly was a very experienced agent.

We arrived at Heathrow. Frank got out and handed some money to one of the airport staff. We all stood on the pavement together to say our goodbyes. Anneliese seemed a bit emotional, but I had decided to work at being tough. Then she said "it's only two weeks then we go to America for meetings then a respite holiday" Anya joined the talk saying that she would meet us in the U.S. and come on holiday with us. I was finding it hard to keep it together. Anneliese chimed in. "I will send you the itinerary, so watch for it."

The porter that Frank had tipped brought a trolley for the girls. They only had two cases each, and as they all walked towards the entrance, Frank called Anneliese back. He stood smiling and whispered to her. She re-joined Anya and the porter and headed into departures.

Frank and I got back in the car. And all the time I could see how alert he was to everything around us. As we motored around the M25, Frank started to talk. The first thing he said was that when we were going to the U.S not to take the gun.

"Although it's pretty easy to conceal, it's not worth the risk. When you arrive in the U.S you will be provided with a gun and more." Being curious, I then asked if he had given any news to Anneliese. "Well, that's a good sign" he said "you do keep your eyes open. I told you earlier that they were searching high and low for you. They were finding it difficult due to Anneliese's new passport. But I had new information earlier that they have got over that problem. So what I said to Anneliese was that we had switched the girls' flights. They were now flying Lufthansa rather than B.A. On the Lufthansa flight, they will have protection all around them. It's been arranged".

"The question that our people are investigating is where the Russians are getting their information? Anyway, once they get back to Tunisia they will be relatively safe. Our African agents, especially the Dutch South Africans are the best in the world".

Frank got me back to Deal. My adrenalin dropped to negative. I had stepped back in time. It felt like a different life! He seemed a reliable guy who I would like as a friend, not just a minder. And as he got in the car he reminded me he was only down the road about 20 minutes away, in Canterbury. He had sent a text with phone number to my phone earlier. I planned to have a serious study of the phone in the morning as it was all new to me!

Chapter 29

Down To Earth

Monday is here. Back to work. I decided on the way to work I would accelerate through this week, slog it out with very late nights if necessary. And it was necessary! But all my guys were extraordinary. Most I already knew but some had just joined the team. No complaints from anyone and they were all very likeable, progressive, helpful guys. No ladies in the mix, but it wasn't the type of function that females entered at that time.

By the end of the week we had agreed a fabulously all-encompassing system that was durable and would give us all the information we required to select global suppliers. I was cream-crackered by the end of the week but also astounded by how much we had achieved. A real bonus in this team was a new guy we poached from Cologne. An Egyptian working in Cologne as a Gasterbeiter (or guest worker). He was so pleased to get the job he was willing to go to the moon and back to please everybody. To start with, he was a gopher, but he quickly became a solid character that we all relied upon.

The news came through during the week that Berlin Plastics Plant was just starting to run. I expected they would be next in line to put bids in for plastic parts. I was continuing to be apprehensive about getting involved in the early days and whether I should have done so. Still, it was water under the bridge. Anneliese would probably know who the investors were and shed some light on the whole affair.

During the week Frank phoned, indeed he phoned every day and would say "just checking in ". He also had a thing about being very careful if eating out. He had received intelligence that the KGB had become very accomplished at injecting food with a fluid containing heavy metals which almost immediately caused surging heartbeat, kidney failure and then coma.

Also they were intensifying their work on perfecting nerve agents that will kill you with a minute pin prick. I said "Frank, don't worry I'm not getting time to go out to eat, and in the future, if I do, I will remember what you have said".

When I sat back and reflected on what Frank had told me, it sank in that this was very scary stuff. Anyway, I was involved up to my neck with no way of escaping. The good news was that we were working to protect the West and getting well paid for it! And I would not give up Anneliese and Anya.

Over the next week we would receive quotes from the Tier 1 and Tier 2 suppliers, the companies that were bidding to manufacture the key, most important, components. My guys would begin evaluating the quotes using our new procedures and system. The suppliers were basing their quotes on outline designs previously provided by Engineering. But an essential element of their bids was to secure design features that were seen by our Engineers as the best-in-class.

My intention, if all this played out was to take details of the quotes, financial evaluation, design achievements, with me to the Detroit meetings with Gordon. Essentially, this would all support me in providing a recommended list of Tier1/2 suppliers for all the key components.

At times, I felt as if I had reneged on my aspiration to become one of the supremo's of Ford. But, I suppose, in the company's eyes I was still working hard and giving it good value for money. What I was unsure about was how much the top people knew about my involvement with CECD. It was that thing that Anneliese said about my position on the world car having been engineered for me. It sort of irritated me as I had always wanted to achieve on my own merits!

I suppose the comforting thought in this was that I knew, I was totally convinced, this was the most fantastic Company to work for. The Senior Management were superb, and if they knew my circumstances, they would be with me and support me all the way.

Come Saturday morning, Frank arrived to pick me up. On the way to Heathrow I asked him to divert into Ford's European HQ. I was only a few minutes dropping off my Dictaphone tape that I had made whilst in the bath the previous evening. It was just a big thank you for their blood, sweat and tears. And I knew they would get a good laugh out of the water and bubble sounds. They had heard it all before!

We set off to Heathrow, and Frank and I started to chat. I explained I had the "preferred supplier" list. He understood every element of what I was talking about. Then he said he wanted me to listen carefully. First he asked "did Berlin get into the preferred list ". "No, because we decided to leave plastics out as Berlin are new and we didn't have all the quotes in anyway". "That's great, but it may be revised" said Frank. "Why, I don't understand "I replied.

"The venture capitalists that predominantly own Berlin are Russians. Not visible but definitely behind the dollar bills. They want in so they can extract much more information about the Ford Corporation. They think it will gradually get them more insight into the U.S Government and enable them to manipulate different adverse scenarios. Counter Intelligence are monitoring their every move and in doing so one thing, and it's not new, has come up. It is the latest thinking that there is a double agent within the U.S Government. We suspect a guy that you have met. He was given misleading information by Anneliese. She is such a clever woman. She was trying to nail him with info about the Middle East. He was a diplomat in Tunisia named Harry Grenke. We may be totally wrong but we don't think so. He is a very clever guy. He covers every one of his steps".

All the time, I was thinking, should I tell him about the note in Anya's bag? Then, I thought no, it may implicate Anya and I have no evidence that makes complete sense.

Frank spoke again saying "You need to remember the KGB are out to de-stabilise Ford and other parts of the U.S economy. If successful it would be a devastating blow to the U.S Government and probably result in a tsunami effect throughout the Western World. Anneliese and the rest of us in her team have a crucial role to play in preventing this. I will tell you now that Anneliese will use your Preferred Supplier list to the best possible effect. She will be disingenuous to the KGB using counter intelligence methods that are tried and tested and almost completely effective. This is her area of expertise".

"When we board our flight" said Frank "you, Matthew, will be in Business Class. I also will be there but just across the aisle from you. All I would add is don't have too much to drink and stay alert. You must not indicate, in any way you know me!"

"Two more things to remember. First of all, after we pick up your car at World Headquarters I shall give you a couple of tools you may need. We will leave the airport in separate taxis as I have to pick up a few things. I will meet you at WHQ so watch out for me. Second of all, Anneliese will need an afternoon during the week where she can be excused. She is going to her old University at Ann Arbor to meet some people we may need …CIA people. You should mention the afternoon off to Gordon. Just say you agreed for her to go back to her old Uni."

The flight was fabulous. This time BA, and also pampered throughout. Not as much as first class with Pan Am but really enjoyable. I always enjoyed these business flights even though I do not like heights. Flying is difficult but it definitely beats sitting on milk crates in the early morning delivering milk to the masses with a friendly milkman for my boss (remembering early years in the East End). I did literally anything in my early to teen years to earn a few shillings to keep myself going!

We landed at Detroit airport, early afternoon with sun shining and high humidity. I headed out to the taxi rank, found a cab, and asked the driver for Ford WHQ in Dearborn. I arrived, got my car keys from security and went to the carpark to find the vehicle. This one was a Lincoln Town car, a powerful, large three box design vehicle. As I was opening up, Frank tapped me on the shoulder, he was checking around all the while, then we got in and headed out.

As we drove to the Ritz Carlton Hotel, only a few blocks away, Frank handed me a parcel "When we get out, put it in your luggage" he said, "what is it" I asked. "You like Mont Blanc pens" he replied, "well this one is special. Press the clip on it and it fires a dart 40 feet. The dart is coated with a paralysing fluid. So whatever you do, be careful not to shoot yourself!" We both laughed out loud. "The other item" he said "is a Breitling watch". Before he could say anymore I replied "I absolutely love Breitlings, what model is it?" Frank gave me a brief, silent stare, "Matthew, who cares what model, this may save your life! If you pull out the time adjust button, it emits a weak nerve gas, but it will knock anyone in the vicinity out, in five seconds."

"Matthew, are you absorbing all this" "Yes of course" I said, "but it's still all a bit crazy" Frank was always very pragmatic, "I understand this is all new to you but you have to get it into your brain that you are now involved in life or death scenarios. I don't know how you got into this but you are. And I am detailed to look after you. So please help me, take your thought processes to a seriously higher level to protect both of us! And remember, before you pull out the time adjust bottom, take the watch off and get away".

Those words were a wake-up call. He continued "this package contains a Beretta pistol, I know you can handle it and while we are here wear it! The pack includes a thin unobtrusive shoulder holster. And as you wear a suit every day, it will just sit there, quietly, for when it may be needed. Stake your life on it!"

As we arrived at the hotel, Frank said "good luck, I will see you when I see you ". He jumped out of the car and disappeared into the hotel before I could say anything. I exited, and under the hotel awning, stuffed the packages into my pilot case.

Booked in; the hotel was fabulous and new; then went up to the room. By now it was 6.30pm and I'd not heard a thing from Anneliese. Did all the usual things. Showered, laid on the bed for a while, and started to worry. Then, thank God, I had a text message. She would be arriving about 8.30pm. Her plane had been delayed.

She walked in on time, I was sitting waiting in the bar. Wearing a summer dress which flowed over her hourglass figure, hair pulled back into a single plait, as always she exuded elegant femininity. We just exchanged polite greetings. I remembered all the instructions about appearing professional. But really all I wanted to do was to grab hold of her.

We got a couple of drinks and went to sit in a quiet corner of the bar. Before I could say a word, she uttered "Matthew, you must listen carefully to this. I have received some certified intelligence. The Russians have always trusted me due to information I have given them previously. But that was always weak, ineffective intelligence, and even though we set them up with Berlin, the clever bastards in their back room intelligence have put me on their "red alert" list, and that's why they are looking for me. I will get them back on the hook if I can give them something big. That something is the "Preferred Supplier List." They are keen to start infiltrating suppliers so they can move ahead with their de-stabilising plan".

I interrupted her to say, "But I don't have a complete list yet. Maybe by the end of the week!" "That doesn't matter" she said. "I intend to send them a very professional looking document on Ford headed paper that shows them, not only the Preferred Suppliers but also all the metrics and quantified data that led to the decision. I need you to construct it while we are here. Can you develop such a report?" "Well yes, I suppose so" I responded, "but I would need you to help me, Anneliese, with the computer skills. I usually have my secretary do things like this but obviously, I can't involve anyone else". "Yes, of course" she said "and one more thing to give it authenticity. A covering letter signed by Gordon would do it".

"If we can get this done this week, I am sure it will convince the KGB that I am valuable enough to trust and retain. This will give us a win/win situation in terms of disrupting their plans while buying us time with their future trust".

We finished our drinks, glanced into each other's eyes, and Anneliese said "now it's time to relax, it's been a long day" she showed me her key with number 313 and smiled.

We had a scintillating night together. I now feel that we are just one soul because the togetherness is perfect. Having had breakfast, we set off for work in the Lincoln. Anneliese reminded me "don't forget I am Karen in work". When I replied. "Oh, yes" she grabbed my wrist and stuck her nails into it until I screamed in pain "you must remember" she said.

We did all the usual meet and greets and then had two solid days of meetings with Gordon and his staff and some other teams from HR and Manufacturing. In the evening, when most people had left, we would find a private room with copier to work on the document that Anneliese needed.

As most of our meetings with Gordon's people involved the ratings of European suppliers set against U.S. suppliers (and U.S suppliers included Japanese and South American) as the week progressed, we gained more data to include. Anneliese had an objective to include 40% accurate and 60% false data in her document. She was excellent at this sort of stuff!

Wednesday morning we had a meeting to review all the currency exchange rate projections through to 1989. Not much input to this as we were not the experts. However, over lunch, and I think it was probably because he had been bored with this meeting, Gordon cornered me and Anneliese and asked if we would join him, after work, for a game of pool in his neighbourhood bar. He really was a down-to-earth kid that had made his way up through the system like I was trying to do!

Gunfight At The Ok Coral

Anneliese reminded us both that she was about to leave to return to her old University, Ann Arbor. Both Gordon and I were disappointed but then she said she would try to be back by 6.30pm. Gordon immediately wrote down the address, but then apologised saying "it's a bit of a scruffy bar but they do fabulous beer and chili hot dogs."

So everything was agreed. We would go for a beer and play pool. About 5.30pm, Anneliese had gone to her meetings at Ann Arbor. I ended up sitting in a quiet office on my own reading the documents we were trying to consolidate for Anneliese. Sitting quietly reflecting on everything, suddenly I realised that I was enjoying every moment of what was going on. But I was still not accepting it as any more than a fantasy.

This was absolutely real. It was dangerous. I had to become a Frank. I had to ensure I did everything to protect everything and everybody I loved. I could not carry on being naïve. I had never been like it in my previous life. So it dawned on me, it was my epiphany that I had to step up to the world I was now in.

Gordon stuck his head around the office door just as I was filing some of the papers away in my pilot's case. "Hey, Matthew, looks like we've got it all moving in the right direction", he said. "If we leave about 5.45pm you can grab your car and follow me to the bar. Is that ok with you?" "Yes

Gordon, that sounds good. I will meet you outside the main entrance "I replied.

Gordon was driving a 5 litre Mustang and had a lady sitting in the passenger seat, I followed them down Southfield, turned off left at the exit then did a couple of lefts and then rights. Looking around, I knew we were now in a less than prestigious area where you needed to be streetwise!

I pulled up behind him when he parked on the road outside a ranch-style bar in a fairly downtrodden area. Gordon jumped out of the Mustang, ran round to the passenger door and helped his passenger out. She was his secretary, Mary. She was a real chirpy cheerful lady who always was ready to help if you had a problem. She was also a looker, a babe, and knew it.

They waited and turned towards me as I walked up. I did the usual greetings of handshakes and kiss on the cheek for Mary. Gordon strode off towards the bar door.

As I approached the door, what hit me was it was like something out of the Wild West. Cowboy town double saloon bar swing doors. I looked around expecting tumbleweed to come rolling down the road and Wyatt Earp to appear!

Inside it had the appearance of a large wooden shack in somewhere like Tombstone. There were only four or five customers and we went straight to the bar. The barman, full of smiles, appeared to me to be Mexican, but had a strong American accent.

Gordon chose Budweiser and Mary asked for a Red Dog beer. I thought that sounded unusual so decided on the same. As we started chatting, I looked around. There were four American pool tables with one taken by a couple of locals, both dressed in tee shirts, jeans and the obligatory Detroit Tigers baseball caps. Gordon said that Mary had offered to join us to keep Karen company. I thanked her, but she responded saying she loved to be out having a drink and some fun! A very down to earth person who, strangely, was very similar to Anneliese. Same height, same hair colour and impressive business attire. But not the same lovely face and eyes that always entranced me.

Gordon suggested we start having a practise on the table nearest where we were at the bar. Mary seemed quite comfortable on her bar stool and said that when she had finished a few more drinks she might join in. She laughed and said she was very good but only when she had had a few more!

We had a few shots on the table then Gordon went to get another round. I could sense he liked a drink when he was relaxing. At that point my brain kicked in and I reminded myself that, here I was, playing pool and drinking with a guy that was almost top of the heap in Ford, just one step away from being on the Board of this great Global Company. I calmed myself and just as I did, Frank ambled in with another guy. They came straight over. Before I could say a word, he clasped Gordon's hand and introduced the two of them. Frank introduced the other guy as Dan. I could tell both Gordon and Mary took to Frank immediately.

Frank said that Karen would be here in a few minutes with another of her Ann Arbor colleagues. Frank and Dan had also been at Ann Arbor with Karen and they had all agreed to have an annual get together.

At that point, Gordon began to ask questions about their degrees and what they were doing now. As I was just about to practise a cushion shot, the saloon swing doors smashed open. In strode a mountainous moose of a man, looking local with red baseball cap, white tee shirt and red shorts. The eye-catcher was the gun in his right hand. It was large, like a Colt 45 out of the westerns.

Then all hell let loose. He started to fire in the direction of the Mexican barman, but also all around poor dear Mary. My mind went numb. I just reacted, diving at Mary and knocking her off the bar stool onto the floor.

By now, the gunshots were completely indiscriminate. My mind started analysing, it's the Russians looking for Anneliese and they thought Mary was her!

I was crawling under the pool table and everybody else seemed to have taken cover. Next it all went quiet, gun shots stopped. I poked my head out. The moose man was lying on the floor about six feet away from me. And standing over him, pool cue in hand, was Karen (Anneliese). I was euphoric, but then he started to move, rolled over and was getting up!

Then Frank's previous words to me screamed in my head. I put my hand into my inside pocket, pulled out the pen, aimed and pressed the clip. It was accurate, the dart hit moose man in the thigh. Sirens were now surrounding us. Frank rushed to me and dragged me out from under the pool table, he whispered, go and stand in front of moose man and hold Karen (Anneliese). I realised later that was to provide him with cover.

Frank had moved in on moose man who was completely paralysed. He pretended to be checking him but pulled the minute dart out of his thigh, just as the local sheriffs entered the bar, guns drawn.

They handcuffed moose man and then commenced questioning us. In between times, I checked on Mary. She was fine, and the new guy with Karen (Anneliese) introduced himself as Ron. While individually, we were talking with the several Deputies, Ron and Dan went over to talk to the Sheriff.

They went outside with him for a few minutes. Moose man was then dragged out and the fun was all over.

We congregated at the bar. Drinks all round. Then the chatter started. Gordon was so impressed with Anneliese. He was not aware of my pen trick and I wasn't going to tell him! Frank whispered a "well done" and we all carried on getting to know one another. But Karen's (Anneliese's) performance was to be revered. Frank saw her enter the bar just behind moose man. He started firing, she reached for a pool cue, as cool as anything, unscrewed the handle, did a jump to reach, and smashed him over the head.

Mary grabbed my arm and pulled me close. Gordon also came over. Mary, still smiling but with tears in her eyes, kissed me on the cheek and said "Thank you, thank you, you saved my life". Gordon was slapping my back and ordering more drinks. Karen shouted "get him a whisky, Gordon, he probably needs it".

We gradually finished up, Gordon and Mary said their goodbyes leaving our party to saunter out to the sidewalk. Once outside, Frank and Anneliese got us into a huddle with Ron and Dan. Anneliese explained that these guys were CIA agents and that after the shooting, they had talked with the sheriff.

This was all simply a domestic. Nothing to do with the Russians. Moose man had found out his wife was having an affair with the Mexican barman. He is known to the sheriff's office and has previous for violence. So that all seems to confirm there is nothing more to worry about for the moment and that the KGB have still not located Anneliese. The CIA would continue to work with Frank to monitor and maintain surveillance.

We all quietly slipped away, back to our hotel. When we arrived back, went into the Ritz Carlton bar for a couple of drinks. There were very few people around but none that I recognised from work, so we sat, enjoyed and relaxed.

Anneliese was so complimentary about the way I had handled a dangerous situation. In return, I said I couldn't believe how such a beautiful, reserved person could be so intrepid and competent, wielding a pool cue. She replied with "how do you think I have survived this life so far. I adore living on the edge, I have had years of training and I always have a fearless survival mind set".

She then smiled and said she was so proud of the way I handled the Mont Blanc dart, the accuracy and then how I had worked with Frank to extract the dart, unseen, from moose man.

"That was a superb dry run for any future trouble. Frank is getting you a new pen for tomorrow. Joking with me earlier, he said he is giving you the nickname Nib"." You are so accurate with a pen!" I said to Anneliese. "This is the second or third incident that had nothing to do with our work or the Russians "she replied, "they were just bad luck but good practice for you!"

Once again she gave me a view of her room key. We set off to our rooms separately and I would go to her later. My heart was pounding.

When I got to her room, we sat and talked for a short while. We had two more days in the North American office, then she and Frank would accompany me to Fresno for training. We would fly Saturday morning and it would be four days for me. However, she stressed that it was essential that she had a really convincing "Preferred Suppliers" document by close of business Friday.

I was sure I could do that and said so. She said that if she had that she would not be able to stay with me for the whole four days, because she had to get it into the KGB arena and soften them up. But Frank would stay the whole while. I definitely was not looking forward to this, but somehow, hearing that Frank would be with me was calming.

Anneliese seemed to have found my heroics stimulating and so we moved, no we stormed, into love-making. This was even more special than before. Every piece of furniture became our props, with a breakfast bar stool being the last of the gymnastics that finished me off. I was totally exhausted and just lay next to my love constantly kissing her. Sexual unity is wonderful but lying with your loved one, exhausted, is the most satisfying and comforting thing if you manage to find it. Our love was sublime and, from this night, I knew it would last forever!

Next morning we ventured back into work. Back into the real world. As soon as we arrived, Gordon called me in and asked us not to say a word to anyone about the previous evening's events. It would not be appreciated, being involved in some sort of incident, which included violence, in a neighbourhood bar. "Of course, I understand" I said.

So we closed that subject, although Gordon and Mary continued to smile and pamper us with coffees and doughnuts throughout the morning.

Anneliese and I worked through the whole day on the two "Preferred Supplier Lists". The correct one and the fraudulent one. By mid-afternoon, the fraudulent document was finished and appeared very professional on Ford headed notepaper. I prepared a covering letter as I needed Gordon's signature to run with it. Addressees were the Purchasing Directors and Vice President.

The next part of my thinking came into play. I took the covering letter into Gordon with the incomplete correct list and explained that although this list wasn't finalised, I needed his signature on the letter. I carried on to take him through the details of the list and discussed with him, a few minor pieces of information, and a couple of quotations that my team in Europe were still working on. He was very understanding, but said he would rather wait for completion before he signed the letter!

This was crunch time! I explained that the timing plan through to vehicle job 1, required me to provide Purchasing and Engineering with the list by Monday. They understood it would not be 100% complete but at least they would have something to work with. And if I had further information from my guys in Europe, I would incorporate it tomorrow, Friday. This needed to happen this way because I was going on vacation and Gordon was away preparing to move to the U.K.

I was very thankful, when he said he understood and this all sounded eminently sensible. After he signed, I took the letter outside to Anneliese. She was in raptures. Immediately, she went to the photocopier, so that the photocopy signature with the fraudulent list would soon be on its way to the Russians.

I explained to Anneliese that I had, at the last minute, included Berlin Plastics Plant in her list, despite not having any financial evaluation or quotations. I had, however, added a footnote stating that Berlin had been pre-selected as it was strategically advantageous to Ford to support expansion of control over the family of plastic components. This gave the KGB Russian investors an assurance that they would achieve significant influence in the direction of the Corporation. All completely false but Anneliese thought it was a brilliant tactic that would get her back in their good books!

Having said our goodbyes to Gordon, Mary and the U.S staff, we said we would see them in about three weeks. I was heading off on vacation while Karen (Anneliese) was returning home to see her parents.

Swimming With Seals

The fact was we were off together, me for some training and Anneliese to join me afterward for some vacation time together. I really could not wait to get going. In the morning we would fly to San Francisco to meet up with Frank and then drive to the training ground somewhere near Fresno. This was all going to be an experience to relish, or so I thought! Little did I know that I was unknowingly entering a different dimension....different in every aspect compared to the world that I knew.

We flew early and arrived in San Francisco about 10.30am. Frank was standing at the gate waiting for us. He was always on time, completely reliable. I was disappointed when it was explained that we did not have time to look around. But we would after training was over. That pleased me. I was a great fan of Tony Bennett and had the "I left my heart in San Francisco" ringing in my ears.

But it was not on the cards yet. Frank had a car ready and we set off to somewhere near Fresno. It was only about 220 miles away, but with the U.S. 50mph limits that was about 4 hours travelling. What added to the anguish was the non-descript Ford Bronco which had a bit of a hard, rough ride.

After Anneliese and I continued complaining about the uncomfortable ride in the Bronco, Frank clearly had had enough. He said "Listen guys, I know it doesn't compare with the Bentleys and Lincolns but this is the car that may one day save our lives. It is an all-terrain vehicle that has also been adapted by our people. Our engineers are the best in the business for innovations."

Frank continued "one day this car will be famous for something spectacular. You, Matthew, should believe that and believe in the car! When we are training, I will show you the adaptions. Under the rear chassis it has been fitted with two machine guns aligned with the exhausts. Under the front chassis is a small rocket launcher. Not many cars have a strong enough chassis to take such weight! More than that, it has all sorts of electronic equipment including satellite navigation, heat shields and protective armour. So a hard ride should be the last thing on our minds".

We arrived in Fresno just after midday. It was a typical U.S town with low buildings and the usual motels and chain shops. We were all hungry and Frank decided to drive into a Denny's. A bit of a come down from recent haunts, but way above the class of the pie and mash shops I had spent my early life in.

The food order arrived on plates the size we would have a turkey on at Christmas. We were all taking it slowly because the mountain of food was daunting, then Frank said that I had to be at the training camp by 4.00pm. I asked Anneliese what her plans were. She said "I will do some training with you until Monday evening. I need to upgrade myself".

Frank interjected, "don't forget we are with American Servicemen; they don't know us from Adam, and Anneliese is a very attractive woman. Don't answer questions like why are you here? Divert all questions to whatever is going on at the time, the type of training etc."

We were half way through the food mountain. I was eating pancakes with eggs, bacon and many fried vegetables. But this was going to be too much for me. Anneliese looked like she had already surrendered. Frank, who obviously had an enormous constitution, was ploughing on and almost finished. He stopped, dropped his utensils, looked straight at me and said "do you want to know what your training includes? The Bronco will be the first then, firearms, which you should do well at. But then it will get more difficult. Surviving under fire in buildings. Self-defence, Jiu-jitsu, knife defence. Then how to fall, although football training should help with that! The worst bit is a survival trail on Shaver Lake. Sounds great doesn't it!"

On the last leg of the journey to Shaver Lake, Frank told us how it was famous for being the area where Bigfoot was supposedly seen. And apparently this creature has been seen by several people! From Frank's description it sounded like a cross between a Gorilla and a Yeti (from the Himalayas).

Shaver Lake was a one-horse town in the middle of an enormous woodland. It took two minutes to drive through the town on to Shaver Lake. The lake is man-made but looked completely natural, surrounded by forestry. This area is just south of Yosemite National Park so now I understood why the U.S army and Special Forces used it as their training ground.

I am going to pull the blinds down on the training itself as I was sworn to secrecy. Other than to say it was not enjoyable. It was the most stressful, intensive and punishing thing I have ever attempted. And to be factual, for most of the elements I achieved mediocre results but I did find myself improving. The Americans did not accept excuses. If you got it wrong you were penalised, mostly with press-ups. So I did my best, sometimes over and over again!

Anneliese and Frank were sensational beyond belief at almost every element. But to be honest, they also gave me so much moral support. Even though sometimes I felt like crying, they would drag me out of it and convince me that this was training that could save my life, indeed, all our lives.

One thing that helped me through this was that something kept reverberating through my mind. In my teenage years, I went with my mates, good mates, to a gym in the East End. The guy that owned this house, and it was just a house, was a guy called Wag Bennett. He had converted the house into a pretty basic gym.

We, me and my mates, would take it pretty casual, but I used it to help me build leg muscles for football, and I'm sure it did! But there were lots of body builder types and we would watch them flexing their muscles in front of a mirror. However, I never put myself through excruciating pain and agony, like these guys, who saw it as a way out of their deprived life.

One of those guys was Arnie Schwarzenegger and look what he has achieved. So, although every part of my mind and body was being subjected to punishment, I continued to think that if they could suffer it, so could I. Indeed, I was already out of the deprived area, and therefore, had no reason to complain.

The last day of training involved working with the U.S NAVY SEALS on Shaver Lake. They call them the Special Service. Instead of "special" they should have been named "relentless". They never give in, never concede, and in my case, trying to get me to succeed in water was a thankless task.

They were in a motor boat, Anneliese with them. They were trying to teach me to be picked up as the boat was speeding by. This involved a loop to put my arm in, as they sped by. I tried six times but missed each time. I was tired, very tired, treading water. On the seventh attempt, I missed, the boat hit my head, and I don't remember the rest. Until I was rescued by Anneliese, I am a pretty good swimmer but not in Anneliese's league.

As I recovered, I was looking up straight into Anneliese's face. She was lightly slapping my face and massaging my temples. As my mind came back into play, I sat up and the commanding officer asked if I was ok? The next question was "do you want to try again?" These guys do not accept failure! After saying yes, and Anneliese chiming in with "no wait a while", the next thing I knew was I was thrown bodily back into the lake.

The next pass, I very nearly succeeded but needed my grey matter to be in a better state. The boat drove some 200 yards away and turned towards me. I was crazily treading water. The boat was coming at one hell of a speed! The loop came nearer and nearer. My focus got better and better. This was the one, I was in. The impact nearly tore my arm out of my shoulder socket, and was so powerful it threw me into the boat on the pass without any help from the SEALS. But that was still not enough for them. I had to do it twice more, and I did!

So for now, training was done, finished, over. However, it wasn't all good news. In the evening we met with the Commander for our assessment and wrap-up meeting. I was told I would be doing it again in six months. My performance, or what the Commander called an "aspiring performance" was rated "satisfactory". I suppose, to put a smile on some of the faces in the room, he repeated my performance rating saying "so you are not confused, I did not say inspiring, I said aspiring performance".

At that point, people in the room chuckled, but my ego inflated slightly when Frank and Anneliese applauded loudly. We were now all too tired to even think. We agreed to head back to our cabin bunks to sleep. Oblivion was the inescapable temptress. We would attempt some form of celebration tomorrow night.

In the morning we drove to the town of Shaver Lake, Anneliese had asked her two Fresno –based people to come to us for a U.S Imports meeting, early evening.

We booked into an innocuous motel in the main street. Across the road was a small restaurant/bar and next to it a shop. This was about all there was in the town.

The motel could have been modelled on the film Psycho. The rooms were the typical one-storey building and set back from it was a large dark detached house. As we drove up, an old man was sitting on a rocking chair on the porch. As we stopped, he stood up, beer can in hand and began to stagger over to us. We had a quick polite chat with him and booked into two rooms. Anneliese asked if we could reserve other rooms later to accommodate her staff, if they wanted.

The man laughed and said "of course sweetie, the whole place is empty and available".

Later on, the three of us went across the road to the restaurant. A lady with glowing red cheeks came to our table to take our orders. We asked for a bit more time as we hadn't even got to looking at the menu. However, when we did, it didn't require much thought. It was mainly basics like omelettes, burgers, fries, eggs, bacon and pancakes.

When she returned, the first thing she said with a real warm glow was "welcome to Papa Bears". We ordered several items, agreeing to share, as we were all starving hungry.

Just before we left, Anneliese asked if we could come back for an evening meal and what was the earliest time.

Apparently six o'clock seemed best. She, by name Shelley, went on to explain that if we liked music the woodsmen and loggers would be in about 8.00pm for a jam session. And they were coming down from the forests to get haircuts from a local barber. " It only happens every six months or so" she said. "Don't be put off by the way they look. They are great guys who always make my customers welcome".

During the afternoon, I had a little walk around with Anneliese, then a rest. Frank knocked on our door just as we were ready to go to Papa Bears. We arrived and were seated about 6.15pm. Anneliese reported that her two guys from Fresno would be arriving about 7.00pm. Their names were Gerry and Tony.

The waitress, Shelley, brought us some local beers, just bottles, no glasses. Of course, the beers brewery name had to be Big Foot Beer! I was really enjoying it as we had not been allowed beer whilst in training.

Anneliese grabbed my wrist and said that I would feel at home with Gerry and Tony as they were both English. I replied "so what are they doing working here for you?" "Well" she said "they are both high intellect chaps that I hired straight out of Oxford University They have succeeded in every element of training and have proved to be very accomplished. Moreover, Americans love their aristocratic English accents, as I do yours. Although your accent has the added attraction of being gritty and almost coarse. With that she smiled and pinched my thigh.

Gerry and Tony arrived just after 7.00pm. It made me think of my early days getting berated for being late. Five minutes or less! Anneliese did the introductions and they obviously both knew Frank. I immediately had the feeling that they had a tremendous amount of respect for Frank, as did I.

After some polite talk, without any forms of questioning, everyone started to look through Papa Bears menu. Tony turned to Anneliese and in a very posh voice said "my dearest, you really do know how to treat us knobs to a sumptuous business supper!"

We ordered, but before the food arrived, Anneliese said in a quiet voice, "have you managed to access all the army personnel assigned to new duties in Europe. That's the best financial strategy we have to increase U.S import sales in Europe." Gerry responded "Yes Anneliese, its going fantastically well. The U.S servicemen have a real penchant for the Explorer and especially the Navigator. But for most, the pinnacle is the F Series pickup up truck. They really do sell themselves."

Anneliese then, in an even quieter voice, looked at both of them and said" ensure you also keep on top of the information part of your work. There is a mole in the U.S Government system so try to pick up anything that may lead us to this character" Tony said "yes mam, we have some fragile leads and are working at it constantly. Alphonse and Mia share information with us every day".

With that, Shelley appeared and the plates gradually filled the oak table,. As everyone started to participate in the heart stressing victuals, I could not resist the chance to show off a cockney boy's knowledge regarding elegant designed wearing apparel.

Earlier I had been attracted by the cut and quality of Tony and Gerry's business suits. The closer attention I paid, the more I became sure that these were Simpson's garments. In fact, although I had never been a fully-fledged sales person, I had worked in sales several times and felt I had either seen or served these suits. Indeed, I was such a fan of clothing, I was convinced I recognised the style, the cut, the material and the overall impeccable look that these suits created.

Tony wore a dark grey and aubergine hounds tooth, whilst Gerry's made an exacting contrast. It was a very light grey Prince of Wales check which I believed was entitled "the weekender".

I took the plunge and said, "Looking at both you guys, yours suits are marvellous" "oh, thank you Matthew, very kind of you to say so" I think Anneliese guessed the next segment, as she smiled and looked in my direction. "I would guess that Gerry's is that part of a men's London fashion collection with the sought after label named "Weekender" that figured in Vogue. Not so sure about yours Tony, but for some reason I recall a collection marketed as serenely historic, called "Winchester". Tony responded immediately, "Matthew, you are a guru. The prestidigitateur of men's fashion". Looking at Anneliese and Frank he said "where did he gain such knowledge? He is like someone out of Mastermind answering fashion questions correctly. Let's all have another drink, I'm buying. And Matthew, the next time I want to buy clothing, I will get in touch with you first!"

We were all starting to bond with these guys. They may have been posh but they were very likeable posh. In fact, their way of talking, walking and their demeanour strongly reminded me of my dear gay friend, Mr Charles. In the meantime, Frank sat enjoying all this banter whilst finishing off the left-overs. Anneliese was part of all the chat but could not leave my thighs alone, under the table. It's strange how our minds work but, all the time, it kept taking me back to what I had seen, under the table, with the Grenke character. I had to get over this in some way.

⊶⊷⟨⟩⊶⊷

Chapter 32

They Fired Their Guns

It was now close to 8.00 pm. Shelley came over to our table, and the caring person that she was, asked if we were going to be disturbed by the music. We were all getting in the mood, so with one voice, replied that we were looking forward to it. I paid her for what we had consumed to that point and gave her a large tip. She was clearly ecstatic and said that if we were enjoying ourselves, to stay as long as we liked.

Sure enough, just around 8.00 pm, in came the jam session. One after the other, they clattered through with their instruments, falling over tables and apologising constantly. The place, luckily was two rooms. We were in the first restaurant section. Through an archway, it took you into a slightly bigger room where these guys would practice and, hopefully, give us some enjoyment. There was about 8 – 10 loggers, I can't be sure because they were coming and going. But they got started, quite loud, but it was fabulous music which mostly I knew. Some skiffle, some blues, some rock'n'roll.

But when I looked at them, they all looked like a Big Foot. Long hair, massive untidy beards, and all had big strong physiques.

Everybody in our group was starting to feel the results of the liquor. Maybe the exception was Frank who sat, with a small bottled beer, scanning around. I could see that Anneliese was close to the point of wanting to dance. All of a sudden, it came to me that she was a woman on her own. I needed to pay her more attention.

Us blokes were all having a good time. Then the next episode began. The door opened and in walked four U.S servicemen. They entered looking rather worried that they were in a place they may not enjoy. They went straight to the bar and started knocking them back.

I went to the bar to buy a round and could see from their flashes and badges that they were with the 81st Stryker Brigade Combat Team. At the bar, they were quite friendly, although they were starting to sound a bit drunk.

One of them, standing next to me said "are you a Brit, what are you doing here?" Gerry and Tony came over to help with the round. Having heard us talk to one another, the guy said "are all you all Brits?" Gerry answered the original question. He said "we work with U.S forces going to Europe to get them the car they want, and yes, we are British".

This guy kicked off straight way, getting very loud and belligerent "my brother is in our forces in Germany and you sold him a load of shit. Nothing but problems, he can't get it fixed and had no help from you guys". We got together and went back to our table. Frank whispered to me "be careful, they are out for trouble. That guy is a psycho! I can see it in his eyes! Don't know if they are paid undercover Russians or just idiots out for trouble, so Matthew, watch me every moment".

The loggers were enjoying their jam session. Anneliese sensed something was building. The next event was that the Stryker Soldier, the nutter, went up to the mike, grabbed it out of the loggers hand, turned to the guy playing the lead guitar and said "would you play the skiffle song, Battle of New Orleans please". He didn't look over the moon about it, but, nevertheless, started to play slowly. Bass, drums and then the banjo player joined in.

The Stryker nutter started singing at the top of his voice, as well as swinging his arms about erratically and posturing as if pointing a rifle at us.

This behaviour was obviously aimed at taunting us Brits. Gradually, as his colleagues joined in with the singing, the nutter's body language and facial expressions became more intimidating.

For people that don't know the song it goes:

- We fired our guns but the British kept a coming
- There wasn't as many as there was a while ago
- We fired once more and they began a running
- Down the Mississippi to the Gulf of Mexico

This chorus is used over and over again to heighten the insults and obvious abuse of the British. The nutter even tried to get a reaction with rude finger signs. He did get a reaction but not from us. One of the loggers grabbed the mike from him and pushed him off the small platform used by the jammers.

He came hurtling off the stage. Anneliese and I were standing at the bar together. Nutter came straight at us. We both took a step sideways and he crashed into the bar between us. He pushed himself up using the edge of the bar, looked slowly around and lunged for Anneliese. The next thing happened so fast, it is a bit of a blur. He put his arm round Anneliese's waist, pulled her towards him attempting to kiss her. I grabbed his arm and said "Hey guy, don't be silly, you can't do that," With that, he smashed his elbow into my face, but simultaneously Anneliese brought her knee up and his manly bits took a crunching knock!

He dropped to the floor. Immediately, his cronies charged across the room and were throwing punches at me. The next amazing thing was Frank, to be frank! He joined the Melee, pistol whipped all three of them then stood screaming at us "Let's get out of here?", the loggers now came across saying don't worry, we will keep them occupied. But just as we were leaving, the nutter sat up and shouted "you have upset a lot of people. If you get away from us you won't get away from all the rest"

Frank herded all five of us out to the Bronco, giving us cover all the way. We were heading off towards Fresno. Gerry remarked in his usual posh voice "So you did not want to spend the night in the Shaver Lake Motel?" Anneliese responded, "I am very sorry guys but we will get you back to Fresno and you can pick your car up later. And if not, I will get you a new one!"

We had been travelling about 30 miles when Frank said "we are being tailed so be ready for some fun". My heart beat substantially increased. It was a large Dodge Ram with bull bars on the front. It just came closer and closer and then on the first bend, they tried to ram us off the road.

They were never going to win with Frank driving. I had watched him drive the Bronco on the training course. There wasn't an obstacle that he could not overcome. When the next bend came up they attempted to power through on the inside of us. Frank hit them with a solid broadside forcing them to pull back. As the Dodge closed on the back of us again, Frank activated the machine guns. A small screen shot up from the dash panel, clearly slowing the Dodge Ram front end with an indicator for target accuracy. We slowed for a second then Frank commenced firing.

The noise was deafening. It seemed to echo through the complete underbody. I would guess about twelve rounds hit the front end of the Dodge. Both front tyres were shredded, steam poured from the engine compartment. From the ground up, the front of it was obliterated.

It was not going to win any off-road competitions. Tony, in his posh voice screamed "oh this is so much fun, Frank, what else can you do?" At that point, one of the Stryker's had got his window down and started firing at us.

Frank got a really serious look on his face. "I've had enough of this "he said. He hit the accelerator hard, turning the wheel full lock. The Bronco spun in the mud and we were now facing the Dodge Ram. Frank said "this is not something I enjoy but they leave me no alternative!"

He put his hand under the instrument panel and appeared to pull a lever. There was a whirring sound that increased in intensity, followed by what felt like an earthquake that shook the whole car. My eyes followed a stream of smoke trailing to the Bronco. It only lasted one or two seconds then a horrendous explosion. Frank had released the front end missile. The Dodge Ram just exploded in front of our eyes. Nobody could have survived that blast. We watched the fireball drift upwards.

Gerry had to get his oar in. "I know Tony asked what else can you do, Frank, but I didn't think you would conjure up Christmas on Christmas Island!"

Frank, still looking extremely serious, turned in his seat so he could also see the faces in the rear. I was feeling very shell-shocked but I suppose I was beginning to accept the violence. Frank was steely-eyed, staring at all of us, waiting to see if we were composed.

"Those Strykers were not U.S. Army. I have spent time with that brigade. Everything about them was wrong. Their uniforms were tatty. Badges in the wrong place. And they all had the wrong boots. They were mercenaries paid by the KGB. That is bad for all of us. Anneliese thought she would have got their trust back, but this episode indicates to the contrary. So we have to be very alert. Watch each other's backs constantly. You, Gerry and Tony are alone in Fresno, but I think you will be ok. Until tonight you could not have been on their radar. And the Strykers won't be feeding any information back!

"So summarising all of that, my orders for you guys, Gerry and Tony, are as follows. Anneliese, stop me if you have any issues with what I'm about to say". Anneliese was still sitting quietly in the back as if all of this had been like a walk in the park. Frank continued "I will get you back to Fresno. Anneliese, Matthew and I are going back to San Francisco. We will be there a few days to meet up with Anya for a short break. Meanwhile, I think you should get out of Fresno. It's too near to where all this occurred. Fly down to Phoenix and we will meet with you in a few days".

"Are you both comfortable with that. We love you guys and do not want to leave things to chance". I suppose emotion got hold of me, so I piped up "yes, we do all love you!". With that Tony, one side of me and Anneliese, the other side, grabbed my head and planted kisses all over my cheeks. Seriously though, only one evening with these guys and I could not bear the thought that anything bad might happen to them.

Frank said "So do we all agree that this is the plan?" we all replied as one voice "Yes we do", this speaks volumes about how we all felt about Frank! He continued "Gerry, book yourselves into the Embassy Suites in Phoenix, This time of year, it's so hot;

not many people will be around. So, and I know you will love this, you won't need much more than tiny shorts!"

Now Frank turned to Anneliese. "From what we are experiencing and seeing, I think it's clear that the KGB are presently dedicated to finding us. They have decided that we are not trustworthy and a negative for them. The CIA have been in touch with our central intelligence and reported that the Russians have been tipped off that the "Preferred Suppliers List" that they were given is a dummy. In consequence, we are all at risk of attack until or, if we can find another approach to alleviate or nullify their beliefs".

We Travelled to San Francisco in the knowledge that we were now dedicated targets. Anneliese had reserved us rooms in the Four Seasons hotel in central San Francisco. Despite being under severe threat, Anneliese was calm and relaxed and, as we arrived, assured all of us that defence would constantly surround us.

I suppose we all took the lead from her and decided to act as normal as possible in the circumstances. Anneliese and I left to book in while Frank drove to the airport with Gerry and Tony. Both of those guys wished us luck and assured us they would be waiting in Phoenix. As we said goodbye, their speech and body language was effeminately comical, but that made me even more confident that they were survivors. They were hard as nails!

We went and had a couple of drinks in the bar. Frank arrived about 40 minutes later but sat at a corner table, didn't talk to us, but acknowledged us with his eyes.

It had been a long and eventful day so we set off to our room about 9.00pm. Once we were in, Anneliese did her normal tour, checking the room for any suspicious equipment or listening devices. She gave it the all clear so we went to bed. Even after all this time, nerves still got hold of me and although I did my best to appear strong and confident, I usually managed to do something clumsy. This night was relatively ok.

Early next morning, Frank tapped on the door. He came in and spoke very quietly to us. He was due to meet up with another of our agents late morning. The meet would be on the tour boat that visits Alcatraz Island in the Bay to give tourists a view of the prison. He asked if we would like to come along, then after lunch, he would go to the airport to pick up Anya. Anneliese said how much she was looking forward to seeing her and was about to say we would come too. But Frank cut her short saying, it was probably better if we waited at our hotel, for security reasons!

We agreed to meet at Pier 7 at 11.00am. We all should appear and behave like normal tourists! Frank would meet the intelligence agent on the main deck. He would provide Frank with the latest intelligence information. We should head upstairs to the roof deck while he was conducting this business.

By way of explanation, this intelligence agent was part of the central intelligence team. Intelligence was the culmination of deciphering, interpreting encrypted messages and analysing any information or data received from other operatives. And there were many around the globe. Mia and Alphonse, Tony and Gerry submitted substantial amounts of data, information and suspicions gleaned from American service personnel accessing the U.S Imports Programme. Some may be where a soldier said something that indicated allegiance to Communism or the East, disillusion with Western Governments, or just mental health issues presenting themselves as antagonistic towards society.

Ultimately, this information was used by front line agents to help them survive, or deter or prevent serious destruction or challenge to our way of life!

Chapter 33

The Alcatraz Tour

Next morning at precisely 11.00am, we were in the queue on the quayside by Pier 7 to purchase our tickets for the Alcatraz tour boat. Frank was a few places behind us and, for obvious reasons, maintained a distance.

It was an absolutely glorious morning. The sun was beating down, glistening on the bay and emphasising the bright red ochre of the Golden Gate Bridge.

Looking along the line, everyone appeared as you would expect normal tourists to look. Most people in bright summer clothing, a couple of guys in Hawaiian shirts and girls in floaty dresses. The only thing that seemed somewhat strange was a bearded man carrying an umbrella. However, I put that down to the fact we might experience sea spray as we got out into the Bay.

Once on the boat, Anneliese and I climbed the steps to the upper deck. We had fabulous views across the Bay to Marin County and could see Alcatraz off in the distance. We could also see people walking and milling around on the main deck, but no sight of Frank, although he was probably in the seats inside.

We cuddled up together, my arm around Anneliese's waist, and admired a view that, in my whole life, I had never imagined I would see. I said to Anneliese "This feels unreal, almost as if we are in a cinemascope movie and soon may see Burt Lancaster, the Birdman of Alcatraz, sitting on the rocks surrounding the prison".

We were now closing in on the prison and were starting to feel spray from the waves hitting the rocks. Looking down at the people on the main deck, most were enjoying the feeling of the water mist in the heat of the day. Peering around the main deck, I noticed a young couple that did not look dissimilar to Anneliese and me. Similar clothing, hair colour and body language. I remarked to Anneliese that they appeared as much in love as we were!

A commentary about the prison commenced but it was muffled by engine noise and the waves crashing against the rocks. We were on one of the cheap trips that only went around the prison, rather than in it for a guided tour! I suppose because none of us wanted to see the inside of a prison and Frank was only doing it for business reasons.

Now we had almost completed 360degrees around the island and were sailing into calmer waters as we headed back to Fishermans Wharf. That's the area where all the boats and ferries sailed from and it included dozens of different piers. Along the Wharf stretch are a myriad of restaurants so finding some sustenance after we docked would not be a problem.

By now, we were only about 5 to 10 minutes away from docking. Then I noticed a power dinghy coming towards our ferry. He was moving quite fast, straight at us, but then at the last minute he turned and drifted in alongside the ferry. Both of us were now looking along the main deck to Alcatraz in the distance.

The bearded gent, now wearing sunglasses, was still carrying his umbrella. He was about to pass the loved-up couple and as he did, the umbrella tip seemed to scrape the back of the lady's leg. We watched as she bent down to rub the painful area. Within 30 seconds, she collapsed on the deck. Her boyfriend, obviously distraught, started shouting and screaming for help. He was on his knees next to her, his hands behind her head trying to get a response. The next thing we saw was Frank arriving on the scene. He also tried to revive her, but to no avail.

Anneliese had begun to scan the other side of the deck. She shouted to Frank, whilst pointing " this side quick, this side, the small dinghy". Now I picked up on it. The umbrella man had begun to run to where the dinghy was alongside the ferry. Frank gave chase. As I turned to watch, I realised Anneliese was on her phone.

Umbrella man jumped over the side, landed on the side of the dinghy and fell backwards into the water. His accomplice grabbed his arm and hoisted him into the dinghy. This all happened just as Frank streaked past below us. He jumped up on top of the safety rail and threw himself at the dinghy. However, it was only seconds before the dinghy powered up, white water spewed up all around it and it took off like a bat out of hell. Frank got one hand on the edge of the dinghy but could not hold on as it sped away.

We both ran down to the main deck. I threw a life buoy to Frank and several people helped get him back into the ferry. Just then, we began docking and within minutes the Pier was full of police and ambulances.

Most people disembarking had no idea what was going on. Frank went over, covered in blankets, to talk to the police. A few minutes later, a black Ford Navigator arrived. Two guys joined Frank and the police. Frank told us later they were CIA. They took over and Frank was allowed to sit and recover.

Anneliese was a woman of few words. She held my hand, very tightly, and led me through the melee of police, ambulances and confused people. I stopped her and said "what about the poor girl, and what about Frank?" She looked straight into my eyes with that authoritative glare and said "the girl is going to hospital. Frank will be OK and will catch up with us later. The CIA will look after him". Just at that point, a car drew up alongside us. The driver, a young thin faced Asian looking girl, said "please, get in quickly".

Once in the car, Anneliese attempted to convince me that we should leave Frank to handle it. We should go to the hotel and Ellie, the driver, would help collect our stuff, settle the bill and take us to another hotel.

I was straight with Anneliese. I wasn't happy with that plan. We were arguing as we arrived at the Four Seasons. Obviously, it was too dangerous to stay in San Francisco!

We began to enter the hotel to collect our belongings. In reception, Ellie went to the desk to explain we had to check out and to pay; Frank strolled in. He was such a composed guy who always appeared totally in control.

He called us all together and said the plan should be as follows; Ellie would finish paying the bill, she would then drive us to the airport to meet Anya. We had plenty of time, an hour or so. He qualified this by saying we had to leave San Francisco for security reasons. Apparently, he had received more information and would explain later. Then we all would fly to Phoenix, Arizona.

Ellie would stay with Gerry and Tony in the Embassy Suites. Ellie nearly wet herself. She was so excited firstly because she loved Tony and Gerry and secondly, because she had never been to Phoenix but had been told it was the hottest place in North America. I whispered to Ellie "you do know that Tony and Gerry are gay?" "Why yes, that's why we get on so well. It's like being with two girlfriends!"

Frank continued "Anneliese and Matthew, you are booked into the Wickenburg Inn on the Wickenburg Ranch. Matthew, I hope you can ride because this is a semi-dude ranch, so you will be expected to work with the cattle early morning. But by semi-dude, I mean it is luxurious. You will definitely have the chance to complete your vacation, so hope you enjoy it." My ego could not keep quiet. I said "Listen guys, I love to ride. Western will be a bit of a challenge for a day or two but my trainer, Jason, is the best in the business and his dad, Ian, is a magical horse whisperer! So I can't go wrong!"

Frank pursued his explanation. "This is the best plan I can come up with after taking advice from central HQ. Nobody will expect you to head to Arizona. And with Gerry, Tony, Ellie and myself there, you will have round the clock protection and support. Wickenburg is only a couple of miles outside Phoenix and the CIA advise that they use it as a safe house so the necessary few at the facility will also provide support and security".

We met Anya at the airport arrivals gate about 7pm. She was ecstatic to see us all there to meet her. Anneliese and I were her focal point for enthusiastic embraces. She was so tired having had a long flight from Tunisia. Anneliese and I were left to give her the bad news. For her, travel was not at an end.

As we explained we were staying in the airport and flying to Arizona about 9.30pm, I saw her face drop. But this was a very strong willed person. When we continued to give details of the Wickenburg Inn, and that this would be our vacation, her eyes opened wide and it felt as if the sun had just started shining.

I must admit, I had been fixated with staying in San Francisco for at least a few days. It's strange how we human beings lock onto things from our childhood and find it so difficult to let go. As I mentioned earlier, the only thing I knew about the place was from listening to Tony Bennett's songs. The place itself did validate the feeling that the music had given me. It was a vibrant, glorious, enthralling place that I could spend the rest of my life in. Instead, we were off to pastures new and, hopefully, one day I would return to hear the clang-clang-clang of the trolleys on the hills of San Francisco.

Frank, as if reading my thoughts said that the young woman attacked on the ferry was a case of mistaken identity. Our intelligence people and the CIA had both concluded that this had been a murder plot orchestrated by the KGB and really meant for Anneliese. The woman was now serious, in intensive care. She had been injected with a nerve agent.

Internal flights in America always seemed strange and bemused me. We all just strolled up to the airlines ticket desk, bought our tickets, and walked to the gate. Just as easy as going on a bus ride in London.

We were flying with South West Airlines on a BAC 111. We took our seats in business class, almost commandeering half of it. The flight time, according to our hostess, would be two hours. Sure enough, the flight was on time, landing exactly at 11.30pm. Poor Anya slept all the way and only awoke as we were close to Phoenix.

Landing at this airport is a weird feeling. Coming into land, the plane seemed to climb above some mountains then drop like a brick. Indeed, I am pretty sure the pilot cut the engines after the climb before we dropped safely onto the runway. It was this sensation that woke Anya.

Now she was awake, she became almost hyperactive, talking non-stop, very excitable and clinging to my arm. Just like a child arriving at her holiday destination!

Having collected our luggage, Frank organised two taxis. Frank and Ellie in one, going straight to the Embassy Suites in Phoenix. I commented to Ellie that I was certain Tony and Gerry would be waiting for them. Frank explained to our driver that we were going to the Wickenburg Inn. He laughed and said "Gee, I'm taking a cowboy possee!" There were some handshakes and Frank said they would be near us all the time!

Chapter 34

The Chaps In Wickenburg

As we arrived and entered the gates of the ranch, I could see the Inn in the distance. It was Arizona rustic. A very large timber building surrounded by decking and the customary rocking chair swaying in the evening breeze.

The reception staff were so friendly and welcoming, so I asked if we could get a drink at the bar. Anneliese was very quiet and thoughtful and said "Yes but let's make it just the one, as we want to be bright and breezy tomorrow. No work herding, but we can ride or have a look at Wickenburg. Decide in the morning".

No whisky in the bar, so I settled for an American "Jim Beam" bourbon. The girls chatted away, mostly about how it was going in Hammamet and with Anya telling short anecdotes about Mum and Dad. Anneliese was still very quiet so I tried to get her to open up. Slowly it surfaced.

Anneliese said she could not stop thinking about the loving couple and the woman now laying in a hospital bed. Not much is known about these nerve agents so the doctors may be out of their depth. Anya interrupted saying "The best army medics and scientists will be looking after her and the Americans are the best." All the time, Anya was close to Anneliese, trying to comfort her. I felt totally useless.

I then said the wrong thing. "Anneliese, that was meant for you and what would we do if you were lying in the hospital bed and we were sitting there absolutely helpless". "Matthew, you have just made me feel twice as bad. I am responsible for that poor girl's condition!" She started to cry. Anya cuddled her and quietly said " It is not your fault, it's those bastard Russian criminals!"

With that, Anneliese gulped her wine. I put my arm around her and said "That was a first, I didn't know you could cry!" She had a small choking laugh and held my hand tight. Things started to look better so we tripped off to our room.

Once again, we were all in the same room. A very large room with two double beds and patio doors leading out to a well-lit swimming pool. We all just wanted bed. I got in the one nearest the patio doors and Anneliese got in next to me. I just wanted to comfort and care for her. I was happy to look forward to more exciting nights!

Anya collapsed into the other bed, we all shouted good night to one another and then it was sunny morning in Wickenburg. At breakfast, we were all feeling recovered. So there was quite a lot of talk about what had happened the previous day. Especially, regarding Anya's questions. The poor soul never knew much about what had gone on other than what Frank had said. Whilst we talked, we enjoyed a seriously good breakfast. The girls mostly had cereals and fruit. I had got a penchant for American breakfasts so I went for pancakes, which normally come with bacon. But I prefer eggs, sunny side up, and maple syrup.

All the time we were enjoying breakfast, the girls were planning the day. They wanted shopping in Wickenburg, but also just lounging by the pool getting a tan top-up. This morning it was 42c. Most mornings around Phoenix, it is that sort of temperature. It falls in the winter, but not far.

I managed to get a few words in. Looking out of our room, beyond the pool, I could see a small coral or training area for riders. So I suggested we go to reception and get an appointment to meet our horses.

I wanted to spend an hour or so getting together with my horse and getting the feeling for a western saddle. It is totally different and you ride with long stirrups. Your arse has to get used to this. It may be painful and may take a while!

Reception arranged for us to meet the horses at 11.30am. I said to Anneliese I wanted to go for a wander in the grounds. She wanted to come and so did Anya. We only got just outside Reception when I caught sight of a small bird. Then I noticed many more of them, they were humming birds attracted by the insects on this large bush. I probably got over-excited and said to Anneliese I would hurry back in, to get my camera. I love nature and had never seen anything like it before. I got the camera while the girls stood in the area posing for photos.

I took many photos of the girls to keep them happy, but mostly the humming birds. What a spectacle of nature. We trudged on and saw a few brightly coloured snakes crossing the road. What a nature reserve this place was!

At 11.30am, I was on my way to see the horses. The girls were off to the ladies to check their make-up and would catch me up in about 10 minutes. I could tell they were very confident about their riding, and really, just wanted to get a look at them and take a few photos.

All three horses were in the coral. A wrangler was with them, giving them water. His name was Chuck. He said they had worked early morning and after we had been, they would go in the stable out of the heat.

The biggest horse, about 16 hands, would suit me best said Chuck. His name was Tonto. He was a brown and white piebald. What the Native Americans call a paint pony. I liked him a lot. When I got close and put my hand near his mouth, he had a smell and then his huge tongue came out to lick me.

The girls arrived and said hello to Chuck. Their horses were a bay for Anneliese and a palomino for Anya. Their selections, were both beautiful examples of American Quarter Horses. Chuck said "You can help me get them in out of the heat and groom them for a bit, if you want". We led them into a large shed, but did only ten minutes of grooming due to the heat. As we were leaving, Chuck said the round-up would start at 6.30am in the morning and we would work until about 8.00am. It was voluntary but he assured us that most people enjoyed it and learned a lot about a Western Ranch.

Walking back, the girls were keen to get on the road to Wickenburg for some shopping and then they planned to return to the swimming pool to catch some rays!

I suppose I would describe Wickenburg as a two horse town (on a scale of 1 – 10). The girls' faces said it all. There was a saloon, a ladies dress shop and a very large Western store, that was our first target.

Chapter 35

Chaps Look Great And Prevent Chaps

The store had everything from boots to cowboy hats, to a massive array of western clothing, belts and leather goods, as well as saddles, bridles and equipment.

The girls got in the mood and bought all types of Western goods. Jeans were a real favourite, a pair of boots each and then they found the chaps. Both girls came out of the fitting room wearing chaps over their jeans and modelled with delight. It was eyes on stalks for several men in the store.

I was less adventurous. Two pairs of jeans, two hand crafted leather belts and a couple of neckerchiefs. The final bill tally was enormous; Anneliese whacked it all on her credit card.

Now we all wanted a drink so we quickly went to the Ranger Pickup that the Ranch had given us to use, loaded all in and I was about to head for the Wickenburg Saloon. Anneliese stopped me in my tracks and said "Let's go back to the Inn, get some drinks and relax by the pool". So that was what the boss wanted and we agreed.

Because the sun was so hot, we spent the rest of the afternoon in and out of the pool, on the sunbeds, back through the patio doors to the room and so on. I could not stand more than fifteen minutes at a time in the sun and the girls could not take much more. A lot of time was taken up applying sun cream and lotion. A totally enjoyable experience for us all.

Dinner was typically ranch style. The choice was steak or more steak. Gigantic T Bone steaks were selected with a couple of bottles of Californian wine. It wasn't quite haute cuisine but with background country and western music, the mood was undeniably potent.

So we took more bottles of wine, and a bottle of bourbon, back to the pool with us. Although about 7.30pm it was still over 30 degrees. We gathered around the pool. I immediately felt as if I was melting. Anya, probably due to the heat, said "I'm, going back to the restaurant to get some fruit for us while we are out here". I had an idea; "while you are there, ask reception if they could get us a canopy tomorrow. Don't even care if I have to pay for it" Wonderful idea" said Anneliese.

Anya returned after a short interlude with a massive bowl of different types of fruit. Although we had all devoured those tender T Bone steaks, we all wanted the refreshing, cold, sweet fruits.

I asked Anya if she had remembered the canopy. "Oh yes" she said. "They will install one during the morning. If we wanted a large one to cover all three beds, it would mean us making a contribution". "That's fine with me" I said. I kept recalling the beautiful fine linen canopies at the Sousse Hotel!

We continued drinking with background music seeping from our apartment. Anya especially, but Anneliese and myself also became more loquacious, active and amorous. After a couple of hours, the girls, who had been chatting secretively by the pool, announced they were going in to try on the clothes they had bought in Wickenburg.

The sun had lowered behind the local mountain, Eagle Peak. It was dusk and the lights around the pool had come on. I was so relaxed it was as if rigor mortis was setting in.

But I didn't care. I'd not felt the splendour of relaxation for a very long time.

Just as my mind was tripping through the events of the last few years and how my life had changed, the music volume intensified. I became much more awake, pulled myself up a bit and looked around.

Anneliese and Anya were standing at the patio doors. In time to the music, they stepped out onto the patio and swayed in front of me. Both individually and collectively, they created massive excitement. Such a stunning appearance. Although meant to re-enact their past lives, and also be humorous, these two females absolutely blew my mind.

They were wearing the chaps. Underneath were tiny g strings but then they began to gyrate to the music. They turned their bottoms toward me. Both had wonderful curved lines from their hips down. Anneliese fitted her chaps perfectly. Her bottom was like a peach that had been massaged and squeezed to fit every contour. Anya was different; it was as if the chaps were fighting to contain her bottom, like a rabbit trying to escape from a sack.

They pranced around and tried to get me up dancing with them. Playful does not describe their mood. I cried "you don't need to titillate me because your beauty has been more than exaggerated by your performance and has underlined the meaning of erotic". Their dancing moved from intermittent to slow and so we snuggled up together on the bed.

Chapter 36

The First Roundup

My body didn't want to play ball as I rose at 5.30am. It was hot but bearable this time of the morning. Not a cloud in the sky and a very dry heat. I called Anneliese and Anya and as they were rising, I mentioned that we should get some water on the way out. After about ten minutes, Anya announced she had a hangover and would miss this morning. Anneliese teased her, saying "can't hold your liquor, that's a first". She got back in bed saying "I will see you at breakfast, about 8.00am. We moved out to the coral.

Chuck was already there and had watered the horses. No food until they had worked. With a surprised voice he said "Gee guys, no Anya?" I jumped in saying that she had a hangover and would start tomorrow.

Chuck had left the saddling to us. He said "That's how the horse gets to know you". He was correct. I learned early that grooming, saddling and feeding were mandatory to get a good relationship with a horse.

Now up in the saddle, it felt great. Different but great. Bigger saddle, pommel to hold if you needed to, rope and saddle bags, if you wanted them. We both had just one each.

Chuck was leader. We cantered for about 10 minutes. Then saw the cattle just ahead. What they called Shorthorns. The horses were so easy to ride, because they seemed to know what was expected. First it was to round up about 50 head.

Tonto was fantastic, Anneliese looked to be an accomplished rider. The teamwork between us and our horses made it look easy.

Chuck was so pleased "You are the best riders I have worked with this season. It will make it so much fun and easier on all of us!"

That said, with the cattle moving constantly it was so dusty. My hair and eyebrows were almost white. We carried on after cutting out the 50 head who were all being shipped off to market later that day. The last half an hour was to watch and listen to Chuck explain roping. Tomorrow we would be expected to capture several calves that required injections. The usual vets' protection.

We both had several goes at riding around the coral roping the calves. We both started to get the roping. Where it got really difficult was jumping off your horse and hog tying the calves. I suppose, after a couple of attempts we were getting the feeling for the process, but also very tired. To be honest, Anneliese was the star. Once you get the calf on the ground, it is essential to lean on it, spread your legs wide and then scramble to get the rope round its legs. Neither of us were great, but Chuck said we were pretty good!

We were back at the coral and I was looking forward to breakfast. Chuck said "if you want to come back about 11.00 ish to groom the horses you are welcome. If not, don't worry, this is your vacation and I can do it". God, I couldn't even think to answer, I just wanted breakfast!

Anya was feeling better. And as usual, she looked stunning. Anneliese had gone off for a shower and would be about 10 minutes. I could not be bothered, white hair and eyebrows and all! I just wanted the grub, coffee, orange juice, the lot.

Anneliese arrived at the table, just as Anya was collecting her second bowl of fruit. She said "it's an aphrodisiac and clears a hangover." I couldn't help myself. "You don't need an aphrodisiac" She smiled and grabbed my thigh!

The rest of the day was so relaxing. Swimming pool, drink, food, photos of the place and, especially humming birds. And a bit of a sleep in the afternoon.

In the middle of all this, I did wander down with the girls to pamper Tonto with a grooming. I could sense we were getting a serious relationship together.

In the evening, out by the pool, Anneliese cuddled up to me and said "are you happy with this as a vacation?" What could I say, I'd never had such fantastic holidays. I had loved my holidays, picking hops in Faversham and Canterbury. But this was a grown-ups holiday in another country and a fabulous location. Yes this suited me down to the ground.

We loved the rest of the evening. Wonderful company, food, drinks, music and marvellous surroundings. As dusk turned to darkness the light around the pool lit the surrounding areas. And with a glorious full moon, we could see some distance. The heat of the evening, drink in my hand, the lights and the view enhanced that feeling of euphoria. Looking out to the valley, the shadowy majestic shape of the Saguaro Cacti, throughout the hills, was entrancing. I constantly reminded myself how lucky I had been to find Anneliese and this spectacular world. Even though I regularly thought about past events, and the fact that we were targets for the most dangerous people in the world, I had unadulterated love and support from everybody around me. This world was now my world, and I would take whatever it threw at me.

I got together with Anneliese and Anya and said "why don't we get dressed up and go into the bar and have a party. These people have not really had the chance to get to know us and I want us to carry on enjoying ourselves. This was one night where I wanted more!

It did not need much coaxing. The girls were immediately off to get spruced up. I went to reception and informed them. "We want a fun night and don't care what it costs". They were ready to accommodate.

We all went to the bar about 45 minutes later looking and smelling fabulous. There were about a dozen people in so we acknowledged them and then I stepped out of my comfort zone. I stood at the bar, turned around and asked them all if they would like a drink.

It was like a tidal wave, 10 or so people came to the bar and started chatting. All different nationalities and mostly all there to get to see a working ranch in parallel with sincere but subtle relaxation.

The reception manager came over to us and with smiling eyes that teased out dimpled cheeks announced that the canopy had now been installed next to the pool. "I'm very sorry it arrived late" she said, "But the installers have been overwhelmed with demand".

We laughed it off saying we were just happy it had been done. To be honest, with all that had gone on, we had all completely forgotten about it!

Chaper 37

Lets Have Shagging At Our Party

I felt that I should ask Lucia, the Reception Manager, if she would stay for a drink with us. She had replied "Oh thank you, I would love that ", when a voice boomed across the room. "Heyyy Matthew, I'll have a bourbon with you". It was Chuck, his smile almost as wide as Texas! I should never have mentioned that, recently, I'd been drinking bourbon. He loved the stuff as much as I love the girls. Lucia had a superb accent which sounded Spanish. With her dark very attractive features, I assumed she was Mexican.

Obviously, she was a great friend to Chuck. She immediately invited him to get behind the bar and pour our drinks. Such a dangerous thing to do. His own drink was at least half a pint and the rest of us got drinks triple the usual size.

Looking around, everybody seemed to be getting in the party mood. The music volume was increased by someone and a few people began western style dancing. Several different dance styles came and went. There was some line dancing that was right up Chuck's street. He was a Texan and could not resist being a brash flamboyant leader.

Chuck was clearly attracted to Anya. He dragged her out to perform various line dancing steps and she quickly proved a really excellent dancer. But then, she had the physique, no

I should say body, for that type of dance. Chuck was as proud as punch as men drooled over Anya!

I could not keep away from Anneliese. We chatted, laughed, had some serious chat, but all I wanted was to be with her and look into her eyes. But then the peace was shattered! Sex reared its ugly head, enough to make us both collapse with hysterical laughter.

Lucia advanced on me as the music beat changed. With a very tempting look on her face and that very sexy accent she said "I used to live and work in South Carolina. This music is the dance music of that region. So would you care to have a shag with me?"

I just took a second to look at Anneliese and we both exploded with laughter. It was just the funniest thing that I'd heard in a long time. I pulled myself together, took Lucia's hand and we had a go… not a shag… but at the South Carolina dance named as such.

I have to say, I didn't do too bad. Lucia said she was impressed because it's like ballroom with a lot of static footwork. Chuck appeared, still not getting any noticeable effect from the Bourbon. He stood talking to me about "the shag" and the wonderful Lucia.

As we were talking, my mind drifted into surveying Chuck. He was about 6 feet tall. His eyes always seemed to be smiling. He had bushy red hair, a very square dimpled chin and his facial skin looked as tough as old boots with a rugged complexion. But the colour and texture was like leather.

I suppose his clothing and the way he smelled, he smelled of horse and cattle, were typical of a cowboy. Usually, he wore a dirty grey floppy domed Stetson cowboy hat. And well-worn chaps covered in dirty lines probably caused by taught ropes. But not tonight, the hat and chaps had been left in the bunkhouse. Instead, he had opted for a pristine light blue check shirt with a dark blue neckerchief. He was quite some human American cowboy specimen!

Whilst talking with Chuck, I told him Lucia had asked me for a shag. He looked bewildered. So I took off explaining why it was so humorous to Anneliese and myself. Anneliese joked" he has never had any woman come straight up to him and ask him for a shag!" Once he had managed to get the whole picture, he called Lucia over. Chuck insisted we all got into a sort of rugby scrum. Arms around each other's necks in a circle.

It started quietly, Chuck explaining to Lucia what the name shag meant to people from the UK. He did it slowly and carefully. Lucia stopped him a couple of times, asking questions. But then the dawn came. Lucia started chuckling, giggling, laughing, and then seismic uncontrollable laughter. We were all falling to our knees, overcome with hysterics!

Gradually people drifted away to their beds. Anya, Anneliese and I decided we would go by the pool to finish our drinks and get a feel for the new canopy.

Chuck came with us after we all said a big thank you to Lucia who was quickly and efficiently clearing up. Under the canopy we were amazed at how large it was. It was like our own marquee.

Later, I was telling Chuck that I needed to get some boots as my calf muscles had got seriously chafed riding earlier. So I was planning to go back to the Western store after round-up in the morning. Chuck, with his usual authority said "No don't do that, when you come in try some I have in my place. I have enough boots to kit out a centipede!"

Tomorrow was the end of our work week so we then had a couple of free days to look forward to. Chuck said us guests were given two days on, two days off. Of course, all voluntary, "But beware" he continued " tomorrow is a big one, so you will meet four of the ranch wranglers who will drive a couple of hundred head up to Sedona, red rock country, for a big sale. You will assist until they get them clear of the ranch".

Chuck was dead keen on Anya. Whilst it was just us boys, he asked "What is Anya to you. Is she your sister?" "What, with her accent" I replied. "Well I thought she sounded different but thought maybe you and Anneliese had brought her away on a vacation with you".

"Well, it goes like this" I said. "She is Anneliese's best friend". "And so she is ok with sleeping in the same room as you two love birds?" "Yeah, we are all fine with it because she also has become my best friend!" But if you are keen, just go for it, but remember, Anneliese and I are her guardians". "OK, thanks" said Chuck and wandered over to the two girls. I watched with interest as Anneliese strolled over to me and sat on my knee. We poured, what I hoped was a last drink and Anneliese became very amorous which livened me up.

As we watched, but deliberately appeared not to, Chuck was very polite and courteous to Anya. She also to him, but she did keep looking over at us. Next, apparently she announced to Chuck that she was so tired and had to go to bed. She stretched up to peck him on the cheek. He could not accept that and locked his arms around her back. Such a strong guy, he lifted her off her feet, kissed her on the neck and then cheek. As he put her down he shouted to us that, in the morning, she would come on the roundup.

At precisely 5.30am, we got the alarm call from Reception. I said "Morning Lucia, how are you today?" "I'll tell you in a few hours" she responded. The girls were coming round. Very quickly, I was ready to go. My head wasn't straight but physically I was ok. I told Anneliese, I needed to go to try on the boots. She understood! Chuck showed me a row of boots and the third pair I tried were perfect. Already worn in and soft and flexible. I said to Chuck that these would help me get through the day. He looked excited and said "the only thing that will get me through this is if Anya turns up!"

Just then, Anneliese and Anya walked in. they were both ready to go and, as expected, looked like rodeo models on a fashion shoot. What kept going round in my head was the difficulty I had experienced with Western riding. Neck reining was second nature to me but long stirrups take a lot of getting used to. In fact, it's a real pain in the arse and I knew it would worsen today!

Chuck could not wait to chat to Anya. Put his arm around her shoulders and edged her towards the door. He had already tethered our horses outside the bunkhouse. The girls' horses were named after a famous outlaw and gunslinger which seemed appropriate, Anneliese's was Jesse and Anya had Bat. Chuck said to Anya "really he is named after Bat Masterson, but more like because he can fly, so grip tight with those fine little legs of yours."

With a cloud of dust, the four wranglers arrived. Chuck shouted "don't dismount cos we have to get going" But then, pointing to each one he named them. First a beautiful tanned girl named Cassie. Then the three men; Rueben, Luke and Aaron. None of them appeared very biblical!

Before we left, Chuck explained that we were trying to cut out the biggest strongest cattle. The four wranglers took off to make a start. My God, how they could ride. Chuck stayed with us, almost glued to Anya. However, she decided to show him she was no slouch. She pushed Bat to almost take-off speed, turned him on a sixpence, jumped every ridge and fence, and went down through every gully.

And all the time, her gorgeous bottom moved around in the saddle like it had a mind of its own. I actually commented as much to Anneliese and, as she looked across to Chuck, she said "that's how she has always mesmerized mankind!"

It was a tough assignment but we came through with flying colours. Once again, about 8.30am, I just needed a good old American breakfast.

Chapter 38

Sunset Ride

As we walked from the stables, Chuck said that if we wanted, he would accompany us on a Sunset Ride tomorrow evening. It was a special treat for most visitors and he promised to make it something we would remember. He would come to the ranch Hotel about 7.30pm and we would take a picnic. We should remember our cameras as there would be spectacular scenery and sunset views. We all agreed it was definitely for us!

In an almost timid sort of way, Chuck asked if we would mind him joining us by the pool tomorrow afternoon. I spoke up first, saying that would be great. Anya just smiled at him.

Back at breakfast, Anneliese couldn't seem to take her eyes off me. Although Anya seemed pretty quiet. In the last couple of days, she had given off some strange vibes.

Just tucking into my eggs and pancakes with Anneliese giving me glowing looks, Frank came into my mind.

Carefully and quietly I said "haven't heard anything from Frank, do you think he's ok?" Anneliese smiled and said "he's fine. You may not have seen him but that's because he's trained to be elusive. Ever since we've been here, he's been around, no more than a couple of hundred yards away."

Then, as we tried to draw Anya into the conversation, we talked about arrangements for tomorrow. I shuffled my chair close to Anya and asked if she was ok. "Are you not enjoying yourself" I said, putting my arm around her; she looked at me with a pitiful, tearful look. "Of course I'm enjoying it, but like everything, it will have to end, and I can't stop hurting with that thought!"

"Anya, please listen to me, just take one day at a time, and never expect too much. We are in a fabulous place and tomorrow we can just relax and have a glorious day in this sunshine beside the pool. I've even got a canopy which we can all share, what could be better than that?"

She then began to become agitated, gripping my hand very tightly. "I am not a kid anymore. I am at the point in my life where I need more than this. I know exactly what I want but every time I get close, it seems to find a way to elude me!"

Anya got up and said she would go to get her bikini on for swimming. When she was out of earshot, Anneliese said "the only thing she craves, Matthew, is you. I can't do anything about it and neither can you. It's not a physical thing. It's an emotional need and I don't know what to do about it".

We enjoyed a great afternoon and evening by the pool relaxing. But none of us were totally relaxed because we carried on worrying about Anya.

Early evening I ordered a great selection of food for us by the pool. Wine flowed throughout, Bacchus, the God of Wine, would have been proud of us. But the impact of the wine and relentless concern for Anya, made me explain to Anneliese I felt under pressure. She understood and said she felt the same. Anya was sitting on the edge of the pool, dangling her feet in the water.

Anneliese said "Maybe it's time to try something different. Go into the bar, find Lucia and ask if she would like to join us. And also would she get in touch with Chuck so we could have a fun night."

I did just that, it was a great idea! I found Lucia and she seemed ecstatic to be invited. But, one problem, she had to work until 9.00pm. That was only an hour away, so I said "of course, there would still be mountains of food". She whispered, "I can always get more if we need it". "And what about Chuck," I said. "Oh, I'm pretty sure he will come" said Lucia. But then, with her sexy Spanish accent, she asked "Just one more thing. I have met a guy that I would like to accompany me. Is that ok?"

She was such a lovely lady so I asked "is he American, local, one of the residents?" "No" she said "he just comes into the bar occasionally and tells me he's English, but to me the accent sounds Australian". I was intrigued.

I explained all this to Anneliese. She said we could analyse the guy when he arrived. Psychology was her forte but I seemed to have a basic understanding. We had been splashing around, getting even more inebriated, and at 9.05pm they walked in, Chuck beaming as usual.

That meet and greet I always find rather stressful. However, I knew them all, or so I thought. Lucia arrived behind Chuck, but as he moved towards us, I was elated with her friend. It was Frank. He was charming in the introductions, but all the time his facial expressions said you must not let on.

I can't, even now, explain how pleased I was to see him. He was a character that would accept dangerous situations as if they were like sitting having pie and mash, in an English café. Anyway, we all got started. Wine flowed, food was gobbled and the party was, again, underway.

I managed to get some Dire Straits music playing on the sound system and Frank and Lucia started the dancing. Frank had a couple of dances then cornered me by the drinks and said "I know you are going for a sunset ride" I interrupted "how do you know that?" "Doesn't matter. Just remember to bring your gun and be very alert." He moved away silently.

Anneliese was so professional, she hadn't really acknowledged Frank other than to say hello when they had arrived. Lucia was a really lovely, indeed beautiful, lady that clearly had the hots for Frank. He had this quiet way of adjusting to any environment.

From the ground up, he looked impeccable. He had Chelsea boots, not cowboy boots. His trousers were grey with angle cut outs at the boots. His jacket was navy blue, three quarter length, which gave him the appearance of Wyatt Earp in Tombstone. An impeccable white button down shirt twinned with a white silk handkerchief protruding from his coat breast pocket.

But above all this, it was his composure, his slow deliberate movement and speech, together with an undeniable presence.

It was early the next morning when we finished. The end game was us all sitting around telling stories and jokes. Chuck had a marvellous sense of humour. Sometimes, rather near the knuckle, but he managed to get Anya laughing which was a feat in itself.

Whilst everyone was finishing drinks and eating the last few pieces, I took my drink down by the end of the pool and stood looking out at the vista created by the moon reflecting on Eagle Peak.

Frank strolled down and stood beside me. He reminded me so much of my brother! As we stood, quietly, I asked Frank "What do you think may happen tomorrow?" "It is just intuition from my surveillance. I think they may be planning an attack tomorrow. I am convinced they have found Anneliese and you. You will be in open country, no protection, or that's what they are probably thinking. But I won't be far away".

We walked back into the midst of our group as they were saying goodbyes. Lucia couldn't wait to grip hold of Frank, saying that he was driving her home, just a couple of miles away in Phoenix. Anya and Chuck kissed passionately, which put chuck on cloud 9. As we strolled to the gate together, he said she had told him that she was still trying to get over a relationship and needed time. Chuck was not one to give in easily! "I will see you tomorrow afternoon. You guys have given me the best time since we put a man on the moon!"

Anya reverted to her dismal state and went straight to bed. So Anneliese and I sat comfortably on a couch sipping our last drink of the night and recounting the evening's events. It was fabulous just being alone with her and my emotional sense began to overwhelm me.

We were talking about how Frank and Lucia seemed very keen on one another and how they appeared suited. My mind now became overcome by my emotional state and I asked Anneliese, "Do you really, really, believe that we are a perfect match?" "Of course, I do "she replied. "There is something magical with us. I can't describe it, but my feelings for you are so strong that the force, in itself, will never allow me to be without you. And I hope and believe you feel the same." Just at that point the background music swung into The Carpenters. The track playing was "I won't last a day without you."

That reached my soul! I looked into Anneliese's eyes and, I know that she was feeling the thoughts in my mind. I could not contain myself and in a shaky voice asked "Will you marry me?" Her reply was immediate. "Yes and we should because I have been having the same thought for several days." We kissed and embraced lovingly for a few minutes and then, as Anneliese eased away, she became excited.

"Let's have a wonderful day here tomorrow. We can have our Sunset Ride with Anya and Chuck. That will help the romantic stakes for all of us. And during the day we can tell everybody. We can tell them that we are going to fly up to Las Vegas on Saturday to get married!" Now she was in trembling mode. "I can ask Anya to be my bridesmaid and Chuck could be your Best Man." "Hold your horses, young lady. I think I should be allowed to pick my Best Man. As much as I have grown to like Chuck, I would really like to ask Frank if he would be willing. I hope you agree" I said.

"Yes, oh yes. I am so excited. We need to get flights and everything organised tomorrow. Lucia will help I know. We can come straight back here afterwards and have a wedding party. I can get all my wardrobe up in Las Vegas. I joked "For the first night you won't need much!"

We carried on for a little while longer, a couple more drinks and was almost suffocated by the emotion of the last hour. But then Anneliese took my hand and led me off to the bed that I needed. Emotion can be draining and we were both exhausted!

Next morning, it all seemed a dream. One of those happy, exciting dreams that make you feel good when you wake up. My childhood had been full of those dreams and I'd not experienced them for many years.

While we were getting ready, I quietly asked Anneliese "When should we tell Anya." She said "Let's get breakfast over and tell her at the end." I asked "Will she be ok with it?" "I don't know but we will manage it!"

When we were all ready to go to breakfast, I told them that I needed to go to the Western store in Wickenburg to buy some stuff. Never said what, but I had to get a shoulder holster based on what Frank had said to me. In all the travel, mine had gone missing. My idea was to wear it under a waistcoat because the weather was so hot. This also gave me a way to get out of the scenario when Anneliese informed Anya of our intention to marry.

Breakfast finished and done, I left the girls to explore and discuss our plans. Walking through the hotel, I didn't get far. Everybody kept stopping me, shaking hands and saying what a great time they had at the party. Next came Lucia. I told her I had to go into Wickenburg. But it went further, I asked if she could get a couple of days off. She asked why. "Well yes, I probably could" she said, so with my brain working overtime, I just said "Please talk to Anneliese "and rushed out to the pickup truck.

No parking problems in Wickenburg. I parked right outside the store, and got help in there. I explained what I needed, nothing bulky, almost undetectable, narrow thin material. They had just the thing. It was a beautiful leather construction but very thin tooled leather and fitted perfectly. Also, a waistcoat that covered it comfortably.

I felt I was under pressure and in a rush. I got back to the hotel only 45 minutes after I'd left it. I wanted to know how it had gone with Anya!

Anneliese was sitting by the pool on her own. I sat next to her. She looked at me, trying to hold back tears. I never had a chance to speak. She said" Don't be worried, these are happiness tears. I've never been so happy. Nothing, until you came along, has made me feel this way."

I kissed her hands and said "but how did Anya take it? Was she pleased for us?" "Oh yes" she said, "She could not be happier. Initially it was a shock, Anya said, and she was correct. She and I would always be together, partners against the world. But when I explained how strong my feelings are for you, she became almost euphoric and went into overload when I asked her to be my bridesmaid. I have also spoken to Frank and he is delighted. He said he will make all the arrangements for our Las Vegas wedding."

Lucia is going to arrange a wedding party for when we return. I was still feeling concerned for Anya so I asked "Where is she now?" "Oh, she's gone down to the stables to check on the horses for our "romantic" eve of wedding, sunset ride. She will make sure everything is perfect!"

Anya arrived back with Chuck early afternoon. Anneliese was just explaining that tomorrow, the travel arrangements were still uncertain, but we probably needed to be ready to go fairly early. Not to worry about clothing, Frank had it all arranged.

It didn't take a moment for all the talk to become about the wedding, traversing everything else. Chuck and I settled into drinking. We ordered some food and it would arrive shortly. The chat with Anya was mostly questions; what are you wearing? Where will you live? It was unsettling because I sensed a hint of sarcasm in her voice. I tried sitting next to her, giving her a cuddle, but compared to the way we used to be, it seemed resistant.

Lucia came in, what a fabulous woman. The girls all talked with her about the wedding celebrations and she said she was so proud I had picked Frank to be my Best Man. She had brought us a picnic to take on the Sunset Ride. Chuck said he would take it in some saddle bags on his horse along with a couple of bottles of vino!

After saddling the horses, checking we had everything we needed, we set off about 7.30pm. Chuck led the way, out of the ranch towards Eagle Peak, along a dried up river bed.

There were boulders both sides all along the fringe of the river bed. It was probably a beautiful river in winter time that supported all types of natural habitats. Chuck said that in the height of summer, the boulders and rocky crags were a magnet for snakes, rattle snakes in particular, and to keep a look out for them. Apparently, a rattle snake can strike twice its body length.

Following the river bed led us into a long gully with hills either side. It looked as if it was about a half mile long. As we picked our way through the rocks and boulders, I sensed something behind me. It was a small black Dobermann puppy which had, obviously, followed us out from the ranch.

I was last in the line with Anya just in front of me. All this pup seemed to want was to get to Anya and her horse. It was annoying Tonto by trying to weave through his legs. Then I got another surprise. Again I felt something trailing us, I turned in the saddle to look and was shocked to see a large skinny wolf attempting to get to the Dobermann, snapping at it's heels! I shouted to Chuck. He looked and called back that it was a Coyote and there would be more soon because this was the time they were trying to feed young and the Dobermann would make a worthwhile meal for them.

We were all getting jumpy with the Coyote moving really close to the pup and the horses. Then it stopped in its tracks and started to howl. With that, the pup cried and whimpered under Tonto's belly.

By now we were half way along the gully and the whole pack of Coyotes began to appear and gradually surround us. They were vicious looking beasts that circled us silently!

Anneliese shouted "Chuck we can't go on like this. I'm going to get that bloody pup and lash him to my saddle. Then we can ride and try to lose these ugly Coyotes!" "No, don't do that. Now the pack is here, and hungry, they may even attack a human" Chuck screamed.

But too late. Anneliese had already laid across her saddle and dropped to the floor. As quick as those rattle snakes, she grasped the pup, pressed it next to the saddle pommel and very quickly used the leather lash straps to tie him to the pommel and saddle.

As Anneliese was about to get her foot in a stirrup to mount, Anya screamed "No, stop, don't do that, stay where you are!" I could not believe what I was seeing and hearing. I looked at Chuck. His brain seemed to have gone into spasm as if he did not believe his eyes. First off I thought Anya may have seen a rattle snake. But no!

Anya was pointing her little Derringer pistol at Anneliese. "Don't mount that horse, I knew you would have to be Joan of Arc and save the pup. But now he's going to be the death of you." The Coyotes now had come even closer and were growling and snarling at Anneliese.

Anneliese, once again tried to get a foot in the stirrup. Anya's expression now turned completely evil. Her veins stood out on her temple. Her face became taught and white and her gun hand shook, like in the midst of a tornado.

I just blurted something out, my brain had joined Chuck's. I think I said "Anya, what are you doing, what is this?" she immediately turned on me with a ferocity that I could not believe, even today, as being Anya. "You, you bastard have left me for her. I've always had to be the subservient one in the background. The one she relies on. Then you come along and I thought, eventually, you would see I was for you. But no, you decided to dump me and be the idiot and marry that whore. And then you both decided to insult me, asking me to be bridesmaid" It was obvious from Anya's whole demeanour that she had become completely psychotic. Demented to the point of uncontrollable, ferocious anger.

A disturbing noise worsened the complexity of this fearsome situation. A dull whirring sound which grew in intensity. It was a helicopter coming closer and gradually descending.

I thought that this would distract Anya, but not a chance. She appeared so fixated with destroying Anneliese's world that her weird gaze hardened, her gun arm stretched out further and the trembling increased.

At that point my whole being reacted without thought, blindly but powerfully. I suppose my mind concluded that Anya's mental state was going to be disastrous. I pulled my horse whip out of my boot, and with one terrifying swipe buried the whip deep into the hind quarter of Anya's horse. It reared with such power that all hoofs left the ground.

Anya was thrown backwards with a tumbling motion. The back of her neck and head landed on the lip of a large boulder. The crack, then crunching sound, seemed to echo as the horse galloped past us, Anya's right foot caught in the stirrup, blood pouring from her mouth.

I am sure that she was killed immediately she hit the boulder. The horse was in shock and gained in speed as it dragged Anya over boulders and rocks for about 200 yards along the dried up river bed.

We began to ride to her but as we got closer, I could see that her whole body was completely broken. Her head, face and body were completely mutilated, with flesh and blood on almost every rock.

I held my arm in front and across Anneliese and Chuck to stop them going any closer. I didn't think it could worsen, but it did. We sat, in total shock. The Coyotes, smelling blood, tore into her body. It was absolutely grotesque. I can't describe it. My anger boiled over. I pulled out my gun and rode Tonto straight into the middle of the pack. Three shots, at close range dropped three coyotes. Chuck arrived and killed another. The rest ran off into the bush at the side of the gully.

My heart and soul were fractured. Every piece of me was shuddering and shaking and Anneliese was exactly the same. It was as if the terror, the pain, the worthlessness of everything had all arrived with the Grim Reaper. I felt that half my soul had been lost for no good reason. I had always been happy to think that Anya would be with me and Anneliese forever!

The horror of the evening would not end. About 100 yards on the east side of the gully, the helicopter had landed. Two guys were walking towards us, both holding guns. A third man stayed sitting in the helicopter pilot's seat.

These guys had picked the wrong time. We were all tormented by the horrific, excruciating things we had just evidenced. My mind, however, was now tuned in, remembering Frank's teaching. I watched every movement intently as they approached.

Very quickly I placed one of them. It was Harry Grenke. As he got closer he shouted "Hi, you guys, can we help? We saw those terrible events so I thought we may be able to do something for you?"

That jovial voice made me angry. I wanted to explode, I wanted to kill him! But I was learning, especially from Anneliese. Her voice was a bit stuttery but she coolly managed to say "Hello Harry, what are you doing here?" "Well, you know my dear, you still owe us. You owe us that list! Anya had promised she would get it for us but her trouble was she couldn't decide who she had allegiance to. She had always been a Russian and has been feeding information to me for years. But she also loved you, Anneliese, and then this prick Matthew came along and complicated things even more. Anya was supposed to kill you today, but couldn't even manage that. So fuck her to hell cos I have to sort it out."

"So, Anneliese, the bottom line is, we want that list! We have invested a lot of time and money in this, and you! So where is it?"

Harry Grenke raised his revolver, pointing it straight at Anneliese's face. He had one of those ugly grimaces on his face which then developed into a smile that said he would get what he wanted.

That was the second time today that Anneliese had been the target, which was really getting under my skin. I was quickly flicking through options in my head, as Frank, pragmatic Frank, had taught me. Then the sound of a rifle shot stopped me in my tracks!

Then there was a second crack, so close to me, blood splattered on my chest. The first shot had dropped Harry's partner. The second shot went straight through Harry's shoulder, the blood spraying on my shirt and waistcoat. Harry's revolver fell to the floor along with him, clutching his shoulder. I kicked it away!

The helicopter rotors started to whirr. No more than 30 seconds of the rotors gaining speed when a tremendous explosion made us all duck and crouch on the ground. As flames flew into the sky and things quietened, a voice came from nowhere. "Frank said we should call you Nib our little fashion guru. You are looking fabulous in your little leather waistcoat today". It was Gerry wandering down the hill with Tony just behind. Tony joined in "Looking so fit in that tight little waistcoat, Nib is an ideal name for you."

Whilst joking was their style, it certainly didn't obviate their intensely tough characters. They walked with their effeminate elegant poise straight past me, tapping my bottom as they went. Harry Grenke was their target. Well he had been earlier so this was the second occasion. Tony kicked Grenke's revolver even further away.

Gerry knelt beside Grenke. "Oh darling are you in any pain?" Gripping Grenke's shoulder, fingers pressing hard on the wound, Gerry asked does this help?" Grenke screamed in pain. "Well, dear I think we need to get you to hospital" said Gerry indicating to Tony.

Tony pulled Grenke's good arm to the injured one and in a flash slapped handcuffs on him. Grenke continued screaming and moaning as two vehicles drove towards us down the hillside. The first car I recognised, it was the Bronco with Frank driving. I felt so relieved. The other car, a Ford Navigator, drove down almost parallel with the Bronco.

Two guys, suited and booted, emerged from the Navigator. Frank walked in the middle of these unknown characters, his arms around their shoulders.

Anneliese and Chuck sat quietly on their horses. Frank said "These friends are CIA and will take over with Harry Grenke. They have been well briefed and know and understand what happened here today. They also have complete information and have seen all the intelligence reports. So I want to let them get on so we get as little disruption at the ranch as possible. The Americans want it to continue to be useful!"

Both the CIA guys acknowledged Anneliese first. They either knew her from before or knew her work. She was responsive but remained almost rigid in the saddle. Both of these guys had obvious sympathy for Anneliese. "Ma'am, sorry for your loss" they both uttered.

They started to head away, dragging Grenke to their car, still moaning. Frank went over to Anneliese. "I know what a shock this has been to you. Anya was a fabulous person, and none of us had any idea about her work for the KGB. But Anneliese, I have known you a long while. You are strong enough to get through this and now you have Matthew to work with you and love you." He raised his voice. "Tomorrow you are giving your souls to one another. You are getting married. All arrangements are made and I don't want anything to get in the way!" Anneliese seemed to relax and gave me an affectionate smile!

Tony and Gerry took off, with the CIA guys, and Grenke laying in the back. Probably heading to hospital, then a penitentiary.

Frank, talking to Chuck and Anneliese asked them to ride back, taking the two rider-less horses to the ranch. Frank wanted me to ride in the Bronco with him. Anneliese understandably protested. She would not leave Anya's body to the Coyotes or any other creature.

Frank agreed, but just as he was speaking, two very large pickups drove up the river bed. They were F Series 350's, one with a coffin and with professional funeral directors in the cab. Anneliese still was not satisfied enough to leave. "Frank where are they taking Anya?" He thought for a moment then said "it may be her home city in Russia" Anneliese replied that she needed time to process that but, at the very least, she wanted a funeral in the West so she could be there. I added my voice saying I wanted the same.

With that, Frank said he would ensure that would happen. But now we all needed to get back and regroup. Chuck and Anneliese, with the two spare horses, rode off slowly. Chuck's face looked like he had been through the ringer, but I knew he would recover!

I climbed into the Bronco with Frank in the driver's seat. As we were setting off, I asked him "what happened to the helicopter?" "Look behind you" Frank said. "I couldn't let it get away to warn any other insurgents they may have around." I turned and looked in the rear. Lying on the floor pan was what looked like a massive gun. "Frank, what is that?" I asked. "It's a fantastic weapon, a portable anti-tank rocket launcher. The Americans have used it since World War II. They call it a Bazooka. If you can handle it, it can destroy heavy equipment from armoured personnel carriers to Centurion tanks."

Frank continued "We need to get back to the hotel and I will explain as we go. The KGB leave very little to chance, so they most likely would have other operatives out searching for the supplier list. So the hotel rooms would be the place for them to start. I would guess they used Grenke to keep you guys occupied. When we get back, take it slowly and carefully".

We walked up to Lucia in hotel reception. She was all smiles and about to be polite when Frank whispered "have you noticed any strangers or vehicles you've not seen before?" "Why, no I haven't". "Lucia, just stay here and prevent anyone going in the direction of Matthew's room".

As we closed in on our room, I could see the lock had been busted and the door was slightly ajar. Frank, just behind me, slid across to the far side of the door and eased his revolver out from the holster. Looking into the room, I could see one guy ripping through the drawers. Then an arm and shoulder came into view. The second man was in the far part of the suite.

I signalled to Frank not to move. His expression was quizzical as I snapped open the Breitling bracelet. The next move was crucial. I pulled out the watch time adjuster, opened the door wider and tossed this neat time piece into the room. I grabbed the brass door handle and pulled the door tight shut. Frank also pulled, both leaning back to add weight.

We held this positon for about two minutes, then Frank eased the door slightly open. Smiling, Frank said "quick back to reception. Those guys won't be waking up for some time!"

Frank, standing in the corner of reception called someone on his mobile. "They will be here in five minutes". Lucia asked who was coming. "Our CIA colleagues!" He explained to Lucia what had gone on and said not to let anybody go into our room. The gas would dissipate in fifty minutes and the CIA personnel were bringing breathing apparatus with them.

Chuck and Anneliese arrived just as the CIA guys were heading to our room. Obviously, Anneliese realised there had been an incident and wanted to know what. Frank began laughing and said to Anneliese "Nib here learned a lot on that training course and he must have been listening when I explained the Breitling to him". His raucous laughter continued, "The issue is he may be late for the wedding because he's lost his watch!"

Around midnight we all met in the bar. I had spent the last two hours comforting and talking with Anneliese. We did talk about deferring the wedding but jointly concluded that other than further misery, there was nothing to be achieved by it. But that two hours helped the grieving process and we were both going to get through it.

After a few drinks, with all our friends around us, everything was travelling towards cheerful. Everybody turned up including Gerry and Tony, who were the life and soul. The nickname of Nib was definitely sticking like superglue. Poor old Chuck was continuing to look lost and vacant. But even he began to get in the party mood, especially when Frank pulled him aside and invited him to the wedding.

About one o'clock, Frank, supported by Gerry and Tony, held an audience at the bar. Once again, he resembled Wyatt Earp so everyone listened intently.

Chapter 39

Ding Dong The Bells Are Gonna Chime

Frank commenced with his usual strong, charismatic approach. "You guys all know tomorrow is a very special day, not just for Anneliese and Matthew, but also for all of us. We will witness the wedding of two people that are the best any of us will ever meet!"

"But now to arrangements. I have made them simple so Nib can be there, even without a watch or a pen! All you need to know is to be outside the hotel at 10am. You have plenty of time to do your ablutions and have breakfast. You will obviously pack your smart wedding attire. But, be warned, also bring some shoes to handle a short walk through rugged terrain. We will arrive back here about seven o'clock, and Lucia has arranged some music and, if you are in the mood, some dancing. You may even have a shag if you want! Now I will hand over to Tony and Gerry who will buy you all a drink."

It was a really hot morning. We should have been working but the wedding was the priority, and work was voluntary. It didn't stop me feeling Controller Paul was reminding me of commitments.

We were both in a much better mood. I emphasised to Anneliese that, although we had both lost Anya, we had each other. And nothing would change that!

There were several people at breakfast along with most of our wedding guests. We both just went for the buffet breakfast and several cups of coffee to help us recover from the previous night.

It was time to head out onto the steps at the front. As we left the restaurant, everybody stood up, applauded, cheered and wished us good luck. It really did bring a lump to my throat. We all congregated on the steps at the front of the hotel, or Inn, as it was known.

Nobody was sure what was going to happen. No sign of Frank. No cabs, no coach. But then it burst onto the horizon. The noise became deafening. A helicopter. No, a massive helicopter! It landed about 150 yards from the hotel. Frank casually exited and strolled towards us indicating that we should get to it.

It was a U.S. military Chinook helicopter. It was so big we could have taken another 30 people. We had acres of room. Luggage was no problem. I settled next to Frank, behind the pilots. "How did you manage this? " I said. Frank replied "With you two getting married, the U.S. military were overjoyed to help".

I thanked Frank, embraced him as I left, but he pushed me away saying "I am British, we do not do that sort of thing!" I went back and sat with Anneliese and our entourage. She was ecstatic with the love and affection from everyone.

It wasn't long before we landed, about 50 minutes. The confusing thing was that we weren't in Las Vegas. The engines quietened, rotors stopped and Frank stepped out in front of us all.

Frank explained that he had organised this with a Company, the oldest wedding company in Las Vegas. They were the first to provide ceremonies back in the 1960's. They are called The Chapel of Flowers and could have done this in their Victorian Chapel in Las Vegas. But Frank thought this option gave us fabulous views of Red Rock Country next to the Mohave Desert.

We would have lunch first, on a terrace with a fantastic vista, and then the wedding would be at 2pm. Frank took me to one side and said although there would not be a chapel, church or building, a Minister would perform the ceremony in the open air, with spectacular views across Red Rock Canyon. I said to Frank that all this was amazing and we would be grateful forever.

Also, if we wanted, after the ceremony we could have a twenty minute helicopter ride above Red Rock Canyon and then there would be photographs in the Canyon. "One last thing" said Frank, "this is also the safest way I could come up with. We can see anyone approaching and could be out of here in minutes if necessary. But none of that will be necessary!"

The food was sumptuous, a vast choice. Then the ceremony. A wonderful white haired Minister with a beautiful southern drawl. It was somewhat pious and religious, which seemed to fit with everything we felt for one another. I'll get emotional if I become more descriptive but it was all done in a way that was completely soulful, and we needed that boost after the Anya episode.

Anneliese's eyes were now sparkling. We were now man and wife. I asked for time with our guests before we took the "Chapel of Flowers" helicopter ride. We stood on the terrace with our guests, each with a champagne flute. And as the song goes "Love was all around us". We gathered ourselves and set off, a walk of around 100 yards to the helicopter.

As we took off, the scene was absolutely consuming, with all our guests, our friends, waving frantically. Our guests began to assemble together. We could see they were infused with the magical beauty of Red Rock country. As we climbed higher and our gaze left our friends below, Anneliese, looking tearful whispered to me "I'm sad that we could not have Mum and Dad here with us". All I could do was to cuddle her and say "they will be pleased and proud of you and we will make it up to them when we get home".

The helicopter whirled around and was heading for a large, protruding escarpment shining ochre red in the sunlight. As we travelled over it, all the ground, merging into the Mohave Desert became an almost deep spiritual red!

Concentrating on the details of the landscape reached our souls. We were almost in disbelief at the beauty below us. The ground contours, the rock shapes, which in places almost created monuments, indeed, cathedral towers of red rock. On our wedding day, this really made us sense we were close to God.

We turned back towards the wedding venue and, I suppose, because of the emotional impact of our experience, I said to Anneliese I was reminded of a poem I wrote, for school homework, as a kid. Anneliese said "Oh please say it, tell me!" I took a few seconds to compose myself and get it straight in my head. I made a tentative start, but then with belief, I uttered:

Who made this earth?

Who made these skies?

It was not man

Who lives and dies

Anneliese was as close to me as she could be, looking into my eyes. I said "sorry darling, it's just a silly poem that emotion brought to mind! The original was longer but I can't remember the rest. "Don't worry, it was beautiful and it will remain with me forever" she replied.

We landed, without a bump. We sat peering at one another for a minute or two. Anneliese looked absolutely stunning, ever more beautiful. Although she did not have a traditional white wedding dress, a beige satin mini-dress suited the occasion. Even the stout walking shoes looked sensational!

Looking across at the Chinook, Frank already had assembled our guests by the helicopter ready to leave. He indicated to us that we should transfer directly to the Chinook. Once in the aircraft, while all our guests were chattering away about the day, Frank quietly said he had thanked all the staff and Minister and explained that this had been a military wedding with necessary security caution. He said they were intrigued but understanding.

It seemed we were back at the Wickenburg Inn in the blink of an eye. Having a bit of a joke with Frank, I asked if I should take a collection for the pilots, like traditional behaviour on trips to Margate. I don't think he quite got it, so at first thought I was being serious. Then he saw the grin develop on my face. "What a comic you are Nib, I just hope you have ink in your pen for tonight!"

Our guests led the way into what had been prepared as a wedding venue. As we walked through it was all pretty quiet, but they ushered us through the hotel, out to the pool. As we walked out through the patio doors, the spectacle was unbelievable. All the hotel staff and guests were there. They had transformed the canopy into a magical marquee totally covered in fairy lights. The music immediately increased. It was Don McLean singing American Pie. The words said a lot about both of us and it was our favourite. It you ever listen to each section, the details reflect many social developments from the 1950's to 1970's. Anneliese and I once spent a whole night deciphering the segment meanings. But for me, my life started delivering newspapers, I loved whisky and also pickup trucks. Those are my basics. Anneliese had more in-depth psychological views!

So that song was a great fit and got us off to a good start. Next thing we knew was that food had been prepared. A glorious BBQ type spread, lots of salad, salsas and desserts. Then a wedding cake, made by the hotel, which looked spectacular.

It was a steaming hot night so the cake took priority. Clearly, nobody could complain about the food. But then we had the traditional cutting of the cake. Chuck came to the table with a massive Bowie knife. It was almost a machete, but as he explained, that was a traditional thing in this area.

We managed to do the tradition. And kissed afterwards. Now the music started, very loudly. Frank came over to us and said that it was planned to have a Shagging segment as I had appeared to be so good at it. Lucia had taught me earlier, so I went to her and said could we try again when the shagging segment commenced. "oh, of course" she said, "I would love to shag with you." If I hadn't just married Anneliese and loved her so much, I would have gone for it. Her face was enticing me with a sort of salacious gaze. But instead I opted to restrict myself to the dance!

I was better this time, not a lot, but marginally better. I don't care what anyone else thinks, but weddings are totally stressful. We were all having fun but the stress and pressure of the day was taking its toll. I was feeling frazzled, Anneliese never ever showed it but I could see that she was feeling the strain.

The music and dancing were reaching a crescendo. Most people were close to feeling the effects of alcohol. Trouble was that made them all more affectionate and wanting more of everything.

Frank had been missing for some time, then he appeared in the doorway. It was in no way strange for Frank to go missing. It was his trademark. And one that he always used to good effect. But not in this instance. His face was glum as he beckoned me to go over to him. He was bereft of his usual sparkle. He spoke even more slowly than usual, probably trying to hide his emotions. Straight away I knew this was serious!

"This is the worst night for this, but you and I know each other well enough to work through it together". I started to say what is it but before I'd got all the words out, Frank said "there has been an incident. A terrible incident". "Is somebody hurt?" I asked. "Somebody injured?" "No, well I don't think so" said Frank. "Let's take this outside." Frank and I walked out to the front steps. I looked at Frank and was dreading what he was going to say. He put his hands on my shoulders. "I am so sorry Nib, but this is not easy to say on your wedding day." I knew this was really bad because Frank always appeared unconcerned and in control. But not now. "When I disappeared for a while I went to meet up with one of our intelligence gatherers. Its tragic news I am afraid."

Chapter 40

We Were Climbing The Walls

"Several different sources, including the Soviets themselves, have reported that Anneliese's parents have been abducted." "But why Frank? What use are they to the Russians?" "There is not much information out there at the moment, Matthew, but my guess is it goes something like this."

"There are two things the KGB want. They cannot make any headway in their strategy to disrupt the Western Car Industry and consequently, Western economies without the "Preferred Supplier List". You have already experienced how much effort they have put into finding that Holy Grail. And secondly, they want Grenke because they are terrified he will name their agents operating in the West."

"A short while ago, CECD and particularly the CIA issued a "red notice" for Grenke meaning he should be captured and detained at all costs. That clever bastard got wind of it and has been in hiding until he turned up here. Now we have him and they want him back".

Frank took a deep breath and continued, "That is all important information but we have a more pressing priority." I was still trying to distil it all in my mind. "Matthew, we must tell Anneliese and do our best to keep her calm and thinking straight. The question is, do you want to tell her or would you rather me do it?"

"Frank, no question I will talk to her. But I would like you to be with me. She will be frantic and have lots of questions which I won't be able to answer. And maybe you won't either, but your experience in this arena will help search for answers." "I was hoping you would say just that" said Frank. "So shall we get on with it? The quicker we handle this, the quicker we can get on with solving how to rescue those poor sods!"

Dancing, music, everybody seemingly enjoying the evening. Anneliese was chatting with Chuck and Lucia but also looking around, probably for us. Sure enough, as we walked up Anneliese said "Where have you two been? They are about to put more shagging music on and Lucia is champing at the bit". Lucia held onto my arm but Frank said "Would you guys excuse us for a few minutes?" I took Anneliese's hand and we went off to our room.

Once inside the room, I held both her hands and said "sorry but I have some bad news. Would you like a drink first?" "No" she said "just get on with it, I've handled bad news for years."

"Anneliese" I stuttered "there is no easy way to say this but it seems the KGB have abducted your parents in retaliation." Just one or two seconds of it sinking in, then she began to scream, an angry scream, bending over, head in hands and stamping her feet.

As this subsided, she stood erect. "Those bastards, how can they stoop so low? They will not win this. I will get my parents back and kill as many of those Ruskis' as possible, I swear it on my life!" She began to calm down. Frank spoke. "OK, Anneliese what do you think about meeting tomorrow to work out the next steps in this maze." "Yes that's ok but first I want to know where they've taken my Mum and Dad. Is there any surveillance information or any indication from the agents we have all over, or were they all asleep, drunk or just idiots?"

Frank replied "listen Anneliese, I know you are upset. There is information but nothing definite or backed with evidence. The information is that they have been taken to East Berlin. The West German authorities are attempting to assist, but as you know, the Soviets surround the whole of Berlin and the East German police, the Stasi, are in complete control of the Soviet Sector.

Frank said "get some sleep and we will re-group in the morning". Anneliese, pacing up and down, said "No Frank, please organise some way to get us to Berlin tomorrow. I can't just sit around waiting for someone else to do something. "Frank said "no problem, but we should still talk in the cold light of day in the morning."

Frank left, Anneliese continued pacing. Then she got on her phone, straight through to Mia. I could only hear our end of the conversation. Mia already knew. She and Alphonse had contacted all agents, asking them to increase surveillance and put out all the feelers, but nothing so far. Anneliese said that we would be in Berlin sometime the day after next. Mia told Anneliese that all the Western sectors were involved, the British, Americans and French and they would come up with something soon.

Mia then alleviated substantial amounts of Anneliese's pain. She said negotiations between the West and the East were already ongoing. She had been told that a significant amount of progress had been achieved and thought it would not be long before Anneliese's parents were released.

Mia explained to Anneliese in some more detail. We were in the mid-1980's. Gorbachev had been in power for several months and was out to make an impact. President

Reagan and Gorbachev were in friendly mood and talking constantly. Gorbachev was a dove! He desired reforming the Soviet Union. He was preparing to withdraw Soviet troops from Afghanistan and next on his shopping list was to meet with Reagan to agree limitations on nuclear weapons.

Therefore, releasing Anneliese's parents would enhance his friendship propaganda stance and assist with appeasing the Berlin subversionists who were constantly advocating the need for the Russians to "release the peace". In other words, pull down the Berlin wall and give East Germany freedom.

Anneliese was definitely impressed by Mia's assessment. The pacing up and down decreased. Anneliese was much less anxious and eventually we hit the sack.

In the morning, she seemed to begin to get agitated again. At breakfast, Frank arrived. We sat and talked quietly over breakfast. Anneliese explained to Frank Mia's theories. Frank, with a really honest look said to Anneliese, "That all sounds eminently sensible, but let's get out there on the spot, and make it all happen!"

Anneliese's face said it all. She trusted Frank implicitly, as did I. Frank had made arrangements and explained that a U.S. military helicopter would pick us up at 6.00am.It would take us to Luke U.S. air force base on the outskirts of Phoenix and they would fly us to Berlin, refuelling somewhere on the way.

I was amazed that Frank had arranged all this in such a short time and was starting to realise how much respect he and Anneliese commanded amongst the U.S and European military.

Right on time, the helicopter arrived. We were ready and now most of the hotel residents had been wakened by the noise. So we needed to get away quick so the guests did not crowd us.

Frank met us in reception and he had brought his buddies, Gerry and Tony along. They were his and Anneliese's backup team. Next it was the U.S Air force base and a quick transfer into what appeared to be a type of military troop transport. Not luxurious in any way, but food and drink had been installed. However, it was very noisy.

After about 5 hours flying, we landed… at Montreal. They were topping the tanks up for the trip across the Atlantic. Anneliese, after about 30 minutes was showing her agitation. Then Frank came to the both of us and presented us with our new "married" passports. It lightened the mood, with us all commenting on the passports and then recollection of the wedding.

Back up in the air again, the plane flew whilst we slept. We were all so tired, not even this noisy, uncomfortable plane could keep us awake. We landed, with sunshine and cloud, at an isolated airport in Kent called Manston. Another military airport that had been so good for us in the Second World War

It was early morning. This time we had landed to change pilots. That was understandable considering time in the air, noisy clattering flight and quite some turbulence. The next stage would be the last… Berlin in our sights!

We arrived at a non-descript, quiet military base midday. All the buildings were covered with camouflage netting and we only saw a few military personnel. A large American limousine was waiting alongside the runway.

Frank checked the driver's credentials, military identification badge and security pass and then we were on our way. As we drove I asked Frank where we would be staying. He replied "Matthew, if I told you I would have to shoot you and I like you too much for that. It is a safe house that only I will have the address of. Better safe than sorry".

Anneliese gripped my hand and said "Trust us". Eventually we stopped outside a detached grey house, with a reddish brown tiled roof and wooden shutters to every window. Although I never said anything, I had seen a sign that said Charlottenburg, which I seemed to recall was somewhere in the region of the Berlin Plastics factory.

It was beginning to rain so we collected our luggage and entered the house quickly. The door was opened by a statuesque German lady, just as we reached it! I had my pilot's case and a small soft leather luggage holdall. After the long journey, I was feeling pretty grubby so started to wonder whether I should have packed more clothes. I only had a couple of days' worth, which I probably would be able to stretch to a week.

Once inside, the fraulein went off to get us some drinks. Frank said it was important that we all listen. The first thing he did was to open a large walk-in cupboard and pulled out an armful of machine pistols. One for each of us in case the house was attacked. The German lady brought a selection of beers and fruit juice in. After she left the room, Frank continued, "We all need to get a good night's sleep. We will take turns at guard duty. Two hours each!"

"But now for the good news that I have just been handed by our driver. We may be out of here by tomorrow night. Our intelligence people tell me that arrangements have been made for an exchange in order to get Anneliese's parents released. The exchange is scheduled for mid-day tomorrow."

The quiet but euphoric sighs of relief were prevalent. Tony actually grabbed me and gave me the strongest ever embrace! I responded using Frank's repertoire "we do not do that, we are British!"

Frank said more. "When we are on our way to the exchange tomorrow, I will tell you where it will be. When it all begins, be very alert because the notorious East German Police, the Stasi, will be involved and they are the most barbaric, inhuman characters you will ever meet. You, Matthew, and Anneliese will stay in the vehicle whilst the exchange is happening. Gerry, Tony and I will provide cover, but unseen. Then you will meet us as you leave".

Anneliese said "Frank, I suppose I don't really care who we are exchanging, but are you allowed to say?" "Why yes, you will be very pleased to hear its Grenke. I don't imagine the Stasi or the Soviets will welcome him with open arms because they are aware that he has provided us with a substantial amount of information, including the Russian silent investors in the Berlin Plastics Plant. And most of them are vulnerable as they are closeted in the West! I suppose they want him back to ensure they avoid further damage."

With hindsight, we clearly had reached a point where the Soviets had accepted that their plan to disrupt Western Industry and, consequently, economies had now edged towards complete failure. And the new Russian approach now that Gorbachev was in power, meant they were becoming willing to step away from traditional aggression!

All of that thought stimulated a new concern. I had to let Gordon know I may not be back with Ford for some time; if at all. I collared Anneliese and said exactly that! What a clever, intelligent woman I had married. She smiled her angelic smile which always melted me. "It's ok Matthew, I sent Gordon an e-mail on the Ford Communication System. Remember I am your P.A. I told Gordon we were married but also that we worked for the Government as undercover agents for National Security and did not think we would be able to return to the Mondeo. His response was astounding. He had been briefed by Government personnel early on. And as Gordon had seen us in action in that neighbourhood bar, he knew his country was in safe hands. Also wished us all the best in married life and invited us to visit at any time. I replied that we would keep in touch". "What a fantastic person he is!" I turned to Anneliese and jovially said "He may be fantastic but he's also employed. Sounds to me as if I've been done out of my job!"

"Matthew, as you know, I always plan ahead" said Anneliese. "Once we have Mum and Dad safe and have given Anya a decent funeral, we should both get out of all of this. We should get away and make ourselves a happy normal life. And financially now, we are more than secure so we can do anything we want!"

We got through the night, each taking our two hour guard duty. The morning was a very tense affair. Everybody, especially Anneliese, was on edge. We all tried to be jovial at breakfast but it seemed jaded.

The transport arrived just after 1.15pm. It was not a car. The U.S. military had sent an armoured personnel carrier, which Frank said Anneliese and I would travel in. An armoured scout car arrived for Tony and Gerry. In addition, a small U.S. jeep would be in our convoy.

We set off with drivers that already had been given instructions. However, Frank was driving the scout car. All the vehicles were equipped with 2-way radios and after about half a mile, Frank came on our radio. The point of exchange had been agreed as the Glienicke Bridge across the River Havel. The Bridge separated East and West Germany. We would travel through the U.S. sector of Wannsee to the Bridge.

About ten minutes into our journey the radio kicked in again. This time it was U.S. central command. Our driver pulled over to listen. The exchange location had been changed by the Russians, or maybe the Stasi. Now we were to get to Checkpoint Charlie, the final point in the city centre before entering East Berlin. This checkpoint was on the corner of Friedrichstrasse, a crossing through the Berlin Wall. In fact, there were two walls separated by about 100 metres of no man's land, called the Death Strip. We were informed that the exchange was still timed for mid-day!

Frank came on the radio commenting that the Russians had probably made this last minute change to cause some psychological disruption and uncertainty, and not to let it worry us. Anneliese remained very composed.

The driver obviously knew the way and our speed increased. He used his horn several times, and seeing military vehicles, cars moved over for us. The stress and pressure of that period was intense.

We arrived at Checkpoint Charlie with only two minutes to spare. Then came to a halt at the barrier manned by American marines. A sign in front of us said "you are leaving the American Sector".

In the distance, I could see guard towers in the entrance to East Berlin. They presented a threatening presence. Where we had stopped, by the American barrier, were large, several storey, tenement buildings that appeared grey and bleak like the whole business we were involved in.

At the barrier, was a prefabricated shack manned by the U.S. military. All around this small building were sandbags and also behind it and on the other side of the road.

As I looked around, I realised there was no sign of the scout car or Frank. That made me feel very exposed. Just as I was about to speak to Anneliese, who sat very quietly scanning the area, another U.S. army vehicle arrived and parked next to us. This one was a fully enclosed armoured unit.

On the radio came the announcement. It was time to exchange. Two U.S. marines got out of the armoured van next to us. They opened a rear door and assisted a person to get out. It was Harry Grenke.

He peered in our direction with a huge grin on his face. His hands were bound. He was man-handled by the marines up to the barrier, which began to open. With a swaggering arrogant walk, Grenke was led by the Marines to almost the centre of the "death strip".

In the distance, two elderly people came towards Grenke from the East side. They were escorted and assisted by two guards who called them to a halt about five yards from Grenke and the Marines.

Anneliese said "it is my parents" and appeared to be going to exit the vehicle. I held onto her and said "No, please wait". Just as I spoke, they all moved forward and the exchange occurred. The East German guards in their tower were aiming their rifles in the direction of the exchange.

Seeing her parents smiling, Anneliese pushed past me and jumped out of the vehicle. She sprinted to them, throwing her arms around them simultaneously. I wasn't far behind and joined the group hug. My brain then clicked into gear and I said "come on, let's get in and get out of here".

Just at that point, Frank, Gerry and Tony appeared. Frank began to detail what should happen next. Loud voices, almost screaming, interrupted his flow and we all turned to look.

Grenke was standing two thirds of the way across "death strip", one guard behind him trying to push him. The other Stasi guard was in front, with Grenke screaming at him. He wanted the guard to free his hands but the Stasi was refusing. Instantaneously, the guard behind Grenke raised his rifle above his head and brought the rifle butt cracking down on the back of Grenke's head. He dropped to his knees and the Stasi hit him again.

These guards were definitely Stasi. One wore an East German military uniform. The other, a full length dark grey overcoat and trilby hat. Both had serious pugnacious faces with sadistic violence reflected in all their body language.

Grenke was comatose, if not already dead. They grabbed his coat collar and dragged him to within a few yards of the wall at the foot of the East German guard tower.

In full view of the onlookers, and by now there were many on the West Berlin side, the Stasi in the civilian long overcoat, reached inside it and pulled out a revolver. He looked straight at all of us, as if to say this is what a turncoat traitor will receive.

This spectacle was too much for Anneliese's parents, and indeed, most of us. They turned away to Anneliese and Frank for comfort. I was rooted to my spot, disbelieving the horror we were witnessing.

There were four shots, his torso bounced off the ground as the bullets pounded him. More East German soldiers came running out and dragged Grenke into East German territory out of view! Frank immediately ushered us all into the armoured personnel carrier.

Once we were on the move, Anneliese's parents, Joe and Frederika, had questions about what had led to all this. Anneliese, with great compassion for their bewilderment said "I love you so much. All this is my fault but it is very complex. It will take some time, but I will explain gradually. Right now, we must look ahead and ensure we are all safe", She added, out of the blue, "Mum and Dad, please meet my husband, Matthew. He will make sure we all have a very happy life together, in safety! I could not have expected a more wonderful response. They both embraced me whilst Mum began to cry. The euphoria continued for several minutes and then, as it quietened, Frank tried to break in but I butted in and said to Mum and Dad "this is Frank, and these two fellows are Gerry and Tony. They are the best friends we could ever have. They have done a splendid job of looking after your daughter."

Frank, with an enigmatic smile continued, "I would like to get us out of Berlin tonight if possible. It's not a safe place for us. Gerry and Tony and some others have helped make all the necessary arrangements. But before I give you more details, I need to ask a couple of questions. Frederika and Joe, is there anything you need that can't wait until tomorrow. Do you require any medication or anything else that's essential?" The response was negative. They had been given all necessary medications by the East Germans. Apparently they had been very kind to them.

Anneliese chipped in "do you need clothes? I need clothes and I would love a shower, but can manage without for another 12 hours. You men can last a week, but it's not in a female's nature".

Frank came to the rescue. "We have all your luggage, ours and Joe and Frederika's. It would be good if you could manage with that until tomorrow." "My pilot's case, my life is in that" I asked. "Yes that's with us in the scout car which is following". So is everybody happy they can last until tomorrow?" The answer from everyone was an emphatic yes!

OK, Frank continued, "The plan is this. We are going to get out of the military world and into the civilised world. We are heading straight to West Berlin airport. Getting a flight to Amsterdam, first class. Hopefully all the comforts you have missed; we will be met at Schiphol airport and travel straight to one of the best hotels in Amsterdam where you will be pampered".

"In two days' time we will attend Anya's funeral and pay our respects". With that Joe and Frederika gasped. Anneliese said" I'm so sorry Mum and Dad but I've had no chance to tell you. I will explain all tomorrow".

"So, are we all in agreement with that plan?" said Frank. It was a resounding yes! "Just one more thing" said Frank, passing a package to Anneliese, "these are new passports for Joe and Frederika. Their old ones had run out. These ones give them U.S citizenship with visas for life, just like yours, Anneliese, and Matthew!"

Chapter 41

Where We Began

The plane journey to Amsterdam was a joy. The comfort and food and drink were just what we needed after our stressful days in West Germany. And once we had flown over East Germany, I felt as if our escape was complete. A couple of drinks later and we were really beginning to relax.

Anneliese had sat with her parents in a three seat middle section. She had spent most of the time since take-off describing all the events from the start. I knew there was no possibility of her completing the story before we arrived in Amsterdam. Every few minutes I heard gasps, what? why? How did that happen?

As we landed at Schiphol airport, I looked across at Anneliese. She returned a massively happy smile. I was sure it meant that Joe and Frederika had been very understanding. Then they both gave me a wave that really lifted my spirits.

We were met off the plane by Dutch police and escorted through the airport and immigration. We were given celebrity fast track treatment. A small buggy was provided for Mum and Dad and we were outside the main entrance in 30 minutes.

Dutch soldiers met us, as well as an American soldier who spoke Dutch. He had been designated our interpreter, but Frank assured him that some of us were Dutch speaking.

He replied "that's good but I'll travel with you anyway because I relish an easy assignment".

He was a big handsome American who attracted immediate attention from Gerry and Tony. I could see from their gleeful faces that this guy had made their day.

A minibus was parked waiting for us. The Dutch soldiers loaded all the luggage into the boot and assisted Anneliese's parents onto the bus. Gerry and Tony moved to the bus, either side of the American soldier, chatting to him as they climbed on board.

Frank was the last, standing outside for a few minutes, surveying all the surroundings. Once again, Anneliese sat with Mum and Dad, probably continuing to explain. When Frank got on, he came and sat next to me. Gerry and Tony were in the last row of seats laughing and joking, loudly, with the American interpreter. The Dutch soldiers, six of them, took the intermediate seats, chatting and smoking.

We departed from the airport and as road noise increased, Frank brought me into the picture. "Matthew, listen, we are not out of the woods yet and it may be sometime before we are. The Russians are not stupid, so they may have worked out where we would go to bury Anya. So, please do not relax. I know I might be a pain in the arse with my concerns but believe me, I have proved in the past that my concerns sometimes prove valid".

"Frank, we are good mates now and I have the utmost respect for your judgement. I will always attempt to do whatever you want me to do because I know you are the best at protecting all of us, so on the Bible, I will do my best!"

We arrived at our secret, and protected, destination. I was overjoyed. Anneliese also! It was almost as if our past was deemed to provide a safe home for us over the next few days. We had stopped outside the Sonesta Hotel. The place I had the good fortune to stay just a few doors down from Anneliese in her Red Light District.

Everybody helped us, and we all helped one another. The stress of the last few days caused us all to feel very tired, and the few drinks on the plane had not helped.

Once inside the hotel, I clasped Anneliese and said "How lucky is this, it's like a sign from the Almighty, its nostalgia multiplied by millions. This place led me to you, and after all we have been through together, and now married, we have arrived back on the doorstep where we started".

Anneliese put her arms around me and pulled me close. "Matthew, you are such a sensitive, but also strong person. I am feeling what you are feeling. This is exactly why I have always known we were meant to be together! But look at me. We both know that this is our destiny. Someone is orchestrating this for us, but we have to carry on working to finish where it is meant to end. So we both have to stay strong and implement whatever the final part of the journey involves!"

At that point, Frank arrived, Emotions were running high but I composed myself, as did Anneliese. The parents had already gone to their rooms, totally wasted by the tough days they had experienced. We sat in a quiet area of the hotel with Frank. He spoke, but very calmly "Listen you guys, we have arranged a funeral for Anya. I never get emotional, but like I love you two, I loved her. I don't know what happened with the Russians getting inside her mind. But they did, and we have ended up with what we have got".

"I don't know if I have done the correct thing but the funeral is to be held at a Russian Orthodox church in Amsterdam. It's called St Nicholas of Myra Church. It's in the old town district of Jordaan, near to the railway station. I've been there and it's a beautiful church with a very peaceful cemetery. Lots of trees that I know she loved! The funeral is scheduled for Thursday at 2.00pm. The day after tomorrow. Then we will leave for, I can't l tell you where, you are still under my protection!"

During the last few weeks we had very little time to ourselves. Almost no time to relax and care for one another. The time had been loaded with incident and so, when night arrived we were both exhausted.

Now things were looking brighter, so when we got into our bedroom, we both needed each other. The first hour or so, in bed, tender passion took command and anointed our married union. Sleep, very sound comforting sleep, followed!

Next morning, on the way to breakfast, we called for Joe and Frederika. The breakfast offerings were splendid. Cooked breakfast, croissants, a variety of pastries, fruit and cereals. Anneliese and I collected the parents' choices and then our own. The whole of breakfast was buffet style with the exception of coffee and teas which were brought to our table.

Chapter 42

With A Little Help From Her Friends

When we all were comfortable, Anneliese spoke about the funeral arrangements. "I will be missing for most of the day today because I have decided to try to find some of Anya's friends to invite them. She had several good friends and, although it was a long while ago, I hope I can find some of them." Anneliese continued, speaking more to Mum and Dad, "the Church that has been selected is a Russian Orthodox Church called St Nicholas of Myra here in Amsterdam."

Frederika said "That's wonderful dear, Anya told us that although she didn't attend Church regularly, she did go occasionally and as she had been baptised in a Russian Orthodox Church, that was her first choice." Joe joined the conversation and said "I know that Church, I have seen it and it's a fabulous old Church. I think it was built in the late 1800's and is quite close to here!"

Just then, Frank, Gerry and Tony strolled in. Anneliese told them about her plan to go to find Anya's friends. Frank was uncertain about the idea, saying it was too risky. But after several minutes discussion, almost arguments; it was agreed. Frank said "it will be best if Gerry and Tony stay with Mum and Dad as their protection." I would accompany Anneliese and Frank. Joe and Frederika wanted a say. They assured

Frank that they would be OK just relaxing in the hotel and maybe have a swim in the pool.

Frank would not hear of it. "We can't take any chances and Gerry and Tony can go and have a swim with you". Tony said, "That's settled then because I would like that, and afterwards we can partake of the chef's cuisine for lunch, and maybe sit and chat!"

With that all settled, we three collected what we needed and set off. We had only passed a couple of shop windows when Anneliese took us in. The lady was in the middle of business but would only be a few minutes more.

Her name was Greta. Anneliese explained, using a bit of a cock and bull story, and then Greta said she would definitely attend. Also she would contact a few other girls. Greta said they all loved Anya and would be devastated.

Anneliese moved us onto a pole-dancing club called "Twirling". Apparently Anya had worked there at one time. While Anneliese was talking to the club owner, I went to the bar with Frank and sat having a lunch-time drink.

We got talking to a couple of Dutch guys who worked in the Amsterdam Diamond industry. They knew Anneliese and so I told them we had just married. Whilst generally chatting, I had an idea. I'd never had time to get an engagement ring for her.

I asked the two gents if they could get me a two carat diamond single stone set in platinum. I needed it by tomorrow, early afternoon, to be delivered to the hotel. One of the gents, Louis, said he would deliver it himself. It would cost about 5000 U.S. dollars. I was somewhat embarrassed as I did not have that sort of cash with me in Holland. Frank said "no worries, I will bring it to you tomorrow and you can pay me back later".

With all arrangements made, I thanked the guys just as Anneliese joined us. I suppose we all appeared a bit sheepish, trying to conceal the surprise. However, Frank saved the day, introduced the two gents and got Anneliese a drink.

The guys left and we three got comfortable on the bar stools. Anneliese, whilst drinking a large glass of Chablis, said things had gone very well and she was pleased with how things were turning out. "I had a good talk with Marco, the club owner, and he volunteered to organise things with Anya's friends. He would send runners out around Amsterdam to pass the message and give people details of the Church and time, 2.00pm in the afternoon".

Anneliese had now finished her large glass of Chablis. Feeling less inhibited she said "Marco thought the world of Anya. She was his best girl for a whole year. The Club would put on a special act on a Saturday night where a member of the audience was invited on stage to make love to the girl working that night. Anya was the very best, never complained, and the punters loved her. She made him a hell of a lot of money!"

So Marco said, even if he had to lay on a coach, at his expense, to get everybody to the funeral, he would consider it a privilege.

Anneliese's description of the conversation with Marco indicated that she still held a view that licentious sex was simply a liberated way of life. At that time and before, a Dutch approach to life and sex! But she had married me, committed to me and I knew she was sincere.

I then asked Anneliese if she thought we should have a wake after the funeral. "Oh I forgot" she replied, "Marco has invited all of us back to Twirling for the wake. Obviously, I thanked him and said it was very kind of him. There won't be any shows on so Mum and Dad won't be offended, but I just may do some pole-dancing as a tribute to Anya." She developed a teasing smile!

Now back in the hotel, Anneliese went to our room for a rest and prepare for the evening. I suppose she felt like me, a long night ahead of us waiting for Anya's funeral. It had the feeling of waiting for execution. The gallows or electric chair came to mind.

I sat with Frank in the bar waiting for the Gem man, Louis. He arrived at 4.00pm. He was exceptionally pleased with the jewellers design. He brought the box out of his pocket and flipped open the lid. It was exquisite, simple but definitely exquisite. Louis asked how I decided on a two carat diamond. My Mother had the same and called it her two carrots! Frank asked Louis about sizing "Oh my God" I blurted out, "I forgot that". "Don't be concerned "said Louis. In his attractive Dutch accent he continued, "I had a good look at Anneliese's beautiful hands. I can visually measure fingers. Its years of applying my mind to the size of fingers. She is an L. "Indeed she is" said Frank, "she's one hell of a lady". Frank then pulled a packet out of his pocket and Louis was all smiles. Putting it in his pocket, without counting the $5000 he smiled again and said "I trust you guys." "Good luck with everything" as he departed. All I was left to do was to decide the best time!

Chapter 43

Looking Back Helps Going Forward

Gerry and Tony bustled in looking a bit hot and bothered. They had been for a walk and obviously it took them through the Red Light District. There was no other route from our hotel, but it was possible, along the way to take a seat by the Voorburgwal Canal and enjoy watching the canal traffic, mostly tourist boats.

After they had got their breath and settled down with a cool beer, Tony decided to tell us the story. As they walked past the girlie shop windows, every girl waved at them. Naturally, Tony and Gerry attempted sign language to demonstrate they were not of that persuasion. The girls didn't understand the signs and gradually, one by one, came out of their shops. Eventually, Tony and Gerry were surrounded by scantily clad young ladies. The girls seemed to think that these guys wanted some unusual, erotic act or position. As the crowd grew, the police arrived and collared Gerry and Tony, taking them to one side in the street.

Luckily, one of the "Politie" spoke English. Gerry in his emphatic effeminate way, explained that girls were not for them. The policeman turned to his colleagues and told the story. Belly laughs exploded all around. The police told the girls, who giggled and laughed so much, bodies were shaking to the point of evacuating the tiny bits of clothing protecting their modesty.

The "Politie" left thanking Gerry and Tony and shaking their hands ferociously. But it didn't end there. Several of the girls surrounded them again and pulled them into one of the abodes. They apologised, plied them with drinks and chocolates and thanked them over and over. The thanks involved kisses from all the girls and that was why Gerry and Tony had looked so flustered when they arrived.

That story had Frank and me in fits. Throughout, we had continued drinking and I could tell this was going to turn into a drinking and story-telling session. We ordered more booze and now I moved onto Scotch. It always loosens my tongue. Gerry and Tony both decided to hit the Gin and Tonics. Gerry asked for Pink Gin and was pleasantly surprised that they had it. Then Frank surprised us all by ordering a Jack Daniels. None of us had ever seen him drink. Maybe a small beer but that was as far as it went. He was enjoying himself, although I knew he never really relaxed, was always working, and thank God that was his character.

Gerry and Tony were first into the stories. Firstly, just recounting the events at Shaver Lake when we were being chased by the Stryker nutter. Tony said, using the special talent he had for imitating people, but with an effeminate angle "and when Frank threw the Bronco around and said I don't like doing this sort of thing, I thought he was getting out to relieve himself, instead, there was the massive explosion, and it was me that nearly crapped himself!"

More drink after the laughter subsided. With my jaw loosening, I told the story of my colleague, Mr Charles at Simpsons, trying to figure out why he couldn't sell a suit to the man and his wife, When I got to the bit about climbing on the chair to look over, Gerry said "Oh no, how could you do it? Are you a voyeur? Because if you are, you can come shopping with me anytime my darling!"

I was in full flow now so I moved onto the next anecdote. Everybody seemed to be enjoying themselves for which I was grateful. All we had beyond this was a bleak day tomorrow!

Tony and Gerry's eyebrows raised when I said "at a young age, I had worked in the London docks" Tony said "But you are not big and muscular". "Tony, your eyesight maybe perfect, but I'm average height, wirey and have muscles in places you can't imagine. I was a professional footballer until the age of 19 and you have to be fit for that". "Oh darling, you are now seen in a different light". Frank said, "Watch out Matthew, don't go too far."

Now, I have the opposite story to Gerry and Tony's earlier. It was not with beautiful girls in a Red Light District. But it captured my mind at the time. I started to tell the story. Tony and Gerry appeared to be listening intently. Frank was in the middle of ordering another round.

"I had decided to find a future. I was ambitious and that was not working for me in the London Docks. I wanted to do anything that would provide wealth, advancement, clothing like I eventually worked with in Simpsons, and clothing like you guys are all wearing!"

"Anyway, it was my leaving party with my mates. We were working in Millwall docks, so we all agreed to go for a celebration night in the City Arms. And that night, they had music and some acts. We got together in the bar, about a dozen guys."

"I was probably the youngest. After a short while I was drawn to a beautiful young lady sitting at the bar. So well dressed for a pub night, a long sequined dress, with beautiful long blond hair. I mentioned her to one of my mates. Immediately, they all began encouraging me to go and chat to her. There was an empty bar stool right next to her. I suppose the crucial final factor was that I was feeling really horny. "

"I ambled in beside her, trying to appear nonchalant. My opening gambit was, "What a lovely Frock". She sort of winced at the word frock, but we grew into conversation. About two drinks later, I was feeling that maybe I would be taking her home. By now, all the guys, Tony, Gerry and Frank, were hanging on every word. Earlier I had said that I'd not had sex before so this might lose my virginity, Tony made me laugh by saying that he could help me with that. I answered I love you guys, but from a distance."

I carried on with the story. "Her name was Brenda. Halfway through the second drink, with my mates shouting "go on Matthew, get in there Son". The sound system blurted something out. She turned to me and said she had something to do, but would be back in a minute.

She headed to the stage, needing to inch her dress up to get on it, but then took hold of the mike. I was proud of the way she looked, so professional. And I was getting close to the professional singer, or so I thought! But no, this was where it ended. With Brenda on the mike, she said "hello everyone" in a very deep voice. She followed this with "well Good Evening Ladies and Gentlemen and the rest of you know what you are!"

All my mates were rolling in the aisles. My potential girlfriend's name was really Barry. Tony, Gerry and Frank were splitting their sides!

Now it was Frank's turn. He chipped in with a story about when he was with us in Wickenburg. He was at the bar chatting to Lucia. Fancied her a lot; the more they talked, the more he wanted her. His libido was on fire. And then the more drinks they had, the more they bonded. Eventually, she asked, "Frank, how do you hold your liquor?" Now partially inebriated, Frank replied "Lucia, it's usually by the ears!" it took a few seconds, but when it had sunk in, she absolutely collapsed with laughter. Frank had found a way with humour to the melting point and was going to see her again.

Anneliese walked in and joined us. She asked why we were all laughing. I said we had spent a couple of hours having a lad's afternoon. Drinking and telling stories. "Will I spoil things if I stay?" she replied. Frank cut in and said "Of course not, we need the feminine touch to rein us in a bit!"

Goodbye – Wipe A Tear From Your Eye

For the next hour or so we talked about the funeral. Procedures; would the hymns be in Russian; was it something like a Catholic service. None of us really had any answers. We poured over many maybes. Many guesses. Then Tony asked "How do we address the Vicar in charge of the service. Or is he a Priest?"

This was one question I knew the answer to. One lesson in School that had partly sunk in was about Russian religion. So I said "I learned one thing that is a start with all of this. The Vicar in charge of the funeral service is to be addressed as Patriarch followed by his name, or I suppose just Patriarch may be enough"." Very well done Nib" said Tony.

"Chipping in with that has jogged by memory on a couple more things. Everybody should attempt to wear dark coloured clothes, preferably black, or at the very least, sombre colours. And men should wear ties. Now, also important. They stack the church with flowers, roses mostly. And pink, I think, not white!"

Anneliese put her hands to her face. "We must get lots. I will go to reception and beg them to arrange it" She apologised to us and went off to try to arrange the flowers.

We carried on with our lads' time, drinking, telling jokes and anecdotes. I think it was because we were all resisting thinking of tomorrow.

Anneliese returned about half an hour later, all smiles. She had a friend with her, a lovely lady who Anneliese introduced as Vera. First thing Anneliese announced was that reception would arrange a massive array of roses, mainly pink and red. It was going on our bill but if Anneliese was happy so was I. She said it would be from all of us.

Now Anneliese asked Vera to speak. She said she was Russian and remembered Anya, and would be at the funeral. The Patriarch was named Nikolai and spoke English exceptionally well. He would do his best to translate the proceedings as we moved through.

"Usually "She said, "Anya would be placed in the casket during the service, but in this instance, as the congregation were predominately western, she would already be at rest." She continued, "At the end of the service, if you wish you may kiss Anya's hand. Also, it's a tradition in Russia to place any article, anything Anya may need in the after-life, in her coffin. But these are choices that will be left to you".

Then Vera said she had to get back to work and would see us tomorrow. We all chimed in and said to Anneliese that she had really delivered and probably prevented us all from appearing as morons.

I now felt it was time to be assertive and check everything. Firstly, I asked Anneliese, "Vera will be a fantastic help. She already has been, but who is she. Anneliese smiled and said, "She is from the shop windows four doors down. All these girls do this job because circumstances led them into it. But they are all fabulous people when you get to know them. Vera is God loving, she attends the St Nicholas Church almost every week. She will be a massive help tomorrow. To be honest, I can't remember her, but she frequents the hotel and reception helped me to find her".

I turned to Frank, Gerry and Tony. Do you guys have any questions, any concerns. "No" Said Frank, "in the minimal space of time we have had, you guys have done a superb job. We all responded as one. "Thanks Frank, but you get the Victor Ludorum for all of this."

A people mover vehicle arrived at the Sonesta at 12.30pm. We had all managed to find, beg, steal or borrow sombre clothing. Some were even pieces of hotel uniform. Once in the car and on our way, Tony and Gerry began to joke, laugh and generally lighten the mood. Just their effeminate way of speaking raised my spirits and even Anneliese giggled on occasion.

We only drove for about ten minutes, and that would have been less if the traffic in Amsterdam had not been so monstrous. Arriving at the Church, we stopped behind a coach as many people were getting off. Tony and Gerry said they would accompany Frederika and Joe.

As good as his word, Marco had organised the coach for Anya's friends, mostly the girls from the Red Light District. Everyone began to assemble in the Church grounds which had pristine paths and grass areas. The Church itself was beautiful, a typical 19th century building with splendid arched windows and flint brickwork.

I looked at Anneliese. She seemed in control and occasionally said polite and courteous hellos to the girls. We guys just stood around like spare parts in a car warehouse. Frederika and Joe stayed with Gerry and Tony.

The time came for us to enter the Church. As we started to file in, I noticed that the graveyard, with an open grave chasm was to the rear. Statuesque tall trees, all around the boundary, provided shade across the gravestones.

Anneliese gripped my hand. Just inside we were greeted by the Patriarch. He was dressed in a black tunic and a large black rectangular hat. This attire was immediately softened by a wonderful welcoming smile, his eyes glistening as if to try to lift our mood. As soon as we spoke in English, he replied in English, saying "Welcome my children to the Church of St Nicholas of Myra." I still don't know how I remembered, but I managed to say "Thank you Patriarch Nikolai for the warm welcome".

The interior of the Church actually took my breath away. It was incredible. The serenity of the atmosphere in this building brought heaven to us. Anneliese gripped my hand extremely tight. We both stood in the rear of the Church amazed at the glorious spectacle surrounding us. Glimmering gold painted icons. Historic statues and effigies, interspersed with beautifully decorated tubs of fresh flowers everywhere. The fragrance from the flowers mingled with incense candles burning near the altar. I love the tranquil soul-rewarding sensation you feel in churches. This was one of the best ever.

Chapter 45

Every Time We Say Goodbye

The service was largely conducted in Russian by the Patriarch but he did insert some English by way of explanation. He began by saying in Russian something that ended in Panichide. Then, in English, he explained the Panichide was the Funeral Mass.

The most difficult thing throughout for both of us was the coffin by the altar. It was an open coffin with Anya dressed in a beautiful white gown. I really did find it hard to hold it all together. Anneliese managed better than me, but Frederika was crying.

We were near the end of the service. The Patriarch then asked if anyone would like to say a few words. I turned to Anneliese, but she was almost in tears already. "No I can't do it" she said. I sat for a few seconds looking around. There was about 70 people in the pews. My mind said No!, one of us had to say something! I stood up. This was curtain time. The lights, usually keeping my head clear, dimmed. Consciousness abandoned me as I walked down the aisle toward the pulpit.

As I passed Joe and Frederika, they gave me a tender smile, as did Tony and Gerry. The Patriarch was standing at the foot of the pulpit, only a yard away from Anya's casket. I continued towards him, my legs feeling like concrete.

Nearing Nikolai, I could only look at Anya. Getting close, a feeling of serenity engulfed me. I became overwhelmed by a spiritual presence so intense it seemed I was having an out-of- body experience. Nikolai smiled and said "you may use the pulpit if you wish. It has a microphone!"

Now my legs were light as feathers and the next I knew, I was staring out at the faces of the congregation. I was no longer fearful. I started to speak, indeed the first thing I said was "I am here but really don't know what I am going to say" I carried on, "I need to say something. Whatever it is, it is on behalf of all of us. My wife, Anneliese and her parents, Joe and Frederika, especially".

Words now started flowing without prior thought "I spent some time recently with Anya in Arizona, perusing the natural God given world. One evening we saw fireflies. Anya was a firefly. Wherever she was, however dark it was, she brought light into everyone's life. And it was always spectacularly bright and reached our hearts. Then on another day, we stood and watched, and photographed humming birds. Anya was our own little Humming Bird. Small but so beautiful. Like a Humming Bird, her wings were so powerful. She was athletic, she could ride a horse like a rodeo rider, and nothing ever daunted her. But most of all, she had sincere love for Anneliese, Frederika, Joe and myself. And all of you also. She had an ability to live! Anya was spring all year round!"

All the time I was saying this, the patriarch was doing his best to keep up with me with a Dutch translation. I think he seemed to be getting the message across.

"I am close to finishing but because she meant so much to us all I need to say a few more things. Looking around the church now, I see her face in every flower, and I will carry that with me forever. Anya, Anneliese and I loved music and would spend lots of time listening together. Some words from songs now seem fitting! And with these words my tenderness grows!

It's just the thought of you that we will remember through our tears. God, take Anya's hand, she is a stranger in Paradise. Every time we say goodbye, we die a little! Thank you so much for listening and being here for Anya!"

The congregation were so quiet as I walked back to my seat. I began to wonder if I had done anything out of order. Then the Patriarch went into the pulpit and took the mike. He said "that was a wonderful experience for me. I knew, I could feel, that Jesus was with Matthew, and Anya was holding his hand. That will be remembered in this Church forever."

When I got back to the pew and sat next to Anneliese, she was very tearful. She put her soft hands on my cheeks, turned my face to hers and said "Thank you, thank you so much, my fabulous husband!"

The Patriarch, Nikolai, said, "We have all experienced something very spiritual today. And I am sure, we, all Jesus's flock, will feel the presence of that throughout our lives. But right now, I believe we need to feed both our souls and stomachs. So if you would like to go to the back of the Church, there is Russian black bread and vodka. Please enjoy before we go to lay Anya to rest" I suppose this tradition is intended to ease the pain in the final chapter, the burial.

It was time for us men to initiate the final curtain. Frank, Gerry, Tony and I went to the casket and lifted Anya onto our shoulders. To a slow, solemn beat, we carried her outside and placed the casket next to the open grave. It was fully lined with dark blue velvet.

Anneliese and her parents were sobbing all the while, I just could not take any more! I ushered all three of them back to the waiting mini-van and we watched from afar. It wasn't long before the chapter was finally finished. Nikolai walked out to the car and gave us all a blessing. We all thanked him profusely. Such a re-assuring person with a heart-warming smile and personality.

We took off to Marco's. We all needed to relax with some friendly chat and pain-easing alcohol. Once inside, Gerry and Tony took over. They had become such great mates to us, along with Frank, and I really wanted to find a way for them to be around forever.

Anneliese and I were enjoying the first drink. Joe, sitting next to me, said "Matthew, please excuse me for asking but after another drink, could you get us back to the hotel. It's been a long, stressful day and Frederika will need to relax in her bed". "Joe, of course, not a problem. Would you like me to stay with you as well". "Oh no, please, be with Anneliese and come back when you want."

I spoke with Anneliese and explained Joe's request. She said, "That's fine but come back to me won't you". After the next drink, Joe asked "could we go now Matthew?" I had already organised a taxi and a barmaid said it was outside. I started to explain to Gerry and Tony but Gerry would have none of it. "I will take them, you need to be here with Anneliese. And I will ask the hotel people to check on them every half-an-hour. I think I will also order them some food room service, so that's the deal!" Joe was fine and understood. Gerry with Tony, escorted them out to the taxi.

About an hour later, Gerry came back in. He came straight to me and said he had given the hotel our mobile numbers and if there was any concerns to call us straight away. Just as he was speaking, Marco came over. I stood up and thanked him for all the arrangements. "It was the least I could do" he said. His English was impeccable.

The evening was now getting pretty boisterous. The girls were all back. The coach had broken down, but it had got fixed and now the girls were all demanding a good time. They were all still beautifully attired, most of them looking like American movie stars that had just stepped off the plane. I did wonder as the night went on, how long the conservative clothing would last.

One after the other, the girls came to see Anneliese. They were all beautiful and very sincere in their condolences for Anneliese. Some chatted and told stories, others just expressed their sympathy. Anya had made a massive impact on Amsterdam.

Now things sparked into party-mode. The drinking speed increased to rapid. Gerry and Tony had begun talking to the girls. One by one and then sometimes in groups, the girls were talking and flirting with them. All the time, Frank was in a corner of the bar, enjoying a drink, but doing his intensive surveillance.

Anneliese and I had recovered. We were both getting back to normal. Then she said "Where have Gerry and Tony gone?" Holding her close, I scanned the whole room. People dancing, people drinking, people talking. Then I saw them. They entered from the girls' dressing room area.

The next thing was they were up on the pole-dancing stage. People began to crowd around. I couldn't believe what I was seeing. But it was funny. Both of them strode onto the pole-dancers stage as if they had done it forever. But the funny thing was, they were both naked, other than small G string-like pants to protect their modesty.

Anneliese now came out of her semi-doldrums. She began to giggle. The more these guys presented themselves as comical and theatrical, the more she laughed. They attempted the pole, with disastrous results. They attempted pretend sex but Tony fell off the stage. They attempted sexy wiggling about. This raised the roof and drew massive applause.

The girls had applied make-up to the faces of both lads. They now had exaggerated beautiful female faces. With toned, muscled, tanned bodies, they both, even without the cosmetics, had very attractive faces. The whole package demanded attention, whatever the sexual persuasion.

In this instance, it was the girls' libidos that were aroused. As Gerry and Tony finished their playful performance, stepping off the stage, they were surrounded by the Red Light girls, skimming their hands over the sweat-covered muscles, laughing and teasing every gram of testosterone out of these reluctant, but aroused, bodies.

They managed to break away, and ran for the dressing rooms pursued by hordes of girls. Some managed to squeeze through the door before it slammed shut. Gerry and Tony were an awful long while getting dressed. When they did eventually reappear, they looked extremely flustered and went straight to the bar.

Frank, Anneliese and I were in fits! These were two very tough hard nuts that wouldn't shy away from any form of violence. They had been trained to deal with it very effectively. But now they had met their match in the form of a bunch of girls that wanted, indeed craved, changing their sexual preference!

Several minutes later, they joined our party. Anneliese couldn't resist asking them, "Did you have a good time with the girls?" Tony answered "To be honest, we had no choice but to surrender. Their attention was mind blowing, there was no way we could resist. Yes, as an experience it was completely new and totally different!" Gerry continued, "Neither I nor Tony have ever been with a woman. It's never been part of our psyche. As a one-time, I have to say it was enjoyable. But I will always prefer real love with Tony. He is my lifelong love and partner."

A few minutes later, Frank changed directions. I need to talk work with you all. Tomorrow I have a meeting arranged with CECD and some CIA guys from the U.S. We will discuss and plan the future for Anneliese, Matthew and her parents. There continues to be quite some protection needed for them. I would ask you all to attend with me, I will meet you at breakfast to give times and venue.

At breakfast, everyone was fairly quiet, mainly due to hangovers. Frank joined Anneliese and I on our table. Gerry and Tony were on the next table.

When Frank had enjoyed two coffees, he picked up his knife and fork, then put them down again. He asked Gerry and Tony to pull their chairs across and join us.

"The meeting is at 11am in a spare office here. Is that OK for everybody?" Frank asked. We all silently nodded. "Shall we meet here about 10.30am to get another coffee before we meet". Again nodding silence!

Anneliese said she needed to go up and check on Mum and Dad. They were fine but she would organise breakfast for them. I went to the room with her in case she needed any help. We got ready and talked about how Joe and Frederika were doing.

Anneliese assured me they were fine, but just wanted to know what would happen next,. They would have loved to go back to Hammamet but they understood it would be too dangerous.

I asked Anneliese "Have they completely understood the job that we have been doing. The job that has got them into this and threatened their very existence?" "Yes" she said "it has been a long, difficult process to explain everything, but now they are very proud of us both and so happy that we have found happiness together. They are both convinced that we are doing the right thing, and have told me they want to be with us, wherever the job takes us."

Anneliese finished this by saying, "Mum and Dad are both very ill. Mum in particular. Whatever place sounds right for us, we have to consider if it's good for them. Will they be able to get the healthcare and treatment they need. I want my Mum and Dad with us for many years yet! You heard Frank say this meeting today is to talk about where we go from here. We are not safe yet but they will help us."

At 10.30am we all met in the corner of the restaurant, each of us having collected a drink on the way in. After some chat, Frank led us to a small conference room, then immediately left to meet our visitors.

Frank and four guys, walked in exactly at 11am. Frank did the introductions. Anneliese knew of the two CECD. They were very senior Intelligence Officers named Brian and Donald. The CIA gentlemen were also from the intelligence back room… the people that are talented analysts. They were named Sam and Connaugh (nicknamed Con).

Donald kicked off getting straight to their proposals. He assured us that a vast amount of intelligence analytical work had been applied. Essentially, they had considered many countries, but ultimately they were only left with one country. A country that minimised risk to us and provided the best monitoring and support for us for several years.

The selection was Canada. Anneliese, although smiling, threw a negative straight at them. "It's a cold country. Not sure I could live like that!"

Sam immediately replied, "With the utmost respect mam; that is a fallacy, well mostly! The cold periods on the East Coast, on average, only last five months, similar to the UK. Temperatures from April to October are much higher than the UK. And although the cold months can have low temperatures with snow; that can be great fun!"

Donald continued "And it's the East Coast we are proposing. You would be very close to the U.S border which helps us to give you excellent support. At this point, I would emphasize that throughout this planning process we have collaborated with the Canadian Secret Service known as CSIS. All their views and thoughts have been considered and they are completely in agreement with us."

"The proposal that it should be Canada is mainly due to the Canadians goodwill, indeed their pleasure, at the thought of having you decent, intrepid people live in their country. Consequently they will be providing you with completely new identities throughout all Government systems. They have helped in selecting and securing appropriate property and are also compelled to provide healthcare for you all. That includes any necessity to use U.S.A healthcare."

"A key feature in the selection of Canada, is the country's excellent relationships with the U.S.A. and Western Europe, particularly the UK and France. We could not find any chess pieces that could match that."

Another important element in this proposal is that CECD, supported by collaborating Western Governments, have agreed to support and contribute constant close security. The operatives concerned are Frank, Gerry and Tony. You have done so well as a team, we could not offer this assignment to anybody else. Frank has already agreed, and Tony and Gerry will be considering this over the next 24 hours."

Brian, who had been quietly listening, now stood up to speak. We wondered why, but then he explained. "I am really only here as a messenger." He was a very quiet but eloquent speaker. I guessed by his accent that he was from London. Impeccably dressed in a blue serge suit, not more than about 5'8 but his demeanour made him seem of colossal stature. He came across as a very wise, caring person.

"I am here to tell you how much Western Governments appreciate the work you people did. The work across the Middle East, the work in your early years, Anneliese in Amsterdam, collecting and feeding back information, was invaluable. And then recently, helping us to obviate the threat that Grenke posed to the stability of U.S business and economies in the Western world. I will go on to mention Anya because I know she meant much to you all. We are all sorry for your loss and everybody in our organisation that knows you, appreciates how much you are hurting. We all, at times, make wrong choices and it is so sad that a wonderful, loved, person did just that. My final pitch is to say that you have all become worthy of our continued support. Western Governments with the U.S.A. and Canada wish you well and every happiness from hereon in. But I have also been empowered to tell you both, Anneliese and Matthew, that if after your five year sabbatical, you wished to continue in the service of Western Countries, you would be welcomed back with open arms. From me personally, I wish you enduring success in the future!"

Donald now took over again. "Does this proposal sound attractive to you guys, because if it does, Frank will make flight plans for you two days hence. That will give you time to shop for anything you may need. "Anneliese looked at me. We both smiled. Frank was happy also. So all together, it was yes! With that our four colleagues got up and departed.

Now we guys needed a drink, Anneliese was ok, composed and looking rather pleased with the way it had gone. She sauntered into the bar just in front of us, dressed in a soft cotton pale pink mini-dress, her legs looking fabulous. Indeed, every part of her had been designed and put together like an E-Type Jaguar. Stunning bodywork and classic lines and posture.

She said she was buying this round to thank us all for our support. The barman looked fixated as she ordered our drinks. It always made me so proud when she was admired by other men!

We all sat down and scanned one another's faces. Tony and Gerry were quiet and appeared uncomfortable with the outcome. Frank opened. He said to Gerry and Tony, "Don't worry or feel bad in any way. I think I can manage alongside Anneliese and Matthew!"

"No that's not the thing," replied Tony, "We really do want to be with you guys but neither of us are completely comfortable with living in Canada. It's not a country we know. It's never been on our agenda for places to visit. But we are confounded by the strength of our need to be with you guys. And we are not saying that as colleagues giving priority to our work prospects," said Gerry. "You are the best friends we have ever had. We respect you up to the hilt and you also show us the utmost respect. That means a tremendous amount to us."

I decided I would have a say. "If you wouldn't mind me saying, I've had a sketchy idea. My wonderful little flat in England has probably missed the human touch. Would it work for you guys to go and live there for a few months? It's a great part of the country at Deal, next door to Dover. You can get to the continent in about an hour. And all around you is Kent, the Garden of England."

"After about three or four months, we should be getting organised and established in Canada. Then you could come for a visit, for several weeks if you want, to see if it's agreeable to you as a place to live. Frank and I will manage for three or four months."

"How does that grab you? Tony responded "Matthew, is it ok if we go for a wander and discuss it." "Of course" I said "you don't need to ask, it's a huge decision".

As they walked away, Frank turned to me and said "Matthew, great idea!" Anneliese added, "Yes, you are my very own genius. That's just confirmed what I saw in you". I took a large gulp of my beer!

Tony and Gerry reappeared looking stern as they approached. As they got close, their faces changed into massive, whole face, smiles. "Matthew, your logic is impeccable. How can we thank you and we are sure that assuming Frank is ok with it, CECD bosses will be happy to agree." "So, that's settled then! We can have a couple more days together, all of us, so let's enjoy it and make the most of our time together". I loved these guys like they were my family.

Chapter 46

Frozen Theme Or Canadian Dream

Anneliese, all the time, had been sitting thinking how great this was all starting to appear, then she turned to Frank and said, "Do you know Frank, where on the East Coast of Canada this property is that has been selected for us?" "Yes, I do, and rest assured that if it's not to your liking, you can start house-hunting as soon as you want. I've seen photos and it looks superb. It's on the edge of Lake Ontario about 10 miles outside Toronto." Frank carried on, "I visited that area on holiday several years ago and it is heaven, you are only about thirty minutes from Niagara Falls, and around you are small villages with restaurants everywhere. In summer, they all specialise in outside dining! Niagara Village is a Christmas must see! Extraordinarily picturesque, with festive shops up and down the main street."

"When we arrive in Toronto," said Frank, "I have some plans and want to check that you are happy with them. I'll stay with you for a few days to help you start the settling in process. Then I would like to fly down to Phoenix to see Lucia. I will only be there for a week and may even be able to bring Lucia back with me for a vacation".

"Frank, what a wonderful idea "said Anneliese. "That works for us". Anneliese had other things to talk about. "Matthew, tomorrow could we go back to St Nicholas Church to see Anya's grave and place some flowers. We were finding it difficult on the day of the service, but I can manage it now. Then afterwards, I would like to get a last look at Dam Square and the Royal Palace and then some shopping in the Royal Streets." "Sounds great" I said.

Whilst we were talking, Gerry and Tony had disappeared to the bar, enjoying a drink as young couples do! They reappeared, just in time to hear us discussing tomorrow's plans.

Frank turned to Gerry and Tony and explained his desire to visit Lucia. "So would you guys mind going with us to Toronto and staying a week or so, just to keep an eye on things whilst I'm away?" "No, of course not "replied Gerry. "In fact, that will give us an insight, for when we return next time!"

Gerry and Tony said they thought they would go for a wander around Amsterdam. Tony remarked "at least all the girls know us now so we don't risk getting hijacked!" Frank had decided to have a swim in the hotel pool, but said perhaps we could all meet in the bar at 7pm before finding somewhere for dinner.

Anneliese was going to check on Mum and Dad and ask if they would join us for dinner. So I went up to the room and just got comfortable on the bed.

My mind began its usual meandering and analysis of thoughts that developed in my cranium. The most striking thought was in terms of how much my life had changed. Money and financial security were no longer an issue. So, driving for more was no longer an objective. Keeping what we had was clearly important, so I would defend it absolutely. Then uncertainty raised its ugly head. We were going to Canada to live a normal, well hopefully, domestic life in the suburbs outside Toronto.

Would that be enough for us? I was definitely unsure about me! And what about Anneliese? She had experienced more excitement, more adrenalin rushes than I ever had. Would she get bored with me? Would she want more? I could give her fantastic holidays, but would that be enough? Material things? Well, they were easy to come by. Two-a-penny as we East Enders always said.

It's strange how, when you just let your mind wander around, what it comes up with. I have no idea why or how but Sir Edmund Hilary came into my thoughts. His ultimate objective always had been to climb Everest. He did, but what did he feel afterwards. What would he do now? I suppose we will never know but I'm sure he felt unsure, just like me!

The room door clicked open. Anneliese crept into the bedroom, probably thinking I was asleep. She carefully lay on the bed next to me. I turned over and clasped her waist. She was surprised and said "Hey, Mum and Dad would love to join us tonight, but could we get a wheelchair for Mum as she is not feeling strong". "Yes," I said "of course. I am sure reception will have one or get one for us".

"So what have you been doing? Just lying there thinking?" From Anneliese's eyes I could tell she had more on her mind. "What is it, I know there is something special you want to say?" "Yes, you are reading my mind. We are going to Toronto, hopefully, to settle down." "Yes, so what" I replied.

"I've been thinking about this for a while" she said with a twinkle in her eye. "I really want us to have a baby! I've not said anything before as I was worried about how you would feel. I want us to live in a normality world. We deserve to have a family to ratify our love. So how do you feel?"

"Anneliese" I said as my smile broadened. This progressed into thirty seconds of laughing my head off as I rolled onto the carpet. On my knees at the side of the bed, I spluttered, "Anneliese, I could not be more elated. You couldn't have surprised me with a better present. So let's start now, because I am really in the zone right now!"

I climbed back on the bed, still chuckling and we grasped each other and made our first attempt at making a baby. What an early evening spiritual experience that was!

Reception loaned me a wheelchair, so I went back upstairs to collect Frederika and Joe. It was all pretty easy for me; we took the lift and were in the bar by about seven o'clock.

Frank, Gerry and Tony arrived. After one drink and some banter, especially from Gerry and Tony who asked to borrow the wheelchair on the way back, in case they had too much wine. Frederika refused but said Tony may sit on her lap. A wonderful old lady with a sophisticated sense of humour and an impish smile.

We all ambled alongside the canal not knowing where we were headed. Then Frank enlightened us. "I've reserved a table just along from the corner of Dam Square, so it's only a five minute walk. It's a Greek restaurant so we can all have a go at breaking plates later. They don't mind, it's a tradition!"

As we strolled along, I whispered to Anneliese, "I assume we won't say anything about our plans just in case it takes a while." She put her hand on top of mine on the back of the wheelchair and whispered, "I am so excited, I really want to, but you are right, we should not!"

We pressed on, then Anneliese said to me, "You are so good at wheeling that chair, where did you learn to do it? I can see it's not easy, up and down kerbs, across cobbles and round obstacles, with a weighty person in it."

"My brother is 13 years younger than me and in my early teens, I spent a lot of time with him, looking after him. I would push him around in a pushchair, talking to him, and although he could only say a few words, I loved his expressions and the few words he did say. Since those early days, I have always loved him as if he were my own son." "So where is he now", asked Anneliese. "he has his own family in England. We have always kept in touch. I am very proud of him because, after a difficult start, he has become a very successful business man, with his own company."

"But to continue the answer to your question, Anneliese, a lovely lad in my family is disabled and I wheeled him around for years. Because hardly anywhere is wheelchair friendly, I learned to manoeuvre the wheelchair with expertise. And I loved every minute."

"That's fabulous Matthew, so you are qualified to push our kids all around Canada," said Anneliese with a joyful smile. "Hey, that came out as plural," I muttered, "let's not get ahead of ourselves."

The owner of the Greek restaurant and his family were ready and waiting for us. The family name was Hajiantoniou and he introduced all of them. He was Tony. I did our introductions saying we also had a Tony.

There were quite a few people already at their tables, so we seated quickly and then the evening got underway. Waiters and waitresses appeared from every corner. Most of the starters were Greek salads, bowls of Feta cheese with olives, courgette balls and octopus.

Wine was flowing throughout and everyone quickly became amused and amusing. Then a whole selection of courses for main, Moussaka, Spanakopita and several others I can't pronounce or spell. Followed by another selection of grilled meat and fresh fish.

Anneliese and I agreed we would treat tonight, for Mum and Dad's benefit, as our late wedding feast. They were already in the zone and the mood, and when Gerry told Mr Hajiantoniou that we had just married, he halted all proceedings and asked the whole restaurant community to join in a wedding toast. Joe and Frederika and, of course, Anneliese were in raptures.

Following this, Greek dancers appeared in full Greek costume. They danced for a full ten minutes and the host later told us that the dances were traditional Greek wedding choreography. As expected it then moved onto the plates. The first element of this centred on very spirited and talented jugglers. Then the dancers began to involve the customers. Gerry and Tony did not need an invitation! Their participation was inevitable. It was natural for them to become a key part of the entertainment. Absolutely everybody was in hysterics in response to their deliberately effeminate juggling gymnastics and lots of apologies every time they broke a plate. Joe and Frederika, just like us, were clearly massive fans of these two lads!

Their piece de resistance came when they seconded all of the dancers to join arms with them, shoulder high to perform the famous Greek dance, Sirtaki. Several customers, including me and Anneliese joined in. it was a sensational end to an unexpected and memorable wedding event!

Eventually, having said our goodbyes and thanks, we wobbled off back to the hotel. Tony and Gerry were continuing their boisterous mood, and as we passed the Red Light shop windows, they began calling out names of the girls they had met. Wasn't long before some girls were hanging out of their upstairs windows and some came out and walked with them. It was fabulous for us all to experience genuine loving peace, not war!

Back at the hotel, after some banter and a nightcap, it was off to get some sleep in preparation for a visit to the grave.

We left immediately after breakfast, and arrived at St Nicholas of Myra just after 10am. It was a cloudy morning with early mist that would probably clear later. We entered through large, wooden, ornately carved gates. The church building looked stark and isolated in the morning mist. We walked round the east side of the church towards where her grave lay, gradually slowing as we got nearer. We stood together at the side of the grave which seemed bare other than piles of dying flowers heaped all around it.

Chapter 47

Anya Getting A Memorial

Neither of us spoke, but I could see that Anneliese was choking back her tears. As we stood there together, staring at the pile of brown earth. Eating at me was how lonely the grave appeared.

Just at that point, the clouds separated and the sun started shining brightly. A voice behind us said "the sun is shining on the righteous!" We both turned to see Nikolai the Patriarch, with a beaming smile that competed with the suns' rays.

"God bless you both Anneliese and Matthew! Jesus is praising your soul with sunshine and I am your witness. Of course, you have come to say a last goodbye to Anya, but be assured I will take good care of her. And you will be welcomed by both of us anytime you may wish to call by. Do you have anything you need?"

"Well, yes" I replied. Anneliese joined my sentence and in unison, we said "we don't want her to be forgotten. Her grave is naked without a headstone or some kind of memorial." Nikolai asked, "Have you something you would like to say on a headstone?"

Anneliese said "Yes, I have Nikolai." "I have a pen and paper" replied the Patriarch. "Just write it down for me. Let's go in the Church and do it."

Once inside, Anneliese rested on a pew and wrote as if some force was helping her. She wrote:

Anya,

Died in the service of her country

A brave patriot and loving person

Who will always and forever be in

Our thoughts

Born: April 3, 1959

Died: August 30, 1986

Loved by us all

Anneliese showed it to Nikolai who said it was wonderful. She then asked Nikolai, "Could you arrange to get it crafted and installed for us? I have the money and will add a donation to the Church."

"Of course I will" replied Nikolai "and a donation won't be necessary." "Oh yes" said Anneliese. "You have been so kind and we will never forget the fabulous service and beautiful church."

She pulled out a large roll of Dutch Guilder notes from her bag and handed it to the Patriarch. "That is more than enough", he said. Anneliese took his hand and kissed it. I shook hands and we left, both leaving with sadness in our hearts.

As we slowly walked to the car, I needed to bring happiness back to us both. I cuddled Anneliese and cheerfully said "Darling, tomorrow we will be in Canada on the first day of the rest of our lives together. I'm really excited and I know we will love it". Anneliese lifted her head and smiled as if she had just seen the rainbow." Shopping was next on the bright list.

But on the way to shopping, Anneliese wanted to show me the Royal Palace. We, with an increasing spring in our steps, headed across Dam Square. How I had not taken notice of this building before, I will never understand.

We stood at the foot of this magnificent building. Anneliese said it was originally built in the 17th century as the Town Hall. They were obviously very flamboyant councillors in those days. Now it was the official reception residence of the Dutch Royal Family utilised for state visits, banquets and so forth.

Anneliese gave me a short tutorial. Princess Beatrix had become Queen with her consort, Prince Claas of the Netherlands.

I remarked that I loved our Royal Family and thought it splendid that the Netherlands also had a Royal Family. They had become exalted heads of state in a world where very few had survived.

As we wandered across the front of the Palace, perusing the signs of stability in a changing world, it emphasised that the work Anneliese, Frank and the rest of us had been doing was necessary to protect the heritage of western democracies.

Since meeting Anneliese, every so often my soul was being massaged and uplifted. No longer was life superficial. It had become extremely important!

We drifted into Royal Street and the wallet-wrenching began. In Anneliese's mind she was already buying for our life in Canada. Continuously, I explained that it would not be possible to load everything she liked onto the aircraft. She understood and said she was only window shopping.

After an hour and a half, I was cream crackered. But there was more to come. Anneliese found a children's clothing shop. She wanted to buy everything, but I put my foot down saying that they have massive shopping malls in Canada. Just get ideas for now. I did stress, "You are not pregnant yet, so don't even think about imposing a sex timetable on me. I don't need it". That did get her laughing, but more from excitement than from thinking what I had said was funny.

To a certain extent, I was starting to feel that this must be like trying to escape from the Stasi. But relief arrived. Anneliese took my arm and said "Let's get back to the hotel and check on Mum and Dad". What a wonderful few words. We strolled back, but with several bags, mainly new clothes for Anneliese.

Chapter 48

Dragging On A Fag

As we walked through the hotel, Gerry came sprinting towards us. Breathlessly he said "I'm glad I caught you guys. Hope you had a good time today. I hope you are ok with this, but as you are leaving for Canada tomorrow, a few of us thought we couldn't let you go without a farewell party tonight. We've invited a few of the local girls and they are going to put on a bit of a show... nothing lewd. The hotel are ok with it and have dedicated a small conference room at the rear of the hotel. There are a few famous people staying here and Tony has pulled out all the stops to invite them. Are you ok with it, I know it will be real fun!"

I looked at Anneliese, she smiled and looked at me. We both said "Gerry, sounds fabulous, and we can sleep it off on the plane". We said we would be in the bar by 8.00pm and Gerry went away smiling from ear to ear.

We were both shattered from the intensity of the day, but had a rest and a shower, then we were back ready for the evening. In the bar at 8pm with Frank, Gerry and Tony, I said that it would all be a bit too much for Mum and Dad with the long journey tomorrow. Then the bar began to fill, very rapidly.

At about 10pm, Tony announced we should all follow him to our party room. We did, and as I looked back, the bar was almost empty. We were all crowded by the bar in this party room. There was no sign of the Red Light girls. After about two more glasses, the lights dimmed and spotlights picked out the stage. The girls filed out with Tony and Gerry in the middle of the line. They all wore bikinis. The music began to caress our ears. It was a romantic, sensuous mixture of French and American lounge music. The girls' dancing was enthralling. Slow, deliberate, athletic but romantic. The music moved to the song "I've got you under my skin", more upbeat and with that a male dancer joined one of the Red Light girls and they performed out of their skin!

At the end came enormous applause, but then the mood music changed to a French song, and as it did, a guy wandered out on the stage; a girl either side of him; and started to sing in French. "Darling je vous aime beaucoup, je ne c'est quoi, what to do". I'd never seen him before, but his voice was fantastic and he was enviably handsome. Dark hair with piercing eyes and a fabulous face shape. All the girls, all the audience, Gerry and Tony, were absolutely beside themselves. Totally in raptures.

He finished; there was a lull and we had a short break. Anneliese was loving it, as was I. The music started up again and we all pressed towards the small stage. This time four beautiful girls moved into view. Too much makeup, overdressed but they suited the place. These were Drag Queens from the Twirling Club!

They took turns, taking the mike, telling jokes, enmeshed in stories and making fun of all of us. You did not dare to move, perhaps to go to the toilet, without some quip heading your way.

At one point, I came back to earth and looked around for Frank. I had not seen him for a couple of hours. I scoured the room and then I found him by the door, methodically surveying everything!

"Frank, are you ok, do you need anything, a drink perhaps?" "No" he said, "just go and enjoy; I am with you tomorrow and we can be more relaxed".

I returned to Anneliese just as the last Drag Queen was getting into her stride. She said "Oh, I've just seen Matthew. He and Anneliese are leaving us tomorrow to start a new life in Canada. Do you know they have just married?" with that, there was rapturous applause. His name was Felicity and, with gusto, he continued, "I expect when they get to Canada, in the cold, under the duvet, nature will drive then to try for a baby. Don't need to think protection. No need for condoms or the pill! So I asked Anneliese if this was a possibility. With honesty she replied "Well yes, but I have to cure Matthew of something first". Now everybody was hanging on her every word. Trying to appear nonchalant, the Drag Queen, Felicity, said "is there an issue?" Anneliese said "sort of, he always wants to lay underneath with me on top. So what's wrong with that?" I asked. Felicity increased her volume at this point. "That means just one thing, he can only fuck up!"

The whole room erupted. Felicity had conducted and presented the fictional story as if she was on the Jerry Springer Show. Everybody, including Anneliese and I took a few minutes to gather ourselves. Several people came over and shook our hands. Then Anneliese took my hand and we shuffled through the hordes to thank the girls, the dancers and the drag queens. Felicity was the last. As we embraced, I whispered "You are very perceptive". She giggled a man's deep giggle and kissed Anneliese on both cheeks.

As we were about to work our way back to Tony and Gerry, a man stepped in front of us. Frank's words bellowed in my mind. I prepared for trouble. But looking at the guy, he was not very big and had a huge smile. Anneliese had already recognised him. It was the singer.

He started to say "I wish you...." When Anneliese cut in. "Sacha, may I introduce my husband, Matthew. And Matthew, I would introduce Sacha, an old friend. Indeed, he is a very famous French singer who graced us with his performance tonight."

I suppose his accent was a massive plus, but he was such a gracious person. He grasped my hand as if he would never let go. Looking me straight in the eye, with sincerity written all over his face, he said, "Matthew you are such a lucky guy, your wife is not only beautiful, but her personality lights up every room". I think he could see from my face that I really did appreciate those words, but before I could say anything, Anneliese said "Sacha, would you do one more thing for a fan." "Anneliese", said Sacha, "you are not just a fan, you are a long-time friend. Tu es mon merveilleux ami! And so, of course, I will do my best."

"Would you please sing one more song for both of us? It's my favourite and I believe Matthew will recognise it. Its "Raindrops keep falling on my head." It was a special song for your career and always reminds me of you and our time together in our young years."

Sacha kissed Anneliese's hand and strolled back up the steps onto the stage. After a few minutes, arranging things with the backing quartet, he took the mike and said "Dear friends, this song is a special request from Anneliese. It's her favourite and I hope you enjoy it also".

As he began to sing, the charisma, charm and presence oozed from this guy. You could hear a pin drop in the room. Even us men were taken with his captivating accent, his voice and the beauty of the song he presented.

It took me immediately to the film with my favourite actor Paul Newman, and the girl pedalling her bicycle around a Bolivian forecourt.

He came off stage to stupendous cheers and applause, and moved straight to us. We both thanked him as he started to say to Anneliese, "Nostalgia feeds all of our souls. I will never forget our time in our little junior school in Paris. You were always a good friend and helped me through some difficult times. So when you are settled in Canada, would you send me contact details? I love Canada, and have performed in Montreal several times. I would love to meet up with you both again."

With that he slipped on a fabulous long trench coat, turned the collar up and we accompanied him to the door. "Sacha, we would love to meet up again, or maybe come to one of your concerts. Please keep in touch. Not many people have a friend they went to school with before their age reached double digits."

His chauffeur took his bag and he ventured to the waiting car. We both strolled with him and as we were thanking him and saying more goodbyes', Anneliese was politely opening the car door for him.

We had not seen Frank for a while, but unbeknown to us, he had sneaked out whilst we were talking and was watching from a car just a few yards up the road.

Our Drag Queen friend, Felicity, had parked herself just outside the hotel main entrance and was dragging furiously on what may have been a cigarette.

By now, it was completely dark. Occasionally, the moon peaked through the clustered cloud but only for a few seconds. The only other worthwhile light surrounded

Felicity, picking out her bright red dress and illuminating it sufficiently to accentuate her curves.

The street lights were situated on the canal wall side, such that light to our side of the road was scarce and, therefore, dim. Most traffic, had by now, returned home, so not even car headlights to brighten the spot.

As Sacha's car slowly pulled away, the light from his headlights disappeared with him! Momentarily, the noise of a car engine roared into the space he had left. A black car without lights on!

A figure ran from the alley at the side of the hotel. Dressed all in black and wearing a balaclava. Only his eyes were visible as he closed in on us. But it wasn't me he was after. He grabbed Anneliese around the throat, attempting to throttle her.

My right hand slid under my jacket feeling for my revolver, but before I could get control of it, an arm was around my throat, pressing my Adams apple. The car driver had run round behind me and was now attempting to drag me to his car. He got the passenger rear door open and then, with an undetectable motion, pistol whipped me. As he did, it caused a natural reaction. I still had my hand on my revolver and the shock made me jerk the trigger. I remember the feeling of a searing burn in my side. And hearing a scream!

The arm had gone from my throat. A few seconds recovering my mind and I looked around. This assailant was lying under the car door clutching his thigh. The shot from my revolver had passed through his thigh. It wasn't all good news. I could hardly move. My side felt like it was on fire, but at least I was still upright.

As my head cleared, I could only think of Anneliese. My eyes searched beyond the car roof but nobody was to be seen. I hobbled around the car to see, on the pavement, the assailant with Felicity and Anneliese sitting on his prostrate body. He was screaming with pain, trying to hold his eyes, but Felicity restrained his wrists.

This man/woman was not the naïve innocent she portrayed in her act. Indeed, she was a gutsy, gritty person with a shadowy fearless streak.

Frank arrived, he had driven his car across the front of the attackers' car to prevent any attempt to escape. As he joined the affray, he slapped handcuffs on both guys' wrists. Being an unflappable perfectionist, he yanked at the cuffs to check they were solidly engaged. Both men groaned!

Another couple of minutes and the Dutch police arrived. Frank, Gerry and Tony spent time with them, showing their security credentials and describing the incident. After the "Politie" made contact with Central Command, they gave us the "all clear" and loaded the aggressors in a police unit.

Frank grabbed my arm and helped me into the toilets so we could take a look at my side wound. We agreed that it was just a flesh wound and didn't need a doctor's attention.

I leant on Frank as we stumbled into the hotel reception area. Anneliese stood waiting with a concerned expression, but I forced a smile and said it was merely a flesh wound and nothing to worry about!

Anneliese, fighting back tears, blurted out "it is something to worry about! I'm worrying about you, my parents, everybody around us, all the people I care for. Will this relentless pursuit never end? I am constantly endangering all the people I love. I just want to escape, have a family and live a happy loving life. I got us into this but never ever imagined that payback would last forever!"

Felicity, supported by Tony, staggered in. she was covered in grazes, two large gashes on her left leg and dirt and grime all over. Anneliese yelled "Felicity, I can't thank you enough".

It transpired, from various accounts, that when Anneliese was attacked, Felicity had dropped her smoke, sprinted across and launched herself onto the guy's back, legs around his waist, arms around his neck. She had grabbed his face, ripping at his cheeks with her long, painted finger nails, and gouged his eyes so badly that one eye socket poured with blood. He dropped like a bag of spuds unable to see anything, other than cobbles, as his face struck the ground.

Panties on show, both girls helped one another to stand, although Anneliese struggled due to the male weight of Felicity.

By now, the Dutch Police had taken both characters into custody. Frank had managed to secure a few minutes conversation with a senior police officer and a CECD agent, who had appeared in the aftermath. Frank spoke to both men in a slow, meticulous but cultured way. He wanted to ensure that there would be a very determined interrogation process to try to establish who these guys worked for and how they had located Anneliese.

Back in the hotel, Frank, Gerry and Tony agreed they would keep watch on our room throughout the night. The Dutch police already had indicated they would provide surveillance around the hotel. So with that, we apologised and said our goodbyes' to everyone several times over.

Now in our room we both just wanted to comfort each other. Just as we were getting to the point of switching the lights off, there was a knock on the door. I gripped my revolver as I approached the door. There wasn't a peephole so I prepared myself as I opened the door about 2 inches and peered out.

It was Felicity and behind her, Gerry and Tony. I must admit, until I realised who it was, I became angry, swearing and blaspheming as I went to the door. But they lightened my mood. So in they came. Felicity asked "Are you both ok?" "Could we just have a last drink and talk for ten minutes. I need to cos I'm still shaking and when I met Gerry and Tony downstairs, they thought you would be OK with it".

We sat in the lounge, Felicity, Gerry and Tony on the sofa. We got them all drinks, and a large gin and tonic for Anneliese. I went straight for the Scotch and poured, probably a treble. My nerves needed steadying.

Felicity began the conversation and then continued to be involved in most of the rest. She said "That was a difficult time for you all but I am intrigued. What are you guys involved in, because it is obviously dangerous" Gerry quickly responded, "Felicity, I know what you are thinking, but no, it's not drugs, it's not human trafficking, it's not any form of criminal activity. We work for Governments. We are trying to help keep the world sane. We are trying to protect us all, and especially our democracy."

Having listened, open mouthed, Felicity said "I'm really proud of you all. There is no room for aggression and violence in this world. We have suffered this for centuries and that's more than enough! But we are all entitled to defend ourselves!"

In the morning, when we woke, the previous day seemed like a very bad dream. Our flight was scheduled for 11am. The guys were all at breakfast by 8am and did their best to brighten the atmosphere. We were soon on the road with Frank driving a hired mini bus.

Mum and Dad were as bright as my blazer buttons. They had been to breakfast at 7am and said they were looking forward to seeing another part of the world, especially Niagara Falls. Their buoyancy gradually lifted Anneliese's spirits and one-by-one, we all began to enjoy life again.

Chatper 49

Toronto, In The Big Country

Two CECD agents met us at the entrance to departures. The previous days' events had rung a few alarm bells. They hung back several paces as we all headed into departures and, unobtrusively, escorted us right to the plane. Frank said that all passengers had been thoroughly checked, but none were found to have any suspicious markers in their backgrounds.

We settled into our seats in this brand new BA Jumbo Jet 747A. We were in Business Class which met everyone's comfort requirements. Didn't match up to First Class but as the CECD were paying for this, we couldn't expect more.

Reading a brochure I found in the seat pocket, I came across an article about Canada. I put my arm around Anneliese and said "Do you realise that Canada has half the population of the UK but is 40 times bigger. It only has, on average, about 4 people per square kilometre. And we can live anywhere we want. It's obviously one of the safest countries for us to secrete ourselves away in".

Anneliese was seriously impressed and gushed that she couldn't wait! She began to talk about finding her ideal home and the features she thought would underpin a happy family life.

There were very few people in Business Class, and with that, Tony and Gerry came and sat with us in the five seat middle row section. A hostess arrived and asked if we would like drinks and there was a positive response from all of us. Red wine was the order of the day, and as we all commenced opening our individual bottles, Anneliese said to Gerry and Tony there was something she needed to discuss.

"After your few months sabbatical, back in England in Matthew's flat, you, possibly, may return to be with us in Canada" she said. "The point I'm trying to make is that I would like you to return to the U.S Imports business. It has been very lucrative, but without your guidance and efforts, has recently declined. I know that your CECD assignments come first, but it would be an advantage to us all if you could return to work on it with Mia and Alphonse. Trying to tackle your issue, if you decide you don't want to live in Canada, there is no reason you cannot return to California and work from there. With ongoing communication with Frank, if he needs help with body guarding duties, you could fly up and be with us the same day".

"Anneliese, that's excellent thinking! It's feasible and, to be truthful, we are missing the financial rewards from the business" said Tony. "We definitely will give it strong consideration during our three month break!" But I couldn't leave it there. With my sincerest tone I said "Be assured, our preference is you two working here in Canada with us. We will pull out all the stops to try to make you feel this is the best place you have ever lived. And I know I'm speaking for both of us! And that goes for Frank too!"

Just then, we all felt a jolt, as the wheels locked. The deafening sound of the reversing jet engines kicked in as we hit the ground. We slowed and began to taxi to the disembarking area. We had landed at Pearson Airport, Toronto, in the bright sunshine, so the next few hours of getting somewhere to settle should be easier.

It was as if Immigration had been primed and were ready for us. As we were each called forward, over the yellow line, the Officer delivered a welcoming smile and only a cursory glance at the passport.

In baggage, Frank said, "Listen you guys, we are being met. Everything has been arranged. So no worries, they will get us somewhere to spend the night!"

The airline had loaned us a wheelchair for Frederika. As we came out of departures, there was the usual crowd of meet and greeters. One stood out, a Royal Mounted Policeman in his captivating uniform including the domed beige Stetson hat, holding up a card that read "Frank".

We introduced ourselves to the Mountie, named John. Stripes on his arm said he was the Sergeant. He escorted us outside and two more Mounties jumped out of a waiting mini-van. They assisted us all into the mini-van, Mum and Dad first, then one of them returned the wheelchair to the airline desk.

They drove us out of the airport onto the motorway known as the QE, named after Queen Elizabeth. John, the sergeant, said we were going to a town about 10 miles from Toronto centre, called Oakville. It wasn't long before we pulled into a small suburban development and stopped outside a row of three storey town houses.

Two of these houses were our temporary accommodation. John explained the house selected for us was being decorated, but would be finished in 3 days. They would take us to see it in the morning to check that we were happy with the one chosen.

It we were happy with it, we could begin choosing furniture and everything else we would need to live comfortably. We should do most of the shopping in Sears department store, where an account had been set up for us, and they would invoice the Government direct. What a bonus!

The Town houses were superb. Frank, Gerry and Tony were our neighbours. Once we had entered our house, Anneliese started to search around. The place was clean of all bugs etc. she was very happy when she found that the fridges and cupboards had been stocked with food and drink.

A few minutes later the bell rang. I went to the peephole and saw another Mountie on the doorstep. I opened up and he very politely pointed to the driveway and said he was just delivering our vehicle. It was large! A Ford Windstar, automatic, 5 seats and all essentials. The boys next door had a luxury Lincoln Continental.

Mum and Dad were very happy with their bedroom and so we all settled down, with some munchies and drinks, in front of a massive TV screen. After a couple of hours, jet lag took its toll and we all drifted off to bed.

The morning was spectacular. Bright blue skies, sunshine and warm, which was forecast to become hot later. Anneliese said John, the Mountie, had given her his mobile and direct line. He had sent a text saying he would arrive about 10.30am which gave us quite a bit of time to have a scrumptious breakfast. Along with all her other assets, Anneliese was in the "very good cook league".

I knew it wouldn't be long before the lads next door turned up. Sure enough, they arrived, obviously ravenous. Tony went straight to the kitchen, assisting Anneliese with the cooking. By 10.00am, Mum and Dad and the rest of us were finalising our breakfast efforts. For once, there wasn't a single person in the doldrums.

At precisely 10.30am, John, the Mountie, arrived. I did hold some envy for this guy due to my love of horses as a teenager, I had thought about emigrating and Canada was top of the list because the Mounties sounded an exciting job that you did on horseback. But, as with most of us at that point in our lives, we tend to take the line of least resistance.

This time, John drove us in our Windstar. On the way, we chatted about it., he was enthused by the car. Then he mentioned they were manufactured just down the road in Oakville. The Canada Ford HQ was there and John said they would welcome me with open arms! But, that was for later, now I wanted to get the family settled.

We arrived at the proposed house. Looking at the front, it was like I had always imagined films stars live in. The frontage was enormous with immaculate grass and gardens. To the right, a large double garage. The entrance was via large double doors. The exterior of the building was painted Dove Grey. The surrounding houses were all pristine and just around the corner was a beautiful English style church. It was only 2 minutes' walk from the edge of Lake Ontario and that became my next objective.

But first we would walk around to view the outside of the property. The garden seemed huge. I guessed it was about half an acre, and there was a wonderful patio area with marble-type slabs. Also at the rear was a 50 foot swimming pool with a spring board. I commented to Anneliese that, later, we could get a high board installed. Her response was "Don't you dare!" But she adored the pool.

Walking inside from the patio, there was a generous hot tub. A beautiful kitchen and a family room. A massive lounge and, opposite, an office. The entrance hall, through double glassed doors, was glorious.

A winding staircase, wide with maple wood stair rails, leading to five large bedrooms upstairs. Anneliese appeared as pleased as could be. I commented "This was the house I always imagined as a residence for the rich and famous. " Anneliese was ecstatic. "It is our perfect house, for us now, and for our future family." We both said to John, "We are sold!" He did look relieved. He asked if we were willing to continue and, if so, we would go to Sears.

This part of the excursion was absolutely amazing. John led us into the store and introduced us to the Store Manager. He slowly walked us through all departments. Gradually, as Anneliese selected stuff, the sales people joined us and eventually we had an entourage that was impressive. We finished, with only some furniture excluded because Anneliese had decided she wanted special pieces for certain places!

Whilst they were totalling the bill, I carried on looking around. There was something else I wanted, and I found it. I trundled back and just as they were finishing, said I had seen a barbeque that was something else, looking to Anneliese for approval. I showed the Manager and he said he would deliver it next day and one of their people would set it up. The final total was nearly $40,000. John didn't flinch, just said "shall we move on?"

We thanked everybody and did our best to show our appreciation to the sales staff. Of course, I knew how much that meant to them!

Back in the Windstar, John asked if we would like to move onto Swiss Interiors in Oakville. Anneliese thought for a moment, then asked John, "John would it be possible to continue tomorrow? I think I should get back now and check on Mum and Dad."

"That's ok with me" replied John. "About the same time tomorrow. We can go to Swiss Interiors, I am sure they will have special pieces of furniture that will please you down to the ground!"

Anneliese then asked if we could drive back, but through Oakville. "Of Course, Ma'am, it's a small roundabout tour along the edge of the Lake."

We drove right through Oakville Town. Along what Canadians call the main "drag" or street. Always adjacent to the perimeter of the lake. The whole place was stunning. John, when we commented it was picturesque, said that it was filmed for the movie, Santa Clause The Movie, and we could see why. Even though it was not Christmas, there were lights adorning everything, especially the restaurants which seemed endless right through to the next town, Burlington. It would be even more spectacular in the snow, which was only a month or so away!

Arriving back at our temporary accommodation, we thanked John and Anneliese went to check on Joe and Frederika.

Next day, we were selecting special pieces of furniture. Anneliese and I were astounded by the craftsmanship and quality and came close to letting it run away with us. But, in the end, we were happy with our purchases and couldn't wait to see it all in place in the house.

Now we were at "moving day". We all arrived at our house about 11am. All included Mum and Dad, Frank, Tony and Gerry. We attempted to be helpful, however, Anneliese had very particular ideas.

After an hour or so, Anneliese had become very tetchy. All of a sudden she shouted "Stop, please, all you guys! Line up in the corridor by the office. Against the wall." She was now in the character of a sergeant major. She walked along our line, reached me, grabbed my man bits and said "You are all a hindrance; misfits destroying my plan." She paraded along the other three, stared at Gerry's face and with ferocity exclaimed "If you three don't disappear, until evening, I will personally ensure you learn what it feels like to be a eunuch!"

Frank, laughing, led the way out the door in ultra-quick time. We jumped in the Lincoln and drove off down the QE. Not long before we found a shopping mall with a pool bar. It was splendid with 15 tables and TV's all around showing different sports. The waitresses wore mini-skirts and delivered food orders to a pedestal table by the side of your pool table.

I suppose because we were all in elated moods, we had a grand time. The waitresses loved us, especially Gerry and Tony. We ordered bags of food and had continuous drinks.

We left at about 5.30pm having made our mark in Donovan Baileys bar. The staff said we were welcome anytime and could join a club that would give food rewards. The best reward was when we got home and saw the results of Anneliese's efforts. The house interior was fabulous. Everything in its place and a place for everything. Even outside, the barbeque was there, ready to go whenever we wanted!

Next day, Frank set off to take a flight to Phoenix to meet up with Lucia. Tony and Gerry planned to stay around for his return in about a week's time. Frank seemed joyous and excited to be seeing Lucia, but as usual, maintained a casual relaxed front. Although, he had made quite an effort with his appearance! Haircut, new leather jacket and had even had his teeth whitened. Also, he had treated himself to a new pair of expensive black Cuban-heeled boots. They elevated him a good two inches, so now he appeared close to six foot.

His taxi arrived and as he headed off to Pearson Airport, he had a grinning confident smile, which, combined with his slow precise stride, characteristically reflecting a man of significant ability!

Gerry and Tony joined us on the doorstep to wave goodbye. Both of them were still dressed in precocious dressing gowns, Gerry wearing a cravat and Tony in brightly coloured tartan socks. Gerry shouted to Frank as he entered the rear seat of the taxi, "Don't worry Frank, we will take very good care of them all."

We spent the week fiddling and adjusting everything in the house. We meddled until we were 110% happy with everything. I went to the Missiisauga Mall and bought a pool table, cues, balls and all the other paraphernalia, to install in the basement.

Six days later, Frank messaged saying he and Lucia would be with us by mid-afternoon. It was exhilarating for all of us. Tony and Gerry got the booze in. Anneliese and I cleaned everywhere, especially their room. Even Mum and Dad were excited.

Their arrival felt special for all of us. Lucia, even after the flight, looked fabulous. Wearing a classic Givenchy trouser suit and a demeanour that was always so welcoming. Obviously, learned from her time in the hospitality business. For a joke, as they entered the house, I said "Would you care for a shag now or should we leave it 'til later." She gave me a playful smack on the cheek and a gorgeous smile.

In the middle of the evening, during dinner, Frank stood up and announced that he had asked Lucia to marry him! There was stunned silence for just a few seconds, and as we all began to show our elation, Lucia shouted "And I have accepted".

A week later, Gerry and Tony were preparing to go to the U.K. Frank and Lucia were now living with us, which we all enjoyed.

Gerry and Tony would leave on Wednesday. When the time arrived, there was a very blue mood over all of us. We loved these guys and it would be difficult to see them go.

But when the day came, they assured us they would be back, after Christmas, the latest being March.

On Wednesday, they left for the airport. It was difficult. I, and probably the rest of us, were in the depths of despair. We had grown so close! We got it over as quickly as we could. As I have said before, goodbyes are really difficult for me.

The next few evenings and days were in a sort of vacuum. We missed their faces, their humour, their clothing and most of all, their aura!

A few weeks went by, towards Christmas. Frank asked, would it be OK if he and Lucia spent Christmas with us and then got married at the beginning of April. In fact, he had selected April 1st, Aprils Fools Day! He thought that would add some fun and lighten the mood! I exclaimed "That sounds great because we can get Gerry and Tony back by that time." So this was the plan and we would spend the next couple of months getting it all together.

Early December, we all drove up to Niagara. We veered off the QE and visited Niagara Village. It was snowing; about a foot deep on the ground and as we drove in, it seemed like a scene from "White Christmas". It was what we all imagine when we are youngsters. A fantasy white Christmas in a small village with a seasonal character.

We spent an hour in the Christmas stores. Everybody shopped with passion. After 1 ½ hours we moved on, through the Parkway, up to the Falls. Mum and Dad were already feeling young again and Anneliese was loving their emotional chatter.

The Falls were not frozen yet, and the boats, the "Maids of the Mist" were taking tourists close to the Falls. We stood at our vantage point mesmerized by the spectacle of tons of water per second pouring over the two falls, the Canadian and the American. This had been our first visit to the Falls, but I knew, by everyone's reactions, that it wouldn't be the last.

Christmas soon arrived. In the meantime, Frank and Lucia were in the process of buying a lovely house just two doors down from us. But we all had a wonderful Christmas. Anneliese and her Mum and Dad, together with Lucia, presented a gorgeous traditional turkey roast. Us ignorant guys played pool up to lunch!

It turned out to be what has always been portrayed as a traditional yuletide, but with a secret twist. The house decorations had been designed and exhibited by Anneliese and Lucia, so it was compliments all round. The tree also, dressed in silver, was amazing. Outside it was snowing and had settled to about a foot. All the houses were decked out with lights and holly. Kids were up and down the street on sledges and our local Church, St Luke's, had a choir outside singing carols.

Chapter 50

Our Dreams Come True – To Be Frank

Frank and I had consumed a few beers whilst playing pool so that was working on our appetites. Starters, glorious wine and crackers were the order for the early part of lunch. Frank and I carried in the main course, turkey will all the trimmings.

Joe and Frederika helped with organising vegetables, offering a selection to each of us. Both of them were giggling throughout, listening to continuous humour and banter.

After the main, we returned to the wine. Joe was definitely a fan of Christmas, asking if we would mind him playing music on his stereo. Quiet background music completed the heart-warming Christmas atmosphere.

Anneliese felt this heavenly emanation and decided the time was right. She broke in and the banter and chatter stopped dead. She asked with a gracious smile, "Would you mind if I told you a tiny secret that I can't keep any longer?" Until now, her speech had been soft and gentle. That all changed! She had to stand, and blurted out, "I am going to have a baby, I mean, we are going to have a baby," as she leaned across and grasped my hand.

It's hard to describe how we all reacted. Frank and Lucia gave us both long emotional hugs. Mum and Dad were embracing one another. Mum had her hand over her mouth, attempting to supress a scream.

So, there it was, the secret was out, sealing the most wonderful Christmas present we ever had. From this point, family life really began to evolve. Every day, Anneliese experienced new bodily changes and emotions. Every day, all of us talked plans, searched baby shops and began storing equipment that would be needed. Then came the medical tests, checks and scans.

By the middle of March, we told everybody everything was fine, and we were expecting a baby boy! I was absolutely elated, Anneliese also; she had always said she did not have a preference, just a beautiful baby that was ours!

The next big event in our calendar would be the wedding of Lucia and Frank. Helping plan and organise this was sometimes a welcome diversion down another happiness road.

Faster than the speed of light, or so it seemed, April "Fools Day" arrived. By now, Anneliese and I were going to St Luke's Church almost every Sunday. Many people in the congregation, and the local community, had become good friends. It was a beautiful, pristine, fairly modern church with a very personable, cheery vicar. Frank had asked me to be his Best Man and for the last few weeks I had not stopped worrying about what to say in my speech.

Gerry and Tony had just arrived and were so excited by the wedding. We chatted at the church entrance and agreed we would concentrate on the wedding, and everything else would wait until after it. Tony, had to say, "We've let your flat to a lovely couple and have shipped your material things over." I replied "Oh you should not have bothered". Tony said, "But your football trophies, precious books and ornaments. They are your life". "No Tony "I replied "they are not my life, they are just stuff!"

The wedding was a relatively small affair. About 30 guests, mostly friends and neighbours, and of course, us. The reception was in our garden, with a marquee beside the swimming pool. Lucia, Anneliese and girlfriends had taken charge of the food, with the men, including a local publican, taking care of the bar.

It was a stupendously bright sunny day. About 23 degrees centigrade and a serenely attractive deep blue sky. Even to this day, such a sky, to me, is a "Canada Sky."

Lucia had preferred to have a buffet style wedding lunch so most people stood and sat around on the patio enjoying conversation and the delicious food. Background music, mostly Frank Sinatra lounge music, added a sophisticated element to the whole wedding ensemble.

This, I decided, was the perfect time to make the "Best Man's Speech." Gerry did the honours, tapping a spoon on the side of a glass! I had given it a lot of thought. Frank and Lucia did not have any remaining family, sad but true! I think they had experienced tough early lives, so I thought it best to avoid that subject. Instead, I would take it gently and keep it brief!

I inhaled a deep breath, licked my lips and began. Everybody was so quiet, it was intimidating! "Frank is a man of few words. More a man of action! So I intend emulating Frank, you will be pleased to hear! Frank spent most of his adult life in military service. Protecting and serving our countries and us. When I say us, it is said with sincerity. He cares enormously about people and has helped me and my family through many difficult times. One thing to be aware of is embraces. Although it is natural in North America to embrace men, when they have achieved, or maybe when they are leaving. That is not Frank. He is not receptive to male hugs! Females yes, but probably reserved for Lucia. In fact, until he met Lucia, I had never seen him find any other woman attractive. He was obviously just waiting for the right woman to come along. I will finish with a small word of warning for Lucia. I have seen Frank handle his bazooka and it is a sight to behold! So God Bless you both. One last thing; on Monday Frank and Lucia are moving into their house, 2 doors down, so we should all welcome Frank and Lucia to our community!"

There was a loud cheer and hip-hip-hoorays for Frank and Lucia. Nobody tried to hug Frank! Through afternoon and evening, the friendly atmosphere prevailed. Food had hit the spot for everybody ad we now moved onto drink, music and dancing.

One of the guests approached me with Tony. Arms around each other's shoulders, they had obviously hit it off. The guest, one of the guys from church, said that Tony was initiating this! Tony said with a really gleeful look on his face, "Matthew, this is David." I said "Yes, we met at church." An excited Tony continued "Yes, he plays organ in St Luke's but, the thing is, he has a piano. And he plays. Could we bring it over and have a bit of old-time pub music?"

There was no way I could resist. I grew up with pianos in pubs, indeed my stepfather would play in his local every Sunday. It was "special".

Tony set off with David and a crowd of men to help get it down the road. There were so many, they probably could carry it. They arrived back in ten minutes and, yes, it was carried through the house and in place in just a few seconds.

I turned off the piped music and the dancers all moaned. But within two minutes, Dave was on it. Tinkling for a few minutes, but then people crowded around as he started to play. He appeared a "fresh faced kid" but his fingers did the talking.

He had a fabulous repertoire. He had a penchant for Bobby Vee and played several of his. Elton John and David Dowie crept in gradually. Absolutely everybody was singing, dancing and joining in with everything. The atmosphere was electric.

As the evening slowed, people began to make requests. There were quite a few English amongst the guests. I didn't know all of them and most had been in Canada since the 1960's. I was a bit drunk by now and asked if he knew "I'm forever blowing bubbles." He did, and so I sang at the top of my voice and several joined in.

The piano songs continued as the evening went on. The guest numbers dwindled until there were only about ten people clustered around David at the piano. Drinks and singing continued late into the night, the last song being "Pack up your troubles" which everyone seemed to know! The Canadians were a fabulous bunch which I suppose is only to be expected. We have always had a very close relationship with their country paying homage to our Royal Family and the Commonwealth.

Our community seemed to move through the next few months with constant enjoyment and expectation. Our baby boy was due around the middle of June, and as Anneliese grew in size, the weather grew hotter.

Although Anneliese found the heat too intense at times, she managed to join in most of the discovery trips with Mum and Dad and the rest of our close friends. Toronto CN Tower, the Toronto Harbour and Islands, Ottawa and Thousand Islands of Muskoka. Along with these trips, we frequented restaurants all along the edge of Lake Ontario almost every week.

Chapter 51

A Baby, To Be Frank

Anneliese gave birth to a beautiful baby boy on the morning of June 12th, 1987. He was a good weight, with a full head of almost black hair, just like his Dad.

Next day was filled with a continuous stream of visitors. Mother and baby were both fine so we were able to cope. A day later, Frank accompanied me to bring my Anneliese and new born home. Once comfortable in the lounge, Lucia arrived and went into raptures over the baby. Just a few minutes behind Lucia was Gerry and Tony. They were almost as gushing as Lucia.

After they all had taken a turn at holding him, Gerry asked the expected question! "Have you decided on a name for this cute little fellow?"

Anneliese looked straight at me and said "well yes, we have agreed we would love to call him "… she passed it to me with a telling glance so I continued, "with your agreement, we would like to name him after… Frank." He looked stunned, followed by a controlled expression of pleasure and pride. "Of course, we all agree and think it's a name he's worthy of. His mother has been through a lot, and Dad also," said Lucia. Anneliese said, "Well that's another pleasurable moment to record in his baby book. So his Christian names will be Francis Matthew!"

Frank never ever said more than necessary, but in this instance he was just lost for words! "And while we are on the subject of Frank Junior," continued Anneliese, "we would like to ask all four of you to be his God parents. " Gerry and Tony could not contain themselves. Hugs, kisses, some tears and "of course" and "love to" expletives.

By now, Frank had gathered himself enough to say "You have my word that I will watch over Frank Junior and ensure he never comes to any harm. And I will help you guys bring him up to be a considerate and accomplished person like his parents."

There is no holding back time as we all know. Family life was agreeing with us and Frank Junior was a real treasure. Frank was an unbelievable help along with Lucia. My boy loved these two people and Gerry and Tony figured in his world as his playmates.

Another Christmas approached. This would be different. More enjoyable than ever before because we had Frank Junior to bring into the world of Santa Claus. It was a bit of a difficult run-up because Joe had become ill with cardiac problems. But we got through it. Canadian doctors are first class. A stent and ongoing pills brought him back to us and we had a wonderland Christmas. Surprisingly, Frederika seemed to be growing fitter every day and loved spending every minute with Frank Junior.

A spectacular Christmas followed by a January holiday in Barbados. We had three weeks of sunshine; beach every day, sand castles, lots of lovely food and drink. Lots of help too as Gerry and Tony graced us with their company. They were always helpful and attentive, but at times, I wished they would wear bigger, baggier shorts rather than the tiny G strings that incurred stares from all around.

I did not manage to stop time so we carried on through 1988. After another wonderful Christmas with Frank Junior and our crowd, the other Frank wandered in. We were sitting in the garden watching and playing with Frank Junior in a sandpit. Frederika and Joe, although warmly dressed were sampling winter sun in Canada.

Chapter 52

Heading To The Demise Of The Wall

Frank, after the usual greetings, asked if he could have a few minutes with both of us. We went inside. Mum and Dad looked after Frank Junior and it was obvious he was giving them absolute pleasure.

We sat down and frank delivered a monologue. "Reagan, the U.S. President, was sure that Gorbachev would gain overall power in the U.S.S.R. Reagan had plans to continue to improve relations with the Soviet supremo to extricate the world from constant fear of war caused by the "Cold War". This was his key objective to take his place in the history books."

"The bottom line belongs to the Americans. They need an experienced Intelligence Officer who has detailed knowledge of, and a network in, Berlin. Anneliese fits the bill especially as she is also expert in psychology and communications. So they want to persuade you, Anneliese, to return to work on this project." Frank apologised, but said he couldn't tell us anymore, but would leave us to think about it for a few weeks. The end date deadline was August 15, 1989.

It was clear to me, within hours, that Anneliese had made her mind up. The next day, she managed to arrange a Nanny for Frank Junior. She would arrive tomorrow. Anneliese explained all this to me and asked if I minded. She emphasised that this was important global security and eventually, and hopefully, peace.

"No" I said, "I will do whatever you think will help." In my mind, I was terrified that Anneliese may get into the type of dangerous situations we had experience before. But, to mitigate these worries, I kept telling myself that she was the best there was at fighting these battles and Frank would give her the utmost protection and support.

A short while later, I was in the garden keeping busy tidying to keep my mind off things. Frank strolled in and we sat down chatting by the pool. I poured my heart out to him, saying how worried I was for all of us and especially my little Frank Junior. Frank, in his usual controlled, unemotional manner, said he believed this was meant to be. A while ago, something had happened that, maybe, was a good omen. It was too much of a coincidence not to have meaning! I gave Frank a quizzical look and before I said a word, Frank spoke.

"Matthew, what date was little Frank Junior born?" I replied June 12, 1987! That same day, Ronald Reagan was in Berlin. He made a well-documented, historic speech, which would advance the cause of freedom and instigate peace and harmony between East and West. The key line from his speech went like this! "Mr Gorbachev tear down this wall."

"Since that date, June 12 1987, the relationship with the Russians has been gradually improving. And now, Frank Junior's mother has been selected to be the instrument that progresses the elimination of evil tensions."

"You know I am not a religious guy, but I have a suspicion that some force for good, some magical, mystical power, had a hand in this. There is no person more qualified than Anneliese to lead and design whatever is necessary to secure a safe and stable world for Frank Junior, and ultimately that will probably involve dissolution of the U.S.S.R."

That night, Anneliese and I talked for some hours about the change in our life that was imminent. Anneliese would begin planning and preparation tomorrow. She envisaged she would work from home for a couple of months, using her networking with the intelligence operatives in the field. She would start with Mia and Alphonse as they were on the spot and had access to other agents and information. After that, she wasn't sure, but would get direction from CIA, CECD and maybe even the Canadian CSIS.

About 9.00am in the morning, the new nanny arrived. Lucia had recommended her and she would start immediately. She was a young, stocky Mexican girl with a very pleasant smile and demeanour.

We chatted with her for about an hour whilst Frank Junior played in his gated floor space. The nanny, named Rosa, had pretty good English. Anneliese had written out instructions, meal times, where to find this and that. She was definitely a kid-lover because she couldn't take her eyes off him and eventually got on the floor with him. Anneliese said just to find us if she needed anything and we left the room, leaving them to get acquainted.

Over the next few weeks, Rosa and Frank Junior developed a close relationship which was a joy to watch. But we made sure we had plenty of time with him. My time was mostly taking him to the park opposite or down by the edge of Lake Ontario, whilst Rosa tidied the mess he constantly made.

On Fridays, we all, and I mean all, would go to a child's play park on the edge of the lake in the next town, Burlington. Our gang comprised Anneliese, Frank, Lucia, Gerry, Tony, Rosa, Me and Junior. After the play park, we would go for mid-afternoon lunch in a great restaurant called The Landing. We all had agreed this was our weekly break time and it was always crazily fabulous.

Anneliese worked on her computer most of the day. Anything she did went straight to CIA HQ and was encrypted. All messages she received had come through the same route, had been decoded, cleaned and cleared. From the things she told me in the evenings, mostly whilst relaxing with a bottle of wine after Junior had hit the sack, indicated that she was making immense progress. A major propaganda event was 3 brothers who successfully executed a rescue!

Her strategy seemed to be to mobilise every operative, and motivate each one to build a network to publicise the need to use all possible forms of propaganda against the Berlin Wall and the Stasi. She held a belief that the Wall had provided many thousands of jobs for the Stasi and their families and henchmen, and breaking their hold on the Wall would start to open the door that would lead to a totally different Soviet psyche.

Frank would sit and work with her for hours. I could tell they were beginning to feel their networking and scatter gun propaganda was working. Early August, they had a call to tell them they were required to go to a meeting in the Pentagon. Anneliese asked if I could attend also. They went away to check and we hung on for a while. "Yes, of course" was the answer.

Frank made all the arrangements through the CIA and CSIS. Early next morning, we were picked up by a driver in a Ford Explorer. Straight to Pearson Airport, onto the edge of a quiet runway used by private aircraft. Our plane was a small Lear jet, and once seated we were off.

Just over an hour and we were being escorted down the corridors of power in the Pentagon. What a story to tell Frank Junior one day.

We were shown into a small conference room. Within a few minutes we were joined by several people, five men and 2 women. They all introduced themselves and as we started to do the same, the guy who seemed to be the boss said "Its ok, we know you very well!" He was a tubby guy with a friendly smile and very smart appearance. As he took his jacket off, his trouser braces, or suspenders as Americans refer to them, were stretched to their limit by both hands. He leaned back and lit an extra-long cigarette. This was the Director of the CIA.

The door opened and in came a lady pushing a coffee trolley with a selection of pastries. She left the trolley and exited. One of the Director's assistants, a business suited blonde lady pushed the trolley around to each of us and served. Whilst this was going on, the Director began to speak.

"Well now Frank, Matthew and, star of the show, Anneliese. We know you have accepted this assignment and have been avidly following your work. Frank informed us a while ago that Anneliese had begun work immediately she received our request. I am immensely impressed, knowing you have been on leave for quite some time, and now have a youngster!"

"I suppose you are wondering why we asked you here. Well, in essence, we want to bring you up to date with our work and intelligence information. But before we do, I personally want to thank you. Your efforts, your planning, your ingenuity, have surpassed anything we expected. The results have been spectacular. You have managed to massively accelerate the fight for freedom in Berlin. And this has become widespread throughout Soviet territories. In consequence, the relationship with Mr Gorbachev, has moved up to a level of diplomatic friendship."

Chapter 53

All The Presidents Men

"Mr Gorbachev and President Reagan are definitely now on the same page. And they are close to turning to the next page, which initiates détente, a world without fear, a world with peace".

"Anneliese, your skilful use of wise propaganda, human interest stories, people in your command, imparting knowledge for a common peace mandate, is beyond commendable, indeed, the President has asked me to give you his personal thanks, and hopes to meet you in the future."

"The President, and we all, thought your expose of the story about the three Bethke Brothers, with the detailed account of how two of them flew a light aeroplane over the wall to rescue the third Brother, was a magical propaganda piece. Your use of this type of human interest story has been key to the advancement of the peace process."

I could tell that Anneliese had enjoyed every minute of this and so had both Frank and I. However, Anneliese remained unpretentious!

The Director continued, "But now I would like to move on to the future. We have also been working diligently to secure in-depth intelligence. There is widespread unrest in the Soviet Bloc. There is turmoil in some Soviet cities. And there is a wave building that has potential to cause a tsunami of revolutions. This is being spurred on by church groups, environmentalists, non-government groups, mostly in Berlin, but spreading far and wide. And most of all, this has been initiated and underpinned by your teams skilful propaganda and rhetoric."

"We have recently received substantiated intelligence that subversive groups are joining forces in Berlin and, sooner rather than later, will attempt to take matters into their own hands to dismantle the Berlin Wall. Our concern is that this could cause a very dangerous response by the Soviet military and, particularly the Stasi."

"The Stasi have most to lose in this scenario. The existence of the Berlin Wall has provided the Stasi's and their families with thousands of jobs along with a very lucrative lifestyle. The West Germans want to neutralise the Stasi with a pre-emptive strike. They are asking for all our intelligence information on Stasi personnel, names, addresses, hierarchy and so forth. We are considering this request as it may be a valid approach to the issue."

All these factors have led us to formulate what we believe and hope may be a plan that gives us a very good chance to achieve a win/win result. I will outline this and would ask that you save any questions until the end."

"Firstly, we believe we need to continue targeted rhetoric and propaganda. This, combined with our support for all peaceful protests and subversive activity are critical to President Reagan's request to Mr Gorbachev – pull down that wall."

"The next element is crucial. The execution of our strategy must, at all cost, avoid bloodshed! The risk, or perhaps I should say, the very high risk with the way things stand, is that the many and varied protest groups, subversive groups, and other factions will go it alone. In which case, they may be met with a severe Stasi response. Killing a few people wouldn't mean a thing to the Stasi. Any media criticism would be thrust aside under the Soviet banner of ownership of East Germany and the Wall."

However, Ladies and Gentlemen, a fully coordinated and synchronised response would have a great chance of success. We believe a simultaneous mobilisation of all the various factions, to protest at a point in the Berlin Wall, is the best way forward. Masses of Berliners, both West and East, protesting at a single point, supported by TV coverage are not likely to come under attack from the Stasi. The Russians definitely won't get involved because they are already receiving the Gorbachev doctrine on military values and economic reform that is also being applied back in their home towns."

"One final point, the dominance of the U.S.S.R is already under threat. Their pillars are beginning to crumble. If we get this right, we will also release many other countries from their grip because the house of cards starts at the Berlin Wall. I think I've said enough about the overall situation. I know you have all listened intently, especially you Anneliese. So my question to you Anneliese, and I am sure it will be difficult for all three of you. The whole of the Western world, all governments, agreed we want you to lead this operation. It will involve spending the next several weeks preparing with your team and then being on the spot in Berlin for about three weeks from mid-October. Before we go any further do you have any questions?"

Anneliese looked at all the faces around the Director and then straight into his eyes. She said "Thank you, Sir, for such a clear and detailed delivery of the situation." Anneliese glanced across at me, held her stare for a few seconds, smiled and then turned to the Director. "Sir, I will gladly accept this assignment. This world has seen more than enough bloodshed. Two World Wars and virtually constant military violence involving innocent citizens throughout most of the world. This may signal the end to all this nonsense and give us all a chance to have respect for everyone. I want, and will always work, for a safe and secure world for my son, where peace and love predominate."

The Director looked surprised at her rapid decision, and across him and his whole team was a display of humungous smiles. At that juncture Anneliese said "Mr Director, Sir, there is one proviso." The smiles eased. "I am absolutely against the ideas from the Germans. I have known the terror the Stasi can inflict. If there was any attempt to disrupt their organisation, they would immediately intervene with barbaric reprisals. We would not have any chance to continue with our softly, softly approach. Violence would commence and when you are dealing with deranged sadists there is no telling where it will take you!"

The smiles on the Director's team reappeared. "Anneliese" he said, "I agree with you and as you will be leading this we accept your decision. We will inform the Germans and ask for their total support for you and your team. Incidentally, we have earmarked a Central Command centre for you in Berlin and we will install all the latest technology to assist you with communication and monitoring equipment. And just so you know, we will be with you every step of the way."

So the scene was set. Next would come the Command Performance. We arrived home and sat round the kitchen table. Frank left us but asked if he could return in about an hour. We got drinks and started to discuss the meeting.

I couldn't move onto the concerns in my head without telling Anneliese how proud I was of her. I hadn't realised how much clever work she had done in the last several weeks. It obviously had been perfect, so much so, that it had moved the whole programme forward more than anyone in Government had expected. Anneliese, across the table, clasped my hands, and with a tortured expression exclaimed, "Matthew, I know you! You are worried about where this is leading us. I am so worried and uncertain too! I'm concerned leaving little Frank Junior, you, Matthew and Mum and Dad! And once again I am dragging Frank into the firing line. Having said that, I'm confident that we are capable of bringing this home. It won't take long, and it will mean so much for all our futures, especially Little Frank Junior."

I began to feel better about the whole affair. But my emotions took over. "Darling, I am just so worried about your safety and little Frank. For this reason, I have decided to stay behind with Frank. He's too young to understand and I think it's essential that one of us stays around. It's been difficult deciding what to do, but I think its for the best." Before Anneliese could speak, Frank and Lucia came in. They sat with us and in his usual relaxed casual way, Frank said "I bet you are both feeling stressed." I got them drinks with tears bursting my eyes. Sat down with eyes that told the story!

Frank carried on, as I gulped my glass of whisky, "I've given Lucia the lowdown and she believes in us all. I think I'm right Matthew, when I say you will be staying with Little Frank Jr. I could read your expression earlier and I can understand. I would do the same. If you are here, I am happy to get this finished with Anneliese, and I am convinced we can do that. Lucia is fine. It will only be a few weeks away and she will help you, Matthew, with everything."

Rosa knocked then came in at that point, gave a glorious smile and said with accented words that were enshrouded in flamenco tones, "Our little Frank es domida en la cama. Perdon, he is happy and asleep. So if ok I will ir...to my room."

Anneliese smiled and replied "of course, Rosa. Thank you so much for caring for him today!" Rosa smiled and left.

We all began to feel relieved, the pressure of the day was over. I got us all more drink, large ones, and then Gerry and Tony arrived. It gradually slipped into being a happy, then euphoric party. We told stories about how the CIA were so impressed with Anneliese, the words of the CIA Director and detailed descriptions of the Pentagon.

Everything was on the incline until a drunken Gerry banged the table and everybody stopped to listen. Gerry, rather slurred, spoke in quite a loud voice, probably due to alcohol. "Frank and Anneliese, this is a formal request, Tony and I want to come with you to Berlin!"

Frank slowly stood up and moved to the corner of the kitchen. "I have already considered this," Frank said. "I would love to have you guys with me, but it's impossible. Our job is security for this family. So Anneliese can't influence this decision! I am responsible and my proposal, which you may find difficult, is as follows. I want Gerry to accompany me, when the time comes, to Berlin. Tony should remain to support Matthew. For safety's sake he should move into this house. I'm sorry guys, but that is how I believe it needs to be organised!"

Gerry and Tony quietened down, considerably! With that everybody left and got to their bed, which we all needed.

Anneliese was up very early next morning and it wasn't long before Frank Jr. joined her; Rosa also. Together they gave Frank Jr. his breakfast, and they seemed to really enjoy that time together, both laughing and giggling with our son.

I began the chores as Anneliese settled down in the office to begin her work on the "Wall". This became the reference to her work, "The Wall".

After a few days, she explained to Frank and me that her strategy and processes would use East German informants and agents in East Berlin, and would primarily target propaganda. Also, Russian and East German military and as many Stasi personnel as could be identified. She would use Mia, Alphonse and their staff to solicit all factions protesting at the Wall; Church Groups, Environmental Groups, Subversive Groups; for any information regarding identification of East Germans involved with the Wall. And Importantly, Theatre Groups in East Berlin.

The second wave strategy would be to implement methods to coerce these East German people targets into anti-wall sympathy and, eventually, protestation. In particular, this would include students, especially those with family members in West Germany who may be able to stimulate dissent.

The final wave would mobilise all protestors at specified times. People to be targeted just prior to the climax would be the German media in general and, as a priority, the two East German news programmes. Contacting the media would be reserved for last minute action to avoid the perception that the West was deliberately applying pressure to the protest movement attempting to take the Berlin Wall down."

Anneliese and Frank immersed themselves in this work, constantly discussing ideas, constantly contacting Mia and Alphonse and occasionally, using me as a sounding board. Every communication was routed through Central Intelligence HQ to assure total security.

The pace picked up as we rolled through September. The spread of information and propaganda from Anneliese's intelligence machine was developing into an infection in East Berlin. The protest level in West Berlin was being maintained at epidemic proportions.

There has been, in recent months, several encouraging speeches by Mikhail Gorbachev and Anneliese had published nourishing excerpts throughout Berlin. Earlier in the year, Poland's elections had been strongly contested and a wave of protests were spreading across the Soviet Bloc. Anneliese and Frank found ingenious ways to use this ammunition to increase awareness.

The message was stoking the fire raging in the hearts of Berliners who cried out for a peaceful revolution. East Germans had been fleeing to the West for months, and recent times had seen a dramatic growth in escapes. Significant numbers of East Germans risked all to escape to the West, by various methods; jumping out of buildings adjacent to the Wall, ramming vehicles through the Wall, even flying hot air balloons over the Wall. Anneliese used all such revelations to nourish and feed the propaganda effort.

The dissemination of every possible piece of information critical of the Berlin Wall grew. Through early October feedback from Mia and Alphonse was excitable. They lived there, so they could see and feel the atmosphere growing expectant, moreover they sensed that fate was soon destined to eliminate years of repression!

On October 14, 1989 CIA Headquarters made contact with Anneliese. As she was talking, answering security questions, Frank arrived. He had already been contacted and asked to join Anneliese. This was the moment I had been dreading for weeks!

Various intelligence reports had been received and validated. Senior CIA commanders had reviewed all these, in detail, with their staff. Their conclusion was that a flash point, in the next few weeks, was highly likely. Direction from the CIA was that Anneliese and Frank should be in Berlin within the next 36 hours. They should assemble their key people in the Command Centre and monitor the situation and deploy resources, as events unfolded. Code name for the operation was "Epiphany".

Finalising the call, the Director came on and wished them all the very best. A dormitory had been installed in the Command Centre, and they should contact him any time, day or night, if necessary. The last thing he said was" You know this is crucial. However, I am certain, Anneliese and Frank, that you guys will deliver!"

The phone line went dead. All I could do was breathe deeply to hold back the tears. Anneliese stood up and stepped away from the green shaded banker's table lamp. Standing in a shadowy corner of the office, I knew she was collecting herself and gathering her thoughts. Frank had gone to the kitchen to get us all a drink.

Our drinks arrived and Anneliese stepped forward, out of the shadows. She held her glass out and said "I would like us to make a toast. God bless the two saints in my family, Saint Matthew and Saint Francis." We all clinked glasses. Anneliese continued, "Our Frank Jr. and you also, Frank, indirectly are both named after Saint Francis of Assisi. At university I learned some of the things he said and they have always seemed important. The first we should all focus on while we are tackling "Epiphany".

Start by doing what is necessary, then what is possible, and suddenly you are doing the impossible.

The second will drive me through "Epiphany" to ultimate success!

When you leave this earth you can take with you nothing that you have received… only what you have given!

That evening, our goodbyes' tore us all apart. I have given my heart to Anneliese absolutely and completely. She spent ten minutes with Frank Jr. in his room and couldn't speak when she came out. She composed herself and whispered as she kissed me, "It won't be long. Please care for my other little love."

Frank and Lucia were also quietly saying their goodbyes. Typically Frank, shouted to Lucia as we got in the car, "Save yourself for me darling, see you in a couple of weeks!" Fifty minutes later, they were in the Gulfstream Jet taxiing onto the runway. The cabin crew said this aircraft had a fantastic range and would fly through the night direct to Berlin. So Anneliese said they should try to get as much sleep as possible.

They landed in Berlin about 11am and were picked up in a Windstar people-mover car. The driver and his sidekick were U.S. Marines but dressed in civilian clothes. It took about 45 minutes, through West Berlin traffic to get to a large building, previously used by the German Government, probably a diplomats building. They could see the Brandenburg Gate out of the windows and as they walked through the corridors, Mia came running up to Anneliese, followed closely by Alphonse.

They showed us around; first port of call, the Command Centre. It was a very large rectangular room with high ceilings, shutters on all the windows and splendid furnishings. Several desks were set against one wall with several phones and mobiles lying on each.

Alphonse explained that they also had computers that would be installed next day. But that was the limit to technological communication devices. Cameras and surveillance screens were not possible because they would be too obvious on the streets. Instead, they had several personnel that would be out and about, feeding back information constantly. Most of them were involved in dissident and subversive groups, and they had organised a meeting for tomorrow with them to explain what was required.

⚓

Chapter 54

Start By Doing What Is Necessary

Anneliese then asked Mia and Alphonse if they could convene a meeting for 4pm that afternoon to get the ball rolling. Anneliese had, as St Francis's sayings had taught her, decided to begin by doing what she thought necessary.

Mia then showed them the dormitory. Anneliese said it reminded her of school and university, but nowhere near as much privacy. It was an excellent room with quite large beds, but it would be necessary for sexes to mix. A "take your turn shower room" and less than brilliant heating. Anneliese noted all this but had no complaints. Frank didn't seem perturbed and as they ambled along, whispered to Anneliese, "We'll only be here a few weeks and too busy to care!"

Sandwiches and coffee for lunch, then more information from Mia and Alphonse. Demonstrations were continuing to grow. There had been peaceful demonstrations early and mid-October in East Germany. Around 70,000 people had taken to the streets. Mia said that the word on the streets was that several protest groups were organising a mass protest by East Germans, expected to happen on November 4th. Possibly in Alexanderplatz. Anneliese grabbed this by the horns. "We must massage the message on this and ensure we make the most of this chance."

The three civilian dressed guards on the entrance door began to allow people in around 3pm. One at a time with gaps to avoid drawing attention from the street. By 4pm, the headcount was 13 including Anneliese, Frank and Gerry.

Just after 4pm, Mia asked, in German, if the group would come to order. Mia introduced Anneliese and her two colleagues and said, essentially, that Anneliese had taken command and wished to speak.

She stood in front of the group, her erect, statuesque posture radiating an air of authority. The room was silent, she stood quietly thinking, brushing her blue waterman pen across her lips. She began to smile as she transferred the pen to her left hand and stroked her hair to rest behind her cute ears. She looked up to the ceiling and then directly into the group; Guten tag jeder und willkommen... another surprise she spoke Deutsch! After good day and welcome everyone, she asked if they were ok with her continuing in English to help her colleagues, Frank and Gerry. A guy in the front, in a wheelchair, spoke up saying "sure, we are all pretty good with English."

Anneliese thanked him. She began to pace across the front of the group and back again and stopped in front of the wheelchair guy. "May I ask your name?" "It's Boris" he replied, "and we are very grateful for your help!" "Boris, you have just clicked my brain into gear. I was in Berlin recently and it was one of the most difficult times; no the most difficult time in my life! This visit is going to be different. It is going to be a time where we change the world and make it a much better place. You guys, and I am proud to be part of your group, will write the history books! You will reach the world!"

Anneliese took a deep breath, and said, "Recently, I read a report that described a U.S. television interview with an East German Foreign Ministry spokesman. He told the interviewer that the Soviet Bloc was about to adopt the "Frank Sinatra Doctrine." That grabbed my attention because he is my husband's favourite singer. Anyway, this German diplomat went on to say, Sinatra has a song "I Did It My Way." The East German diplomat said that is what is happening! Each country will decided its own way!" "In the case of Berlin, you, the people have already decided that repression must end and the "Wall" must come down. And we are here to help because the whole of the Western world supports you. Berlin will, once again, be done your way! The people's way!"

The whole group erupted into applause. Frank and Gerry's smiles shone across the room. Mia kissed Anneliese and then the room gradually settled. Anneliese said, "Just to finalise today and let you get home to your loved ones. We won't do any more tonight, but tomorrow we will begin to slowly and carefully encourage both East and West to see this as an opportunity that must not be missed, so, tomorrow, if you could assemble at 9am, I will give you my strategy, my thoughts, my plan in this early stage." To Anneliese's surprise, the young guy in the wheelchair stood up, out of the wheelchair and applauded. She went to him and said, "Why are you in that chair?" "I'll tell you more tomorrow, but the reason is; its camouflage. Everybody thinks I am nondescript in a wheelchair. They talk over me. Don't think I exist, so that provides the best chance to get intelligence. Mia will tell you I am, by far, her best operative for solid intelligence."

Anneliese met with Mia and Alphonse early next morning. Gerry and Frank posted themselves by the window so they could watch the street. Mia said that from her feedback sources, the pace of demonstrations was continuing to increase and would soon reach a stage that would overwhelm East German politicians.

Anneliese was grateful for the input and she would go through all of that with the team at the 9am meeting. Right now, she wanted to detail a few things, for this core group, that were too sensitive for the 9am meeting.

"From this point on, I will work with Mia and Alphonse on a particular angle. The CIA and CECD have several secret service agents and informants in East Germany. They are always in danger and, therefore, have the highest security rating. As we move forward on "Epiphany" the danger level for these people will, doubtless, increase." "I plan to use our people to access influential East Germans. This will be done stealthily and only when I believe the timing is perfect for each targets mindset to be opened, based on psychological and environmental factors."

"Mia and Alphonse will help me with necessary communications to our agents. Also, they will assist me in analysing information they supply. Is all that clear?" everyone nodded.

"Frank and Gerry will remain with us in this building as security." "However" she continued, "I would like you both to head the field team and we will address them shortly. Of course, you should involve me if you are unsure on any issues." "Very good," said Frank.

It was now time for the 9am meeting. After a polite welcome, the first thing Anneliese covered was the way everything had to be handled. "The absolute top priority is the need to always ensure you do not say or do anything that may incite violence, or indeed, get amplified by antagonists in order to incite or justify violence. Every minute, remind yourselves, this is crucial to avoid derailing Epiphany."

"Let me also tell you that our efforts to add to the momentum of peaceful protests and demonstrations, over the last month, has been a great success. Now I want us to press for more. If we do and we get it right, I am absolutely certain that within the next few weeks we will secure our objectives. The Berlin Wall will be dismantled and Germany will again be one single democratic country."

"Presently there is unrest in all the 15 Soviet Republics. East Germans are being allowed and helped to escape through most of these weak building blocks of the Soviet world. The human chain, the "Singing Revolution" across 370 miles of Baltic republics was an astounding event. Those people, singing and marching for independence, should enthral us all. We will be able to do similar things for freedom. And an important part of your job, while you are out amongst your fellow Germans, is to convince them that this will happen without violence!"

So let's get down to the nitty gritty. For anyone not understanding that English, it means the details of what I think will help most. A priority is to get as much information into East Berlin as possible. Our latest intelligence says there will be a mass rally of demonstrations on November 4th. Probably in Alexanderplatz. With things moving so fast, there may be some other event before the 4th, but if so, we will re-group."

⸺⊹⊱◈⊰⊹⸺

Chapter 55

Next, Do What Is Possible

"We also need to keep the warmth glowing in West Berlin. Spread the word carefully, restaurants, bars, on trains, buses, everywhere people congregate. Be inventive. Messages for East Berlin could, for example, be on message boards held up at windows in the tenement buildings adjacent to the Wall. This is a shitty suggestion, but the sewers go into the East. Leaflets could be left in the tunnels!"

"Boris, there is a special assignment for you. Please take your message to Theatres in West Berlin. I am sure those producers, directors, actors, find ways to talk to their counterparts in East Berlin. The Theatre groups in East Berlin are very active in demonstrations and lobbying the media. So push hard, get your wheels rolling, and get around as many as you possibly can."

"Just one last thing! How many of you have family in East Berlin, separated from you?" Boris and three others raised their hands. One of them a lady called Emma spoke first. She was probably in her mid- 40's and said, with sadness in her voice and expression, she had been separated from her parents, brother and sister, and of course, the rest of her family, since she came to West Berlin for University. Anneliese said, "I am so sorry, and do feel your anguish." Then she asked if Emma had found any way to make contact with them. "Oh yes, all of us that have families in the East usually manage to find some way to get messages to them!"

"So that's a method we can use to arouse East Germans and build activity to grow the pressure. You guys are key to this. Try to find everyone you can that have family in the East and get their help to spread the word as wide as some words in your German language."

That piece of humour drew several chuckles. "So now we should call a halt to this and get into doing mode. Please go and enjoy every moment that will lead to the end of oppression and a return to democracy."

The core group, Anneliese, Mia and Alphonse, supported by Frank and Gerry, continued to work 18 hour days, using every piece of intelligence from HQ and using their encrypted service to contact and influence every potential activist. The best results in East Germany were coming from theatre groups that had predominated in the ascent of protests and demonstrations.

On November 1ˢᵗ, the news came through that East German politicians had approved a request from several theatre groups for peaceful demonstrations. This lifted the spirits on both sides of the Berlin Wall!

The progress reported by Anneliese's team was very positive. It seemed that the demonstration on November 4ᵗʰ would be a mass demonstration. The key now was to avoid violence. Anneliese used every ounce of her psychology expertise to influence protagonists on both sides of the Wall, particularly Stasi, Military and Politicians. The Stasi were beginning to run scared, so she was finding it much easier to make in-roads with them. Anneliese told her core group that feedback and results confirmed that her strategy of "massaging the minds" of influencers should continue to be their main thrust in the coming weeks.

Chapter 56

Now We Are Doing The Impossible

In the days prior to November 4th, it was reported that a cabal of East German creatives and intellectuals had openly demanded democratic reform. It was clear to Anneliese that this was a direct reaction to persuasive lobbying she had applied under her banner "massaging the minds."

There was an air of expectation everywhere on the day of November 4th. By 9.30 am hordes of East Berliners were arriving in Alexanderplatz. Also, from all over East Germany! A protest march into the square began as people formed groups that joined together as they marched into Alexanderplatz.

Very quickly, the demonstrators numbered over half a million. The Platz was awash with placards calling for the Wall to be dismantled, some reading "D for Democracy", others demanding a public say in policy making. The variety of protest placards was enormous and inventive.

The demonstrations lasted for three hours and at one point it was reported the onlookers headcount had reached one million. The whole event was streamed on live television, probably due to Anneliese's massaging activities with the News Stations.

Hard hitting dissident theatre groups performed and made a massive impact. A makeshift podium had been assembled and a stage fashioned on a parked truck. Around

20 artists, novelists and academics took turns pleading their case. Politically charged satire was a constant part of the show, with stage and screen actors and the Deutsches Theatre forming a cabal of influential creatives and intellectuals.

Even high ranking members of the ruling East German Socialist Unity Party contributed, despite being booed by the massive audience. There could be no question that this day would be the catalyst for change, inevitable change that would bring democracy, a power shift to the people and unification of Berlin and Germany.

All the time, West Berliners were partying, watching with euphoria. They knew it would not be long before they could, after so many years, embrace their families, parents, brothers, sisters. Indeed, the whole Western World were on the edge of their seats, totally amazed at what they were witnessing.

Next day, November 5th 1989, Anneliese convened a meeting of the whole team. She stood in front of them. They were busily, noisily, excitedly discussing the previous day's demonstrations. Anneliese couldn't, didn't want, to do anything other than stand and smile because she was so pleased for them, and understood how much it had meant to them. This team, her team, had put their heart and soul into November 4th. They deserved their reminiscing pleasure and excitement!

After a few minutes, the room quietened and they waited for her to speak. From a head bowed position, she slowly brought her face into view with the happiest smile. Then with athletic prowess, she threw her arms straight up, above her head, and began to bounce whilst shouting "You did it, you won yesterday." Her team began to embrace one another and shout "Danke Anneliese."

As the room quietened again, Boris loudly asked, "Anneliese what should we do now?" She stood quietly for a minute. "Boris, the German people, East and West, did this. You have helped them find their way. The success yesterday will undoubtedly have paved the way for the fall of the Wall. So all we need to do is keep doing that we have done so far. There is a saying where I come from that says, "If you keep doing what you did, you keep getting what you got." Usually, it is used as a negative. In your circumstance it is a positive. We will keep doing what we did, because it will bring us a successful conclusion. And you know, you all know, we did a bloody good job!"

Later that evening, Frank and Gerry came to Anneliese and asked if they could have a word. Frank said he and Gerry had spent some time out on the streets with the team. The atmosphere, although optimistic, seemed to be building frustration, with some quarters beginning to demand urgent actions. Gerry questioned Anneliese saying "Have you any thoughts on where we go from here because there is a distinct danger that this will develop into something uncontrollable."

Anneliese was meticulously clear in her response. "Gerry, yes, I have thoughts on this because my instincts indicated we would reach such a point. We will talk with the whole team tomorrow. But as you guys have asked, I will tell you my thinking now! Using techniques I have described before, I think I have managed to influence East German politicians. One in particular, a member of the Politburo is scheduled to speak to East Berliners soon. Right now, the date is November 9th. You will understand this could change."

"He is living and working with a backdrop that is worsening daily. The economy is on its knees. The industry in East Germany is failing, but the populace can see that West Germany is achieving great things. The result is that the pressure on East German politicians is beyond them, they are cracking!"

"So, I think we need to get in the driving seat. I, personally, will take on the task to get my tame East German politician to announce in his speech that borders will be opened, for everybody. I have a period of five days to work on this but I am convinced I can make it happen!"

"I won't explain it in this way to the team because it implicates the West in involvement in attempting to get unification. But as I view it, you guys should continue to spur our team towards November 9th. Convince them that it is the date when their voice should be heard, and will be heard. I will then give you the location that will be the focal point just prior to the event. Frank, I know we can help these people and make it happen. And if it works, I would like you to get us out of here by November 13th. Can you organise that and alert everybody to be on standby on that date."

Chapter 57

Prologue To The Wall's End

Frank seemed stunned. "That is excellent. I didn't realise your "massage the mind" would be so influential. I totally accept and believe you will succeed so I will organise the 13ᵗʰ."

The sentiments from Anneliese with the Team next morning were the same, everybody could sense victory. Essentially, however, Anneliese restricted it to information the team should impart to the people. November 9ᵗʰ was the date!

All of them worked constantly, like they'd never worked before, through to November 9ᵗʰ. From the very beginning of that day, there was a buzz throughout West Berlin. Our team were on the crest of a wave. They had put every ounce of effort into building the parapets of expectancy from the ground up. All of Berlin, both East and West, were holding their breath anticipating that the architect, Anneliese, had created an enduring moment in history.

They were made to wait until early evening. At various points around the Wall people gathered, waiting for anything, perhaps everything to happen. The early evening news in East Berlin lit the touch paper. Anneliese's tame Politburo member had called a press conference.

Gunther Schabowski stood in front of the cameras, shuffling papers and appearing dishevelled and confused. He announced that private travel between East and West would be allowed without prerequisites. No passports, no visas, in other words, a unified Germany. A news correspondent asked when? He shuffled papers again and then said "As far as I am aware, it is effective immediately! This news was all over television!

A border soldier that was in charge of the border at the time, had watched the press conference. He was beside himself. Didn't know what to do. The crowds that had formed at the barriers were immense. He did what a good soldier would do. He phoned his supervisors for instructions. None came. So this lowly military man, seeing the pleading expressions facing him, gave the order. "Lift the barriers." East and West Berlin were no more. Germany was whole again. Families were re-united, heaven had arrived on earth.

Families, now reunited were excited into action. At the Brandenburg Gate, people began to climb the Wall. They brought implements. All around, everybody was hugging, laughing, celebrating, and completely joyous. Chipping away at the Wall, sledgehammers went on all night!

This was later described as a "human steamroller". It was, indeed, it had been driven by Anneliese. The world was now going to be a much better and more secure place.

Next day, but midday, our team met up again. Everyone bleary eyed. Anneliese, with Frank and Gerry went around the room shaking hands and embracing people. Mia and Alphonse stood amongst the team, but Anneliese moved into their midst and pulled the two of them out to join her. Mia and Alphonse were asked if they could speak first. Mia spoke, quietly at first, but as her confidence built, she said that she had worked with Anneliese for several years. "This lady," indicating Anneliese, "Has left her 2 year old to help us. And she has helped! But it has been more, much more than that, she has been instrumental in gaining freedom for all of us, our families, our country. The worst of it is, is that all I can do is to say thank you! My partner Alphonse, and I thank you with all our hearts. You have given us a liberated life in our home town of Berlin and there is no way we can ever repay that!"

Anneliese stepped forward and said, "I have only been here with you for a short time but I understand the horror you have lived with for years. I was here a short while ago and it impacted my family.. So now you will, and I will, relish the fact that the wheel of history has moved to a good place. It can never turn back.

"We will be leaving soon to go back to our families and friends. So I want to leave you with the thought that I am so proud of you and your people and I will never forget you. I love you all and hope we will meet again one day."

As she turned away, Gerry clasped her and whispered, "You are fantastic." Mia and Alphonse joined in and it was cheers all round. Frank stood smiling at the group and said, "We have delivered President Reagan's request. The Wall is on its way down, bit by bit, as we speak." He turned and whispered to Anneliese, "I know you said we would leave on the 13th but my guess was you were giving yourself a contingency. As we don't need it, I have arranged for us to leave tonight. I assume you are ok with that." Anneliese nodded and said "I am grateful."

They were on the Gulfstream ready for take-off at 8pm. Everyone was excited at the thought of what they had achieved and that now they would soon see their friends and loved ones.

Chapter 58

Home And Dry

Frank, sitting next to Anneliese, leaned across and said, "I've got something great to tell you! Just as we left, Central Intelligence got to me, to say well done, fantastic job. The President is delighted."

But that wasn't the best of it. "The greatest intelligence minds we have believe today marks the end of the Cold War and, consequently, the pursuit of you is almost certainly close to ending. They project that the Soviet Bloc will continue crumbling and be completely dismantled in the next 12 months. So your life of normality looks assured!"

"Frank, you are the most wonderful friend. I can't explain how that makes me feel, I can't wait to see Matthew and Frank Junior and to have our friends close means everything to me!"

Once the seat belt signs turned off and we were cruising at 30,000 feet, Gerry stumbled along the aisle and came to talk to Anneliese and Frank. "Just wanted to tell you chaps that I have decided I want to be domiciled in Oakville with you, and I am sure Tony will agree. In fact, he said as much to me before we left." Anneliese, already euphoric, put her arms around his neck, pulled him close and gave him a resounding smacker on his cheek. Frank grasped his hand and said, "Big man, you have just made our day, not that it could get much better!"

They all arrived home to me and Frank Junior, early afternoon. We had been told to expect them by the CSIS, but anticipation can never beat the real thing. All our reunions were joyful, it was marvellous to see the look on Frank Junior's face when Anneliese came up the path. Rosa had been a Godsend and would now be one of the family, and irreplaceable as far as Frank Junior was concerned.

Tony and Gerry embraced for what seemed a lifetime. Frank and Lucia stayed a few minutes then rushed off to re-establish their union!

Anneliese and I talked for hours, almost the whole night. The news about our families' futures in terms of safety and security was amazing. Mum and Dad were doing well and were so proud of what Anneliese had achieved in Berlin.

All our lives changed over the next year. Even Frank relinquished his OCD for scanning and surveillance. We were all adapting and loving every minute. However, humans always need something to work at. Gerry and Tony got stuck into the U.S Imports which continued building our wealth. Anneliese started a North American travelogue Company with Frank and Lucia. They did most of the travelling and fed information to Anneliese. Alphonse and Mia continued their European work on U.S. Imports. So where did all that leave me. I was happy, at the moment, just spending time with my son, seeing him was fabulous.

One evening, we were all sat in the lounge, relaxing and chatting. Out of the blue, Frank asked Anneliese, "How did we manage to achieve all that; I mean bringing the Wall down?"

"I think it was like this" said Anneliese. "You have heard the saying "The pen is mightier than the sword," well there is another saying! A Psychology Professor exclaimed that there are three ways to communicate and motivate people. They are metaphors, or clever words; semaphore, clever signals: and lastly, a piece of two by four; hit them with it! Our team used the first two every day for weeks."

"I used the last one with the East German politicians. They all knew the people were close to winning. Democracy was close to winning. So I threatened them constantly, saying that, in the end, they would be arrested and would stand trial for "War Crimes"!"

During the next year, we all had a gleeful time watching Frank Junior grow and enjoying one another's company. We even got together and bought a fabulous log cabin on Muskoka Lakes where, during the summers, we would enjoy living together, fishing in our boat, bar-b-ques and noisy relaxation.

It was still the same for me. I could never take my eyes off Anneliese. She was the most glorious creature and had such an intellect. Physically, there was no possible equal. Only Anya came close, and I miss her.

At the end of the year, George Bush, the new President, met with Mikhail Gorbachev. They seemed to have a great rapport and announced that the Cold War had ended and diplomatic channels were open for all future concerns.

Our past was now present day history. But I often wondered if our exhilarating lives would ever return. I could never be sure because history sometimes repeats itself!

THE END